PRICELESS
CLARITY COAST OMEGAVERSE

DEVYN SINCLAIR

INFINITE ENDINGS, LLC

Cover by Devyn Sinclair

Discreet cover concept by Mayflower Studio

To all the fat girls—

You deserve every bit of love you never believed you'd receive.

AUTHOR'S NOTE

Dear Readers,

Priceless is not a book that's meant to be dark. However, as with most of my books, there are some sensitive themes and situations. Particularly, in this book, fatphobia and the treatment of people in larger bodies. If you feel like this could be a problem for you, please protect yourself. No work of fiction is worth your mental health.

The full list of content warnings is available on my website, or through the QR code below.

Writing a plus-size heroine:

For those people looking for a badass plus-sized heroine who loves her body in spite and defiance of everything around her, I'm sorry to say this is not that story.

Neither is this a story about weight loss, or having to change your body in order to love yourself or have other people love you.

Ocean, like many people who live in larger bodies, has good days and bad days. She has moments of both body joy and body horror. As a person who has also lived in a larger body my whole life, I understand this.

Ocean does have trauma related to her body and weight. Those buttons will be pushed. There is fatphobia in this world and it will be dealt with. But she will also experience so much love and joy and acceptance that it will help her healing.

And hopefully yours!

A note on Floriography:

Floriography, or the language of flowers, has been around for a long time. Though we're not nearly as aware of the complex meanings the victorians understood and used, flower language is still used today in things like red roses for love; pink carnations for mother's day, and white flowers—often associated with purity—for weddings.

In *Priceless* every chapter header is a flower with a vintage botanical illustration. I've included meanings with those flowers that are somewhat related to the chapter they head. However, flowers can have many different names and many different meanings! If there's a flower in the book that you believe means something different, it is entirely possible that it's true.

I have done my best to match appropriate illustrations and meanings, and you can find a few of my resources at the back of the book.

Fig 1. Marigold
Meaning: Cruelty; Despair; Grief;

OCEAN

"*T*ighter."

I swear if that word never came out of my aunt's mouth ever again, it would be too soon. It was her favorite word, at least when it came to me.

"Ma'am," Ruby huffed a breath, even more exasperated than I was. "It's as tight as it will go safely."

Aunt Laura scoffed. "No, it's not. We've gotten it smaller before, and the dress shows everything. Make it *tighter*. She has to look perfect."

I met Ruby's gaze in the mirror, and I saw the protest on the tip of her tongue. Instead, I gave her the tiniest shake of my head. It wasn't worth it to fight. If she protested more, Laura would simply take over lacing the corset herself, and it would be far more painful than what Ruby would do.

Sighing, Ruby forced the laces tighter, and I closed my eyes, sinking into a place I already knew well. Behind a glass wall in my own mind, where nothing could reach me and I could ignore the aching pain of my body being forced into something too small for it, and the ache that would fester until after this party when I could finally take it off.

Laura crossed her arms and stared into the mirror triumphantly. "See?"

Neither Ruby nor I said anything as she went to the rack and picked up the dress she'd chosen for the party. Excuse me, the *gala*. She corrected me every time I said anything different, and it wasn't worth telling her that her party never compared to the ones my mother threw, and they never would, even if she desperately wanted them to.

Tying off the laces in the center of my back, Ruby helped Laura lift the dress over my head. It fell down in a silky wave. It really was pretty, and I *felt* pretty in it. Royal blue, with a one-shoulder neckline, it flowed down like water and made me look graceful.

This was where I had to fight myself. Because I loved the way I looked, and I knew that I wouldn't like it nearly as much without the corset I was stuffed into like that last shirt you tried to fit into a drawer even though it didn't want to close. But I was still in pain, and I desperately *wished* I would like the way I looked without the corset. Even with it, I was still fat. There was no hiding that, no matter how small they laced me. Physics were a thing, and my matter could only be compressed so much. And I didn't have the energy to explain the laws of physics to my aunt.

"There," Laura said. "That will have to do, I guess. People will start arriving in fifteen minutes. Thanks for making us cut it so close." Her voice was poisonous. "Make-up, Ocean. Not too heavy. Do *not* be late."

1

She disappeared in a cloud of the powdery perfume she preferred, which I hated, but was better than her natural scent, which was dusty and dry. But not in the good *old books* way. More like cardboard.

It made sense. She was stiff enough for it.

"Are you all right?" Ruby asked.

"I'm fine." I sat down at my vanity, hiding the wince and my inability to breathe. At least this dress was long enough to hide wearing flats, because I wasn't going to be able to sit down much.

"Are you sure?"

"Yes."

She looked like she wanted to say something else, but thought better of it. "Let me know if you need anything," she murmured before closing the door behind her.

My shoulders wilted, and I took a labored breath, trying to get used to the tightness. It would be easier if I wore the corsets all the time, like women used to in the past. When Laura told me she wanted me to start wearing them for events because 'regular shapewear wasn't going to cut it,' I went down the rabbit hole. This wasn't what they were meant for. Corsets were just bras, and the horror stories people used to vilify them either weren't real, or were so far an outlier they weren't worth mentioning.

Laura didn't see it that way, so I couldn't just wear a well-fitted corset every day and get used to it. If I wore *this* every day, it would be hell.

Slowly, I eased my breathing and let my body get used to it before I started doing my make-up. I'd make my appearance at the party as short as possible, and then get the hell out of all of this and retreat to the greenhouse. While it was summer, once the sun went down the greenhouse was still lovely in the evenings, with the breeze from the sea flowing through the portion where the windows opened.

I startled at the sound of my phone ringing, squirting a little too much foundation on the sponge. Part of me wished it had fallen on the dress, but I still selfishly liked the dress too much to ruin it.

Isolde's name lit up the screen. Finally. I laughed as I answered the call and turned it to video, propping it up against the mirror. Trinity hadn't quite made it on the call yet, so it was just Isolde, cuddled up in a sweatshirt that was way, *way* too big to be hers. I grinned.

"Finally coming up for air?"

She blushed, but nodded. "Yeah. That was... well, I'll wait till Rin answers, but it was incredible."

"Good." She'd just had her heat, helped through by the pack of incredibly hot men she'd hired to take her to her sister's wedding because her asshole of an ex was the best man. Both Trinity and I were convinced they were already in love with her, but Isolde was stubborn, so I couldn't wait to hear what had happened.

"You look pretty," Isolde said. "Where are you going?"

I sighed. "The Caldwell Gala."

Her eyes went wide. "That's tonight? Why didn't you tell us?"

"Tell us what?" Trinity popped into the video, her platinum hair a messy halo around her head.

Isolde hid her smile. "That the Caldwell Gala is tonight."

Rin gasped. "Ocean."

Pulling back from the mirror enough to give them both a look, I raised an eyebrow. "Because both of you would have been able to come?"

"No," Isolde grumbled. "But I could still know about it."

I laughed, and it turned into a cough because I still couldn't take a full breath. "It's okay. I'm aiming to make an appearance and then escape as quickly as possible. Laura is in rare form tonight. But don't worry about me. I'm not the one who called."

"Yeah," Rin said, throwing a handful of cheese-chips into her mouth. They were her favorite and better for her diabetes. "Please tell us how you got repeatedly railed by five smoking hot men who do nothing but drool over you."

Isolde laughed, but her eyes were sparkling. "It was amazing, and I do have something to tell you both."

Rin and I waited, staring at her.

"We're scent matched."

"Excuse me, *WHAT?*"

The shrill tone of my best friend's excitement crashed through the screen, making both me and Isolde wince. But she was also laughing.

"Yeah. So, I owe you dinner and coffee and flowers for the rest of my fucking life," she said.

I ignored the pang of jealousy and pain that dug in under my ribs. It wasn't a kind reaction to one of my favorite people in the world finding her scent matches. She deserved it. But that didn't mean it hurt less.

"So what does this mean?" I asked. "Are you staying here? With them?"

Isolde had moved away after her ex broke her heart, and it was great to have her back.

She nodded into the oversized hoodie she wore, which clearly belonged to one of her new pack members. "Yeah, I am. I honestly have no idea what's going to happen after the wedding. I'm kind of playing it by ear. Don't know where I'm going to work, don't know how long it'll take to get the rest of my stuff from the apartment, but I don't really care. We'll figure it out."

I pulled out the rest of my makeup and finished my eyes and lips with the light, barely there makeup Laura and my uncle preferred. I took a risk with some nude shimmer on my eyelids, but no more.

Rin and Isolde kept chatting, and I managed to smile and be happy for my friend when one of her guys came in and sat with her. But I felt hollow. Isolde had her pack and was starting a new phase in her life. Trinity had been promoted and was diving into her dream job, even if she was overwhelmed.

While I was here. Stuck in this house with no way out and no way forward because of a fucking contract. And there certainly weren't any romantic prospects knocking down my door.

"*Ocean*." Laura snapped open the door and glared at me. "Our guests are here. *Now*."

I winced and glanced at my friends. "Gotta go," I whispered. "Talk to you later."

"I told you not to be late." Laura somehow managed to hiss the words through her teeth.

My phone clearly displayed the time where I'd left it on the vanity. There wouldn't be anywhere for me to carry it in this dress, and if they thought I was hiding and on my phone for the whole party, I'd never hear the end of it. "I'm not late. And regardless, no one is waiting for me to be there."

I pushed past her into the hallway before she could say anything. Because it wasn't anything I hadn't heard before. I was a part of the Caldwell family, and I was *expected* to be there. One of these days I was going to snap and tell her I was the only *real* Caldwell left.

Instead, I allowed my face to take on the mask I always wore at these events. Or anytime I was in their presence. Some people thought I should just give them what they had coming to them. Those people didn't understand I had five more years of this, and there was nothing I could do about it.

We reached the ballroom, and there was barely anyone in it. Maybe two people. Our *guests*. Most people wouldn't arrive for at least an hour. Joy to me.

"At least the dress isn't lumpy," Laura muttered, brushing past me into the room and heading for my uncle.

I sighed. The flowers looked beautiful. One small bright spot. There was a negative percent chance I would be thanked for that, despite giving them the deal of a lifetime on the flowers themselves. But we were family, and family did things for each other.

Funny how that only worked when I was the one giving things to them.

Was it too early to start drinking? Because I could use one, and if I was going to make it through this party, I was going to need it.

4

Fig 2. Petunia
Meaning: Anger;
Resentment; Disdain

MICAH

"*Y*ou have to be fucking kidding me." Everett's voice was colder than ice.

The man at the end of the table spread his hands apologetically. What a lie that was. He didn't care, nor was he sorry. I'd bet every dollar in our bank accounts that inside he was giddy. "Unfortunately, I'm not. *We're* not."

Even Cameron, sitting across from me, had a frown on his normally easygoing face. "It seems a bit antiquated. Surely we can find something a little more modern to help with our image."

Joseph cleared his throat. "I'm offended you think we didn't go through all the possibilities before we came to you."

"All the possibilities *without speaking to us*," Everett snarled. I didn't pull him back. These assholes deserved it. Seven men sat across from us, and they were currently handing us our asses on a platter. It wasn't a common sensation, nor one I liked.

Still, I kept my mouth shut and watched them.

For the moment.

"For fuck's sake," Bill shook his head and leaned back in his chair. "You can't expand into a family market without appealing to families. And forgive me, but the three of you aren't fools. You're probably the least family friendly pack in the country."

I stifled my smirk and saw Cameron do the same. But my packmate cleared his throat. Again, it wasn't remotely true, but outright denials would only make them more insistent. "That's why we have an excellent marketing team. When was the last time the owners of a company mattered for marketing?"

"I'm not even going to dignify that," Joseph said. "The minute we announce that Zenith Inc. is purchasing Firefly Clothing and *all* of its subsidiaries is the minute we have people protesting that the kings of lingerie and sex are taking over children's clothing. You think it's not a big deal, but it is."

This time it was my turn to roll my eyes. Sure, our company was known for our lingerie and sex toy brands, but that wasn't all we did. It was just the only thing people paid attention to, because the old saying was true. *Sex sells*. And it did. Very, very well.

"A few well-timed press releases and a quick showing of the plans for the lines will put those protests to bed," Cameron said mildly. "Getting married is an extreme solution to a mid-level problem."

I glanced at Everett, who was still as a statue, and strung so tightly I wondered if his spine might snap. It wasn't the idea of getting married that pissed him off. No, it was our board of directors coming to us and trying to tell us what to do with our personal lives.

A few heads turned toward Joseph, and I narrowed my eyes. It seemed like we'd let the board have too much autonomy, if they were suddenly banding together and looking to him for guidance. But that was a problem for a different day. Any action on that front would only be seen as a defensive attack and not a move of strategy.

I should have been paying more attention. The way we divided things—me with design, Cameron with public relations and marketing, and Everett with the nuts and bolts of the business itself—it was easy for me to set those things aside. But I still owned this company, and this was just as much on me as it was the others, even if Everett might not agree.

Joseph's mouth hardened into a line as he stared at us. "We won't approve the acquisition."

A dark chuckle came from Cameron. He might be the one who was always smiling, but he was just as ruthless as Everett. "We're the majority shareholders, Joe. You really think that's going to stop us?"

"If we all resign and publicly declare why we're doing it, it will."

My eyebrows rose into my hairline. "You feel that strongly about it?"

The acquisition on the table wasn't nearly as dire as they were making it out to be. But the entire board resigning and openly admitting they didn't have confidence in the three of us? That was a problem. Even I knew that.

Zenith Incorporated's stock would take a nosedive, and not only Firefly Clothing would be in trouble. Every single one of our subsidiaries and their employees would be in danger. The Board understood the dynamics. Which was how I knew they weren't fucking around.

"Uh," a Beta named Lee cleared his throat. "Respectfully, we're tired of cleaning up your messes."

"Our *messes*?" Everett leaned down on the table with both hands. "What the fuck are you talking about?"

"He means we're tired of getting called by reporters asking about your latest fuck. Or why you're in the papers in cities halfway around the world instead of doing your fucking jobs," Bill said.

Cameron tilted my head and looked at him. "And it never occurred to you to direct those calls to our PR team? To *me*? Or maybe consider that those stories are either exaggerated or false?"

He snorted. "We know they're not."

"Do you." It wasn't a question. I stood and buttoned my suit jacket, staring the man down. His swallow was visible. Good. He should be scared at the moment. I didn't speak much in Board meetings, and I was glad for it now. My words would carry the weight they needed.

"Allow me to enlighten you then, since none of you felt it was important to come to us directly with your concerns. We haven't been

8

overseas in over a year. The pictures circulating are from a trip three years ago. The pictures themselves," I looked around at each of them, "I assume you've seen them since you're putting such a weight on our public image, are hardly of consequence. The last time I checked, pictures of men dancing with women in a club weren't a crime."

Joseph scrubbed a hand over his face. "Mic—"

"I wasn't finished. Though it's none of your business, we haven't been in a relationship since before that time, because we've been busy doing, what was it you called it, Bill? Our *fucking jobs*. So by all means, throw a temper tantrum and try to force our hand, but do it knowing that this all could have been avoided had you been willing to have a conversation."

The room was so silent you could hear the chairs creak when they shifted their weight. Not one single board member was looking at us. Except Joseph. His lips barely turned up at the corners, and it told me everything I needed to know. "Motherfucker," Everett muttered under his breath.

Cam and I looked at Everett, but he didn't meet our gaze. "You won't stop with this, will you? You've decided this is what you want, and that's the end of it?"

The smile on Joseph's face was at once poisonous and victorious. "Correct."

"Fine. Get the fuck out."

Lee blinked. "But—"

"I said get the *fuck. Out*."

All seven of them did. The spineless ones who hadn't said shit went first. And of course, they all couldn't leave without a parting shot. Joseph nodded like he had any sympathy. "This is for the best. You'll see."

None of us spoke until the door shut behind them.

"Want to let us in on what just happened?" Cameron asked.

Everett hung his head. "They know all the stories aren't true. They just don't care. Joseph practically screamed it at the end. I want to wipe that smirk off his face."

"The real question is *why*?" I asked. "This deal is good for everyone. And this is a made up stipulation, so why have they chosen this hill to die on?"

"Good question," Cam murmured. "But it will have to wait."

"Why?" Everett pulled himself to his full height.

Looking at his watch, Cameron smirked. "Because we have to go home and change before going to the Caldwell Gala."

I groaned, and he shot a glare at me. "We don't have to stay long, but we do have to go. We promised we would. And the last thing we need is for the board to think they've rattled us enough to skip our social calendar."

He was right, and I hated that he was. I usually liked the Caldwell Gala. The house was beautiful, and in general, it was a fine event. No part of me wanted to go out while this anger seethed under my skin, but we had to.

"All right. Then let's move quickly," Everett said.

I couldn't agree more.

Ninety minutes later we pulled up to the gates of the Caldwell Estate and handed the keys of the car to the valet. We'd all calmed down some in the ritual of getting ready for a public appearance, but it still hovered in the back of my mind. Like the pulse of bass from a nearby speaker, or a fly you couldn't find and squash. When you were unable to find the correct color for that last final detail. Nagging and brutal.

Married. Married. Married.

It circled in my brain on repeat.

Why?

Frustration clung to my skin. They'd boxed us in damn well, and they knew it. It was true, we were more powerful than the rest of the board, but the power of public opinion was more than all of us. If they decided to scorch the earth, we wouldn't survive it. Because they weren't wrong.

Our media presence wasn't the most squeaky clean, but it wasn't horrendous either. Mostly it was people speculating about nothing, as they usually did with those who were rich and single. And it didn't matter that it wasn't the truth. Or wasn't the whole truth. All that mattered was appearances. Because by the time the truth could be circulated and gotten into enough hands to be understood and known, it would already be far too late.

We'd seen it happen countless times. We'd just never imagined we'd be on this end of it.

"Let's get this over with," I said with a sigh.

"Don't be too sad," Cam said. "You know Frank always sets aside some of the old bottles for us. And you like this one. I know you do."

I nodded. That was true. Frank McCabe, the owner of the estate, did business with us. He started out as a specialty textile importer and had slowly grown into one of the largest textile conglomerates in the country. We sourced from McCabe Fabrics for probably half of our companies. And if the deal with Firefly went through, we'd certainly be doing more business with the company.

The tinkle of music and laughter surrounded us as we entered. The crowd was already gathered, glasses of champagne shimmering and circulating on waiters' trays. The windows that looked out over the coast let in the orangey light of sunset, painting everything with a lovely glow.

I caught a light floral scent, my eyes drawn to the bouquets on the cocktail tables along the side of the room and with the refreshments. Everywhere I looked there seemed to be flowers. The strange and pretty blend of purple, orange, and yellow that made the room come to life.

A sharp clapping sound drew my eyes, and the man himself walked over to us with a smile. "I was hoping the three of you would show your faces here."

He reached out a hand to shake, and Everett took it first. "Wouldn't miss it."

"I found a bottle I've been saving for the three of you. I'll have the staff grab it."

"We'll be on the balcony," I told him.

None of us wanted to mingle tonight, and the large balcony circling the second level of the ballroom was a good place to observe. We'd used it before to keep a low profile. Not to mention there were less cameras up there. That was one thing I didn't love about this house. There were cameras absolutely everywhere.

Paranoid bastard.

Frank left, and Cam chuckled. "Told you."

"Yeah."

When we'd first met, he'd offered us a taste of one of his vintage wines, and he'd latched onto it, serving us with expensive and exclusive liquor every time we encountered him. Unfortunately, the three of us weren't aficionados. We enjoyed the taste, but mostly because it made Frank's presence more bearable.

Up on the balcony, I looked out over the crowd, my packmates lining up beside me. There were a couple of other people up here, but not many. The usual suspects from Clarity Coast's society, and those who had come from Sunset City or flown in.

I spotted several women looking up at us and marking who we were. It never bothered me before, but now that we were on the brink of having to find someone to marry or go down in a blaze of fire, the stares felt different.

A hand fell on my shoulder, and Everett laughed. It felt forced. "Cam's right. We need to look like everything's normal."

"It's not fucking normal," I growled.

"You think I don't know that? Act like it is. We all know this battle isn't going to be won by you glowering at the room."

"The rare valid point," I muttered. Then I sighed, trying to bring my mind back to balance. "Isn't the gala usually raising money for something?"

"Cancer," Cam said. "In honor of Gloria Caldwell. But more and more I think it's just a way for Frank to network and make more connections."

The Caldwell Foundation was one of the charities on the long list we donated to every year. Which was why we'd been invited. It was also one of the better ones as far as accomplishing their mission, furthering cancer research and treatment.

The same flowers as downstairs trailed along the railing of the balcony, woven around it. They were gorgeous, though they seemed edgier than the vibes in the room. Slightly darker, with the rich purples pulling you into the pops of orange and yellow. I could appreciate a good design concept, especially when I didn't get to simply do *art* as much as I wanted to anymore.

"Who the fuck is that?"

Looking up, I followed Everett's gaze to the corner of the room near the large, arching windows. A woman stood there, lit up by the setting sun. Tan skin bronzed by the glow, contrasting gorgeously with the royal blue of her dress. Every curve she had went on for miles, from the gentle round angle of her face to the large, lush swell of her hips. She was fucking stunning.

"I've never seen her before."

That was the goddamn truth, because if I'd ever seen her before, I would have remembered. One look and she was seared on my brain.

Cameron whistled softly through his teeth. "Given the meeting earlier today, I know we're not exactly looking, but..."

He didn't need to finish the sentence. One look at Everett's face told me he agreed. She held a glass of champagne in her hand and looked out the windows, barely moving. Not engaging.

For a brief moment, it looked like there was pain on her face, but she sighed and sipped her drink, still looking out at the coast.

"Hell of a time to find someone that attractive," Everett said, subtly adjusting himself. Thankfully on the balcony there was no one close enough to see.

"There you are." Frank held up a fat-bottomed bottle by the neck and grinned in victory. "Cognac. Thought you might appreciate it."

I smiled politely. "We certainly do."

The butler that had followed him had a tray with four small glasses and held it still as Frank cracked the bottle open and began to pour. "I've been meaning to put a meeting with the three of you on the books," he said.

"Oh?" Everett accepted the glass and raised a single eyebrow. "Why?"

Despite doing business with Frank, we rarely met with him.

"The Firefly deal. I wanted to get a head start on arrangements for afterward. It seems like it could be beneficial for all of us."

I narrowed my eyes. The deal wasn't public yet. And everyone involved had signed agreements not to say shit until the ink was dry. If he knew, we needed to tighten our ship. It also made me wonder in what context he heard the news.

Everett's face looked sharp and dangerous. "How do you know about that?"

Frank smirked. "I have my ways. But you know, never kiss and tell."

"Hmm," was all I said.

Out of the corner of my eye, I saw Everett pull out his phone and send a quick text. Good. He was putting our team on exactly how this had leaked and why. Because if this had anything to do with the board forcing our hand, it could be to our advantage.

"What do you think?"

He meant the liquor. It was good, but I'd had better. I smiled. "Excellent, thank you. I hope the fundraising is going well?"

Frank blinked for a moment. "For the foundation. Yes, of course. Well, as you know, this event is the highlight of our year in that regard."

Someone raised a hand on the main floor and caught his eye. "I'm so sorry. It looks like I'm needed downstairs. Please enjoy."

"We will." Cam lifted the small glass and drained it before Frank walked away. He put it on the tray the waiter held. "We won't be needing any more of that."

"Aiden is looking into it," Everett said. "I don't want to leave until we know something."

"I agree." And in the meantime, there was a beautiful woman in the room I very much wanted to dance with. But when I looked back at where she'd been standing, she was gone.

Fig 3. Wild Morning Glory
(Also: Heavenly Trumpets, White Witch's Hat)
Meaning: Dead hope; Extinguished hopes

OCEAN

$\mathcal{M}$y body ached. I'd already been at the gala far longer than I wanted to be, and there was only so much more I could take. Between the too-tight corset and people who'd known my parents coming up to me and telling me how sorry they were—which happened every year—and telling me stories, I was done. I didn't even want to go to the greenhouse anymore. I just wanted to go curl up in my bedroom, pretend it was a nest, and go to sleep.

Laura and Frank hadn't looked in my direction for a while. There was a chance I could slip out without them noticing. They'd see on the cameras later, but then I'd already be gone.

The entire mansion was laced with cameras, inside and out. I'd never fully understood why, and I hadn't allowed them in my rooms. But other than that? Everywhere.

Part of me wondered if it was to keep an eye on me. My aunt and uncle's constant suspicion of me was absurd, given the control they held. Not that they allowed me to do enough to get away with anything.

"You're Ocean, right?"

A male voice came from behind me. A tall man that I vaguely recognized as being one of Frank's business acquaintances. If he was who I thought he was, he got kicked out of the holiday party last year for being so drunk. "Depends on who's asking."

He laughed like I'd made the funniest joke in the world. I wasn't sure why. My statement was serious.

"They told me you were witty."

I was too tired and in too much pain to play along, and I hadn't wanted to in the first place. "And they didn't tell me who you were at all."

He bowed at the waist, smirking. "Jason Marsh. I work with your uncle."

"Right. Nice to meet you. Have a good night."

"Wait," he reached out but didn't manage to touch me. "That's it? I was hoping to ask you to dance."

The scent cancellers in the room were strong, but I could still smell him. He smelled *green* and not in the good, fresh-cut grass way. I wasn't able to pinpoint it, but it wasn't great, and the idea of standing close to him wasn't appealing. "Thank you, but I think I'm finished for the evening."

"Don't be ridiculous." Hands came down on my shoulders and pushed me toward the man. Laura had appeared out of nowhere. "She'll be happy to dance with you."

"Aunt Laura—"

"He runs the biggest shipping network on the west coast. Give him whatever he wants," she whispered harshly in my ear.

Jason, at least, pretended not to notice that my hand was being forced. I managed a smile. "One dance."

"I'm honored."

He smiled like he really was. But as soon as we were on the dance floor, he pulled me far too close, his hand wandering downward toward my ass. "I saw you as soon as I came in, and it took me all night to come talk to you."

"Oh? Why? I'm not that scary."

He shrugged, pulling me against him. "Wanted to make sure you were the one."

"The one...?" I blinked, not understanding what was happening. His green scent wrapped around me, and I did my best to keep my reaction off my face. Wheatgrass? I wasn't sure. The fact that I couldn't identify it bothered me.

Chuckling, he turned us slowly to the music. "The one I'm going to take home with me."

My mouth popped open, and I stared at him. All Jason did was grin. I shook my head. "Where the hell did you get that idea?"

Leaning in, his breath brushed my ear, and once again I smelled alcohol. He was drunk. "By looking at your ass in this dress."

"That's enough," I told him, pulling back. "We're done."

His brow furrowed. "Why?"

"Because I'm not interested. You're drunk, and I didn't want to dance with you in the first place."

All at once his face transformed into something ugly, and my heart fell. I knew that look. It wasn't the look that meant I was in danger. Not physically. No, this was almost worse.

"You should be grateful. Not everyone's going to want you. I'm offering you a good time. You should take it."

I pulled away, but he didn't let go of me. "I should be grateful that you're hitting on me at the gala that's meant to honor my dead parents? Sure. That makes sense. Take your hands off me. Now."

"No, you should be grateful because as an Omega with a body like yours, no one's going to want you. Take what you can get, Ocean."

The lance of hurt entered my heart even though I didn't want to. Men like him were all the same. Thought they were god's gift to earth while also thinking I didn't know the reality I lived in.

I was fat. It wasn't a dirty word, it was just a fact. Did he think I didn't understand? He couldn't say anything worse to me than I'd already said to myself. And it still hurt, because even if I knew the truth, I still *wanted* things the world didn't think were meant for me. "Take your hands off me," I said evenly. "Right now. Or I will make a scene.

Wouldn't want this to be the second of my family's parties you get escorted out of."

All he did was laugh. "Your aunt was the one who pushed you into me. I don't think they'll mind a scene."

A hand came down on his shoulder. Hard. "She told you to take your hands off her."

The man now standing next to us looked at Jason, and then he looked at me. Stunned. His gaze roved over me like he was shocked he'd intervened for me. He looked like he'd been struck by lightning and was staring into the sun. Like he'd glitched and needed a full system reboot. Like he didn't even know where he was.

Then he blinked, looking back at Jason. "Do I have to remove your hands for you?"

Jason threw his hands off me forcefully and scoffed. "You bitches are all the same. Stuck up and too self-centered to see a good thing in front of them. Especially when it's their *only option*."

He stalked across the dance floor toward the refreshments table and left me standing there. I needed to move. Not only because people were staring, but because in about ten seconds Laura would find me and berate me for not dancing with him longer.

The stranger stepped in and slid an arm around my waist, and suddenly we were dancing. His scent wasn't green. It was bright and balmy in a good way. In a *great* way. A light and sharp scent of lemons undercut with the sweetness of sugar. Lemon bars. The kind of thing that made your mouth water to taste that blend between the two opposing sensations. It was lovely.

"I'm sorry if I overstepped. I don't take kindly to people who don't understand the word no. You looked like you needed a rescue." Warm green eyes stared down into mine, and I couldn't quite find my words. Because this Alpha was smiling at me, and it felt so different it was almost comical.

When you looked like me, you figured out quickly how to tell which smiles, looks, and words were real, and which ones weren't. The way he looked at me was genuine, and I found myself smiling in relief. "Not overstepping. And thank you."

"I'm Cameron."

"Ocean."

His eyebrows rose. "That's a pretty name."

I laughed once. "My mother loved water. She did research on it before she passed. If she'd had more children she told me she would have done more. Like 'Lake,' 'Rain,' and 'River.'"

When we spun, I barely felt it because he was leading me. It was gentle and steady, and I knew without having to think that I could trust him to take that lead. "That would have been quite the family reunion."

"We'd have to wait until it was raining," I said.

"And only have those reunions on the beach. Or lakeside."

"Or," I countered, "we could find a stream and be next to a body of water none of us were named for."

Cameron nodded. "I think that's probably the best way to go. So no one feels left out."

"If it were a real thing, I'd definitely do that. But I'm an only child."

"Ah." His fingers tightened on my hand and my back, where his hand rested. In contrast to Jason, nowhere near my ass. "Me too."

Glancing around the room, he looked back down at me again. "Are you all right? My packmates made sure he left the party, so if you don't want someone else touching you, I understand."

The words stopped me in my tracks. They shouldn't, but they did. His packmates were in on it too? "I could use a drink, I think. Probably just water."

"Of course."

Cameron led me off the dance floor with a hand on my lower back, and I didn't mind that it was there. Because I already knew it was a measure of protection, not possession. When we reached the refreshments table, two other Alphas stood close by. "Ocean, these are my packmates. Micah and Everett."

I grabbed a glass of water before looking and finding the same kind of awed, dazed looks on their faces Cameron had when he first rescued me on the dance floor. One of them looked at Cameron briefly before looking back at me and inhaling deeply. "It's lovely to meet you, Ocean. Like he said, I'm Micah."

"Everett." The second Alpha held out his hand. Dark brown hair and piercing blue eyes pinned me to the spot. A second later his scent curled through the air. It reminded me of cookies my mother used to make. Pistachio and almond, but sweet.

"Nice to meet you," I said. "Your packmate, and you, I guess, saved me from a rather awkward encounter."

Micah held out his hand then, and when I gave him mine, he covered it with his other hand, clasping it gently. "I'm glad. Bad behavior aside, no one should leave a beautiful woman alone in the middle of a dance floor."

I inhaled sharply. Chocolate and caramel. They smelled incredible, and I didn't even have time to marvel about the fact that their pack smelled so good because my brain was busy being short-circuited by how easily he called me beautiful.

Jason, who declared he'd wanted to take me home, had said nothing of the sort.

Taking the moment to sip my water and look at them, they were exactly who belonged at a party like this. Handsome beyond belief, and rich, if the tuxes and watches they wore were any indication. And they'd rescued me from an asshole?

Yeah, I needed to get away from them as soon as possible. Because I'd already had this particular bubble burst too many times. And after Jason telling me I needed to accept pity sex because I was fat, I wasn't prepared to see their kindness turn into pity.

I realized I'd been staring at our joined hands for too many seconds. "Thank you again," I said, gently pulling back. "I was on my way out when he insisted we dance. So I think I'm going to go. But I do appreciate it."

Everett smiled. "Any chance I can convince you of one more dance before you go?"

Yes.

Fuck, yes.

Dancing with all of them would be incredible. But it wouldn't fix the root of the problem. I was already going to deal with the guilt and the loneliness when I got back to my room. Dancing with Alphas who only wanted to make sure I was okay wouldn't help that, no matter how good it would feel to dance with someone who smelled amazing and looked even better. To be held.

"Not tonight," I murmured, unable to hold his gaze and tell the lie. "But thank you for the offer."

It took more effort than it should have to walk away. I felt their gazes on my back, and everything in me wanted to glance over my shoulder. But I didn't, because if there *was* pity in their eyes, I would need more than this too-tight corset to hold me together.

So I didn't look, and left, wishing I'd said yes to that dance.

Fig 4. Lilac (Purple)
Meaning: First emotions of love; First
love; Infatuation; Obsession

EVERETT

$\mathcal{I}$ took a single step after Ocean, and Micah's hand met my chest. The growl cracked out of me so fast I startled myself, drawing looks from those nearby.

"Easy," Micah said, voice lowered.

"*Easy*?" I said. "Please tell me you're kidding. I can't take it fucking easy. Because she's—"

"*I know.*" He nodded his head toward the back of the room and the windows. Away from the direction she'd gone. I could still scent her in the air. *Omega*. Sweetly floral and laced with sugar I wanted to taste. To bite.

To *feast* on.

That woman was our scent match, and I felt like I'd been punched in the stomach. I'd been so angry when we came to the gala, not wanting to be here at all. Now I didn't want to be here so I could follow the trail of her scent, pin her to the wall and show her absolutely everything.

More than everything. Bite her and let her feel just how deep and how far this went and how I never imagined finding someone so fucking beautiful and then realizing they were meant to be yours. I wanted to merge us together so there was never any room between us again.

She was still in the room, waylaid by Laura, Frank's wife. It made sense if she was leaving.

Micah hauled me in the opposite direction, and it was only the thought of frightening her when she'd already had some asshole pawing at her without consent that I let myself be dragged away.

Ocean.

The name echoed in my head along with the rhythm of the waves along the coast.

"She's still here," I said. "We need to tell her."

Cameron looked as devastated as I felt. "Because that would go over well. Hey, we know we just saved you from a colossal dick, but we're actually three Alphas who want exactly the same thing and are using scent matching to excuse it."

I snarled and checked myself. That's not what he was saying, but how it would be perceived. "Fuck." I ran a hand through my hair. "At least tell me you're losing your mind too, because I feel like I'm having a heart attack."

"It hit me in the middle of trying to get that guy off her," Cam said quietly. "And it took everything in me not to pull her into a closet and mark her. So, yeah."

I watched her disappear from the room, that silky blue dress and shining dark hair I wanted to run my fingers through. She'd been stun-

21

ning from afar when we stood on the balcony. Up close, there was no comparison. I wanted to touch every part of her body until I had it memorized. Make her scream until she knew she was mine. And that was before her scent changed the very fabric of who I was.

It was a good thing we were in the corner where it wasn't glaringly obvious I had an erection harder than a fucking diamond.

"She's leaving." My voice was strained. "We don't even know her last name."

Micah put his hand on my shoulder again. "Ocean's not a common name. We'll find her."

"And then figure out how to explain that we're not stalking her," Cameron muttered.

Right. She wasn't feeling this in the same way we were. It was clear there was interest. I saw the way she took us in, scenting us. She was attracted to us, but because Omegas couldn't scent match outside of their heat cycle, this torture was ours alone.

Fuck.

It didn't make sense.

One second the world had structure and order and the next second I was ready to tear everything apart at the seams simply to take another breath of that *scent*.

"Oh good, there you are. I'd hoped the three of you had made your way back to the party."

Frank McCabe was the last person on the face of the earth I wanted to see right now. In comparison to the scent I craved, he was sickly. Like a fruit that was a few days past ripeness. I'd never noticed it before, but now I knew every scent would be compared to hers.

"Of course," Micah said, ever the diplomat. "We might not stay much longer, but thank you for having us."

"I'm glad you came. About that meeting. Can I have my secretary call yours and put it on the books for sometime next week?"

My eyes narrowed, brain snapping out of its Ocean-induced fog for a moment. That was the second time he'd asked, which meant he wanted something. Badly. The first rule of a business negotiation was never to show your hand too early. If you did, you lost all your power. Frank was on the verge of giving everything away.

"Sure," Cameron said, clapping the man on the shoulder. "I'm sure we can find some time."

I reached inside my tuxedo and retrieved my phone to see if the text I sent had yielded any results. The work we asked Aiden to do was just on this side of legal. Well, most of the time. We tried to use his out-of-bounds skills as a last resort. But the Firefly deal leaking to Frank was a situation that warranted the caution. Plus, he worked fast.

Sure enough, there was a text with a link. I clicked on it, the documents opening up to show me what he'd found. I managed to keep the shock off my face.

McCabe Fabrics was in trouble. They were almost bankrupt, and in the red in almost every sector. Why? They had enough clients for a thriving business. What would have made them tank so quickly? I could have sworn the last time we made a cursory check, they were fine.

No word on how the deal was leaked though. Aiden was curt.

AIDEN

Nothing on how it got out. This level of cleanliness usually means it was in person and verbal.

"Frank, would you excuse us for just a moment?" I asked him with a smile. "Work never stops."

"Sure." His own smile wavered, and he took a step back, looking around the room. For being the host, he didn't seem to be mingling. Instead, he looked like he stood apart. Odd.

I handed my phone to Micah, and Cameron looked over his shoulder as they looked at the text and the financials. They looked up at me and I nodded.

"Well, that explains why he wants a meeting," Micah whispered.

Cameron nodded. "Yeah. And gives us an idea of how Firefly leaked. Maybe someone thought they were doing him a favor and wanted to help him?"

"I don't really care why they did it. They shouldn't have," I said. "But you're right. This should be interesting. I'll have him dig more."

Taking back the phone, I texted Aiden my thanks.

EVERETT

Thank you. I'll take whatever you can find on McCabe Fabrics' current financial status.

AIDEN

Will do.

EVERETT

One more thing.

AIDEN

You know I live to serve.

I rolled my eyes. We'd known Aiden since college, when he came over from Albion to study. I could practically hear the cheeky fucker and the accent that used to make women fall all over him.

Zenith's Board is trying to force our hand and make us get married.

Congratulations?

Fucker. It doesn't make sense. They're making up bullshit reasons, and they seem desperate. Can you check?

It'll cost you, but sure.

Doesn't it always?

The Board could make up their bullshit reasons, but they weren't the truth. Until we knew what the truth really was, my mind wouldn't fully settle.

Not that being married bothered me as much as it had an hour ago. As long as it was with the luscious Omega seared into my mind.

We needed to find her.

And I needed to hit the gym, the pool, or the shower with a bottle of body wash and my own hand if I were going to make it through the night without turning into a literal stalker. My hand curled into a fist, and I closed my eyes. I usually had more control than this.

"Feeling a little on edge, Rett?" Cam asked. He grinned, and I wanted to punch him in the throat.

"You're not?"

"Oh, I am." The look in his eyes, deadly serious, told me that. "I'm just reliving that dance in my head to dull that same edge."

"Fucker," I muttered, which only made him smile more.

Micah laughed, but I heard the strain. "Let's get the hell out of here before one of us does something we regret."

"Fine by me."

"We're heading out, Frank," Micah said, holding out a hand. "Thank you again for having us. But I did have one question."

"What's that?" The hope and naked interest on the man's face was nearly embarrassing.

"Who did your flowers? The design is lovely. I can't stop looking at them."

"Oh." Frank stopped and tried to hide his disappointment. Now that we knew what was behind his request for a meeting, it made sense. The last thing he expected us to ask about was flowers. But he shouldn't

24

be that surprised. We were involved in every part of our business, and especially in the design side.

Micah was right. The flowers were lovely. But they didn't smell half as lovely as *our* Omega.

"They were designed by my niece. I'm sure she'll be happy to hear you liked them."

"Your niece?" Cameron asked, frowning. I joined him. This was the first time we'd heard of her. Not that we kept track of the families of our business partners, but in the many events we'd been attended alongside Frank, it seemed strange she wouldn't have come up if she made creations like this.

Frank nodded and looked around the room. "The daughter of my wife's late sister. Felicity Caldwell."

The others met my gaze in shock, and I made a mental note to add one more inquiry to Aiden's list. The fact that we hadn't known there was still a living Caldwell *did* surprise me. The Caldwells were one of the old families on the west coast. Everyone knew them or knew of them, at least until the last son and his wife had died.

I was still young when they passed, but we knew of them by reputation, and the legacy they left behind. Hence there being a gala in their honor, for one of their charities.

"What's her name?" Cameron asked.

Frank still glanced through the crowd, frowning. "Ocean. I can find her and introduce you if you like."

My body went so still it might have been electrocuted.

Ocean was his niece. Ocean *Caldwell*.

My Omega.

"That's all right," I said, not wanting him to track her down. Now we had enough information to do it ourselves. "Thank you for telling us."

He smiled, but it was bland and uninterested. "No problem. I'll call about that meeting."

"Please do." I was already moving across the ballroom and toward the exit by the time the others caught up with me.

Cameron huffed a laugh. "You'd think your shoes were on fire."

Saying nothing, I grabbed the keys from the valet. My mind was moving now. It had a singular purpose, all revolving around a stunning Omega in blue.

Our enemies, business and otherwise, grumbled that the DuPont pack always won, no matter the cost. That wasn't always true, but today it was. Because I knew how to get us everything we wanted.

I smiled and turned the keys in the ignition.

Fig 5. Dog Rose
Meaning: Ferocity; Honesty; Pain and pleaure

CAMERON

*M*y assistant was waiting at the elevator for me. Which honestly wasn't a good sign. "Oren?"

The male Omega made a face. "Yeah, I know you hate it when I meet you at the elevator."

"But you're still doing it, which means it's important or you have a death wish."

He chuckled, but held out a hand to stop me from going closer to my office. Micah and Everett's offices were on different floors. It made it both easier and harder. Easier since we all did slightly different things. Harder, since we constantly needed each other's feedback.

Our assistants were very good friends.

"You have someone waiting for you in conference room B."

I frowned. "I don't remember having a meeting scheduled this morning."

The look on his face told me I wasn't wrong. "Nope. You didn't have one. But he was here this morning before I arrived, and said you'd agreed to meet with him. All three of you, actually. And he refused to leave or reschedule. I put him in the conference room so I could talk to you, because I didn't want to make a scene with security."

My phone was already in my hand, ready to call security or the others. "Who is it?"

"Frank McCabe."

"Seriously?"

"Seriously."

I sighed. "Thanks. Let's take the back way to the office."

"Fine by me," Oren muttered. "Man's annoying as shit."

Allowing my smirk to shine through, I was glad we weren't the only ones that found Frank generally insufferable. "Did you get him coffee?"

"You mean did I make his overly particular and pretentious coffee order? I did. With a smile on my face. I didn't even put salt in it like I was tempted."

"Oren." I choked on a laugh.

He sat at his desk and gave me a look. "What? I'm allowed to be tempted."

"Well, get off your ass and be tempted to get my particular and pretentious coffee order, will you?"

He saluted and did as I asked. Good thing too. Because coffee really was the only thing that was going to hold me together today. I hadn't slept well, and I didn't think I'd be able to focus for five straight minutes in a row today. The only thing on my mind was getting to her.

Ocean.

Ocean Elise Correa Caldwell. We'd looked her up last night on arriving home. There wasn't much about her publicly. But the few photos I saw of her reminded me of just how stunning she was, and a couple of the stories told me what I already knew: our Omega was beautiful on the inside too.

Shaking my head to clear my thoughts of dark eyes and her warmth under my hands, I dialed both of my packmates. Everett picked up first. "Miss us already?"

"Frank McCabe is in my conference room."

Micah made an annoyed sound. "He must be desperate. Has it even been twelve hours?"

I checked my watch. "Barely. Did Aiden find anything more?"

"Not that I know of. He's fast, but not this fast. The things he found were just surface level, but I looked into the actual financials he sent a little more. They're behind on paying most of their suppliers. A couple warehouses are in danger of eviction. The whole thing looks like it's a house of cards about to topple."

Dropping my briefcase by my desk, I sank into my chair. "What do you want me to do? Send him away until later this week?"

"I don't love going into the meeting unprepared," Rett said. "But if he's this desperate, we'll have an advantage. And that's something we want right now."

Yes. It was.

My cock went hard again at the mere thought of her. The whole last night had been torture, thinking of her sweet curves under my hands and see how much more I wanted to touch them. Worship them and her. Get inside her mind and figure out why those dark eyes felt so sad. Tell her how I felt after being drawn to her from across the room and then being slammed with the best, brightest, *hottest* scent of my life as soon as I was near her.

We'd talked about Everett's idea, and it would work. Granted, we thought we'd have a little more time to implement it, but he was right. This was to our advantage. It would solve our problem and get us closer to our sweet Omega.

I didn't know much about Frank as a person, but if he was as insufferable in his personal life as he was in business, I wanted Ocean as far away from him as possible. Already, my protective instincts were going crazy after I'd almost had to pull that creep off her.

Still up on the balcony, I'd seen her face, and I'd moved before I was fully thinking. The others backed me without question. We were a team and always would be.

"Well, get your asses down here and use the back way to my office," I said. "Let's get this done."

"Give me fifteen minutes to put something together," Everett said. "Glad I couldn't sleep and was already working on it."

"Done."

Oren put my coffee down on my desk and raised an eyebrow. "Satisfied, my liege?" The sarcasm dripped through.

"You're lucky you're good your job."

"And you're lucky you pay me so well." He flaunted his walk all the way back to his desk, earning a laugh from me. Oren was the best assistant I'd ever had. Plus, he was a character. I'd have him out on his ass if he didn't do good work, but half the time he knew what I needed before I needed it.

Everett and Micah walked in together, and the former looked at me. "Ready?" He held a couple of paper folders in his hands.

I grinned and grabbed my coffee. "Born ready."

Frank sat at the large conference table with his phone in his hand and a sheen of sweat on his forehead. Given what his financials looked like, he should be nervous. I still didn't understand what had happened, but for the next few minutes, it didn't matter. All that mattered was that he could give us what we wanted.

Micah was the first one through the door. "I thought you said next week, Frank. I didn't think you meant this morning."

He laughed nervously. "Right. Sorry to intrude."

It was Thursday. Whatever he had in mind could have waited until Monday. Ours, however, couldn't.

"You're here now." Everett unbuttoned his suit jacket with one hand and sat down. "Why don't you tell us what brought you this kind of urgency?"

Frank cleared his throat and took a sip of his coffee. "Some poor decisions." Then he sighed and his shoulders wilted. I glanced over at the others to see what kind of read they were getting, but they gave nothing away. "It's always been my intent to expand beyond textiles. I hoped that in doing some strategic investing I might have the capital to move past that sector.

"But the firm I hired to make the investments didn't manage the funds well. And with things in the market being how they are..." he shrugged. "I'm—"

"In the red in every possible way you can be?" Everett finished the sentence. "We're aware."

Shock rolled across the man's face. He was an Alpha, but he'd never felt that way to me. Not that I put all the stock in someone's designation. "How?"

"We have our ways. But you know, never kiss and tell." Everett mimicked his words from last night. "What I really want to know is how you let it get this bad?"

He had a point. Everett was the business mind among us. There was a ruthlessness in him that served us well in these deals. And Frank should have pulled these investments long before now.

"I didn't know."

"You didn't *know*?" Micah sounded incredulous. "How?"

"They assured me things would bounce back. I didn't realize how deeply the market had shifted."

I frowned. Our own investments were doing just fine. So what had caused this? For the moment, it didn't matter, but it needed to be looked into.

"And what are you hoping we'll do about it?" Everett asked.

Frank winced and pulled his hands off the table. They were shaking. He was nervous, and he should be. Still, I gave the man credit for asking for help instead of blindly driving the company into the ground out of pride.

"I was hoping for a partnership. I'm aware the Firefly deal is private. But if you're willing to purchase a company like them, perhaps you'd be willing to work with us." Leaning down, he retrieved a small folder from the briefcase beside his chair. "I brought this."

I caught it when it slid across the table and glanced through it. Yeah, that wasn't going to work. All this did was give him money and gave us essentially nothing. I passed it to the others and Everett snorted a laugh. "This is your offer?"

Frank said nothing.

"As I said, we have our ways too." Everett tapped the folders he brought with him and then set them side by side. "And I took the liberty of putting these together. This," he pushed one of the folders forward, "is the normal offer you would get."

He didn't ask us *why* we had proposals ready. Frank took the first folder and scanned the contents, his eyes going wide and anger taking root. "Are you fucking kidding me?"

"We don't joke about business," I said. "So no."

"No. The answer is no. I'd rather lose my company than that."

Everett smiled. "Which is why I prepared this. Much of it is the same, but with a few key differences. McCabe Fabrics will still be brought under the umbrella of Zenith Incorporated. We'll buy you out of the majority of your shares and leave you as the minority holder. You'll also be allowed to remain in whatever position you want, with supervision, of course. We're not going to let this happen twice."

Snarling, Frank reached for the folder. "Doesn't sound particularly generous."

I smiled. This was the real Frank. He *was* nervous, and he was weak, but he also wasn't the pussy-footing and subtle man who'd come into the office this morning. He was more like a dog backed into a corner.

That was fine. We preferred dealing with people who were honest.

Everett kept his hand on the folder, not letting him take it yet. "We'll cover all your debts and make sure that the company is in good standing and ready to continue operating. That's a hell of a lot more than what someone else would offer you."

"So let me see the offer."

"There's one more thing," Micah said. "And it's not negotiable."

"You see," Everett smiled. "The only reason we're not giving you offer number one, or letting your company fail so we can pick up the pieces, is because you have something we very much want."

Frank's fingers drummed on the table. He was getting irritated. "And what is that?"

"Ocean."

Confusion clouded his face. "What?"

"Ocean," I said, repeating her name. It tasted sweet on my tongue. "Your niece."

"I know who she is." His brow furrowed. "I'm just not sure what she has anything to do with this?"

Micah stood, stretching and moving to lean against the wall, the picture of ease. "The Zenith Board of Directors, for reasons I won't go into now, has instructed us to marry. We want Ocean."

The expression on Frank's face went from blank to shock, and then he burst out laughing. "What? Why? Of all the people in the world, you want her?"

He stopped laughing when he realized we were all glaring at him. The table creaked where I gripped it, the point of contact the only thing stopping me from launching myself over the table at him.

"Ocean must agree to marry us for a minimum of one year," Everett said, finally releasing the folder and sliding it across the table.

I glanced over at him, and Micah caught my gaze. I read the message there. *One year is just the start.*

"Either that, or it's offer number one."

Frank glanced through the folder and straightened. His sudden haughty attitude grated on me. "If I'm going to sell my niece to you, I deserve to know why."

"Bringing Firefly Clothing into the fold requires us to look more wholesome than our previous exploits currently allow," I said. "Marriage will help that."

He glanced up at me briefly before looking down at the paperwork again. "I guess that makes sense. More sense than the three of you wanting someone who looks like her. And after the year is up?"

Everett was clenching his jaw so hard next to me I heard it crack.

"She is free to go her own way," I said, even though the words burned. There was no way in hell we were going to let her go, and I

31

didn't doubt she would feel the same once she knew the truth. But it was a long road from here to there.

I saw him think it through as he looked at the paperwork. It wasn't a good deal. Not for him, at least. But he wasn't in a position to refuse. Sure, he could approach another company, but with the state of his financials, he'd be lucky to get something as good as our first offer, let alone this one. He knew it too. The resistance was all for show.

"I'll need some time to talk to her," he said.

"Listen to me very carefully," Everett said. "You will not force her into this."

Frank frowned. "I thought it was all or nothing?"

"It is," I said. "But we're not monsters. There are other people we can marry if we choose." My mind *rebelled* at the very thought of it. "Ocean must marry us willingly."

Not only because it was the right thing to do, but because if she were forced, it would be that much harder for us to show her how much we wanted her. How much she was everything.

One scent, and none of the world mattered anymore. Zenith Incorporated—our life's work and our whole future—could burn to the ground tomorrow, and if we had her, I wouldn't care.

She was ours. On the deepest level of our souls, she was meant to be ours. No one fully understood the power of a scent match. I certainly hadn't until I put my hand on that man's shoulder, caught her scent, and the entire universe shifted.

"Like I said, I'll need some time."

"You have until Monday," Micah said. "At noon."

Frank nodded and then left the room so quickly you would have thought the building was on fire.

Chuckling, Micah shook his head. "I don't think that's what he expected."

"What happens if she says no?" I asked.

"Then we court her."

I stared at the wall for a long second before speaking. "He's going to try to force her. There's too much on the line for him not to."

Everett grinned, showing me the smile only our enemies saw. "Let him try. If he forces her hand, we'll take him for everything he's worth. And then we'll court our Omega anyway, in the way she deserves."

Taking a long sip of my coffee, I nodded and smiled. I couldn't wait to see her again, but fuck, Monday felt like a long way away.

Fig 6. Aloe Vera
(Also: Immortality Plant,
Crocodile's Tongue, Savia)
Meaning: Bitterness; Dejection; Grief; Sorrow

OCEAN

I liked the days after parties.

It was always quiet in the house. My aunt slept late and babied herself with her inevitable hangover, my uncle dove into work and solidifying whatever connections he'd made the night before, and I was left entirely alone.

Which was a good thing, because there were still a bunch of things to do before Ellie's wedding.

Isolde's sister was a sweetheart, and I was thrilled to do the flowers for her wedding. Everything for the ceremony and reception was sorted, and my girls were getting ready to make the pieces.

At the moment, I was finishing up the final designs for the boutonnieres. It should have been done a long time ago, but I hadn't been able to decide what message I wanted to send to Isolde's ex. Finally, I'd decided on a petunia, with some hemlock and basil, representing anger, disdain, hatred, and death.

It made me smile.

The flowers at the party last night, though they'd been exactly what my aunt and uncle had asked for in terms of colors, were similar. They never asked about the meanings, and I never volunteered them. One more small way I rebelled whenever I could.

My phone rang, Sally's name on the screen. "Hey," I answered.

"Hi, boss."

"Everything okay?"

"Yeah. Just picked up all the roses. Most of them are still closed, so they'll be gorgeous on Saturday. There weren't as many lavender ones as we ordered, but they replaced them with white. If we get them into some ink water they should be an okay replacement."

Not ideal, but we'd made worse things work. And it wasn't like I was there to insist the vendor give us what we asked for. The roses would soak up the dye from the water, and Sally would monitor to make sure they didn't turn too dark. "That's fine. I'm sending you an email with the last boutonniere. Nothing crazy. But if you guys need anything, let me know."

I heard her car door shut over the phone. "I think we'll be okay, but I wanted to make sure you'll be there on Saturday? We've got all the plans, but you know you're the one with the details in the brain. And you still have that thing I can never manage to do."

My eyes rolled on instinct. Sally was my right-hand woman. Mainly because the work I could legally do thanks to my aunt and uncle was severely limited. I needed help to run my business, and honestly, I was lucky they even let me have one at all.

Sally insisted I had a way with the flowers in person that she didn't, and that whenever I touched something, it looked better. It wasn't true. She was just trying to keep me involved, but it was very sweet.

"You know I'll be there. And you're more than capable of making things look perfect."

"Still," she said. "We need our fearless leader."

"Your fearless leader says to get those roses back to the workshop before they wilt in the back of your blazing hot minivan."

A loud cackle came through the phone. "All right. I'll check in after I make sure we have everything."

"Thanks, Sally."

I'm not sure how it got to be afternoon already, but it was. Hell, it was almost evening, and I didn't even think I'd eaten today. My stomach growled at the thought, and I rolled my eyes. "So demanding," I muttered.

But this worked out well. It was early enough that I could slip into the kitchen and eat something without anyone noticing, and avoid whatever dinner Laura and Frank had planned. If anything.

The days after a party they sometimes let me take a tray in my room.

Here was hoping.

The kitchen was blissfully empty, and it felt like a grilled cheese and tomato soup kind of day. I smiled when I saw there were two pieces of bread left, because that was perfect, and I never got so lucky.

Before I forgot, I added bread to the housekeeper's list on the side of the fridge so she knew we were out. My headphones were still upstairs, so I hummed to myself as I heated up the tomato soup and grilled the sandwich to perfection. It smelled amazing.

"Michelle, I need a sandwich or something. I know we're eating soon, but I was in the office all day and I'm starving." My uncle strode into the kitchen expecting to see the cook, who wasn't here. His face morphed into disdain. "What are you doing in here? And where's Michelle?"

"I forgot to eat too. And I don't know."

He inhaled deeply, like he was keeping himself from reacting. "Right. Because you could ever forget to eat. Guess I'll make myself a sandwich then. Though I don't know why we're paying for a cook when she's not around to do her job."

I was wincing before he even went to where the bread was stored, because I knew there wouldn't be any. I turned off the stove and plated the sandwich quickly, putting the dishes where Michelle preferred I leave them.

Frank turned to me slowly. "Did you take the last of the bread?"

"I wrote it down for Isabel to get more."

"We've had this discussion, Ocean. You don't take something if there's nothing left of it for anyone else. It's selfish, rude, and you don't need it anyway."

"Sorry."

"Give me that. You shouldn't be eating the carbs. Don't want to end up diabetic like that friend of yours." He picked up the plate and was almost out of the kitchen when he turned. "You're going to meet me in my office at six sharp. I need to talk to you about something."

"Okay."

I scowled at his back as he left, once again wishing I had more of a spine with my aunt and uncle. I didn't have the energy or mental bandwidth to explain to him, yet again, how inaccurate that assumption was. Or that he was an asshole for mocking someone's disability. Or that he was an asshole in general.

There was never a problem when he and Laura weren't around, and even though those Alphas had ended up rescuing me last night, I'd still stood up for myself. It was just them. When they were around, the fear clogged up my throat and I couldn't seem to think like the smart person I was. Instead, I turned into a ghost. Or a wet noodle. Someone who couldn't stand on her own two feet.

No. That wasn't true. Someone who was afraid of the power they held over her and didn't want to make it worse.

Tears blurred my eyes, and I blinked them away.

I needed to get upstairs before he came back because he forgot something and found me crying. It never ended well. He'd think I was crying over the sandwich, and the last time I'd cried over food in front of him, I'd barely been able to eat for a week because he told the staff exactly how much food to give me.

My thoughts went down a familiar spiral, and I knew from experience it was easier to just let it happen than to fight it. Why had mom and dad done this? Why had they given Frank and Laura power over everything until I was thirty-five?

I would have said it was a joke, but I'd seen the documents. Plus mom and dad's signatures. It was real. And those documents said that Frank and Laura held custodial power over my finances until that age. It was why I couldn't leave and live on my own—they wouldn't let me have enough money in my accounts to get my own place, even if I didn't want to live in the home that was rightfully mine.

Technically Frank and Laura still thought my flower business was a hobby. As long as I didn't show them too much money, they never questioned it. Because they didn't consider that I could have that kind of ambition.

It was why I had to pay Sally a salary that was far above what a normal manager might have, because she had an account on the side that was for me. With a debit card attached to it. I didn't deserve her.

I'd even offered to make her co-owner of *Entendre*, but she'd declined.

Isolde and Trinity knew, of course, but they didn't *know*. Not the day-to-day digs and the level of control they held over my life. And I didn't want them to know. Not really. Because they were a bright spot, and just like those Alphas, I didn't want them to feel any kind of pity for me.

And there was nothing they could do. Why would I want my friends to feel as helpless as I did?

I curled up in my favorite chair and slowly ate my soup. It was good. It wasn't enough, but it was good. I already knew I wasn't going back to the kitchen tonight. Not if there was a chance Frank would see me. I just didn't want to deal with it.

The words hurt more than I wanted them to, even if I'd heard them a hundred times before.

I didn't hate my body. I might not love it, but I didn't hate it. There were good days and bad days, like everyone had. What I really wished was that I could *love* my body. But the truth was, no matter how much I wanted to love it, I didn't, because Frank, Laura, and even Jason, were right.

I wasn't small. I was fat, and no one wanted a fat Omega. I'd resigned myself to it a long time ago. I was healthy and I took care of myself. My body was simply bigger, and though I'd accepted it, it didn't fill the aching hole in my chest wishing someone would look at me the way Isolde's Alphas looked at her. Hoping that someone would love me even though I looked like this.

Praying that maybe someone could make me believe that I should love myself as I was, instead of trying to make myself smaller to fit into a world that didn't want me. Wanting someone who would be able to scoop me up and allow me to feel cherished and precious even if I wasn't what everyone thought I should be.

A single tear slipped out, and I slapped it away.

No.

There'd already been too many tears over this, and I didn't want Frank to think he'd gotten to me. I wasn't a pretty crier, and if I started now, even in the couple of hours before I needed to meet him in his office, he would know.

Nope. No more crying.

I finished my soup and grabbed one of my sketchbooks to work on a party we'd been booked for next month. The client had some pretty ideas, and I had some thoughts. I wanted to give her some sketches and a list of possible flowers on Monday.

Due to my... limitations, I didn't manage or even design every event. But there were some who came to me because they knew through word of mouth about my hybrid work, or my knack for creating meaning with the language of flowers, and asked for me specifically. I loved it when that happened.

Maybe in a few years I'd be able to expand and do more things myself. Sometimes I felt like I was rotting inside this house. I wasn't a prisoner, technically. They allowed me to leave. But Frank and Laura asked so many questions every time I did that I had to decide which things were worth it. Like going ballgown bowling with Trinity and Isolde.

Glancing at my phone, it was almost six. The last thing I needed was to be late and get a lecture on top of what Frank wanted to talk to me about. Whatever it was, I doubted it was good.

As soon as I approached the door to his office, I heard Laura's voice. Fuck. Them together?

Good thing I didn't cry. Because I might have to do it later. Trying to master the fear and dread in my stomach, I closed my eyes and knocked.

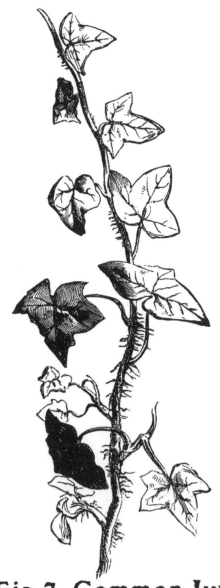

Fig 7. Common Ivy
Meaning: Endurance, Dependence;
Marriage, Matrimony

OCEAN

"*C*ome in."

Pushing the door open, I found my aunt draped across one of the couches in my uncle's office, wrapped in a silk robe with what looked like a cosmo in her hand. If I had to guess, I'd say she'd never gotten dressed today. But if I'd done the same thing she would have called me lazy.

I hated that part of me would have believed her.

· Frank stood near the giant fireplace with a drink, though it was too warm this time of year to have a fire indoors. The plate with my grilled cheese still sat on his desk, with the sandwich only half eaten.

"Glad you're on time," Frank said.

I said nothing.

After a second, he cleared his throat and took a sip of his drink. "You probably know that the business has been having some trouble."

"Yeah." I didn't know what, but I heard enough to know that things weren't going well. Yet another reason why they wouldn't pay me what I was fucking worth for all the flowers I did for the gala.

"We received an offer today. It's a good one." He winced. "Well, it's a decent one, and we're going to take it."

I frowned. "Okay? What does that have to do with me?"

"You're part of the deal."

It felt a little like the sounds of the whole world went fuzzy and I had to lean in to hear him properly. Because there's no fucking way he actually said what he just said. "Excuse me?"

He huffed out a breath, looking annoyed at having to repeat himself. "You're part of the deal. The Alphas making the offer want a wife, and they want you. So you're going to marry them, and while you do, you'll help us take their company for our own from the inside out."

My jaw dropped, and for a second I wondered if I'd hallucinated this whole thing, or maybe the soup had been expired and I had food poisoning. "Are you fucking insane?"

"*Watch your mouth.*" My aunt was on her feet and charging toward me. "You think you can suddenly talk to us like that after everything we've done for you?"

"Done for me?" I gaped at her.

"Yes. Done for you. You should be grateful we took you in at all."

My jaw trembled and the words I'd wanted to say my entire life hovered behind my lips. As if they could take me in when the house we lived in was *mine* and they were staying in it on borrowed time. As if anything they'd done in my entire life had caused me anything but pain.

But they still held the keys to fucking everything, which bound my tongue. Rage swam behind my eyes and my entire body shook with it. My hands curled into fists with the urge to reach out and hit and hurt and take back everything they'd *done for me*.

"No," I said.

"You ungrateful little shit," she hissed. "You will do this."

I shook my head. "No, I won't. You might control my entire life, but you cannot make me marry anyone. I don't care."

"You want us to be thrown out of this house because you can't see this for the opportunity it is?" Laura's voice was rising, echoing off the walls. "Frank said you'd do this, and I thought you would be happy."

Part of me snapped. "Why on earth would you think that?"

"Because someone would finally fucking want you."

I didn't intend for the gasp that came out of me. My rule was never to show how hurt I was. Never give them more power over me than they already had. Yet, with that single sentence, it felt like I'd taken a knife to the ribs.

That was the worst part. Laura believed those things, and an aching, not-so-small part of me believed them too. Hadn't I just said the same thing to myself?

It wasn't just the desire to be wanted romantically. Was it too much to ask that my own family want me?

The pain drained out of me, replaced with bleak devastation. She was right. It would be easier to take what I could get and try to find some happiness within it. Then at least I'd be away from them and I wouldn't be alone.

Five more years of this stretched in front of me like a path into nothing. Just a desert of the same conversations and the same hurts over and over again. I almost said yes.

The tiniest glimmer of my soul that wanted to be loved for me instead of what I could give someone rebelled. It took all the strength I had. "No."

"I thought you might say that." My uncle crossed the room and leaned back against his desk. "But you're going to say yes."

"The hell I am."

"You are," he said calmly. "Because the agreement is only for a year, and at the end of that year, if you do this, I will sign your trust over to you early."

My aunt's head whipped around so fast I could have sworn I heard a crack.

"What?" we both asked at the same time.

His eyes went cold. "Stop making me repeat myself."

More pain spread through my chest, making it hard to breathe. "You could have done that this whole time? Signed it over to me?"

"It's not easy," he said with a shrug. "A lot of hoops to jump through. But I need you to do this, and because you've never been helpful a day in your life, I knew you would need motivation."

Hot tears flooded my eyes, and I turned away, breathing through the sharpness of my grief. "Why do they want to marry me?" I asked, voice watery.

"Some kind of PR problem. I don't really know, nor do I care. What I care about is signing the paperwork that will save McCabe Fabrics, and you are a part of that paperwork."

One year instead of five. One. *ONE*.

My mother died when I was twelve. I'd already survived eighteen years of this. I could survive one more. Especially if it wasn't with them. One jail for another. At least there would be different scenery.

There wouldn't be anything to tie me to this marriage when the year was over. The implant in my arm was more than enough to prevent any accidental pregnancies. I'd tried to get the surgery Isolde had, preventing them entirely, but no one would perform it on me because of my size. One surgeon even went as far as to say I wouldn't need it at all. Like me having sex was a crime against humanity.

One year, and I could be free of all of this.

"I want it in writing," I finally said, looking at him and disgusted by the victory in his eyes. "I want it in writing and notarized, with lawyers and *witnesses*."

"Fine."

The ease with which he said it made me want to crumple. It wasn't hard, he just hadn't wanted to do it. They never wanted to do it because it wasn't worth it to them. As long as they controlled the estate, they could do whatever they wanted and held all the benefits that came with it. No matter if they couldn't touch the money that was mine. They would still try.

Maybe that was why the paperwork had been thirty-five. Maybe Mom and Dad thought that their closest family wouldn't hesitate to sign the estate over to me when I became an adult.

I closed my eyes, and a tear finally spilled over. I didn't bother to wipe it away. "Then I'll do it."

"Good. I'll have the paperwork here for you, with your notary, lawyers, and witnesses, on Saturday."

"Ellie's—" I stopped. "Isolde's sister's wedding is on Saturday. I did the flowers, and she's my friend. I have to be there."

Laura crossed her arms. "I'm sure the flowers will be fine without you."

"What part of *I have to be there* wasn't clear the first time?" I snapped.

Her eyebrows rose into her hairline and she took a step back. I never spoke to her like that. Well, I did, but usually in my head.

Frank interrupted whatever she was about to say to me. "I meant what I said, Ocean. This is an opportunity for all of us, and I will need you to get me information."

"Sure." Whoever it was, if they were doing this, I doubted they were stupid. They knew who Frank was, and they weren't going to let me anywhere near the kind of knowledge he was talking about. I could try if he wanted me to, but that wasn't on my priority list. My priority list was his signature on the document guaranteeing my freedom.

"We'll get everything set up. Sign the papers for you on Saturday, and the rest of the deal on Monday. I'll see if they can come and meet you on Saturday."

"That's fine." I was already retreating into my own mind, making plans and dealing with the repercussions of what I'd just done.

"Do you want to know who?"

I looked at him. "Does it matter?"

"No." Laura snorted. "You're lucky they're even looking at you."

It looked like Frank was going to say something else, but I didn't let him. "Saturday *night*. I'm going to the wedding. Let me know when they're going to be here."

Then I walked out, and I didn't look back.

Fig 8. Garden Ranunculus
(Also: Persian Buttercup)
Meaning: Attractive; Beautiful; Fascination

MICAH

I clicked through the various photos on the website of Ocean's business. Her work was fucking beautiful, and the pictures of her staff all looked joyful. I'd looked into her business because I couldn't help myself—anything and everything to do with Ocean fascinated me, and until I could see her again, I wanted every scrap I could get.

Entendre. The flowing script dragged across the screen. Navigating to the section about the business itself, I sucked in a breath. A picture of Ocean was on the page, and she was fucking breathtaking. Wind in her hair as she sat on the beach smiling at something off camera.

I wanted to be the one messing up her hair just like the breeze, and at the same time I wanted to be the one brushing the hair back from her face so I could see those eyes.

Reading the little blurb had me smiling, and then laughing out loud as I realized what she'd done.

> *At Entendre, we do more than create beautiful flower arrangements for your events. We create stories. Flowers and plants have a language— otherwise known as Floriography—and whatever message you want to send with your flowers, we'll create, combined with the aesthetic you want to achieve.*

Entendre. As in double entendre.

My Omega was fucking clever.

Leaning back and closing my eyes, I tried to remember the flowers at the gala. Other than the basics everyone knew, like roses and daisies, I couldn't claim to be any kind of expert. Was I out of my mind to be searching images of flowers to match what had been there?

Maybe.

But I was desperate.

I wasn't the only one either.

Cam was locked away in his office, working on things that weren't needed for weeks and months. I'd already drawn enough to make my fingers ache, and it didn't solve the restlessness. The last time I'd seen Everett he'd been in the gym, pounding away on the treadmill and drenched in sweat like he'd been at it for a while.

I definitely wasn't the only one suffering while we waited for a response from Frank. It hadn't even been a whole day. I had no idea how I was supposed to make it the entire weekend.

There. In a list of common flowers, I caught sight of one I recognized. Big and almost fluffy with the amount of petals. Peony. All right.

Shortly after that, I recognized a couple more. Petunias, and I knew there had been orange lilies in the arrangement.

I looked for a while longer, but didn't find more. This would have to do until I could ask her. So what did these flowers mean?

Another search had me both chuckling and realizing I was in *way* over my head. I'd heard of floriography over the course of my design career, but I'd never given it much thought.

My skills were in painting and drawing. I'd dabbled in graphic design for a little while before I turned my attention to fashion and other practical designs, but my heart still rested with the traditional art. That's what I recognized. This was Ocean's heart.

I didn't know shit about flowers, but if it was something Ocean loved, I'd gladly learn everything about it. Turns out even the color and sub-type of flower affected the meaning.

And orange lilies meant...

I shook my head, thinking I must have misread the screen in front of me. But no. The list of interpreted meanings was very clear. Dislike, hatred, passion, revenge, and desire. Desire felt like an afterthought in this list.

Petunias brought more of the same. Anger and disdain. Resentment. Peonies were listed as anger, bashfulness, and shame.

Sitting back, I frowned. With what Ocean said on *Entendre*'s site, there was no way this was an accident. And though I didn't know her well, Laura didn't strike me as someone who handled the details of a gala like that. More likely they'd gone to Ocean with a color scheme, and she'd done what they'd asked.

This is what she'd given them.

Interesting.

We hadn't known who she was when we saw her across the room. Now I wanted to know everything about her. From the second we saw her on the balcony she was captivating, and inhaling her scent was taking a match and tossing it on gasoline that had already been poured, making that draw and interest catch fucking fire.

This design choice only made me more curious, if that were possible.

I needed to see her again.

How in the hell had we never encountered her before? The number of galas and Frank popping up everywhere...

"Careful," Cameron said, leaning against the door.

"What?"

He nodded to my hand, where it was gripping my desk so hard I was about to break it. I released the wood and shook my head. "I'm going out of my mind."

"Tell me about it. I just sat at my desk and tried to work, but I couldn't. Nothing came to mind for any of the projects I'm working on. I just kept thinking about her. The way she laughed when we danced. Her by the windows with the sun in her hair."

"Look at this."

His breath went short when he saw that picture of her on the beach. "That—" Cam shook his head. "She looks so free. It barely seems like the same person. Fuck, she's beautiful."

"I have an idea about why she feels different."

"Oh?"

"Come on." I stood and led the way out, seeing the gym empty before finally finding Everett in the kitchen biting into a pear. He still looked out of breath. "How long did you run?"

He looked at me, exhausted, leaning on the kitchen island, and blinked slowly. "I don't know. Would still be going, but I can't. I think I'm losing my mind."

"Join the club," Cam said with a chuckle.

I told them about her business and what I'd found. Everett glared out the windows. Our kitchen looked out over a grove of the magnolia trees that loved to grow here in Clarity. "If they've hurt her—"

"If they have, then we'll deal with it," I said. "And she'll be with us."

"Should have made the deadline today," Cameron breathed with a sigh. "Then we wouldn't be in the limbo from hell."

"With how badly Frank wants this, I hope it will be sooner."

If Ocean said no, we'd find a different way to court her. And if she said no, I didn't need to ask to confirm with the others to know we'd tell the Board to go fuck themselves. We weren't marrying anyone other than our Omega, no matter what they tried to throw at us or our company.

"I'm hungry," I said. "But no matter what Marcella left in the fridge, I already know I don't want it." Because anything that wasn't the sweet taste of flowers—I *desperately* needed to know which one her scent was now—and sugar would be like ash on my tongue.

"Do we know anyone who can render us unconscious for the next three days?" Everett muttered, throwing the core of his pear away.

"I wish."

"Hey," Cameron said, his tone drawing my attention. He stared down at his phone, and the growing smile on his face had my gut tightening with hope and fear. "Check your email."

I couldn't get my hands on my phone fast enough.

There it was. An email from Frank McCabe to the three of us.

It's done. Come over Saturday evening to meet with Ocean. We'll sign the rest of the papers on Monday.

-Frank

"Thank fuck." My whole body released the tension I'd been holding since he walked out of our office this morning.

"Monday my ass," Everett said. "I'm showering, then going to see how fast we can get everything together. I'm not waiting longer than I have to."

Cameron grinned. "Time to go find out what we need to apply for a marriage license. And talk to Geneva and see if she's available for planning. Saturday's probably too soon, but what do you think, a week?"

"You can't make it soon enough for me," I said. "But we'll ask her."

I turned and strode back to my office. I had research to do. My Omega—my *wife*—was going to get flowers on Saturday, and I needed to find the perfect bouquet to say everything we meant.

Fig 9. Cornflower
(Also: Bluebottle, Star Thistle, Bluet)
Meaning: Hope; Hope in love;
Single wretchedness

OCEAN

I didn't think about what I'd agreed to. I barely had time to breathe, let alone contemplate the fact that I'd agreed to marry complete strangers.

The girls all cheered when I arrived at the shop to help them prep for the wedding. Honestly, I hadn't planned on it, but I needed to be away from my aunt and uncle and busy enough to avoid my own thoughts and the strange combination of both panic and relief that swirled through me whenever I thought about signing the papers.

"Ocean," my aunt snapped at me the next morning as I was about to leave for the Caruso Estate where Ellie's wedding was taking place.

"I'm already running late," I said, trying to avoid her.

"I don't care. Stop."

I sighed. "*What?*"

Her eyes narrowed on mine. "Just because you won't be here much longer doesn't mean you can speak to me like that."

My mouth snapped shut, words boiling behind my lips. If I said what I wanted to, this would turn into a blowout fight, and I was already behind as it was. So I plastered on a fake smile. "How can I help you?"

"I have a dress for you to wear tonight."

I frowned and looked down at the dress I already wore for the wedding. "What's wrong with this?"

"More than I have time to tell you. But the other dress will let you wear the corset."

"I—"

"The next words out of your mouth better be 'yes, Aunt Laura.' Because I'm not having you fuck this deal up by not showing your best side."

Just like at the gala, there was no way to avoid someone knowing I was fat. It wasn't like I put on a corset and suddenly I was a fucking supermodel. But my lower lip found its way between my teeth. What if they didn't want me after they saw me, and the corset was the one thing that kept them from changing their mind? I needed this.

"Fine," I finally agreed. "Text me when things are ready."

Her lips curled in distaste. "Don't eat too much cake. We need to be able to lace you in."

I closed my eyes, letting the hurt and embarrassment wash over me before I could breathe fully enough to move again. "I'll see you later."

Today wasn't the day I could wallow in my feelings, no matter what they were. There wasn't time for me to re-tread the path of wondering what I'd ever done to Laura to make her treat me this way. When mom was alive, she'd been nice. Sweet. As soon as mom died it all changed.

But right now Ellie's wedding was my focus. Shit hit the fan with Isolde's ex-boyfriend last night after she'd bonded her pack and he'd found out about it. Again, I was happy for her, but my chest ached with longing whenever I remembered.

Sally and the girls were already waiting outside the mansion. "You guys ready to go?"

They saluted in unison, bringing a smile to my face for the first time today. "All right, let's do this."

My right hand woman had hired extra help for this in order to get things set up more quickly. They had their instructions, but there were always questions, and I already knew I'd have to make some adjustments since the bridal party was changing and I might have said *fuck you* in flower to Isolde's ex while making his boutonniere.

I was in the foyer when someone bumped my shoulder. "Hey, you."

Isolde. I smiled at her, relieved to see her looking so well. She was still in sweatpants and a t-shirt, but she was glowing like she'd swallowed the damn sun. "Hi. You okay?"

Her face dropped a little. We hadn't had a chance to talk about everything. All I knew was some major shit went down at the rehearsal dinner, Beau was no longer in the wedding, and my best friend was now a bonded Omega.

"Yeah. It's..." She took a breath. "You, Rin, and I will have dinner and talk about everything, okay? I don't think I can go through it again today."

One of the new girls came through the door, her arms lined with white paper bags. I pointed to a corner of the foyer. "The bouquets can go there, please. Boutonnieres too." I looked back at Isolde. "I totally get that, and yes, please. I need to get the hell out of my house, and I think we all have things to talk about."

A lot of fucking things to talk about.

"Are you okay?" she asked. Everything about her was genuine. She *wanted* to know. And I felt guilty for keeping so much from her and Rin. "The last couple of weeks—"

Putting out a hand, I stopped the question. Because the three of us were so close, they always knew something was wrong, even when I pretended otherwise. And my friends were going to get a much closer look at my life now than they ever had before. "I can't do it today either, Iz, sorry."

Isolde looked at me for a second, and I felt her trying to figure out what the hell was going on with me. Girl, if you only knew. "That's okay," she finally said. "How can I help?"

I embraced the relief of not having to bare my soul just yet and recruited her to help me fix the flowers for her newly bonded pack member, who would be taking Beau's place walking her down the aisle.

Hawk was his name, and he looked at my friend like she'd hung the moon in the sky.

They all did as they appeared from deeper in the house, pulling Isolde into them like she was the sun they all revolved around. It was beautiful to look at. And painful.

Hawk's words brought me back from my thoughts. "But it's okay, Ocean, I can just wear that one."

"No, you absolutely cannot." I made sure to hold the flowers out of reach.

Her pack looked at me, utterly confused, but Isolde just smiled. "What does it mean, Ocean?"

In spite of how I felt today, I found myself holding back laughter. "It's petunia, basil, and hemlock. Or rather, anger and disdain, hatred, and death."

"Oh my god." Isolde burst out laughing. "That's incredible."

"Remind me never to get on your bad side," Vaughn, another one of her Alphas said.

I smirked before looking at my friend. "I'll take a rose from your bouquet and put one together."

"Perfect."

Hawk and the others tugged her to the side once more, and I had to look away from the tenderness in the way they touched her. It was fine. I didn't have time to focus on it anyway.

The new boutonniere for Hawk done, I helped Sally and the girls finish the arrangements around the ceremony space and on all the tables beneath the big white tent for the reception. Ellie's designer mother supervised, and they really were beautiful. The girls had all outdone themselves.

Something settled in my chest. A feeling of pride and accomplishment I didn't often get.

Arms grabbed me from behind, making me yelp. "Boo."

I placed a hand on my chest. "Fuck, Rin. Warning next time."

"Where's the fun in that?"

"Keeping me from having a heart attack?"

She snorted and looped her arm through mine, guiding me with her to the ceremony space and finding seats on Ellie's side of the aisle. "We both know you're healthier than I am. I'll probably scare myself and have the heart attack."

I laughed softly. Trinity's diabetes wasn't life threatening, but because she did take care of herself, she joked like it wasn't. "Well, you can't off yourself just yet," I told her. "I'm gonna need you. And Isolde."

"Are you finally going to tell us what the hell is going on with you? Because we've been patient, but I've had about enough of you clearly being miserable while also keeping us in the dark."

Guilt crawled up my throat. Not because I felt like I'd been wrong for keeping things close to the chest, but because they *had* been asking, and I'd been pushing them away. They didn't deserve that any more than I did.

"Will I tell you? Yes. Will I tell you right this second? No."

She glared at me for a second. "Fair."

Beautiful cello music floated through the air to start the ceremony, and everything was perfect. Ellie looked beautiful, and Isolde couldn't take her eyes off Hawk or her pack when she glanced at them in the audience. My breath shuddered in my chest. She was so happy, and it was what I wanted.

And I wouldn't have it.

Not until I got out of this marriage, had my freedom fully, and could actually focus on things like my love life.

If I'd ever have it at all.

"She looks so happy," Rin said, echoing my thoughts.

"Yeah." Hopefully my friend didn't notice the way my voice strained.

It didn't matter for long. In what seemed like no time at all, the three of us were on the dance floor, acting like we were still in college and none of us had cares in the world. Isolde's pack watched from their table, and it really was incredible, seeing the way they watched her. But more, it was nice to let go and just... be. Enjoy myself for a little while.

My phone buzzed where I'd tucked it away against my skin to make sure it could be felt.

LAURA

Get back here. Now.

"Shit." The word slipped out of my mouth before I could stop it. The sun was already setting and it was later than I had realized. I did need to get back, because I wasn't taking any chances. They would give me those fucking papers to sign, and nothing was going to stop that.

"You okay?" Isolde asked.

I smiled tightly. "I need to go. I'll call you guys soon."

"O, wait," Rin said. "Give us something, please. Because you're kind of freaking us out."

Both of their faces held nothing but genuine concern, and again, the guilt nearly swallowed me. They deserved to know, even if this wasn't the way I planned to tell them. The rest of it would have to wait.

Gathering my courage, I finally said it out loud. "I'm getting married."

"*What?*" Isolde and Trinity said at the same time, voices rising above the music.

Isolde shook her head. "When?"

56

Trinity followed up. "To who?"

I stared at them, because for once, I didn't actually have an answer for them. "I have no idea."

That was the only thing I could say, and I couldn't wait longer. So I turned and left my friends on the dance floor, hoping to hell they'd forgive me when they finally knew the truth.

"Where the fuck have you been?" Laura asked, following close on my heels as I entered my bedroom.

My patience was already thin, and my anxiety was high because of what we were about to do. "You might want to have your hearing checked. Or your memory. At this point, I've lost track of the times I told you I was *at the wedding*."

Her hand came up so fast I braced for the impact of her slapping me, which never came. Ruby stepped into the room with a dress draped over her arm, and I didn't know if she was the one who stopped it or my aunt's own self-preservation. Couldn't marry me off with a bright red handprint on my cheek.

"Thank fuck you'll be out of this house soon," she hurled the whisper at me.

The feeling was entirely mutual. Whoever I was about to sign my life away to, they couldn't harbor this kind of poison towards me, right? Not when they'd specifically asked for me?

I hoped not.

Nerves fluttered in my stomach. I'd said it didn't matter, but now I was wishing I'd asked who so I could be prepared. Like hell was I going to ask Laura, because she would try to—

Honestly, I had no idea, but whatever she would say, it would only be meant to hurt me and nothing else.

She snapped her fingers at Ruby. "Hurry up."

The corset went on, and my aunt practically shoved Ruby out of the way in order to do the laces herself. Way too fucking tight. "I need to be able to breathe," I managed.

"Not if breathing makes you look bigger and your *intendeds* hesitate even for a second. I'm not letting this deal fall through because you refuse to take care of yourself." She punctuated the words by pulling so tightly that I gasped. I closed my eyes before any of my reactionary tears could escape and ruin the makeup I'd put on for the wedding.

The dress was light, flowy, purple, and pretty. Just like the blue dress. Damn her and her fashion sense. Part of me wanted to mess myself up just a little to see smoke pour out of her ears, but I wasn't sure I had enough breath in my lungs to do it.

Hell, I barely had enough breath to make it all the way to the study.

My uncle looked me up and down when I entered his office, nodding once in approval. And to my shock, he had the documents ready for me, already signed by him. A stranger stood with him. Or rather, someone I recognized a little from Frank's business dealings. Both a notary and a witness, like I'd asked.

He really wanted this to happen, and the ease with which he could toss my life around like a toy didn't cease to sting.

I read the papers carefully, but there wasn't much to them. If I completed my marriage with the DuPont Pack, and remained married for one year, he would sign my trust over to me, fully and completely, with no limitations.

The DuPont Pack.

Somewhere in my mind, that name rang a bell, but I didn't know why. Nor did it matter. This was what I needed. The relief of signing the papers and watching them be notarized almost combatted the pain of having to lean over to sign them in the corset.

He and Laura watched in silence as I signed my life away.

"Good," Frank said, handing one copy of the papers to me. Then he pressed the button on his phone that reached the housekeeper. "Isabel, show them in."

My heart leapt up into my throat. They were here now, and there was no going back.

Fig 10. Peach Blossom
Meaning: Captive;
I am your captive; My heart is yours

EVERETT

*S*tanding in the foyer of the Caldwell mansion, I found myself nervous. It wasn't a familiar sensation. In our line of work, nerves weren't welcome. You needed absolute confidence to run a business as large as ours, especially when the things we sold were so subjective. Any lack of confidence could be perceived as weakness or a lack of clarity, which was the end of more careers than people imagined.

But standing here, ready to meet the Omega who would become our wife once again, I felt a shred of nerves. She was already ours. Biology proved that, and time would prove it as well. But I didn't trust Frank and what he'd said. Or what he'd made her agree to.

I didn't think I would ever forget that first moment of seeing her in the ballroom. It was like the world fell away for a moment and there was only her. Before her scent had punched me straight in the gut and wrapped itself around my soul.

It wasn't the woman who'd let us into the house who approached us now. This was another woman with a smile on her face. "You must be the DuPont pack. I'm Ruby. It's nice to meet you."

I shook her hand. "Hello, Ruby."

"I begged Isabel, the housekeeper, to let me come and take you through."

The three of us looked at her, and Micah spoke. "Why?"

"I've worked for the Caldwells a long time, and I care about Ocean. I wanted to meet who she's meant to marry."

I paused. "The Caldwells?" Ocean was one, but her parents had been dead for over a decade. To say that she still worked for them was an interesting choice.

Ruby waved a hand. "I suppose I should say the McCabes, but I'll always work for the Caldwells as long as there's one around." She began to lead us through the house. I gestured at the man accompanying us to stay. He wasn't needed. Yet.

"What's your role?" Cameron asked.

"Think of me as a personal concierge," Ruby said. "Whatever's needed that falls outside the normal duties of the staff, that's me. I make sure everything's going well and everyone has their needs met."

It wasn't even a thought. I pulled out my wallet and the card with my personal number on it. "If you'd like to follow Ocean, please give me a call."

She paused, making us all stop. "You'd do that?"

Cameron picked up the line without any trouble. "This will already be an awkward transition for Ocean. If there's anything we can do to make it easier, even if it's just a familiar face, I'll do it."

"Thank you."

I watched her pocket the card, unsure if she would take the offer. It stood regardless.

Ruby stopped in front of a set of large double doors. Ocean's scent hung in the air—just a trace of it—and it was so much better than my memories, even while not at full strength. *Omega*.

Knocking once before pushing the doors open, Ruby whispered, "Good luck."

My steps faltered as I stepped inside. The room was *soaked* in her scent. It made my mouth water with the need to get as close as possible and simply breathe her in. To taste her.

My hands tightened on the flowers I held, trying to resist moving forward.

Frank and Laura stood to one side, and there, near the desk, was Ocean. She wore a purple dress that skimmed the curves I already craved, drawing out the deeper tan of her skin and the sultry darkness that was her eyes. She was so fucking beautiful I couldn't breathe.

Which was a problem, because it was all I wanted to do. One more breath of her scent.

Ocean's eyes went wide as she took in the three of us, shock on her face. She looked not only shocked but *stunned*, her hand flying to her chest.

That was all it took to know they hadn't told her who we were, and she'd still agreed. Something in the back of my mind pricked unpleasantly at that. Did she have a reason to want out so desperately? Or had he forced her?

"Good evening," I managed to say. Frank was already on his way forward, holding out his hand for us to shake. "Very good to see you all."

"Likewise," Micah said, but his eyes never strayed from our Omega.

"Ocean," I said. "It's nice to see you again." Frank's head whipped toward mine, and I smirked at him. "We met at the gala, though we didn't know who she was at the time."

My Omega seemed frozen in her place, so I approached her slowly. She didn't seem frightened, more like she was still in a state of shock. "These are for you."

I caught her hand when she reached for the flowers and gently pressed them into her palm. The feeling was electric. She lifted her eyes to mine, voice breathless. "Thank you."

As soon as Micah told us his idea to get her flowers based on their meanings, Cam and I were all in. We each chose a couple of flowers, and the three small bundles could easily be combined into one bouquet. I was sure she could make them look better than we ever could.

My flowers were an orchid I'd come across, which was said to represent beauty and love, and a sprig of peach blossoms, which I had found meant 'I am your captive.'

I'd seen the description, and nothing had ever felt as accurate as being captive to this beautiful woman. Because we didn't know her yet, but every piece of me wanted to.

Cam chose purple tulips for eternal love, and snowdrops for hope. Micah ended up choosing the calla lily, which spoke of magnificent beauty. That was the fucking truth.

I watched Ocean's face as we each handed her the flowers. Watched her eyes flicker over each one and clock the meanings of them. Her eyes flicked up to mine again with more shock, but this time there was pink touching her cheeks. Like it was the last thing she'd ever expected for us to do something as simple as give her flowers.

Clearing my throat, I looked at Frank. "Our lawyer is waiting in the foyer. He has all the paperwork, if you'd like to look it over. There are still some details that needed to be finalized for the signing, which our team requests be postponed until after the wedding. He'll be happy to go over it with you."

"Of course." He didn't look happy that it would take that long for the deal to be finalized. Neither was I, but we would make Ocean our wife first. End of story.

No one moved, and I almost sighed because they weren't taking the hint. Micah stepped in before I could snap at him. If there was one thing I disliked about people like Frank, it was their utter lack of awareness.

"We'd like a few minutes alone with Ocean, please."

Laura scoffed. "Like we're just going to leave her alone with you?"

The softest sound came from beside me. Whether it was a laugh or a gasp, I wasn't sure. But something about that statement made Ocean react. I tilted my head and looked at her aunt. "Yes, we would like to speak to the woman who's agreed to marry us. Alone."

Laura was now pink too, but with an entirely different kind of embarrassment. Her husband had the grace to look sheepish. "Right. We'll just... go speak to the lawyer. Come on, Laura."

They all retreated, and where Ruby still stood outside the door, I caught the smile on her face before she shut it, leaving us alone with *our* Omega.

Fig 11. Wild Carrot
(Also: Queen Anne's Lace, Laceflower)
Meaning: Fantasy; Haven; Sanctuary;
Do not refuse me

OCEAN

*W*here my voice had disappeared to, I wasn't sure, but I would love it to come back right about now.

The three Alphas from the gala were the last people I expected to walk through the door. Cameron, the one who'd danced with me, Micah, and Everett.

The flowers they'd given me— there was no way they could know what they *meant*, right? Because...

I shook my head as the door closed behind Ruby and I was left alone with three Alphas who were far more appealing than they had any right to be. Their scents filled the space, drawing me in, and my same thoughts from that night came back. They were so handsome they were almost *beautiful*. And I was going to marry them.

As soon as the door closed Cameron smiled, shoulders easing. "Much better. Felt like we were all suffocating a bit."

A strangled laugh came out of me.

Everett, closest to me, kept those piercing blue eyes on my face. "Before anything else, I need to ask you, Ocean. Are they forcing you to do this?"

I opened my mouth and closed it again. There wasn't a clear answer to that, was there? Because yes, they'd made it clear that they thought this was going to happen. And yet no, they weren't, because I was making an agreement that benefitted me. I *wanted* this, and I was glad I didn't have to find out what Frank would do if I'd continued to say no. "No," I finally squeaked out.

"But he didn't tell you who we were?"

Shaking my head, I finally relaxed, but I winced. "I didn't ask."

The three of them looked at me with such a blend of emotions on their faces that I couldn't decipher them. Nor did I want to, because it meant I could keep looking at them. No one had a right to look that good simply standing there in a *suit*. Not when I had to stuff myself into a dress like this and feel the ache with every breath.

"Then why?" Micah asked before smiling. "Not that I'm trying to talk you out of it. We were happy to hear you said yes. But why did you say yes?"

That was a conversation that would take longer than Laura would be willing to leave us alone. "I'd rather not talk about that tonight," I admitted. "Not never, but it will take time. But I can promise you I'm not being forced. I agreed, and I have my reasons. We can help each other."

Micah's gaze dropped down to the flowers in my hands and then back at me. "*That's* what it is," he said, taking a step back. "Orchids."

"What?"

"Your scent. I couldn't figure out what flower it was, but with that one," he gestured to the beautiful orchid mixed in with the flowers, "I understand."

My lips popped open. "It's rare that people notice or figure it out," I admitted.

"It's stunning," Everett said, so quietly I almost didn't hear it. He was still staring down at me, and for a brief moment, it didn't feel like he was talking about my scent.

"Thank you for the flowers." I lifted them to my nose and inhaled. They were incredible. Not nearly as good as the blend of the three Alphas in front of me, but lovely all the same.

Cameron stepped a little closer. "I'm glad you like them."

Finally more at ease, I looked between the three of them. "Why did you want to speak alone?"

"Because this is a little strange for everyone, and it's not made easier by having an audience. Feels a little like being in a fishbowl."

I laughed. "You're not wrong. But this will be good. I can help you, you can help me, and a year will go by fast. You don't have to worry about me or even see me. I'll stay out of your way. Promise."

Something touched my hand, and I looked over to see Everett pulling the flowers out of them and placing them on my uncle's desk before taking both of my hands in his. My breath went short, and it wasn't from the corset this time. No, this was entirely from the feeling of being close to him. Which didn't make any sense. He was gorgeous, and he smelled incredible, but this was a business transaction. I had no illusions about them being attracted to *me*, despite their flowers speaking of beauty.

"We need this marriage," he said. "I won't pretend we don't. But just because we need it doesn't mean we don't want to enjoy it. Or for you to enjoy it."

My breath shook, but I inhaled fully before I met his gaze. The look in his eyes was filled with... I didn't know. Something deep and fiery and intense. "I'll enjoy it. Don't worry about me. I can be quite content."

Beside us, Cameron held out a hand to me. I took it, and allowed him to pull me closer, though I was trying not to move too much in the dress. "I would like to touch more than just your hand. Is that all right?"

I nodded, my heart in my throat.

"I need to hear the words, Ocean."

"Yes," I whispered. "That's fine."

Cameron slid his hands up my arms and behind my shoulders, bringing us together like we were dancing once more. It was dangerous for me to be this close to him, or any of them, because I liked it far too much. And the last thing I needed was to fall in love with three Alphas who were only going to leave me in a year. I was getting out of this marriage with my freedom. Not a broken heart.

I bathed in the sharp scent of lemon and the delicious, swirling sweetness of sugar. Probably a good thing I could barely breathe. If I could, I might grab his suit, shove my face into his chest and do nothing but scent him and the others in a constant loop.

"What Everett is trying to say, and failed," Cameron said with a grin, "is that while we need this marriage, we also intend for this to be a *real* marriage. In every sense of the word."

My mind went blank, and I wasn't sure I'd heard him correctly. "You want that?"

"We want that."

I glanced over my shoulder and found Micah and Everett staring at me, both of them with that same smoldering intensity. "You want that with *me*?"

Something passed over Everett's face, but Micah was the one stepping forward and turning me toward him. Brushing his knuckles down my cheek and lifting my chin to see me more clearly. "Yes." His eyes closed, and for a moment he looked pained. "But I understand if that makes you want to change your answer."

I thought about it. The truth was, I assumed it was purely convenience. That was why it hadn't mattered. That I was part of the deal because I was there, and that they needed a wife in name and name only. I should tell them no, because allowing these men to treat me like a real wife would only hurt me later.

And yet, not even a month ago I'd scolded Isolde for not allowing her now pack to take her to bed because of her fear of pain later. Now, standing here in the same situation, I was terrified. They were gorgeous, rich, and so far out of my league, it was frankly laughable that they wanted this at all.

I'd told Isolde that she had a choice, and the day I told her, I truly felt like I had none. Laura had done the same thing she always did, making me feel small and worthless, and I let it get to me. But right now, in this moment, I did, *finally*, have a choice.

And regardless of the pain, I was going to make the selfish choice. The one that would bring me freedom, and however temporarily, three Alphas I could only dream of.

"Ocean?" Micah's finger still rested beneath my chin, and he looked worried.

I'd been silent too long. "I don't want to change my mind," I whispered.

His smile lit up the whole damn room. "I'm glad." His eyes dropped to my lips, and I swayed toward him. "May I kiss you?"

My stomach dropped through my feet, and now me being lightheaded had nothing to do with my corset. Before I could answer, the door to the office swung open, allowing my aunt and uncle back in, along with a man who I assumed was the DuPont pack's lawyer.

I tried to step back, but Micah didn't let me with a hand on my elbow. Even as he straightened, he kept me close. The look on Frank and Laura's faces—I wished I had a camera. So incredulous it was nearly comical.

"My apologies," my uncle said, though he couldn't do it without a sneer. "I do have some questions about the paperwork."

"I will answer them," Everett said, stepping around Micah and into me. He took my hand and lifted it to his lips, kissing the back. "I will see you very soon, Ocean."

"Okay."

He smiled tightly as he strode for the door, gesturing for Frank and the lawyer to follow him. Micah and Cameron still stood firmly in my space, and I didn't mind it. In fact, I felt safer than I had in a long time because I knew Laura wouldn't dare say what she truly thought in front of them.

Cameron cleared his throat. "Are you all free next Friday?"

"What for?" Laura asked.

I had to stifle my laugh at his expression. "Our wedding to your niece."

"*This* Friday?" She took a step back like his words had struck her. "That's a little fast."

Micah placed a hand low on my back, and even through the corset I felt the warmth. I liked it there, comfort without any words. "Time is of the essence." Then he turned to me once more, dismissing my aunt. "A week isn't long, we know. But we've already contacted an event planner. We've worked with her before, and she can get it done. Expense isn't an object. Whatever you want. And though your flowers are incredible, you are under no obligation to design your own flowers if you don't want to."

"I... I'm not sure," I said.

"That's all right. We know it's fast. Take the night to think about that, and Geneva will be in touch tomorrow. I think she already has appointments booked for a dress." Reaching into the interior pocket of his suit, he took out his phone before handing it to me with the contact page open.

When I glanced up at him, he smiled. I could get used to that smile. "At some point, I will need my wife's phone number."

Heat bloomed on my cheeks, but I put my number into his phone, and then Cameron's when he offered it. This was really happening. I was getting married. Not just getting married, but marrying *them*. It didn't feel real. And I imagined it wouldn't until we were all standing at the altar.

"We do mean it, Ocean," Cameron said. "Money is no object. Especially when it comes to the dress."

Laura cleared her throat. "Make sure wherever your planner takes us can accommodate someone of her... size."

This was where I shriveled up and died. Right here, and right now. Apparently I was wrong, and she would say everything right to their face. My eyes fell to the overly elaborate rug on the floor, tracing the ugly pattern in order to keep myself from looking at them and their reaction to her words.

"All of *our* bridal salons are size-inclusive," Micah said, and I could have been imagining the hard edge to his voice. I must have been. "Now, Ocean, the last thing I need from you," he paused, "for *tonight*, are your ring preferences."

My head snapped up. Holy shit. I hadn't even thought about rings.

"With her coloring, gold would be best. Nothing too heavy. She insists on working with her hands, so you don't want her to lose a diamond in the dirt," Laura said.

I closed my eyes and bit my lip, wishing we could go back to five minutes ago when we were alone in the room and nothing felt as awkward as it did right now.

"I don't recall your presence being required or requested," Cameron snapped. "And we didn't ask for your opinion, Mrs. McCabe."

She huffed a breath and stomped out of the room, taking the heavy air with her. But I still didn't trust it.

"Is that normal?"

I glanced at Cameron and flicked my eyes to the door, hoping he'd understand that I didn't believe Laura was truly gone. "She's just concerned. I can be clumsy." Not a lie in the slightest. "And it's all right. It's only for a year. You can get me whatever ring you want."

His eyes hardened. "We'll get you a ring that you love, and there is no argument about it. If you want to think about it, please do. You have our numbers now. And we'll make sure to give yours to Everett."

"Thank you. And thank you again for the flowers. They really are beautiful."

"I hope they tell you a little something about us." Micah smiled. "And we knew you could make an arrangement far better than we could."

Wait. Did they—

I looked at the flowers again and took them in. Most flowers I knew the meanings of by now, but even my knowledge wasn't encyclopedic. There were a couple I didn't know, or wasn't sure what the color variation implied. But the theme was clear: love and beauty.

Cameron's hand touched my shoulder, and he turned me into his body, holding me close. My instincts rose, and I just kept myself from snuggling into his arms and leaning my head on his chest. My Omega liked them, and it was fucking dangerous. "Call us, please, if you need anything for the wedding. Or even if you don't."

"Remember." Micah stole me away, and it was the first time he'd touched so much of me. Just as overwhelming, the heady sweetness of his scent wrapping me up. "What are you allowed for the wedding?"

I swallowed. "Whatever I want."

"Whatever you want." The air felt colder when he pulled away. "I don't want to leave, but I also don't want to leave Everett with the wolves."

"Yeah," I smiled. "Probably a good idea."

The atmosphere felt incomplete, like there was nothing more to say yet *everything* to say and no one quite knew how to move forward. So I picked up the flowers and held them to my nose, trying to clear my head. Not that it would work when the flowers were from them and would therefore bring my thoughts back to them over and over again.

"Like Everett said," Cameron moved to the door. "We'll see you very soon."

I bit my lip, unsure how to say goodbye to Alphas you were attracted to, engaged to, and desperately didn't want to leave. "Okay."

Cameron smiled and ran his gaze over me one more time before slipping out. Micah turned back. "Oh, and Ocean?"

"Yeah?"

"Thank you. For saying yes."

He was gone before I could respond, but I couldn't explain the way those words made my heart flutter and the way they felt like so much more than convenience.

I smiled into the flowers, ignoring where Laura stood outside the study, exactly where I thought she'd be. These flowers needed a vase, and I needed to figure out what the hell just happened, and why I couldn't stop smiling.

Fig 12. Zinnia
Meaning: Friendship; Loyalty; I miss you

OCEAN

*C*orsets weren't any more comfortable to sit in, but I needed to get used to it. At least for the next week.

Laura burst into the kitchen while I was arranging my flowers and informed me that I needed to be on my best behavior between now and the wedding, and that included making sure if I was photographed that I looked my best.

One week. It was a sacrifice I could make. And once again, it was easier to give in than to fight, even if it chipped away at my soul.

Allowing myself to be forced into an improperly fitted corset was the lesser evil. Because I knew if I didn't, the week would be nothing but her forcing her hand in other ways. She would still try, but at the very least if I gave her this one thing, she would let me breathe. Figuratively.

Which was why I currently squirmed in my seat as I waited for Trinity and Isolde at our favorite brunch place. We hadn't been here together since Isolde moved across the country. Rin and I didn't feel right coming here without her.

They approached at the same time, and Trinity fell into the chair across from me dramatically. I'd chosen a table outside because it was such a beautiful day. "I need a mimosa in my hand fucking immediately. Thanks to work, I didn't get to party my ass off last night."

"I think you partied just fine," Isolde said with a laugh as she leaned down to hug me. "Hey, O."

"Hi."

Rin shoved her sunglasses back and stared at me. "First of all, how dare you drop that bomb on us and *leave*. If I'm going to be edged, I would prefer it to be a tattooed Alpha. Or a set of them. Second, what the *fuck*?" She whisper shouted the last bit. "Spill."

"Let's get drinks first and order. Cause I have a feeling you won't want this to be interrupted."

"Damn." She grinned. "Getting serious."

I ordered a mango mimosa and a cheesy omelette. They made them amazingly here. But I knew there wasn't escaping the conversation, so I might as well rip off the bandaid. "You guys know how my trust is locked until thirty-five?"

"Yeah," Rin said. "And it's really fucking stupid."

"Well, Frank came with an offer. A pack who's making a business deal with him needs to get married, and they wanted it to be me. Before you ask, no, I have no idea why. And he wants it badly enough that he agreed to sign the trust over to me early if I stay married to them for a year."

Isolde froze with her mimosa glass halfway to her lips, and Rin slumped back in her chair, staring. "Okay. Wow."

"Yup. Stay like that for three days and you'll be around where I am now."

"You've known about this for three days?"

I rolled my eyes. "That's what you're going to give me shit about? I barely had time to think about it myself while getting everything ready for Ellie's wedding."

"Sorry." Trinity winced. "Still wrapping my head around it."

"You said you had no idea who last night," Isolde said. "Do you know now?"

I glanced around to make sure we weren't attracting attention. Last night I hadn't asked if it was a secret. I assumed it wouldn't be, but I also didn't know if they wanted to make some kind of big announcement. So I leaned forward, and they came to meet me. "The DuPont Pack."

Trinity's eyes went so wide they could have popped out. "Excuse the fuck out of me?"

Looking back and forth between the two of us, Isolde frowned. "Should I know who that is?"

"Probably not. I didn't," I said. "I imagine Rin does from work."

Isolde's mouth formed into a little 'o.' Trinity was a reporter, and though she'd recently been promoted, she'd previously done profiles of celebrities and interesting people. Part gossip, part human interest, part sex appeal.

"Yeah," she said. "They're billionaires. Like literal billionaires. They own half the clothing industry, and if rumor is correct, they do a lot of designing themselves. You know *Cheria*?"

Isolde blushed. Her Alpha Hawk had taken her to the lingerie store and practically bought out the place before a naughty photoshoot he had planned for her.

"Yeah. I'd say I remember." Her voice was hoarse, and she took a drink as I giggled.

"They're the ones who own it," Trinity said. "They also own *Caesura*, the bridal company, Cliff's Edge, Starling Designs, and Extasis. More, but I can't remember what else. They're rich enough that they get attention but also not famous enough to attract paparazzi all the time, thankfully." She looked at me.

That was a good thing. I hadn't even considered it when I did more research last night.

Rin cleared her throat. "They also happened to be smoking hot. They've had a couple of photo leaks, but nothing mind-blowing. Mostly people trying to make something out of nothing. You, my friend, are a lucky girl."

Was I?

I did feel lucky, because of all the Alphas in the world, these men

74

seemed kind, and Rin was correct about how hot they were. "I'm mostly relieved about the trust," I told them. "Frank signed papers. I've already made copies, put them in my safe, and," I leaned down and grabbed the copies out of my bag. "Will you each hold on to one?"

Isolde frowned at the envelope, but she took it. "Sure, but why?"

"I don't trust them not to 'lose' it when the time comes."

"Wait—" I saw Trinity's mind working. Then I saw her reach the conclusion I had. "If he can sign it over early... *fucker.*"

"Ocean," Isolde said. "Why do I get the feeling you have a lot more to tell us than just about this marriage? Which I still have a lot of questions about, by the way. But this first."

"Because I do. And before I do, I just want to say I'm sorry. There are a lot of things I should have told you before now, but I didn't want to make you feel as helpless as I have. You'd want to help, and there's no way you can, so it didn't matter. But now I'm getting out."

Trinity raised her hand, already wanting a refill on her mimosa. "Looong brunch. Got it. Start from the beginning."

We all burst into laughter. Fuck, I loved my friends. They always made me feel better, and telling them this felt like lifting a weight off my chest.

So I started at the beginning.

Trinity looked at me and slurped the bottom of her third mimosa. "If I didn't love you so much, I'd kill you for keeping all of that to yourself."

Isolde snickered, but she felt the same. "I'm sorry you felt like you couldn't tell us."

"You know it's not that. I just..." I sighed and shrugged. "There's nothing I can do. It's shitty, and I'll never understand why my parents made that choice, or why Frank and Laura never changed it if they could all this time. But this is helping. I'll finally be able to get away from them. And don't get me wrong. They're awful, but let's not pretend I don't have a lot of things going for me. I run my own business and I live in a mansion. Things could be worse."

Grabbing one of the dessert menus the waitress left, Isolde handed it to me. "You live in a mansion where you're verbally and financially abused, and physically, based on the fucking corset. Just because you're better off than someone else doesn't negate your pain, O."

I wasn't so sure about that. No one could argue that I didn't have a good life, even if there were painful aspects to it. "Yeah. Just another week, and then it won't matter."

75

"Tell her to fuck off," Rin said. "Seriously. The papers are signed. What is she going to do?"

"The papers don't do much until the actual wedding. Until then, she can and will make my life miserable if I don't give in on some things. It's a wedding for a marriage lasting a year. I don't have to have everything perfect for something that's temporary. She can have some of it if it gets me to the finish line."

Both my friends' faces told me they didn't agree, but they'd already made that clear while I told them the story.

"I'm ordering us cake," Isolde said. "You had to leave before the wedding cake last night, and that's a travesty."

I laughed. "Was it good?"

"Delicious. And no, Warren did not smash cake in her face. They were painfully adorable."

A cake. Fuck, I hadn't even thought about a cake. It was a good thing they'd hired a wedding planner, because this was already overwhelming.

"Are we invited?" Trinity asked.

"Yes." The answer was immediate. I might not be insistent on everything, but this was one. If I was getting married, even if it was fake, I wanted my friends there. "I don't imagine it will be a big wedding, since it's so fast, but I want you there. The only reason they're probably going through the actual motions at all and not just having it at a courthouse is the public relations aspect. Please don't tell anyone about that," I added.

"We won't," Isolde said.

I looked at Rin and stared at her until she held up her hands. "Cross my heart, hope to die. I won't tell anyone. And I won't need to. I told Isolde because she needed the guys desperately. You're literally marrying yours, so there's no need to intervene."

"It's a fake marriage, Rin."

Isolde raised an eyebrow as the cake was set down in front of her. "What was it they said? That they wanted it to be a very *real* marriage?"

"You know what I mean."

Isolde nodded, cutting a slice of cake and giving it to Trinity. "I do. And I'm the first one to say that I'm with Rin, here. I put up a fight, and I was wrong. So I'm proud of you for saying yes, and I'm fully rooting for those Alphas to sweep you off your feet."

That sounded... amazing. But I couldn't believe that. They were from a completely different plane of existence on every level. I would just be a visitor for a while before being cast back down to earth.

"And," Isolde added. "If you say anything against it, *I'm* going to be the one smashing this cake in your face. Got it?" She looked stern as she held out the plate.

I tried to hold it together and failed miserably, the three of us collapsing into laughter. God, it felt good to have time like this with them again. Like I could breathe even though everything was pressing down on me, including the corset.

Something flashed in my eyes, and I recoiled. "What the hell was that?"

It was already bright outside, and I didn't see anything that would have reflected. Then I did. A man with a camera stood down the sidewalk, the lens pointed in my direction. "Fuck."

Both Trinity and Isolde turned to look, and Rin jumped out of her chair. "Hey, fuckface." She was gone before we could call her back. I couldn't hear what she said, but it was loud, her hands waving, and the man looked scared.

I covered my mouth with my hand, stifling a laugh. "Should we help her?"

"No, I think she's got it."

Rin flipped the man off before stomping back to the table. "I know that asshole. Not like I'm friends with him, but I know who he is. He's a paparazzo. So someone must know about you and the DuPonts."

"How? This only happened last night."

"You said you agreed on Thursday, though."

The thought of calling them made my stomach flip with nerves. But if this really was for public relations, then the last thing they needed was a random headline. And they needed a picture of a fat girl laughing and eating *cake* even less.

So I pulled out my phone and found Micah's number. They'd all texted me last night so I had theirs too. I swallowed as I held the phone up to my ear.

He answered on the second ring. "Hello, beautiful."

My entire face flushed with heat. "Hi."

"Ocean?" He must have heard the shake in my voice. "Are you all right?"

"I think so. I'm having lunch with my friends, and a photographer came up and took my picture. I didn't know if this was all... secret or not. I was eating cake, and you probably don't want the first image of your new wife to be with a face full of cake."

He chuckled in my ear. But it wasn't a laugh of mockery. Instead, it was warm and honeyed, giving me chills despite the heat. "No matter the photo, I have no doubt it's lovely. But you're right, we were hoping to come out with the wedding pictures all in one go. Do you know who took it?"

"Do you know the guy's name?" I asked Rin.

She shouted it loudly enough for Micah to hear, making him laugh all over again. "That makes sense. He's one of the ones who likes to try to catch us with our pants down. Not that he's ever done that, because there's nothing to find."

"I'm sorry," I said. "I haven't told anyone other than my friends, and they've been with me the whole time."

"Don't be sorry," he said gently. "You telling someone hadn't even entered my mind. But I appreciate you telling me so we can take care of it. Or rather, Cameron will take care of it."

The way he said it made it feel like 'take care of *you*.'

"Thank you."

"Has Geneva called you yet?"

I shook my head even though he couldn't see me. "No, not yet."

"She should be doing it soon. And we still need to hear about your rings."

"I'll..." I swallowed. "I'll think about it."

"Please do. And call me if anyone else gives you trouble. We'll hire you a bodyguard if we have to."

My mind stuttered. "I'm sure that's not necessary."

He chuckled again. I was going to have to build up some kind of immunity to that sound if he—or any of them—continued to make it. There was only so much I could do to keep myself from melting. "If it is, we'll make it happen. Please have fun with your friends and don't worry about this."

"Can they come to the wedding?"

A silence stretched out on the other end of the phone. When he spoke, I realized it was a silence borne of shock. "Of course, Ocean. It's your wedding too. Whoever you want to be there is more than welcome."

"Thank you."

"I'll talk to you soon."

He ended the call, and I stared at the phone until Rin laughed. "You're so fucked, aren't you?"

"No," I said immediately. "And yes, you guys are invited."

"Perfect. Now we can really help you plan."

She dove into talking about the kind of flowers I should request based on meaning, but I kept glancing at my phone. I had a sneaking suspicion that Trinity was right.

I was well and truly fucked.

Fig 13. Canterbury Bells
(Also: Bell Flower)
Meaning: Thinking of you

CAMERON

a knock on the doorframe to my office distracted me from the metric ton of photos I was going through for the new *Cheria* ad campaign. Mostly a formality, but being hands on with the details of all our companies was what had gotten us this far.

I looked up to find Raina standing in the doorway.

"Oh god. What. If you're here with me instead of with Everett, something must have gone terribly wrong. Especially on a weekend."

She wore a raspberry colored suit from one of our lines, and it highlighted her dark skin perfectly. Grinning, she sat down across from me. "May I point out that you're here on a weekend, too? And why does something have to be wrong for me to come see you?"

"Because you're holding a file," I said. "And because it usually is."

Laughing, she inclined her head. "I guess that's fair. But it's not too bad, promise."

Raina crashed into our lives a decade ago as a model. She was using the money to put herself through law school, and Micah noticed her studying on set. She was brilliant and had a mind for numbers that's pretty much unrivaled, despite her choice of law. As soon as she graduated and passed the bar, we hired her, and a few years after that, when she was running circles around everyone in the company, we made her Chief Financial Officer. Her background made her a unique fit for the job.

Which meant she was practically our boss now. Which she gleefully reminded us of at every opportunity.

"Hit me with it."

She leaned forward and handed the folder across my desk. "Just need you to sign off on everything for Firefly. You're the last of the trio there, and I'll tell you the same thing I told the others about the McCabe deal. It's probably not worth what you're putting into it."

I scribbled my signature on the Firefly paperwork. "We know."

"That's what the others said as well. So why are we doing it?"

"They didn't tell you?"

Raina shrugged. "They probably would have, but I caught them at bad times."

Leaning back in my chair, I took a deep breath and thought about how much to tell her. This wasn't a secret, but there were certain things we were keeping to ourselves. Like the fact that we were Ocean's scent match.

I fucking loved it and wanted to shout it from the rooftops. But no one deserved to know before Ocean did. So I opted for as much honesty as I could. "The board meeting."

She winced. "Sorry I couldn't be there."

"It was better you weren't," I tell her honestly. "They wanted us alone. And they wanted to strong-arm us. We still don't know why. But because of the Firefly deal, they're pointing to our PR presence and saying we need to become more family friendly. They threatened to resign and make public statements about why if we don't get married."

Raina's face went deadly still. "Excuse me?"

"That's about the same reaction we had." I chuckled. "So if you can find out why Joseph, Bill, and the others want us married so badly, please let us know."

"I will..." Her brow furrowed. "That doesn't explain McCabe."

My eyes flicked over the images on my screen. All thin and cut models in the lingerie. Beautiful, but they didn't hold a candle to Ocean. I made a mental note to make sure we hired some more models with different body types. All our lines were size inclusive, but our advertising wasn't always. And the thought of seeing Ocean in our lingerie had me reciting ad statistics in my head to keep my body under control.

"There are a few things I can't tell you, and I hope that as our friend, you'll trust us until we can. But McCabe has a niece. Ocean Elise Correa Caldwell. On Friday, we will marry her."

I could count on one hand the number of times I'd seen Raina truly shocked, and this was one of them. "You're bowing to the threat?"

"They weren't posturing, Raina. Every one of them came prepared to walk out of the room right then. So yes, we are. And Ocean..."

There was no way for me to talk casually about her. If I said we only wanted her to fulfill the board's stipulation, it would be an utter lie. It was so much more than that. We wanted every piece of her. And I, for one, couldn't wait to get her away from her bitch of an aunt. On the surface things seemed fine, if tense, but we knew better than most how things could be different than they appeared.

"We want her to be our wife," I finished quietly.

Raina studied me. She was an Alpha with her own pack. A male Omega and a female Beta. They were sickeningly cute, and I knew Ocean would love them once she met them. Which she would.

"This is one of the things I need to trust you on?"

I nodded.

"Well, I do trust the three of you. Fuck knows why. But the deal is still iffy."

"We're getting a better bargain than McCabe is."

"That's for damn sure." She stood, and I handed her the signed papers. "I'll keep you posted."

A sudden thought came into my head, and I knew the others wouldn't mind. "Would you officiate?"

Her eyebrows rose. "You want me to officiate your wedding?"

"Sure. You've done it before. You're our friend, and we would want you to be there anyway."

She chuckled. "All right. Let me know the dress code and the details, and the three of us will be there."

"Looking forward to it."

On the way out, she passed Micah coming in. I sighed. "I'm never going to finish proofing these images today, am I?"

"Ocean called."

That perked me up. I grinned. "Did she say what she wanted for a ring?"

"Unfortunately, no. She was out with friends and a photographer took her picture." His mouth quirked. "She was concerned about it leaking before we were ready. And that the first image of her connected to us would be of her eating cake."

"God." I scrubbed my hands over my face. "You can't say things like that or I'm going to spend the rest of the day imagining eating cake *off* her."

"What do you think I've been doing since she called? But it's that asshole Markus from Sunset Daily. Can you reach out and make sure we have assurances nothing goes out before we're ready?"

"They're going to want an exclusive or something along with that promise. But I'll keep it small. They make stories out of nothing anyway, so it should be easy for them."

He laughed. "You're not wrong."

I picked up the phone as he walked away. Sooner than later was always better with the press. It was the weekend, but there would still be someone I could talk to.

"Raina's going to officiate," I called after him.

Micah looked back and smiled. "That's perfect. Now we just need it to be Friday." So we could get our hands on our Omega.

Fuck, I needed time to speed up and go faster. We hadn't wanted to get married, and now it couldn't come fast enough.

Fig 14. Columbine
(Also: Lion's Herb)
Meaning: Courage; Strength
Meaning (Purple): Resolved to win
Meaning (Red): Anxious; Trembling

OCEAN

*G*eneva was a dream come true. As someone who worked in events, she was the kind of person I loved to collaborate with.

Hell, she already had a binder and a schedule, a breakdown of everything we needed, and a checklist of whether I wanted to make the decision or leave it to her.

I might be a little in love with her.

Or at least her planning style.

Now, as we walked into one of the biggest bridal salons in Sunset City, I loved that she was here. Because of the hour drive, Trinity and Isolde couldn't make it on such short notice. Laura was here because she insisted, and I already knew how that was going to go. She made sure I was in the corset before we left.

Geneva placed a hand on my shoulder after she waved to one of the shop attendants. "Before we head into the dresses, come with me. Mrs. McCabe, Ashley here will show you over to where we'll be trying things on."

"I'll stay with Ocean."

"No," she said firmly. "We'll be right back. Ocean's fiancés have something for her privately."

Laura kept her face in check, but it was only because we were in public. Geneva sent a glare at her as she guided me away. "Say the word, Ocean, and I'll have her removed from the store."

I sighed. "I'm not sure that would make it better. We drove together." And making the hour trip home with her seething wasn't on my list of priorities.

"I'm sure the DuPonts would be happy to have a driver take you home."

Smiling, I looked at her. "And what would happen once I got home?" Her shoulders fell, and I held out a hand. "Thank you. I appreciate it. And I'm really grateful you're here."

"I'll do my best to keep her at bay."

"I appreciate that." I sat in the chair she led me to. "What are we doing here?"

"A couple of things. Here's the sample of the wedding invitation. We don't need them, but your fiancés thought it would be good to have a few."

She handed me a crisp invitation made of cardstock. There were flowing ripples in silver over the white paper that looked like water. Almost like an ocean. I smiled and shook my head. Of course they would pick something that reflected my name.

Seeing my name along with theirs sent my heart into my throat.

"Do you like them?" Geneva asked.

"I do," I told her honestly. "The style and the decorations. But not the color."

"Noted. We'll change it to something that matches your colors? Not white."

I nodded and handed it back to her. "I like the silver."

"Perfect." She typed a couple of notes into her tablet. "Now, Mr. Westbrook mentioned you hadn't told them your priorities for rings. Since you were already going to be here in Sunset City, I had their preferred jeweler bring over some samples for you."

I hadn't even noticed the man standing in the corner with what looked like a giant briefcase. He came over and placed it on the low table in front of me, opening it. It was like a movie, jewels sparkling under the lights as they were revealed. Way too many rings and way too many *diamonds*. Holy shit.

"If you like any of these, perfect. If not, tell me anything you like about them and we'll go from there."

My stomach hollowed out. This wasn't real. The marriage was going to last a year. It might be better to get a ring that didn't cost someone's yearly salary when it was going to be taken off so soon.

"I—" Nothing came out. Like my voice had decided to vacate the premises entirely.

Geneva smiled. "I know it's overwhelming."

"Yeah. I have big fingers. Most rings don't fit me."

"It won't be a problem," she promised.

Everything shone so bright and was so large, I shied away from them. My jewelry taste had always been simpler. Less on the gaudy side and more on the filigree. "Do you think they'll be offended if I don't want a diamond?" I asked.

"That depends. Do you not want the diamond because of cost? Or simply because you like something else better?"

I already knew they wouldn't care about the cost. The fact that I was sitting here with a literal briefcase of gems in front of me was proof enough of that. Oh, and the fact that Trinity had said they were actual billionaires.

"Something else better."

"Then no," she said with a smile. "I don't think they'll be offended at all."

Taking a shaky breath, I pointed to a stone that was a bluish purple. "I've always loved stones like this. The color is gorgeous."

Geneva wrote notes on her tablet. "Perfect. That will look lovely with your skin tone as well."

I smiled, but my breath was tight. Damn corset. "These are all a little..." I glanced at the man who'd brought the briefcase. "Much? For me. I love swirls. Filigree. Simpler. I don't really love circular or square stones."

"Metal?" Geneva asked.

"White gold."

"That is perfect. We can definitely work with that." She glanced at the man. "I'm sending a copy of the notes over to you. Thank you."

The briefcase was closed, and he was gone in what felt like seconds. "They can make a ring in this kind of timeframe?"

Geneva led me back into the main section of the salon. "Darling, with enough money, you can do almost anything. Now, I've already had them pull some dresses for you based on what we talked about at lunch. But we can go from there."

We'd met Geneva early to talk through things, including colors. I didn't want to do my own flowers, but I wanted a hand in picking them, and their meanings, but I didn't say the second part out loud in front of Laura. The last thing I needed was her looking into the meanings of all the flowers I'd ever done for her and Frank.

But the colors were similar to the ring I'd requested. A lovely bluish purple. Periwinkle. And white, with black accents.

Holy fuck, I was getting married. And nothing solidified that fact like walking into a room full of frothy white dresses.

"They own this place, right?"

"Yes, the DuPonts own *Caesura*. It goes hand in hand with *Cheria*. Their lingerie brand. But don't worry. They don't get to see the dress until you walk down the aisle. Even if they're paying for it."

The thought of them seeing me for the first time in a dress like these made butterflies whirl in my stomach. It shouldn't. But I couldn't seem to wipe the smile off my face.

Until I saw Laura sitting on a white couch with her arms crossed and a sour look on her face, clearly pissed at being set aside, even though there was a glass of champagne sitting on the end table next to her.

Well... too bad.

The woman who'd brought her over here extended a hand to me. "I'm Ashley. I'm going to help you today."

"Hi—"

"I've already told her you need a dress that's corseted. And one that's not too form fitting."

Ashley's smile froze on her face, and she blinked a couple of times. It always amazed me how clueless Laura was about how people perceived her, and was then shocked when people didn't react well to her rudeness.

"I have some picked out for you. Why don't you come with me?"

"Thanks."

We walked out of sight, and I glanced back just in time to see Geneva glaring at my aunt. Part of me wished I could see that showdown.

The dressing room was bright and cozy, with several dresses already hanging on the walls. "Now that we're here. I do have several corseted dresses in your selections. But because they lined up with what Geneva told me you wanted, and not because of your aunt's requirement."

"If that's all she's going to push for, then that's fine," I said. "If it will keep her happy, do it."

"Well, if that's what you want. But I'm here to make *you* happy. So let's start with one and see how you feel, okay?"

"Okay."

I hated the first dress. It was a poofy mess of tulle and lace that made me look like a cross between a marshmallow and the abominable snowman. I didn't even bother going out into the salon with it on, because I knew I wouldn't wear it, and I didn't need to hear the comments.

"This is already better," Ashley said, clipping me into the sample of the next dress. At my size, they didn't have the dresses available, so they put you in something smaller and used various clips and ties to keep it in place so you could see what it looked like.

And it was better. This one was silky, with bell sleeves that flowed down nearly to the floor.

It was pretty, but it wasn't the one. "Is it normal to just *know*?"

"Yeah," she said. "I swear it's a primal experience like nothing else. Because you just have this *feeling* in your bones, and once you have it, you can't get the dress out of your mind."

"Will you take a picture for my friends? They couldn't come today." I promised Rin and Isolde I'd include them, but even they didn't get to see me in the snowman dress.

"Of course."

I held up the train and made my way to the mirrors where Ashley and Geneva waited. My wedding planner looked me up and down. "That's pretty."

"But it's not the one. The first one wasn't it either."

"Too form fitting anyway," Laura said.

Closing my eyes for a moment, I turned and faced her. "Despite what you might like, I won't be wearing a circus tent to my own wedding, Laura. I'm already allowing you to push the corset on me. But I am fat. No amount of fabric is going to make me *not* fat by Friday. So please, for once in your life, keep it to yourself."

Her mouth dropped open in shock. Then she stood and approached. "You will watch how you speak to me."

"Or what?"

Even Laura wouldn't do something as brazen as hit me in front of witnesses. And it felt good to stare her down and let her feel a fucking *shred* of the helplessness I'd felt for years.

Rage flared in her eyes, and she settled back on the couch with her arms crossed, glaring. And I glared right the fuck back. For once. Ashley and Geneva hid their smiles as I stepped off the pedestal and went back to the dressing room for dress number three.

Number three wasn't it either. A cinderella ballgown that flared out from my hips and made me feel like I was in some kind of film. But I felt awkward and couldn't imagine staying in it for long, let alone sitting down. Or dancing.

Number four was strapless, satin, and simple. Whereas the abominable snowman dress was too much, this one was far too little. Next.

Number five had me wilting, because no one told you how exhausting trying on dresses like this was. Especially when it was hard to breathe. The corset in this dress was a touch sheer, the rest of the dress filmy and floating. It was gorgeous. Just not on me. Everyone agreed, even Trinity and Rin.

"I know I need to find something," I said as I peeled off the dress and let Ashley help me. "But I don't know how many more I have in me."

She looked at me carefully, like she was analyzing me. "When I pull dresses for a bride, all I can do is guess based on preferences. But now that I've met you..." Her eyes suddenly sparkled. "I think I have the one for you."

"Really?"

"Really." She disappeared out of the dressing room, leaving me in nothing but my corset and underwear. I had no idea how long she would take, so I video chatted the girls.

"Did you find one?" Isolde asked.

"No, and I'm exhausted. But my girl just went to get one she thinks is it. Part of me wishes they just picked one and got it over with. It doesn't really matter."

Trinity made a low, growling noise. "The hell it doesn't."

I glanced behind me to make sure Ashley wasn't about to come in. "It's a dress for my *fake* marriage," I whispered. "Other than the photos they need for the press, it doesn't matter."

"Respectfully, bullshit." Isolde popped a piece of popcorn in her mouth. "You're the one who pushed me forward when I was hesitant, O. And now you're going to do the same. Now keep us on the phone so we can see the dress."

"Fine." I propped up the phone on a nearby chair.

Isolde ate more popcorn. "You look hot, by the way."

I rolled my eyes. "Me and my too-tight corset."

"Well, if you loosened it up so you felt good, I fully support this look. And I'm sure your soon-to-be husbands will as well."

Would they? They said they wanted a real marriage, but it was hard to believe Alphas like them could ever want someone like me. Of course, having sex with the woman they were marrying was convenient, so it made sense. But the rest of it?

I shook my head. Usually, I could resist those kinds of self-deprecating thoughts. But with trying on clothes, the pain in my sides from the boning, and Laura's attitude, I was worn down.

Ashley pushed open the door with a new bundle of fabric in her arms. "So there's two pieces to this dress, but I don't want you to see the second piece yet."

"Okay," I laughed. "Ashley, my best friends are on the phone right there, just so you know."

"Hello, ladies. Let's get you into this." She rubbed her hands together with glee.

I laughed again. "You really think it's the one?"

"I do. I feel it in my bones. That doesn't mean you should tell me you like it if you don't. But I've got a good feeling."

"Then let's give it a go."

She helped me into the dress, and it was a different silhouette than the others I'd tried on. Almost a mermaid style, with the white skirt flaring from my knees. The top was entirely lace, with a structured, corseted top, an off the shoulder neckline, and lace sleeves that went down to my wrists, only interrupted by a puff at the elbow.

It wasn't a dress I would have ever picked for myself. But I couldn't stop staring at my own reflection. Even though I was fat, I still had a waist, and the structured corset hit me exactly where it was, emphasizing the curves in my shape to nearly an hourglass. The bottom, flaring skirt balanced out the shape so I didn't look stuffed into the dress, and the neckline didn't feel scandalous, it felt... pretty.

"Holy shit, Ocean," Trinity whispered. "You look..."

Ashley was right. This was the one. Because nothing had ever made me feel like I did wearing this dress. All the other thoughts in my brain fell away, and all I could focus on was how lovely it was. How good it felt. What they would think when they saw me.

"Now, close your eyes," Ashley said. "I think this will make it even better."

I obeyed, and I heard my friends gasp when she revealed whatever it was. Fabric brushed my shoulders, and Ashley pulled my arms through holes, before arranging something on top of my hair.

"Okay. Open."

My reflection looked like a fairytale. Ashley had added a cloak entirely made of lace over the dress. It fanned out behind me in a train, the hood balancing on my hair in place of the veil. It was perfect.

Tears blurred my eyes, and I had to blink them away. "Wow."

"You like it?"

"I love it."

Ashley jumped up and down and clapped her hands. "I knew it. I *knew* it. Do you want to go and show?"

I shook my head. "No. She won't like it, and I don't care. This is what I want."

"Fuck yes." Trinity nodded her approval. "Don't give that bitch the satisfaction."

"She'll give me hell either way."

"At least this way you'll be happy."

Grinning at my friends, I picked up the phone. "Fine. You're right. I surrender. Now I'm hanging up so I can get measured and get the hell out of here."

Isolde stuck out her tongue. "*BYE.*"

After taking a couple of pictures, Ashley helped me out of the dress and took my measurements. "Thursday we'll do a final fitting. I'll make sure Geneva knows where and when."

"That's perfect, thank you."

Laura was staring at her phone when I came out, and she frowned when I looked up. "Took you long enough. Why aren't you dressed?"

"Oh, we found the right one, and I didn't need extra opinions on it. Ashley's taking care of the order."

Her frown grew deeper. "I want to see it."

"You will. When I wear it."

"I—"

"I'm not putting it back on. I can show you the picture later."

Geneva, who was on the phone in the corner, hung up. "I'm glad you found something. While you're here, would you like to look at some things for *after* the wedding?" Her grin told us exactly what she meant. "We have plenty of options here from *Cheria.*"

Laura snorted. It was under her breath, but we both still heard it. Geneva went to say something, and I stopped her. "Ashley is the one who found the dress. I don't know how she picked it, but it was perfect. And she now has my measurements. So if she wants to pick some things for me, I'm fine with that."

Her mouth was a firm line, but she nodded. "All right. As far as everything else, I'll be in touch tomorrow. Let me know what you choose for the flowers as soon as you can."

"I will. And thank you for everything."

Laura was already on her way out of the salon, and I jogged to keep up. "Was she consoling you because I tell you the truth?" She sneered when I caught her at the doors.

I stared at my aunt. "I don't understand."

"What don't you understand, Ocean?"

"Why you do this. Why you act like this. Why you *treat me* like this.

What did I ever do to you other than have my parents die too fucking early? You act like I'm some kind of poison."

She narrowed her eyes. "You didn't have to do anything."

"Then why?" Emotion was rising, as it did when I was tired and stressed. And after this, I just needed to know.

"Frank and I have worked for everything we have," she said. "And we worked hard. You're going to get everything fucking handed to you, just like your mother, and you're already lazy as it is." Her eyes ran over my body at that last remark. My aunt didn't understand the concept of genetics and the possibility that some people were simply bigger than others. To her, if you were fat, it was a moral failing and always your fault.

Always.

"Did your mother give anything to us in the will? No. She gave everything to you. I'm her sister, and she didn't give me a fucking cent while also declaring me the guardian of her daughter. Because I couldn't have a child of my own, she gave me hers like it was a gift and not an utter slap in the face."

"You have full access to the entire estate," I said. "The accounts that aren't my trust. That's not nothing."

"Only until you have it. Then what? Then we're out on our asses and you get to flit around my house and play with your flowers and never do anything valuable with your life?" Her mouth twisted into an ugly sneer. "So if you want to know, that's why. You've managed to take everything from me over and over again, while your very existence reminds me of the thing I was never able to have. So forgive me for not worshipping the ground that the last remaining Caldwell walks on."

Pushing the door open, she stopped and looked back. "And I heard what you said to Geneva. Don't bother buying anything for after the wedding. Because the idea that these men want you for any other reason than that you're disposable is laughable. Get in the fucking car."

It took me a few seconds to be able to move. Hurt pulsed in my chest. I never knew why, and now that I knew, it still didn't make sense. But with the kind of hatred she threw at me every day, it was never going to make sense. There was nothing I could do to make it better or make me like her more. Frank was the same, though he wasn't as vicious.

My chest lifted. All this time I thought it was something I'd done. But... no. There was nothing. And that in itself made me feel better. I didn't do anything to deserve it, and no amount of trying was going to make it change.

Good to know.

I followed her to the car and put in my headphones, ready to ignore her on the long ride back to Clarity.

Fig 15. Hellebore
(Also: Christmas Rose)
Meaning: Anxiety; Relief;
Tranquilize my Anxiety

OCEAN

$\mathcal{T}$here were movers in the house, and there were locks on the kitchen cabinets. There had been since after the bridal salon. The kind used to keep a child out of where they weren't supposed to be, only amplified with padlocks. In a way, the scale of her pettiness was impressive.

I didn't know what kind of weight Laura thought I was going to lose with only days till the wedding, but she was doing her best to make it happen. Whether she really thought it was the best way or she wanted to take it one step further after our conversation, it didn't matter.

But since the wedding was now tomorrow and my dress fitting was complete, movers were here to take everything over to the DuPont mansion. I hadn't been there yet, but if it was anything like the house Isolde's parents lived in, it would be stunning.

The movers were doing an amazing job. I felt like I should help them, but they were faster than I was. There was just one thing I was worried about. My hand was on my phone to text one of them, but I wasn't sure if it was something I should bother them with.

Them.

There was no easy way to refer to them yet.

"Any way I can take that frown off your face?"

I looked up, startled, to find Everett standing in the doorway to my rooms. "What are you doing here? I mean, hi."

He smiled as he stepped in, and I took him in now that I was over the shock of seeing him at all. No suit this time. Jeans and a long-sleeved shirt that clung to him in ways that were sinful. My eyes bounced away of their own accord. When I saw things like that? I started to think Laura was right about the differences between us.

"I came to make sure everything was going well for the move. And to check on you. We haven't heard from you since the photograph."

"Want to make sure I'm not getting cold feet?"

He chuckled and stepped closer. "You're about to be our wife. We want to make sure you're doing well."

The long, slow inhale as he entered my space was imagined, right? He wasn't scenting me. And he wasn't looking at me with hunger. That was just my stomach after Laura trying to starve me.

"They're doing a good job. Almost done."

"Good."

"Except—"

Everett's eyebrows rose. "Except what?"

"It doesn't matter." I shook my head. "I was going back and forth about asking, and you don't need to be bothered."

He reached out, pausing to see if I would let him touch me. When I didn't pull away, he slid a hand around my waist and drew our bodies nearly flush. I was already wearing the corset, though my skin was slowly being rubbed raw from the tightness and how long I'd been wearing it. Still, I sucked myself in.

"Or, you can tell me."

I bit my lip, and his eyes followed the movement. Did he taste like his scent? Almonds and pistachios and a tang of sweetness that reminded me of cookies made with the same ingredients. It was subtle and spicy and rich and I found myself inhaling him just as deeply.

Shaking my head, I swallowed. I must be hungrier than I thought. "My flowers."

Everett tilted his head. "What about them?"

"I, um, I have a greenhouse here. I breed new types of flowers, and some of the plants belonged to my mother. I'm worried about them if I'm not here to take care of them."

I didn't trust Frank and Laura. Now knowing exactly how she felt, she'd ruin all my plants for spite. As it was, the building remained locked at all times, including when I was inside it.

"We don't have a greenhouse, but we can build one," he said. "Do you have anyone you trust to take care of them? We'll pay to make sure they do until we can make a place for them, and I'll make sure they have no problem accessing it."

"You would do that?"

The smile he gave me was blinding. "I think you'll find there's very little we wouldn't do for you, Ocean."

Because I was saving them in their PR nightmare. Well, I supposed they did owe me for that. "Thank you. My employee, Sally. She'd do it. I just need to ask her. But I wasn't sure they'd let her in."

Everett's eyes darkened. "Why wouldn't they?"

"No reason." The answer was too quick, and I knew it.

They'd already seen the way Laura acted when we were in Frank's study, so they probably suspected. But I didn't want to do anything or say anything until I was already the hell out of here. Even with one day left, things could get worse than locks on cabinets.

Lifting a hand, Everett brushed his thumb over my lower lip where I was biting it again. He freed it and soothed the skin. And I was going to pass out because that was the single hottest thing that had ever happened in my life, sad as it was.

"Once you're ours, I have some questions I want you to answer, little nymph."

"I'm not little." I sidestepped the emotion that ran through me at the word *ours*.

His eyes crinkled at the corners. "Just nymph then. Though last time I checked, I was still quite a bit taller than you. You're little to me."

My face flushed hot. It didn't feel like he was joking or hiding his meaning. He meant it.

"Nymph?" I asked, mouth dry.

"Mysterious, beautiful, and a woman of many talents. Or maybe I should call you a siren."

I laughed then. "I'm none of those things."

Pretty, yes. Beautiful was a stretch. Mysterious? No. With the exception of my aunt and uncle, I tried to be honest and straightforward. And flowers were the only thing I'd ever been good at. So one talent.

He frowned, but didn't correct me. That was fine. I didn't need them to flatter me.

Ruby came into the room. "Mind if I toss a few things in with yours, Ocean? I don't have much here, but I figured this would be easier."

I stared at her. "What?"

She stared right back. "You didn't think I was staying here without you, right? I'm coming with you. Got it all set up with your fiancés." She gave Everett a wave. "Thank you for that."

My mouth was open in shock. She'd been in our house for years doing what was needed and helping me when we had events and such. "That's amazing. Yes, of course, do whatever you need to." I looked at him. "Thank you."

"You don't have to thank me for something like that, Ocean. We're happy to."

Ruby left us, and I suddenly became aware of how close we were, his hand still on my lower back. "Where are Micah and Cameron?"

"Annoyed they're not here with me. But we didn't want to overwhelm you. Annoyed probably isn't the right word. More like feral."

Just when I was about to ask him why on earth they would be feral, my stomach interrupted us. I turned red with embarrassment. "It's been a busy day. Kind of forgot to eat." Oh, and my aunt is on the warpath and actively trying to prevent me from eating between now and when I say *I do*.

Everett just smiled again. "I shouldn't keep you too long. You need to eat something, and if I stay here too long, I'll be tempted to take you home, when that's for tomorrow night."

"Right."

God, it really was unfair how gorgeous he was. Thick dark hair, icy blue eyes I already knew could both freeze or turn so warm it heated you from the inside. I wasn't going to think about his body. Because I couldn't. Especially not today, and especially when I imagined them seeing me after the wedding.

The idea that they might regret it and change their minds. Have an

97

annulment, or even just decide to walk away from me after looking at me...

I shook the thought away. It was the fear I'd had with every partner I'd ever had, few that there were. But dwelling on it right now wasn't going to get me through the night.

"You really are an Ocean," he murmured. "So much going on beneath the surface. Hopefully we'll be able to see it someday."

Then he let me go and cast a glance around the quickly emptying space. "I'll see you tomorrow, wife."

"See you tomorrow."

He strode out of my room, and I had to catch my breath. The way he said the word *wife* was positively sinful.

Ruby came up beside me and bumped my shoulder with hers. "I don't know all the details of how we got here, but things could definitely be worse. Husbands like that?"

"Yeah." I swallowed, voice hoarse. "It could definitely be worse."

Now I just had to make sure I got out of this with my heart intact. Because if they kept calling me their wife in that tone, I would fall for them, and when our year was up, the rest of me would be shattered.

At the very least I had friends I knew would pick up the pieces. And, I repeated to myself, I would rather be shattered and free than whole and trapped for five more years.

I dodged out of the way of a mover carrying a box and shook myself out of the spiral. Almost out. So close. I just had to survive until tomorrow.

Fig 16. Hawthorn
(Also: Bread and Cheese Tree,
Mayflower, Thorn Apple,
Tree of Chastity)
Meaning: Contradictions; Duality; Hope;
Male energy; Union of opposites

EVERETT

———

*T*ime wasn't moving fast enough for me. Only a few minutes until the wedding started, and it was still too long.

All I could think about was Ocean and getting lost in those dark eyes as she looked up at me. I wanted to know every thought in her head. Then I wanted to spend several hours between her thighs. Not necessarily in that order.

More than anything, I wanted her to know how deep this was for us. That it wasn't a game or a PR stunt or anything else. It was forever, because she was our Omega.

But I knew, in the same way I knew that she was mine, she wasn't ready to hear it. Even if she would believe us before a heat, there were things lurking under the surface she needed to face. If there were monsters that needed defeating, we would do it with her.

Still, the thought of being so close to her and not being able to tell her everything made me itch with frustration. I fucking hated it. I was the steady one. The one of us who struck fear into opponents when needed. The one who could tune out emotions and do the task set in front of me, no matter what it was.

All that evaporated when it came to her.

A firm knock sounded on the door. Cameron peeked outside, and I saw his shoulders stiffen. When he opened it further, I saw why. Frank stood there in his suit, looking nervous.

His nerves were different from the anticipation dancing under my skin. *I* was on edge because my whole world was going to be walking toward me down the aisle and I didn't want to do anything but make her feel loved and let her know how much we wanted her. *He* was nervous because he was going to lose his company and he was holding onto it so tightly he was about to shatter it.

That was the thing he needed to learn. When you held things that close, they broke. Without room to move and grow, whatever means you used to bind it to you would dig in—like barbed wire—until the damage was irreparable. But Frank wasn't the kind of person to understand that.

"Frank," Micah said by way of greeting. "Didn't expect to see you back here."

"Just wanted to come by and make sure everything was in order."

The paperwork was with the lawyers. We'd sign everything when we got to the office on Monday. He knew that already, so the words rang false. I kept my voice light with amusement. "Nothing's changed since the last time we spoke."

"Right, right." He cleared his throat. "I also just wanted to thank you for choosing Ocean."

That... was not what I expected.

"Oh?" Cameron asked. "And why is that?"

Frank shrugged, and something in my gut told me I wasn't going to like what came next. "Even if it's only for a year, this is probably the only time she'll have a relationship, so it'll be good for her to have it. That's all."

"I don't understand," I said.

"She's..." Frank seemed at a loss for words, and I wasn't going to supply them. Let him flounder in the silence like a gasping fish for all I cared. He was going to say whatever it was. "She's not your typical Omega. And I understand why you chose her. Because she was available. But you don't have to pretend with me. Everyone knows you wouldn't pick her if you had a choice."

"Again," Cameron said, his voice uncharacteristically flat. "Why is that?"

He sighed and pinched the bridge of his nose. "We know her body is a barrier. Lord knows Laura and I have tried to help her, but she's never been interested. And after you, I doubt there will be anyone else. So thank you. It's a kindness."

Red flashed across my vision, and it was only Cameron's hand in the middle of my chest that stopped me from punching him in the fucking mouth. It was one thing to know they treated her differently because of her body, and another thing to hear it from his lips. The fucker.

Frank looked at me and he looked afraid. Good. I wanted him to be afraid of me. "Let me go, Cam."

"Are you sure?"

"Let me go," I repeated.

He stepped away, and I slid my hands into the pockets of my tux, just in case. I approached Frank slowly. "Listen to me very closely, Frank. If I ever hear you, or your wife, ever say anything of the kind about Ocean again, it will not go well for you. Do you understand?"

Swallowing, he stuttered. "The agreement's been made. You can't back out."

"No," I said. "We can't. Nor will we. But let me make myself clear. Business is not the only way we can destroy you, and if you ever insult our *wife* again, I will make sure of it. The only thing Ocean needs to be thankful for is to be free of the two of you and your poisonous outlook."

He looked confused. "But you can't possibly want *that*."

This time it was Micah who spoke while the hands in my pockets curled into fists. "I suggest you don't try to tell us what we do and do not want. It's none of your business. Nor is how we conduct our marriage. The paperwork will be signed on Monday, so unless you have something of substance to tell us, see yourself out. We have a wedding to get ready for."

I suppressed a smirk. We were already good to go. Had been ready for a while. But he didn't need to know that.

Frank cleared his throat. "I guess I'll see you at the reception."

As soon as the door closed, Cameron groaned. "Any way we could kick him out of the reception? Because I would really, really love not to kill him."

"I would love to kill him," I said. "Slowly. With my bare hands."

The look on Micah's face stopped me in my tracks. "What?"

I didn't recall a time ever seeing this kind of grief in his eyes. "Does Ocean think we don't want her? Because they've been saying things like that?"

The words punched me in the gut. No, Ocean wasn't thin. She wasn't what most of the world would call a 'normal,' Omega. What did I care about that? I couldn't remember a time when I didn't find women like Ocean beautiful. The idea that someone could look at her and deem her lesser simply because of her size made me want to burn the world to the ground.

"I hope not," Cam whispered. "But if that's true, we'll fix it. We'll show her it's the opposite."

All I wanted to do was sweep her away to our house and pin her to the mattress until she was screaming our names. But if she didn't think we wanted her? If she thought this truly was only convenience and not an intentional choice, she would be miserable, and the self-worth they'd already shattered would crumble in front of our eyes.

I wasn't going to let that happen.

Oren, Cameron's assistant, poked his head in the door and looked at the three of us. "They're ready for you."

Blowing out a breath, I shook every other thought out of my head. Fluttering jitters flowed back in. But excitement was there too. I smiled. "Let's go marry our Omega."

Fig 17. Pomegranate
(Also: Garnet Apple, Grenadier)
Meaning: Elegance; Good luck; Good
things; Marriage; Paradise; Prosperity

OCEAN

"*F*uck." The word came out as a whimper.

"You'll thank me later," Laura said, pulling the corset laces so tightly I was practically seeing stars. Not to mention I'd barely eaten anything, so I was already lightheaded.

"No," I rasped out. "I don't think I will. I don't think I'll thank you for anything ever again."

Her only answer was to tighten the laces again before tying them off, and for a moment, the pain was blinding. Still, I recovered enough to stand and face her. "Half the reason I'm doing this is to get away from you. I hope you know that, and I hope you know that my mother would be ashamed of you and how you've treated me."

Laura's hand twitched, and I knew she was itching to slap me. She'd never crossed that barrier—because she knew it was one she could never come back from—and she wouldn't do it now and risk being found out.

"If you'd shown me even a shred of kindness, Laura, then maybe things would be different. But whatever comes on you after this, that's *your* fault."

"You still have obligations. You promised to get us information on this new pack of yours, and you better deliver."

I smiled. "I'm well aware of my obligations, aunt."

At this particular moment, I didn't feel like mentioning that the papers I'd signed made no mention of spying on my new husbands, so I didn't have to do shit.

Someone knocked at the door, and I looked over. "I need to get ready now. So please, get the hell out."

She stomped past me just as Geneva opened the door and let in my friends, barely missing my shoulder in the process. Trinity watched her retreating form and lifted her middle finger to her back.

"Rin," I said, smothering a laugh.

"What? Bitch has been asking for that for years."

I shook my head and sat down at the vanity provided in the bridal suite. The one thing I hadn't been consulted on was the venue. Even for men as rich as the DuPonts, there were only so many venues with an availability for a wedding on such short notice.

That being said, the hotel was beautiful. I hadn't seen the ceremony space or the ballroom, but from the way Geneva's eyes sparkled, I could only imagine what I would find when I walked down the aisle.

The aisle. Nerves clung to me and I couldn't seem to hear anything while the women Geneva hired did my hair and makeup. Isolde seemed to know them, and I tuned back in when someone asked me something. "What?"

Isolde looked at me. "I said I was going to try to get you in for a photoshoot. Erin and Monica are the ones who did my hair and makeup for my photoshoot with Hawk."

"Oh." I met their eyes in the mirror. "I'm sorry. I'm... distracted."

The one doing my hair laughed softly. "You're fine, girl. I get it. But you're actually about done."

I looked at myself, and I'd zoned out so completely I hadn't noticed their handiwork. My hair wasn't that long, but it fell in lovely curls, with some of it pinned back, framing my face prettily. My makeup was subtle, but I loved that they'd emphasized my eyes. I felt *pretty*.

"Wow. I—"

The hairstylist put her hand on my shoulder and smiled. "We'll give you guys a minute."

The door clicked shut behind them, and I stared at myself in the mirror. I was really doing this. And in spite of everything—how much I needed this and how much I needed to get out—I was still scared.

"Ocean?" Trinity asked.

"What if they're not as nice as they seem?" The words slipped out of me and suddenly they couldn't stop. "What if I'm about to make it all worse? What if they see me tonight and decide they don't want me after all and everything falls apart? I can't—"

"Hey." Isolde crouched in front of me, her deep green dress pooling on the floor. "Take a breath for me, all right? Everything's going to be fine."

"You don't know that."

She smiled and glanced over at Rin. "You're right. I don't. But what I do know? Is that I just spent far too much time telling myself that things weren't real and that it was all going to end, and look how it turned out. Ocean, *you* are the one who pulled me out of that spiral. *You* got me to take a chance and come out of my shell for the guys even when I was terrified, and now I'm going to do the same for you."

"But it isn't real."

Nodding, she took my hands and shrugged. "I know. But it's real for now, and if you can, I want you to enjoy it. They chose you for a reason. And if they do anything to hurt you, I now have five men who will gladly kick their asses, no matter how much money they have."

Rin appeared at my shoulder before reaching down to grab my hands. "You can do this," she said. "We've got you."

My breath still came in sharp gasps, but I nodded and let them help me stand, and then help me get into the dress, followed by the cape. It was so much better than in the store because this one fit me perfectly, and even though I was still terrified as I looked in the mirror, I looked like a dream.

"I never thought I could look like this," I admitted.

It was never active thoughts that prevented me from thinking about it, it was simply reality. Fat girls didn't look like this. They didn't get the prettiest dresses or underwear. We took what we could get.

Part of me never wanted to take the dress off.

"You look incredible," Isolde said. "If they don't want you, then they're fucking kidding themselves, because they'll never find anyone better."

I blinked tears away from my eyes before I ruined my makeup. "Thank you."

A soft knock on the door came before Geneva poked her head in. "It's time."

"We'll see you out there," Trinity said, squeezing my hand.

I buried my fists in the lace of my dress. My heart was pounding out of my chest, and I still couldn't believe I was actually doing this. Profound grief struck me in the heart. It wasn't real, and I knew it, but I wished Mom and Dad were here to see me.

They would have been happy. At least, I hoped they would.

"Okay." I took a deep breath and steadied myself. I could do this. I could do this. I could do this.

Geneva handed me my bouquet, all purple, blue, and white flowers. Floriography, like any language, verbal or non, needed context to be understood. A single flower could have any number of meanings. But when you paired them together, that was when they truly began to speak.

I'd given in to my romantic and hopeful side when I chose the flowers. Purple lilacs for first love. Forget-me-nots for faithfulness. Hyacinths, which spoke of true love and said 'I am looking for romance.' Eternal love was spoken for by baby's breath and white roses, which also meant 'to be worthy.'

"How you holding up?" Geneva asked from behind me where she was holding the train of the cape so it didn't get caught on anything.

"Nervous," I whispered. "Really, really nervous."

"If it makes you feel better, every bride I've ever worked with has felt the same. You look beautiful, and even though you haven't seen them, your fiancés are nervous too."

"Really?"

She laughed quietly. "Really."

I wasn't sure it was a good thing that it made me feel better, but it did. At least I wasn't alone in this.

There were no bridesmaids. If I'd had them, it would have been Rin and Isolde. So the only person walking down the aisle was me.

In front of the gilded double doors, Geneva arranged my dress so it fell perfectly, double checked where my hood touched my hair, and arranged the train. "Perfect."

"If I pass out, make sure I'm covered when the dress splits."

"You're not going to pass out," she said. "You're going to be just fine. I promise."

I looked at her. "Thank you for everything."

"My pleasure." She nodded toward the doors. "You're on."

Two hotel employees opened the doors in front of me, and it was a struggle to keep my mouth shut.

Flowers overflowed. Everywhere there *could* be flowers, there were flowers. Purple petals scattered down the white aisle. They draped over the edges of chairs, creating a barrier between me and our guests. Behind the officiant there was an arch of flowers that matched my bouquet. There were formations climbing up the walls, and I had no idea how. Candles dotted the room, almost making the flowers glitter. Everything was that shade of bluish purple I loved so much. Even the vests of the men I was about to marry.

My breath caught in my chest as my eyes caught up to themselves and I saw *them*. All three of them, staring at me like I wasn't real. Like I was a ghost, and they weren't sure if they'd dreamed me up.

I managed to take one step, and then another. Cameron smiled at me, and it made breathing easier. They all smiled. They were so fucking gorgeous. This had to be a dream.

Surely, I got hit by a car and this whole situation was a coma hallucination. Because three Alphas who looked like that couldn't be waiting at the end of the aisle for me.

For *me*.

No matter if it was arranged or for our convenience. This didn't happen to girls like me.

But Micah stepped forward and took my hand, helping me up the short steps to stand across from them. He lifted that hand and kissed the back of it. Everett stepped forward and did the same. Then Cameron. And when his lips left my skin, I was pink with heat.

Every time I was near them I was reminded how good they fucking smelled. Like standing in the middle of your favorite perfume. Drowning in it.

"You all right?" Micah whispered.

"I think so."

A half smile. "Us too."

The female Alpha standing next to us—they told me her name was Raina—raised her voice to the crowd, and everything began.

I couldn't listen. Not really. I was hearing her voice and what she said, but my eyes were on them. Taking in their faces and their expressions.

"Do you, Alphas, take this Omega to be your wife?"

"We do." They answered together. Absolutely sure.

She looked at me. "And do you, Ocean, take these Alphas to be your husbands?"

I wished my voice was as sure. "I do."

"Then repeat after me."

They made their vows. The ones we'd all heard a thousand times before in the movies and at our friends' weddings. Most people could probably recite them by heart. But they felt different when you were the one speaking them. When they were being spoken to *you*.

I never thought about the intimacy of *to have and to hold*. Or the long reaching meaning of *in sickness and in health*.

For a year. We were vowing these things for a year. I needed to remember that and not fall into their eyes.

"The rings," Raina said, and panic struck me. I didn't have rings for them. She extended her palm, and the three rings were there. Each one a little different from the others. She took my bouquet in her other hand to help me.

Micah picked up a gold band and handed it to me. "This one is mine."

"Thank you."

His hand steadied mine as I slipped it on him, fingers brushing my hand as he pulled away. Everett's ring was brushed silver, and Cameron's was rosy and copper. I smiled at the way they fit each of them, and they were smiling back. Suddenly, this felt different, because we were in this together.

We were together.

Cameron took a ring from his pocket and stepped forward. White gold. A little band with stones. I nearly gasped. Opals? The ring curved like it was incomplete when he slid it on my finger.

It was Everett who completed it, a ring with a purple, oval stone that settled right in the curve of the opals like it was meant to be there. And Micah completed the set with another simple band. Three rings.

Three rings that *fit* my fingers. Sleek and simple. Beautiful. I loved them. And when I looked up at Micah, I couldn't read the expression on his face.

"You may kiss your bride."

My whole body froze.

Somehow, in the chaos of getting to this point, I hadn't thought about it. We were going to kiss in front of everyone. I didn't think I'd ever wanted anything more than to feel them kiss me, though I wished we didn't have an audience for it.

But I was reliving those moments with Micah in the study before we were interrupted. He was going to kiss me then, and this time, there was no stopping it.

When his lips met mine, time slowed down. One hand slid behind my neck, guiding me closer. Micah tasted like he smelled. Sweet and rich and overwhelming. It was over too quickly, and I couldn't breathe fully. He'd stolen all my air and I could barely open my eyes before Cameron kissed me.

This kiss was playful and light. Joyful. Insistent and powerful. And too fucking fast. I needed more. Fuck the audience and the clapping I heard from somewhere outside of myself.

Everett's kiss was pure sin. Ice with a sliver of darkness and dominance. But such sincerity, I craved more. If they were serious, and they wanted this to be real, then I would make it real because nothing had ever felt like this. I'd never been kissed like this. Hell, these kisses were better than most of the sex I'd had in my life.

My body followed him when he pulled away, like it couldn't bear to be separated from him even a little. "We made it," he whispered.

"Yeah."

He slipped my arm through his, and I couldn't stop smiling as we all retreated up the aisle together, because we'd done it. I got married, and now I was almost free.

Fig 18. Brook Cinquefoil

Meaning: Mixed feelings

OCEAN

*M*y signature lined the bottom of the marriage license alongside theirs. We were married. *Truly* married.

I couldn't breathe. At the same time, I felt such sharp relief it made my knees tremble.

Geneva took the license and put it in a folder. "We'll have this delivered with everything else. Now we need pictures before the grand entrance. Come with me."

My head was light. Now that the adrenaline was fading, my body hurt from what Laura had done and my lack of food made me feel weak. Pictures. I could do pictures.

A hand landed on my lower back and moved with me as we walked. "Ocean?"

"Yeah?"

"Are you all right? You seem dazed."

It was Cameron. His sugary lemon citrus whirled around me, soothing and invigorating. "I'm okay. Not used to being the center of attention."

The hand on my back slid around one of my hips. "Today I'm glad you are. You look incredible."

His words shouldn't have made me blush, but they did. "Thank you."

I wanted to talk to them. I wanted to be happy and involved and not feel like I was dizzy and drowning. But everything felt hazy. I still smiled, and it was a real smile because I was *free*, and even through the haze, my Omega felt safe.

Pictures with the lace cloak on and off. Pictures with all four of us and each Alpha individually. Pictures where they kissed me, and if I wasn't lightheaded before, I was now. Kissing them lit up parts of me I didn't know existed. And the way they kissed me was far from appropriate for wedding photos. But they didn't seem to care, so neither did I.

"I think that's it," Geneva said with a grin. "We can go make your grand entrance."

"Do we need any with the families?" I asked.

Cameron shook his head. "It was short notice for our families. Most of them are on the East Coast. You'll meet them eventually. And forgive me, I assumed you wouldn't want any with Frank and Laura."

A fair point. I laughed. "You're right."

"See?" He winked. "I know my wife well already."

All the breath whooshed out of me in one go. Again, like when Everett had said it, it shouldn't be so... I didn't even know how to

113

describe it except for heat building under my skin and a longing I couldn't name.

I couldn't even focus on the announcement of us entering because holy *shit* Geneva had outdone herself. The small ballroom for the reception put the ceremony space to shame. More flowers and more candles. Purple fabric draping the chairs. A tiered cake with frosting roses in our color scheme.

"Do you like it?" Micah asked.

Looking up at him, I realized everyone was clapping for us, and the three of them were looking at me. "It's so beautiful."

"I'm glad." His eyes searched my face. "We don't have to stay very long. Promise."

"Whatever you need."

"No." He lifted my knuckles. "Whatever *you* need."

Cheerful screaming approached us, and Micah barely got out of the way in time for Trinity to slam into me. *Fuck*, that hurt.

"You fucking did it. You're married and now I'm the only loser of the three of us."

In spite of the pain and my exhaustion, I laughed. "You're not a loser, Rin. You just haven't met the right one yet. Or more than one."

"Well, maybe your husbands have some friends. I could use a rich pack." She pulled back and looked at them where they waited behind me. "What do you say? Have any single friends or packs looking for an Omega?"

Cameron chuckled. "Maybe."

"Well, if you do," Isolde said, pulling me in for a hug. "Make sure to warn them. She's a brat."

"Fuck off," Trinity said. "I'm perfect."

I hugged them both again. "Thank you guys."

"We're here for you, O," Isolde whispered. "And I swear to god if you ever keep something so big from us again I will kick your ass myself."

"I'll let you."

"No kicking my wife's ass," Everett said, stepping up beside me and interlacing his fingers with mine. "It's my job to make sure that doesn't happen."

"These are my best friends. Isolde, and this is Trinity. You'll probably see them quite a bit."

"If you make Ocean happy, then you're always welcome."

Rin's mouth fell open, and she stared at me and looked at Isolde. "Okay, seriously? Fuck both of you. First, you have a pack that worships the ground you walk on and *makes* you chocolate. I'm still not over that, by the way. And now you have a pack that you've been married to for like five seconds and they say things like this? I'm going to die alone."

I couldn't stop my laughter. "You are not."

"I am," she groaned, then lowered her voice. "My pussy is going to dry up and shrivel up from disuse."

"Okay, miss drama," Isolde pulled her away. "Let's get you a drink and let some other people congratulate the happy pack, okay?"

"Fine." Trinity hugged me one more time. "Don't leave without saying goodbye, okay?"

"Wouldn't dream of it."

Isolde pulled her back across the room where the St. James pack had taken over a table and waited for them. Rowan smiled and raised his hand in greeting. I waved back. "Are there people we have to meet?"

"Have to?" Everett asked. "No. You don't have to do anything you don't want to ever again, Ocean."

"Congratulations," a new voice said. Raina, the female Alpha who'd performed the ceremony.

"Thank you for doing this for us," I said. "It's really nice to meet you."

"It's nice to meet you too, Mrs. DuPont."

I blinked at the name. People would call me that. Did they want me to change my legal name? I wasn't sure I wanted that. My name was the only thing I had left of my family.

"Raina, can you do me a favor?" Cameron asked.

"Sure thing, boss."

"Keep Frank and Laura distracted. Or at least give us a heads up when you see them coming in our direction."

My head snapped toward him, and he met my gaze with steady ease. "Why?"

"You want to see them?"

"I mean..."

One knuckle went under my chin to make sure I didn't look away. His voice was soft. "Tell the truth, Ocean."

"No, I don't. But they won't leave without talking to me. I'm pretty sure about that."

With a smile, he dropped a quick kiss on my mouth like it was the most natural thing in the world. "We'll cross that bridge when we get there. In the meantime, I think it's time we cut the cake."

Taking my hand, he guided me across the room, and I let him. Because they were already taking care of me, and I fucking liked it.

No, I loved it.

I was already sliding downward toward wanting more than they would give, and there was no way I was getting out of this with my heart intact.

Focusing on what Isolde told me, I pushed the thoughts away and vowed to enjoy it while it lasted.

Fig 19. Peony

Meaning: Anger; Aphrodisiac; Beauty;
Bravery; Happy marriage; Healing;
Romance; Shame; Shyness;
Unrealized desires

MICAH

I watched Cam take Ocean to the cake and followed at a distance. All wrapped in frothy lace, she looked more delicious than the cake. And with her sweetness permeating the air, she was the only thing I wanted to take a bite out of.

Raina walked next to Everett and I. "Do I even want to know why we're keeping Frank and Laura away?"

"Unless you want to feel Alpha rage right now? No. You don't."

"Fuck," she muttered.

"That about sums it up."

She turned and looked at us. "When you said you were getting married because of the board, I didn't expect this."

"What?"

Her smirk told me what was coming. "Don't pretend. You look at her like she's... the only thing in the world."

Everett chuckled. "I'm glad you noticed. She hasn't yet."

"She will. Now go get your bride."

Raina retreated to her own pack, her Omega embracing her when she reached their table. Raina looked at him the way we looked at Ocean. Unfathomable love.

Another breath of Ocean's scent had me turning back to my Omega where she stood at the cake with wide eyes. Cam lifted his hand to us, but I was already moving. I touched Ocean on the shoulder. "Sorry, beautiful. We're here."

She looked up at me so fast her curls bounced. Her eyes were such a dark brown they were nearly black, and I didn't think I'd ever seen any eyes like them. I could get lost in them. She mouthed a word, and it took me a second to realize she'd repeated the word *beautiful*. Like it was alien to her.

How much damage had her aunt and uncle done to her that she didn't think she was fucking stunning? It had already been the goal, but my entire life's mission shifted to make sure Ocean knew how perfect she was at any given opportunity.

The photographer was already looking at us, so I took her hand. "Ready?"

"I—" she squeezed my fingers and whispered, "please don't smash cake in my face."

Cameron slid his arms around her waist from behind and pulled her in. I watched her eyes flutter as her Omega gave in. Her Omega knew. Somewhere deep down, even if the scent match couldn't be recognized yet, she was ours. "We're not going to do that," he said quietly. "None of

117

this is about embarrassing you, and especially after you've asked us not to."

"Thank you."

The photographer smiled at us. "Should I count you down?"

"Sure." All three of us put our hands on Ocean's, and we slid through the cake together. There was no smashing as I fed her a piece of the cake, entranced by the sight of frosting on her tongue and the barest brush of her lips on my skin.

"That's amazing," she said.

"Whatever's left we'll have taken home. Hell, if you love it, I'll have one made for you every week."

Ocean laughed. *Really* laughed. It was the first time I'd ever seen her face that open, and I realized how on edge she'd been this whole time. How reserved. Even speaking to her friends earlier, she was holding back.

"Having a wedding cake made every week would be a bit impractical, don't you think?"

"Not at all. If it makes my wife happy, then it's the perfect thing to do."

She still smiled and lowered her voice. "Your *fake* wife."

"We signed the license, beautiful. You are very much our real wife."

"For now."

I glanced at the others where they stood behind her. We couldn't fault her for thinking that. It was the deal we'd proposed. But it wasn't the truth. Ocean was our wife, and if there was anything we had to say about it, she would stay that way.

Holding out my hand to her, I bowed a little. "Will you dance with me, wife?"

She stared at my hand for a breath before she took it. "Yes."

Our guests quieted as I tugged her onto the dance floor. She looked around like she was nervous, but I guided her against me. "It's just us. No one else."

Music floated from somewhere, wrapping around us as we danced slowly. Everything in me wanted to purr and make her relax. Feel the way she would melt into my arms. But Cameron was right. None of this was about embarrassing her, and I knew as surely as I knew she was my Omega that she wasn't ready for that in front of people. She barely believed she should be standing next to us, let alone us purring for her. That could come later.

Or sooner.

"How are you feeling?" I asked her.

"I'm fine." When I raised one eyebrow, she smiled again. "Everything is beautiful, and I can't believe you did all of it."

"But?"

"But nothing." She still smiled. "I know why we're here. We need the pictures for when you announce everything. So whatever we need to do, we'll do."

I kept the frown off my face. "We want you to enjoy yourself, Ocean. If you're not, then we don't have to stay."

Something flashed in her eyes, and I couldn't read it. Fuck, I wished we could bond her right this second so I could feel what she felt and soothe whatever fears she had. Finally, she whispered. "I am. Promise. I know I'll never have anything like this again."

"All right," Cameron said, his hand coming down on my shoulder. "Enough monopolizing our wife. It's my turn."

She laughed as I spun her into his arms, but my heart ached. I retreated to Everett. He knew. "What's wrong?"

"It's..." I blew out a breath. "It's so much deeper than we thought. She says she's having a good time, but I don't believe her. Because I don't think she believes this is for her. She just thinks it's a wedding, and she's playing a role. Hell, she said she knows she'll never have anything like this again."

Everett scrubbed a hand over his face. "Do we leave now?"

"No. There are still people we need to see." We'd kept the wedding small, but Ocean wasn't entirely wrong about us needing to keep up appearances. It was real to us—so fucking real—but there was still the reason we did this in the first place. "But let's start ticking them off."

We did just that. We smiled our way through the crowd while Cameron danced with the Ocean, and he took over the socializing when Everett spun her away. When it was finally my turn again, she seemed dazed. "You ready to go, beautiful?"

She bit her lower lip, and I wanted to free it, if only for the chance to kiss her there. "I feel bad for leaving."

"Why?"

"Because everything is so stunning, I don't want to waste it."

"Geneva will make sure everything that can be used again is either donated or brought home for us. I'm more worried about you."

She leaned on me a little more. "I'm sorry. But yes, I think I'm ready."

"Okay, beautiful." There was doubt in her eyes again, and like hell was I going to have her doubting herself every time I called her that. But it would take time for her to believe it. "What's your favorite flower?"

She tilted her head. "Why?"

"Humor me."

I craved that tiny smile. Hopefully, in time, she'd give us her real one. "I have a lot. I know that's not really how favorites work, but it's true."

"What are they?"

Ocean shook her head slowly. "Probably too many. Roses, of course. Lilacs. Bluebells. Certain kinds of lilies. Cherry blossoms."

Hmm, nothing that quite rolled off the tongue. An idea popped into my head. That could work. "Would you mind if I called you princess?"

That little crease between her eyes appeared. I already knew it meant she was confused and puzzling something out. "Why call me that? You can call me by my name."

"You're my wife," I murmured. "I want something to call you that no one else gets to. There are lots of things I want to call you, actually. And every time I call you beautiful, you look at me like I'm lying."

Her mouth opened and closed. Her throat moved in a swallow. "What else do you want to call me?"

Still moving us gently around the dance floor, I leaned down to whisper in her ear. The way she shuddered had me wanting to sprint with her to the car. I needed to feel that shudder *everywhere*. "I want to call you beautiful. I want to call you my wife. If you'll let me, sometimes I'd love to call you baby girl. But I understand that those might be a lot. So princess will do for now. Is that all right?"

She nodded. I felt it where her cheek pressed against mine. "Yeah."

"Good." I moved back, but only far enough to kiss her. She melted beneath my mouth, the sweetness of frosting still lingering and beneath that, the sweetness that was *her*.

"Let's go, wife. I want to take you home."

She bit her lip again, and that only made me move faster.

After the photographs of us getting into the car in a shower of pale purple rose petals, the four of us were nearly silent as we drove. Ocean looked out the window. I kept her hand in mine, and she didn't seem to mind, but I also knew it was strange for her.

The gates to our estate opened, and I breathed out a sigh of relief. Here we could be ourselves, and hopefully Ocean would feel the same. It was late in the afternoon and trending toward evening. We could take our time and do what we liked.

I knew what *we* wanted to do, and we'd already told her we wanted the marriage to be real, but I wasn't sure she was ready.

"Your things are all here," I told her as the driver pulled up to the door. "I don't think all of them are unpacked yet, but the staff will take care of the rest of it tomorrow. I know Ruby made sure all your clothes are put away."

"That was nice of her."

Our Omega sounded tired.

Everett helped her out of the car and kept his arm around her as we went inside. I couldn't help but look at our home the way she might. Would she like it? Our place was almost the exact opposite of the Caldwell Estate. The place was beautiful, but very traditional. Dark woods and elaborate trim. Stately, almost. Ours was light and modern, open and airy when it called for it.

"We'll give you a tour, of course," Everett said. "But do you want to take off your dress first?"

"Yeah." She laughed. "It's the most beautiful thing I'll ever wear, but it's not easy."

"No, I imagine not."

"Just tell me where to go," she said, though we still walked with her. "And I'll meet you for... you know, the wedding night."

Cameron and I shared a look. Just the *thought* of a wedding night with Ocean was enough to make me hard. But not if it wasn't something everyone wanted. None of us knew how to respond, so we didn't, guiding her up the stairs to the wing where all our rooms were. Her room took up a large corner of the floor, with windows overlooking the coast and her namesake. There was a hidden door to the nest as well.

Cameron opened the door first. Plush white carpet and a huge bed —complete with a curtained canopy—dominated the space. A fire burned merrily in the fireplace, and Ocean's things were spread here and there. The room was a little anonymous, but that could be fixed. "This is your room."

"Thank you." She moved to stand by the bed, looking a little lost.

I went to her, unable to stop myself. "Can we help you with that?"

She flushed, a wave of her scent washing over me. "No, that's okay. I'll, umm..." Her hands fidgeted with the ends of her lace sleeves. "I'll have Ruby help me undress and then meet you—"

"She's not here," Cameron said. "We're all alone for the wedding night."

"Oh." Her cheeks were so flushed, I wondered if she was just nervous or suddenly feeling sick. "Okay."

I turned her toward me, noticing the way she wouldn't look at me. "You're nervous?"

"You could say that."

"I promise you don't have to be," Cameron said gently. "We're not going to hurt you. Or force you. I know what we said, Ocean, but nothing will ever happen that you don't want."

Her lips pressed into a line, so subtle I barely noticed it. But it was there. Clearly, there was something that she was scared of. "It's not that."

I tilted her face up to mine. "Are you uncomfortable with us helping you undress?"

She hesitantly shook her head.

"Then we'll talk about it, whatever it is. But let us help you get comfortable first. Here." I turned her toward the bed and started to undo the buttons all down the back of her dress and supported her so she could step out of it. All that was left was her corset, garters, and underwear. They left nothing to the imagination, and allowed us to see the curves she had going on for miles. If this gorgeous Omega had any questions about what we wanted before the night was over, we weren't doing our jobs.

Her hair fell around her face, so none of us could see her expression. "Let me help with this too." The corset was laced tight. So tight it took me a second to undo the knot holding the laces. "There we go."

Ocean hissed out a breath as it loosened, the sound cut short. It sounded like... pain.

"Ocean?"

"I'm fine." But the waver in her voice told me otherwise.

I glanced at the others, and they were just as confused as I was. Gently, I loosened the corset further, and I saw it.

Ocean's back was bloody. Her skin marred with angry red lines where the boning of the corset pressed into her skin. The top of it dug in so deep it had cut her. This was way, *way* too tight, and there was no way for this amount of damage to be done in just the time she'd been in this dress today.

Not to mention she had been laced into this for *hours*.

"You're bleeding."

"*What?*" Everett snapped.

I tried not to hurt her as I pulled the fabric further away from her skin. But there was no way around it. "Who did this?" I asked, trying to keep anger out of my tone and failing completely. "Who did this to you?"

She shuddered, and for a moment, I didn't think she would answer. Finally, "You know who."

Looking at the others, I saw my own rage reflected back at me. "What the fuck were they thinking?"

"I can keep it on," she whispered. "If it's easier for you. If you don't want to see me without it."

"Who the fuck told you that?" Everett growled.

She huddled in on herself even further, and I glanced at Cameron. "Get a first aid kit."

"Just lace it back up," she said quietly. "I'm fine."

"You are not fucking fine," I said, guiding her over to the bed and sitting her down on it. The only reason I didn't carry her over to it was because I didn't want to hurt her back more. "And you're certainly not going to be bleeding and in pain on your wedding night."

I crouched in front of her and brushed the hair back from her face.

She was so beautiful, and so frightened. As soon as her back was taken care of, I wanted to wrap her up in my arms and never let her go. "They made you wear this?" She opened her mouth, and I spoke again. "Don't lie, princess. You're our wife now. You're *ours*. No matter what they did or said, it doesn't matter."

"Yes," she finally whispered. "They made me wear it. Or something close."

"How long?"

Her cheeks turned pink again, and I saw the way her hands dug into the bedspread. "You've never seen me without one."

"Even at the gala?"

She nodded slowly.

This whole time? I bowed my head until it touched her knees. My voice sounded ragged. "Fuck, Ocean. Why?"

"Because you look like you," she whispered. "And I look like this."

Cameron came back with the kit in his hand. Sitting on the bed, he loosened the corset further and gently began cleaning her back. "You look like what?"

She shuddered when his hand came in contact with the first cut. I stood and took her hands. "Stand up for me, princess. We'll get you cleaned up here in a second." I looked at Everett, and he stepped in with me as I gently took the corset off her and tossed it away.

Immediately Ocean's hands came up to hide herself. I reached out and tilted her face up until she looked at me once more. "Let me see if I have this straight. They forced you into garments like that since we met you? Because they wanted to make you seem like less than you are?"

"I'm... not like most Omegas," she whispered. "I'm not small."

We already knew that. Had already handed her uncle his ass for daring to suggest she was anything less than perfect. I let my gaze fall down her body. She was *luscious*. Where she could have curves, she had them. Full breasts and thick thighs, a stomach which was round and soft, and the idea of getting lost between her legs made me so hard I was lightheaded.

"No," I said. "You're not. But where did you get the idea that's what we wanted?"

Her eyes widened slightly, and Everett leaned in, brushing his nose along her jaw. "I already wanted to take a bite out of you, Omega. Seeing you naked has only made me more eager."

Cameron stood, crowding behind her without aggravating the cuts on her back, so she could feel all three of us around her and believe it.

"It's not a secret that we had to marry," I told her. "We didn't lie about that. And after everything is settled, if you don't want to be our O — our wife, we'll let you walk away," I said, the words burning in my throat. "So it's convenient for everyone. Just like we promised. But we're selfish too, Ocean."

"How so?" Less fear lurked in her eyes now, and more curiosity.

"We needed to marry. But we weren't going to marry someone we didn't like, and we never wanted to put our Omega through at least a year of being with someone she couldn't stand. If we hadn't thought this would work, we wouldn't have married you."

She gasped. "But— it was just because of the business deal. Right?"

Cameron leaned down to say it softly in her ear. "Fuck the business deal. We *chose* you. And fuck them for trying to make you less than you are."

"I don't understand." She shook her head and took a breath. "Why would you..."

Everett growled low in his throat. "Why would we want you?"

She nodded.

I took her face in my hands. "Why wouldn't we want you?" The fear was back, and I didn't let it stay. "If there's one thing I want from this marriage, other than to fulfill our contract, it's to show you how wrong everything they've told you is. So when the time is up, you can decide what you want to do, knowing the truth."

"When *we* decide," she said.

"Of course."

What she didn't know was that we didn't have to. We already knew we didn't want her to go. She was ours, through and through. If she didn't want this, we wouldn't stop her. But I could sink my teeth into her shoulder and bind her to me right this second, and I would be fucking ecstatic.

"Let's get you cleaned up." Cameron guided her back down onto the bed. "Once we've got you bandaged, we can decide our plans for the evening."

"I thought—"

Everett held out a hand. "You're our wife. As much as all of us would love a wedding night, none of us want to see you in pain. Or to drag you into something you're not ready for. So let him finish, then we'll talk."

Crossing to where I tossed the corset, I picked it up. "I'm going to burn this."

"What?"

The fireplace was more than big enough to take care of the torture device of an undergarment. I tossed it in and watched the flames eat away at the fabric. Then I looked back at my wife, thoroughly enjoying the look of shock on her face. "You won't be wearing any more of those monstrosities," I told her. "If you wear a corset again, it will be because you *chose* it, and it will be properly fitted so it doesn't *cut* you."

I knew clothing. Corsets weren't the villains of the fashion world the way people made them out to be. In general, they got a bad rap, mostly because people tried to use them like *this*. And like hell was I going to let someone hurt my wife because they didn't understand the true history or use of my own goddamn expertise.

Her face softened. "Thank you."

I couldn't stop myself. I crossed the room again and leaned down to kiss her, taking her sweet lips. One taste, and I'd never get enough of her. "You never have to thank us for this, wife. You're ours to protect now."

She melted into my body. Every soft inch of her, and I looked at the others. Yeah, no way in hell could we let this Omega go. Now we just had to show her how thoroughly she belonged to us.

Just like we belonged to her.

Fig 20. Sempervivum
(Also: Hens and Chicks, Liveforever)
Meaning: Liveliness; Vivacity;
Welcome home husband

OCEAN

*T*here was no way for me to move. Wrapped up against Micah while Cameron cleaned the cuts on my back and gently placed bandages over them. I hadn't realized my skin had split. The pain had been intense overall, so it didn't raise any alarm bells.

But the way they looked at me—not with laughter and not with anything other than kindness and... *heat*. I couldn't quite believe it or trust it yet, but *fuck* I wanted to.

"I didn't get blood on the dress, did I?"

Everett lifted my wedding dress and turned it over. "Not at all."

"No wonder you didn't want to stay at the reception," Micah murmured, stroking a hand over my hair. "You were in pain the whole time. I'm so sorry, princess."

Pleasure lit me from within. I'd heard Cade, one of Isolde's pack, call her that, but I'd never understood the appeal until now. And it didn't bother me in the slightest to have the same nickname, because to be thought of as *royal* by my husbands was something I'd never imagined.

"It's not your fault. I knew Laura would never let it go, so I just got through it."

Cameron smoothed his hands over my back and the bandages. "I wish we'd known. We would have made it clear it wasn't all right. Hell, we already did it with your uncle."

"What? When? What did he do?"

Everett's face was dark. "He came to our suite before the wedding to thank us for marrying you so you could have a good experience before, essentially, being on the shelf forever. That's what he implied."

I wish I were surprised, but I wasn't.

"Well, I'll still thank you," I said quietly.

Where Micah was in front of me, I saw the troubled expression on his face. But he didn't say anything. "Do you have something you like to wear to be comfy?"

"If Ruby put my clothes away, I'm sure I can find something." I pressed my lips together, still unsure. I was naked except for my garters and underwear, and I didn't want to walk across the room in front of them without clothes. They'd made themselves clear, but the feeling of fear was still too raw.

"I'm sure you can too," he said with a smile. "But I don't want you moving just yet. So tell me what you want and I'll get it."

What did I wear in front of them? What would they think of me in my normal loungewear? It was... well, it wasn't meant to be attractive. But it was comfortable. I needed to believe them. "I would usually get some yoga pants, underwear, one of the soft bras, and a big t-shirt if I were just going to stay in my room and watch a movie or something. But the girl at the bridal store, Ashley, said she was going to pick out some post-wedding lingerie and stuff for me too. So I'm sure that's in there somewhere."

Micah leaned forward and kissed my cheek. "The thought of you in lingerie is enough to make me feral, wife. But I want you to be comfortable. So we can all take our time with this, and each other."

He disappeared, walking around the bed, and I gasped when I twisted, seeing an absolutely gargantuan walk-in closet. I didn't think I would ever need the amount of space in there.

"That's enormous."

They all laughed. "Every Omega needs their closet," Cameron said. "Almost as important as their nest."

Their nest.

Did they have a nest here? I'd be here for a year, so that meant I'd have at least one heat. Would they help me through it? Fire rolled over my body at the thought of it. They were already too close and too inviting.

Everett's gaze rolled over me, scenting the burst of perfume that just exploded. "What's in your head, little nymph?"

"Nothing."

"Mmm. We'll see."

Sliding out from behind me, Cameron put a hand on my shoulder. "I'm going to change and get you some painkillers. Then I'll be back." He glanced at the others. "TV room?"

"Yes," Micah answered. He had clothes in his hands and was coming back around the bed to me, already sinking down to his knees.

"You don't have to help me dress."

"You're right. I don't." Then he looked up at me. "Something you should know about the three of us. We don't do anything we don't want to do. If there's something we don't want to do that's still necessary, we find a way to shift it in our favor if we can. And if there's something we can't or won't do, we're capable of voicing that without making you feel like you fucked up by asking. So no, I don't have to help you dress, princess. I *want* to help you dress."

My mouth was open in shock, and I knew I needed to close it so I stopped looking like a gaping fish, but I couldn't seem to move.

Everett watched from where he stood, a hint of a smile on his face. He was the coldest of them—the harshest. But he didn't disagree. And something told me there was warmth beneath the hard exterior he didn't let many people see. He'd already been soft with me.

Micah tugged the garters and underwear off and helped me replace them. I couldn't even be embarrassed when he had me stand and slid them into place because his hands were on my skin, and that was a far bigger distraction than I'd anticipated.

He pressed a kiss to my stomach, and my entire body went rigid. Micah didn't react to it, helping me dress the rest of the way in exactly the outfit I'd told him about, with the addition of some fuzzy socks. "There." He looked me over. "Perfect."

"Thank you."

Everett inclined his head gently toward the door. "Go change, Micah. I'll show Ocean the TV room. One of our favorite places to relax. Are you hungry?"

"Starving," I admitted as he led me out of the room. "The cake is the only thing I've had today."

"Why?"

Shit. "No reason. Nerves."

His hand slipped around mine, tugging me to a stop in a hallway that was so bright and open, it felt more like a gallery than a house. I loved the atmosphere here already. "Don't lie to us. Please. We know it was bad, and I know it might be hard to say it. But I'm not going to judge you for it. If anything, it's only going to make me more furious with your family. And I'm already so fucking angry with them it's hard to breathe, so you honestly can't make it worse."

"Why are you angry at them?" I asked. I knew, but at the same time, I didn't know the extent of it.

Keeping my hand, he started walking again. "The way he talked about you on more than one occasion. The way your aunt treated you in that study, and the fucking corset. Not to mention your uncle is the kind of businessman that wants to be in it for the appearances of business, not the practicalities, which causes him to make poor decisions. He doesn't want to run a company. He wants to be *known* for running a company."

A laugh burst out of me. "That's so true it's not even funny."

"So tell me why you haven't eaten."

Shivers went down my spine. "I—" I winced, not wanting to say it out loud. Not because I wanted to protect them, but because I was embarrassed that I still let it happen. "When I went to Sunset City to try on dresses, Laura went with me. She was... well, she was exactly who you think she is. I found the dress, and because I didn't want to hear her comments about it, I just ordered it and didn't show her."

Everett's mouth curled into a smile. "Good girl."

Now I shivered for an entirely different reason. "She told me that the only reason you chose me was because I was disposable and didn't speak to me until we got home. When I went to the kitchen later, there were locks on the cabinets and the refrigerator."

He stopped walking so suddenly I was pulled back by his hand. "What the fuck did you just say?"

I looked down at the ground. Maybe it would swallow me whole so I could hide from the horror on his face. "Please don't make me say it again."

With one movement he tugged me toward him, and I nearly stumbled, but he caught me, one arm curling around my back and making sure to avoid the bandages. "Your dress appointment was on Tuesday, nymph. Please tell me you've been able to eat since then, because if they've starved you that long, I don't know if I'll be able to keep myself from killing them."

Something warmed in my chest at that. I wasn't a violent person, but threats looked good on Everett. And threats that protected me? Fuck, I was a goner.

"Yeah," I whispered. "I was able to. I ordered food. Just not as much as normal, but I'm all right."

"But nothing today? Other than the wedding cake?"

I shook my head. "It was really good cake."

"It was—" Everett closed his eyes. "That's why you were hungry yesterday."

He wasn't asking, just making the connection. "I promise I'm fine, Everett," I said quietly. "You've seen me. I have more than enough body to sustain me for a couple of days."

When he opened his eyes, they were filled with fire. "Understand me. I don't have a feeding fetish. I'm not going to try to stuff you with food at every available opportunity. But like hell will my wife go hungry because you, or anyone else, think your body is less than fucking perfect."

A gasp escaped me, and I blinked. "It's not perfect. But I promise I'm not trying to starve myself."

"Good." The word was rough, and he didn't release me, only shifted me to his side with his arm still around me as we entered a room where the television was so large it took up a good portion of the wall. Not so big that you couldn't see the whole thing, but big enough that I didn't think I'd ever need to go to a movie theater while I lived here.

Big, cushy couches pointed toward the screen in a U shape. A bar sat along one wall, complete with an oven, stove, microwave, and fridge. A whole kitchen. I spotted a bathroom branching on the other side, and there was also a basket filled with blankets. "Okay, I love it."

Everett chuckled, but I still heard the strain in his voice. "I'm glad. Now what's your favorite kind of food?"

"It's not my favorite, but I've been *craving* chicken fried rice."

He pulled out his phone with a nod. "Got it. I'm going to change, and I'm sure the others will be here in just a minute, okay?"

"Okay."

I went to the basket of blankets and looked through them until I found one that felt right. Then I chose a seat on one of the couches and cuddled down. I wasn't tired enough to sleep, but I was tired. And these couches were the good kind. Firm enough that you didn't feel like you were being sucked into the void, and soft enough that it was cozy.

"I like the sight of this."

Cameron came around the couch in dark sweats and a t-shirt. He handed me the painkillers he'd mentioned and made sure I took them.

But I was distracted by simply looking at him. It was the first time I'd seen him in something other than a suit, and there was something so incredibly appealing about it. Just like Everett yesterday, which felt like a lifetime ago, he was more touchable. Not the billionaire Alpha who was untouchable. Just someone who was sitting down next to me and hauling me closer, so I was practically lying across his chest.

A rumbling startled me. What—

He was *purring*. For me. My body melted into his. I had to be crushing him, but he didn't seem to care. Instead, he shifted me so I was curled into his chest and could listen to the sound. The fucking incredible sound. I'd heard purrs before, of course, but this one was for *me*.

No one had ever purred for me before.

Emotion flooded my eyes, and I had to blink it away.

"What's wrong?" Cameron sounded distressed.

I shook my head. There was nothing wrong with this. It was what I'd always wanted and never had. "You're purring for me," I whispered.

"Should I stop?"

"*No.*" The word snapped out so quickly I was afraid of the reaction. But it only made him smile and tuck me closer. The way I laid across his lap... I didn't think I ever wanted to move again.

"No one's ever purred for me," I told him.

The sound stuttered for a second from his surprise. Then it came back even louder. "No one?"

"No."

"Not even your father?"

I shrugged. "Maybe. But I don't remember if he did. He's been gone a long time."

"Fuck, sweetheart. I would have done it sooner."

Laughing, I looked up at him. "When would you have had a chance?"

"Any time I've been in a room with you. I would have purred at the reception. Anywhere and everywhere, baby."

"Here, princess." Micah's voice came from somewhere behind me, and suddenly a banana appeared in front of my face.

I couldn't stop the giggle. "What's that for?"

"Everett told me to give it to you and tell you to eat it because the food is going to take a while to get here."

"I think he just wants to see me eat a banana." But I sat up with Cameron's help and peeled it.

Everett strode in, his walk still holding the same power even though he was barefoot and bare chested with sweats on. I—

My mind had completely short-circuited at the sight of him without a shirt. Holy shit. It was hard to think any thoughts. And the ones I had were all good about him, and none of them good about me. I didn't want to eat in front of him now. Not while I was in frumpy clothes and buried in a blanket like someone who hadn't moved from the couch in days.

There were tattoos and I couldn't even focus on what they were cause my brain was screaming *abs! Shoulders! Forearms!*

He raised an eyebrow. "I do want to see you eat a banana. And not only because I'll be thinking about your mouth as you do it." Looking at Micah and then Cameron, the next words were a growl. "They put fucking locks on the kitchen cabinets this week."

I looked down, focusing very hard on breaking the banana into pieces and taking a bite. My energy immediately perked up. Funny how actually eating could do that.

Cameron and Micah were staring at me, but I couldn't meet their eyes. And it was Cameron who pulled me closer to him on the couch again. "Anything we can do to get out of this deal, Rett? I don't want to give that asshole anything."

"No, you can't go back on it," I said. "Please."

They all looked at me now. Frowning. But not angry. Micah made the connection first. "Why did you agree to marry us? I assumed it was to get away from them."

"It was." I swallowed. "But not only that. The trust my parents left me..." My throat burned. It still hurt to speak about without feeling the deep sense of betrayal. "It doesn't pay out until I turn thirty-five. But they agreed to do it in a year if I said yes."

He looked devastated. "So they forced you?"

"No." I hadn't been forced. It didn't feel that way, and now that I was getting to know them, I was glad. "No, they didn't force me. But I did make him sign papers so he couldn't change his mind later. I have copies, and I gave copies to Trinity and Isolde."

Cameron laughed. "Should have been a lawyer, sweetheart."

But Micah still watched me carefully. Coming over, he knelt in front of me, hands running up my thighs beneath the blanket. "As long as you weren't forced. Because that was our one stipulation. We wanted to marry you, but you had to say yes *willingly*."

"I'm willing," I said. "Did I agree because of the trust? Yes. But you needed to get married for one reason. I just happened to need it for a different one." For a second, I looked down. "But I'm glad it's you."

He smiled then. "I can work with that."

The way his hands were on my legs, even through the fabric of my yoga pants, made me aware of how close he was to... everything.

But I didn't have any idea how to start that, and it wasn't exactly something I could search. *How do you start having sex with the infernally hot husbands you married for a business agreement?*

"So... is this what you do?" I asked, gesturing to the screen. "Watch TV?"

"Honestly, no," Cameron said. "We work more than we should, though we're trying to get better. We do sometimes watch movies, but I'd like to do it more often."

"Are you sure that's what you want to do, then? I can fit in around whatever your routine is."

Everett settled on the couch nearby. "It might be time for some new routines. At the very least, we'll pick a movie until you're fucking fed."

I raised an eyebrow at him. "Sure you don't have that feeding fetish?"

He looked at me, but there was the slightest tilt to his mouth that showed his amusement. "Careful."

It didn't feel like a threat. It felt like teasing. Teasing with my husbands. In Micah's words, I could work with that.

Fig 21. Taro
(Also: Angel Wings, Elephant Ear)
Meaning: Great joy and delight

OCEAN

I woke in stages. First, just noticing I wasn't asleep anymore. Then noticing I was squished in a weird way. Where the hell was I?

A warm body pressed up against mine, and everything came back in a rush. We'd all fallen asleep on the couches last night. Micah insisted on curling himself around me, and I didn't tell him no. Because I loved it.

My brain felt tired in that way it did when you slept *hard*. I don't remember the last time I slept so deeply, even while being on a couch.

Slowly, sleepily, I opened my eyes. Micah's skin was close, reminding me that he stripped his shirt off before wrapping us both in the blankets. I inhaled the rich scent of him—the sweet softness of chocolate and the bitterness of caramel. It was sharper right now. And further down our bodies, Micah was hard.

They wouldn't laugh at me. I knew that now. But that didn't mean I wasn't nervous at the prospect of sex with three Alphas who were nearly fucking perfect.

Still, just being this close to him made me happy. There was a scar on his collarbone. I wondered how he'd gotten it. Micah had tattoos too, but they were on the forearms currently wrapped around me, so I couldn't get a closer look. One peeked over his shoulder, but I wasn't going to be able to look at that one either. I settled for moving as slowly as I could to touch the small scar.

A tiny imperfection.

It made me smile.

All at once a soft purr came to life in Micah's chest, and because of the way he was wrapped around me, I felt it *everywhere*.

"Morning," he whispered without opening his eyes.

"Morning." I still had my finger on his scar, rubbing it with the tip of my finger. "I'm sorry if I woke you."

"Mmm." The sound was low in his throat. "I don't mind. My wife is touching me. I don't want to miss it."

I was glad his eyes were still closed because my face turned red. "How did you get this?"

"Hiking with my brothers," he murmured, shifting us closer so his lips brushed my temple. "We were being typical teenage boys and not at all careful. I decided to climb a bunch of rocks. Turns out those rocks weren't stable, and I got caught in the mess of them sliding down the mountain we were on. Broke my leg, had a few other injuries. For whatever reason that one decided to scar. I have a few others if you want to see them."

"You have brothers?"

Micah opened his eyes then. "I do. Three of them. One older, two younger. The younger two live back east, the older one is overseas with his pack."

Suddenly, being with the three of them, even for a year, felt overwhelming. "I don't know anything about you," I said. "I'm sorry."

Moving slowly, he cradled my head with one hand, gripping my hair and releasing it like a reflex. "You can ask me anything, Ocean. Any of us. We have nothing to hide from you. I will answer any question you ask."

"What's your middle name?" It was on our marriage license, but everything about yesterday was a gorgeous blur.

"Thomas."

"Micah Thomas Westbrook," I said.

"Ocean Elise Correa Caldwell," he said back. "I love your name."

"Me too." It was the truth. I'd always loved my name, unconventional as it was.

He groaned, shifting against me. "I should check your back, but I don't want to move. You feel too good."

Laughing quietly, I closed my eyes. "If you keep saying things like that I'm going to start believing them."

"I certainly hope so, princess." He did move then, rolling us on the couch so I was beneath him, and every hard inch of him was pressed into me. "When we told you we wanted a real marriage, it wasn't because you were a body we would have at our disposal and therefore convenient. And not because you're *disposable*. We chose you, remember?"

"It still doesn't feel real," I admitted. "And I don't understand why."

"Does it matter? Other than we're ridiculously attracted to you and wanted you? Because even if your uncle hadn't said yes to the deal, we would have approached you."

I swallowed, my hands finding his shoulders. His skin was so warm and him looking down at me... it was a dream come true. Isolde was right. No matter what would happen in the future, I would regret it far more if I didn't embrace this situation to the fullest. "I'm not used to anyone... *not* having an ulterior motive."

"We wanted you. That was and is our motive."

But only for a year.

The voice in my head stung, even though last night they'd said I could decide when the year was up. Maybe that meant they were open to more? Today wasn't the time to think about it.

"Now," he whispered. "Turn over so I can check your bandages before I strip you naked on this couch and start the honeymoon early."

I laughed and twisted, feeling a little like a caterpillar in a cocoon with the blankets twisted in my legs. But I managed to get to my stomach and enjoyed the weight of Micah's legs bracketing my hips. And the way his palms skimmed up my ribs beneath my shirt, not at all afraid of the way all my fat was bunched up and rolled because of how I was positioned.

"These look good. No blood through them, which is a good sign. We should still change them later. But now, we need to get up. We have plans."

"We do?"

"We do." He got off the couch and helped me to stand as the other two Alphas stirred now that we were speaking at full volume. "Well, we have an idea for plans. If you don't want to do them, we won't be upset."

I narrowed my eyes in suspicion. "What did you have in mind?"

"That will require us showing you something," Cameron said with a yawn. "Good morning."

"Morning," I managed. Cameron rumpled with sleep was a good look. The way his hair stuck up made me want to run my fingers through it. "What do you have to show me?"

"Why ruin the surprise, little nymph?" Everett's arms came around me, hands roaming as his mouth fell to my neck.

Chills ran over my skin. The good kind. They were going to kill me. Fuck a year of marriage. I wasn't even going to last a week.

He tugged the collar of my shirt to the side and kissed toward my shoulder.

"You said you had to show me something, not that it was a surprise." My voice was breathier than I wanted. The symptom of his lips on my skin.

"Well, it is a surprise," Cameron said. "Not for long though. And we didn't officially ask you," he looked at Everett for a second. "Touching you? Kissing you? Are you all right with it?"

I nodded. Probably too fast. "I'm not..."

The warning growl came from Everett, and he tightened his hold. "As our wife, you can do whatever you want, Ocean. The one thing I won't let you do is talk down about yourself. It's not what you really think, it's what's been repeated to you."

The shock rolled through me. I had been about to say I wasn't good at it. It wasn't something that had been said to me, but everything else implied that. But it wasn't the only thing. "I'll say something else then. I don't have much experience, so being with the three of you feels really overwhelming. I'm not saying I don't want that. I just have no idea how to even go about it."

Everett's voice grew even darker. "Are you a virgin, Ocean?"

"No. But I might as well be," I said with a laugh. "I've been with two people. I don't want to talk about them."

He kissed me below my ear. "Who do I have to kill?"

"No killing."

"We'll see. I don't want this morning to be heavy, so I won't ask now. But I'll get it out of you eventually, nymph."

I could barely breathe because perfume was pouring out of me. Being overwhelmed by them was going to become a normal thing, and I needed to get a hold of myself or I'd spend the next year doing nothing but staring and perfuming.

Everett walked me forward with his arms still around me. "Should I carry you to the surprise?"

"*No.*" I pulled away from him quickly. "Nope, I'm fine."

When I glanced at him, I saw something spark in his gaze, but he didn't protest. Cameron took my hand and wove our fingers together. "Let's go."

And then we were running through the halls, him pulling me after him with a giant smile on his face. I laughed and couldn't stop laughing. "Cameron, slow down."

"Nope."

"*Cam.*"

We ended up back in my room, my wedding dress still draped over the bed where we left it. He grinned and spun me under his arm. "I love it when you call me Cam. Do it more often. We call Everett 'Rett,' too."

"Rett?"

"Much to my annoyance," he said, leaning on the doorframe. He crossed his arms, which put everything on display, and the tattoos I hadn't been able to focus on last night. Several thick, black lines encircled one forearm, and thinner black bands bracketed the opposite bicep. They were stark, brutal, and fucking *hot*.

Cam made a face at him. "Don't scare her. He secretly loves it."

"Or maybe that's what I let you believe."

"Grumpy bastard," Cameron muttered before he smiled at me again. "Do you notice anything, Ocean?"

I frowned, glancing around the room. As far as I knew, it looked the same as it had last night. "Like what?"

"Look carefully."

I did, taking in the room. It was light and bright, filmy curtains over windows looking out toward the beach, past a garden and lawn filled with magnolia trees. But I didn't think that was it. Was anything weird?

As I scanned the space, my eyes were drawn to the wall by the bed. It looked strange. There was a recessed piece of it that didn't belong. "Is it that?"

"Why don't you go find out?"

It just looked like a piece of wall, but as I got closer... was this a door?

Micah came with me, catching my hand and pressing a nearly invisible button just beside the panel. It slid back without a sound, opening into a dimly lit hallway.

"Let me guess," I said. "This is where you keep the bodies?"

"Nah. We keep those in a fridge in the basement before we take them out to sea and dump them." Cameron deadpanned.

A laugh fell out of me. "Oh."

"Just kidding, sweetheart. We don't have a basement."

Most places on this coast didn't, so that made sense. But I still didn't know what was in front of me. "Is anything going to jump out at me?"

"No."

There was a door to the left in the hallway, and one glance inside showed a bathroom. A second bathroom. The one connected to my rooms was on the opposite side. I'd already seen that. So why was there a second one?

Wait—

I nearly sprinted down the rest of the hall, dim lights turning on with my movement. The hallway opened into a round, cozy space filled with cushions. They were all white and basic, clearly not decorated. But this was a *nest*.

Now I understood why they had said every Omega needs their nest. Because they knew they had one here.

"Over here too," Micah said, standing at the entrance, gesturing to a doorway I missed. It opened into another glass-enclosed space. A porch that faced the coast, but the windows opened, and there were more bare cushions. Like an extension of the nest where you could cuddle and still have sunlight if you wanted it. It was beautiful.

I went back to the inside and stood in the middle, turning around and looking everywhere. "This is mine?"

The three of them stood at the edge, watching me. Even Everett smiled in that small way he had. "It's yours, little nymph."

"I've never had one before." I could cry with happiness and awe, but I didn't want to stop looking at it.

They frowned, and Micah tilted his head. "The Caldwell Estate doesn't have a nest?"

"No, it does. I just never used it."

"Do we want to know why?"

I wandered to the wall and ran my hand over one of the cushions. "Probably not."

It wasn't just Laura and Frank. It *was*, but it was also because it was my mother's nest. Part of me had wanted to use it because it was a part of her, if they had let me. Another part of me didn't know how to feel about using the same nest as Mom. Yet another thing I'd mostly pushed to the side without feeling it.

"You said you had plans for today?" I hoped they'd let the nest thing go for now.

"Well," Micah said. "If you want to. Call your friends. We want to take you shopping for the nest."

I'd never sprinted for my phone so quickly.

Fig 22. Alyssum
Meaning: Worth beyond beauty

CAMERON

*O*cean looked so fucking happy that I was about to tell Rett and Micah we needed to buy this place. Nestled wasn't something we would normally have under our brand, but it wouldn't be the first outlier we'd acquired.

If we could own a sex toy company, we could own a nesting supply company.

Ocean's friends were with her, staring into the depths of the store like it was a lion they were about to fight. But I was glad they could come. In fact, they said yes so quickly she had started laughing.

"Ocean," I called. "Come here for a second."

Her smile was gorgeous. This was the *real* Ocean. Not the timid woman who was beaten down by her bitchy family. This was the woman full of life that I wanted to see every day. Her dark eyes sparkled as she came close. "Yeah?"

"We have rules," Everett said.

She frowned, that shine dimming. "Okay."

I smacked his arm. "Don't be an ass and lead with that, dick."

Laughing, he pulled her in, kissing her forehead. "Sorry, little nymph. We do have rules, but not the way you're thinking. Forgive me, I need to choose my words more carefully."

"You don't need to change for me," she whispered.

"Not change. But also not say things that unintentionally terrify you."

Ocean closed her eyes and leaned into Everett. I didn't think she even realized that she did it, or that we noticed when her reactions gave her away. Those words comforted her.

"We only have three rules," Everett said. "First, no questioning whether you *need* something. If you want it, get it. Today isn't about needing, it's about wanting."

She opened her mouth, and I shook my head. "I think we all know you've been living with only what you need for a long time now, sweetheart."

"Okay," she whispered. "I can try."

"Rule number two," Everett said. "No looking at the cost. We have more money than we could ever need. Money doesn't matter."

Our wife swallowed and pressed her lips together. A clear sign she was nervous. But she still nodded her agreement. "What's number three?"

"Don't think about anyone but yourself today. You're the only one who matters, wife."

"What about you?"

143

I winked at her. "We'll be just fine."

"Can you do those three things for us?" Micah asked.

"I'll do my best."

Nodding back toward her friends, I smirked. "Go nuts."

She was hiding her smile, but it was still there. And her friends were practically squealing with glee when she returned to them. "Happiness looks good on her," I said. "I'm going to love spoiling the fuck out of our Omega."

"Same." Micah sighed. "But I am going to struggle tomorrow."

"Get in line," Everett growled. He shoved his hands into the pockets of his jeans, clearly trying to keep himself from forming fists. "It's taking everything in me not to drive to the Caldwell Estate and beat the shit out of Frank."

"Ocean wouldn't want that." For all that had been done to her, our wife was soft-hearted.

Micah chuckled. "I'm not so sure about that. She might not want it now, but she could want it eventually, and my fists look forward to that day."

The girls headed into the aisles, and we waved down the manager of the store. We'd called ahead, so they knew who we were. She smiled. "Is everything all right?"

"Perfect. We would like installation tomorrow, please."

"Tomorrow? That's really fast."

Stepping forward, Micah had one of our cards ready. "Yes, it is. But we'll make it worth your while. Charge everything to that. Whatever you need to make the delivery and installation happen tomorrow. In fact, put the card on file. We want our wife to be able to walk in here and purchase anything she wants at any time."

The manager's mouth dropped open, but she recovered quickly. "Of course. She's a very lucky woman."

"We're the lucky ones."

It was one hundred percent true.

After the manager was gone, Micah turned to us. "I told Ocean today that we wouldn't lie to her. That we'd answer any question she asked."

I saw where he was going with it. We weren't going to lie, and if she asked us if we were scent matched, we would be honest. Until then, we would continue to woo her, make her feel like the most precious Omega in the world, and show her how we felt so that when her heat hit, she would know the truth.

"Fine with me," I said. "The more pressing concern is keeping my hands off her."

"She's open to it," Rett said. "But since she's nervous, she's going to need us to take the first step. Hopefully soon."

"Do you have any idea what kind of temptation it was to wake up with all of her pressed against me? *Fuck*," Micah groaned. "I nearly came in my pants and that wasn't the impression I wanted to give her. But I was close. Surrounded by her scent and all that softness?"

"Stop." I laughed. "You want all three of us to lose it in the store?"

Everett raised an eyebrow. "Speak for yourself. I'm perfectly in control." Liar. "But I am going to find something for my wife. Some kind of surprise."

I play up the shock and surprise. "Everett Shaw. Are you having *emotions*?"

"Fuck off."

"Never. And it's a good idea."

"Don't steal it."

I just smiled. I was absolutely going to steal it. Micah was too. Because we were all on the same page. Now that we had her, we were going to spoil the shit out of our wife.

Fig 23. Horse Chestnut
(Also: Buckeye, Conker Tree)
Meaning: Luxury

OCEAN

"*J* have *always* wanted to come here," Trinity said, picking up a fuzzy pillow and squishing it to her chest. "It's like the treasure trove of everything you could ever want."

"Why haven't you?"

"Have you seen this place? I'd want to buy everything. My apartment would be so stuffed to the gills I wouldn't be able to move, and I don't even have a nest."

I laughed, stroking my hand over a different pillow. "That makes sense. I'm already overwhelmed."

Isolde had her phone in her hand. "The nest at our house is great. The guys were worried that I wouldn't like it, but I do. Still, I'm asking if they care about me grabbing a few things while I'm here."

"I'm surprised they didn't come with you and buy everything themselves," I said. "They worship the ground you walk on."

She smirked. "At least I'm not the only one who can say that anymore."

Without even trying, I looked back toward my husbands. The word still felt strange in my mind. Husbands. They were my husbands, and the way they stood together, casually speaking, made me want to go back and find out what they were saying. As a pack, they were so *easy* with each other, and I wanted that. I didn't want to feel like I was stumbling all over myself in every conversation.

Hopefully that would come with time.

"They're being really nice," I said quietly.

"Nice doesn't even begin to cover it," Trinity muttered. She pulled me deeper into the store, into a section that was literally just swatches of fabrics everywhere. They could be used for almost anything, from cushions to blankets. What the hell did I want in a nest?

When Trinity glanced behind us, I knew something was up. "So?" She asked, glancing between me and Isolde. "How was the wedding night?"

"It was good. We had some food and watched a movie. Ended up falling asleep on the couch."

Trinity stares at me. "That's it?"

"Should there be more?"

"Yeah, you should be fucking their brains out."

I cleared my throat. "There's a good reason we didn't." Then I told them what happened, even though it still felt strange to tell them and say it out loud. I'd been pushing down Frank and Laura's cruelty for so long it still felt... illicit for it to be out in the open.

147

"Are you fucking kidding me?" Isolde asked. "Your aunt better pray she never sees me again or I might smack her. More than smack her."

I cracked into a smile. "I'd like to see that, but I also don't want you to get arrested. Your pack needs you, and so do I."

Trinity was typing furiously on her phone. "Rin?"

"I've got some people who work for me on cases. We'll find something on your uncle and then I'll take him down with an article."

"I—" I stopped. "You would do that for me?"

"I *am* doing this for you."

I reached out and grabbed her hand. "No, you're not. I wish I could let you, but he's still the only one who can sign over the trust. He's never going to do that if he's in jail."

Her fingers looked like they were about to crack her phone, but she relented. "Fine. But after you get the trust, can I have him?"

"Be my guest."

"Good. Now let's spend some money."

I didn't even know where to start. There were so many *choices*. Textures. Colors. Shapes. Even as a person who regularly designed, there was almost too much to comprehend.

The sweet, tangy scent of lemons wrapped around me, along with that crisp edge of sugary baked pastry. My mouth watered as Cameron stepped up behind me. "Made any progress?"

"Not yet. It's overwhelming."

"Why?" It wasn't an accusation or a veiled question about what was taking me so long. It was simple curiosity.

Micah had said that he wouldn't lie, and I guessed the others would agree. So I decided to be honest. "It's so permanent. If I make the choice, then I can't make another one, you know? With flowers, it's easy. They only live so long, so you *have* to make the choices so you can enjoy them before they're gone."

My friends didn't even try to pretend they weren't watching the two of us with utter glee. And I saw Isolde hide her smile with her hand when Cam slid his arm around my waist. "You're not following the rules, sweetheart," he whispered. "You're not supposed to think about whether or not you need something."

"It's not that," I insisted. "More like decision paralysis."

"If you want to change it later, then we'll change it later. Pick what you want right now."

"But—"

"No." He was speaking so quietly now that the others couldn't hear him. And my whole body broke out into shivers when his lips touched the shell of my ear. "No buts. Make your nest exactly the way you want to make it. And if the day after tomorrow you wake up and hate everything about it? Then we'll come back and get a whole different style."

I swallowed. "Just like that?"

148

His purr rumbled against my back. "Just like that."

No longer caring that Iz and Rin were watching, I turned around and hugged him. Tucked my face into his chest. It might be needy and clingy and desperate and a hundred other things I'd been told I was, but I didn't care. I needed to feel him closer. "Thank you."

"What for?"

"For being nice."

One hand came up and cradled my head against his chest. I inhaled the zesty scent of lemon, both sweeter and sharper this close. "The fact that you think that's something you need to thank us for makes me so fucking angry," he said.

I was too happy to be angry.

"Now," he pulled back and winked. "Go spend some money. Please."

I managed to keep my smile as I rolled my eyes. "If I have to."

"You do."

Isolde grabbed my hand as I came back. "By the way, I need to see *this*."

I had barely looked at my rings up close. They really were beautiful. Like they'd picked the image out of my brain and had it made. Not to mention they fit my fingers and weren't too tight. So many rings weren't even made in my size. I love that these worked so well.

And that color...

The reason I picked it was because it was my favorite. And that's how simple I needed to keep it. Plus, the lack of permanence gave me the same kind of freedom arranging flowers did.

All the fabrics were arranged by color. So I went to the cooler tones and started feeling the textures. There was no way to explain how I knew what was right, but I did.

Omega instincts were beyond logic. So I let those instincts lead, picking fabrics for the inside of the nest and the cozy glass porch. Isolde picked out some cushions for her nest too, but based on the texts I saw over her shoulder, she and her pack would be making a trip here sooner than later.

Blankets were next. There were too many that I wanted, but I stopped myself every time I was going to say it was too much. In no small part because my husbands were following at a distance, watching with interest.

I watched them too, cataloging their differences and how they reacted to things. But also because I wanted to watch them. For the time, they were mine, and they were gorgeous.

Cameron's easy grace was fun to watch. Always smiling or winking when he caught me staring. Everett was a predator. Smooth and dangerous. But he softened for me. And yet, still hard enough to make me feel like he'd rip apart my enemies with his bare hands, and I didn't hate that.

Finally, Micah was somewhere in between. Reserved but warm. He was watchful, checking in if I needed anything while we wandered through the store. I knew without saying he was watching to see if I was tired or in pain. He didn't like that he'd missed it at the wedding. It didn't matter that I'd done everything in my power to hide it.

"O, what about these?" Rin asked, holding up some sheer blue curtains that were also iridescent. They shimmered like water with rainbows scattered across them.

"Oooh. I love them. But I don't think I have anywhere for curtains."

"Sure we do," Micah said.

I frowned. "In the nest?"

"We never said everything had to be for the nest, princess."

"Yeah, you're getting these," Rin said, taking the choice out of my hands. "I've literally never seen anything that's more *you* in my life."

"I guess I could use them in my bedroom," I said. "I'll have to think about what else could go in there."

"You can get it all right now," Micah said. "We don't mind."

I picked up a hanging, sparkly thing I thought would be perfect on the porch and glanced at them. "I need more time to think about that. Not that I don't want to, I just want to plan it more."

"Fair enough."

Isolde looped her hand through mine and walked me toward the section of pillows we'd abandoned at the beginning. We'd nearly made a full circuit of the store now. "He calls you princess," she said. "And let me just tell you, I fucking *melt* when Cade calls me that."

"I probably shouldn't like it as much as I do," I told her. "Because yes. I love it."

"Revel in it. You deserve it, O."

Approximately a million pillows later, I was done. And even if I wasn't done, I was tired.

Isolde glanced at her phone and grinned. "I should get back. They're competing through text to see which one of them can get me the most riled up. Not that it takes much with them."

"I've been ignoring my notifications while we've been here," Rin said with a sigh. "Which means I probably have crises lined up to take care of. Can we have lunch sometime this week?"

"I'd love that."

She threw her arms around my neck. "And I fully expect details next time. I've gotta live vicariously through you both somehow."

Hugging her back, I leaned into it. "It'll happen, Rin. It will."

"We'll see." The words were chipper, but I saw the shadows in her eyes. Of the three of us, Trinity had always been the one who *wanted* a pack. A partner. Someone. She pretended she wasn't lonely, but she was. Her dad thought he was an adventurer and was always going off on crazy expeditions. He'd been doing it since she was little.

Trinity had spent more time alone than an Omega should. "Text me," I called after her.

She waved, but already had her head buried in her phone, likely fielding the urgent questions from her magazine staff.

"Do you need a ride, Iz?" I asked. "Didn't Rin pick you up?"

"I'm good. The guys will be here soon." She hugged me. "Have too much fun." The opposite of the usual warning.

"I'll try."

Cameron tucked me into his side. "You need anything else?"

"I think I am officially shopped out," I said.

"Well, they'll deliver and install everything tomorrow," Everett said. "That, and one other thing."

"What's that?"

"A greenhouse. It's not large, but we want you to have a place to move some of your flowers and work on them until we can get a proper one built. Think of it as a transitional greenhouse."

Micah disappeared to get the car, and I could only stare at Everett. "You bought me a greenhouse?"

"I bought you other things too, from this store. But the greenhouse is from all of us. We thought your employee could bring you some of the plants you wanted tomorrow, so you don't have to see your aunt and uncle."

There were no words I could say. Because they'd done it without me even asking. No prompting, just thinking about what I would need and want.

Like he knew, he pulled me in front of him, lining his chest up with my back. Everett was tall enough that he could rest his head on the top of mine, and he did while we waited for the car.

I wasn't going to go see Frank and Laura, because fuck them. But the tiniest part of me wanted to, if only to tell Laura that this didn't feel like being disposable.

Not at all.

Fig 24. Garden Sagebrush
(Also: Maid's Ruin, Our Lord's Wood,
Southern Wormwood)
Meaning: Aphrodisiac; Bantering;
Lustful bed partner; Seduction

OCEAN

$\mathcal{I}$t was strange being alone in their house.

My house.

I needed to start thinking of it as my house. Because it was while I lived here. The closet was just as ludicrous as I thought, but I loved it. And Ashley bought me *way* too much fucking lingerie.

Like, seriously, who needed this much?

But I couldn't deny that it was beautiful. All in my size. Now I just had to get the courage to actually put it on and wear it.

I was going to seduce my husbands.

The truth was, I hadn't fully allowed myself to want them, because it was so unthinkable that they would want *me*. I'd been attracted from the moment I met them, but attraction and taking the leap from wanting to action were very different things.

What the hell did I wear to say *hi, I'm nervous but taking a chance on something I really want, please don't laugh at me?*

The lacier, barer things were out. I was already dreading the thought of walking into view in something like that, even though they'd already —briefly—seen me naked. Even though they'd made it clear they did find me attractive. Even though they'd flat out told me they wanted me.

It sucked, but a few compliments didn't erase years of being the most undesirable person in every room. Whether or not it was true, it was still the way I was made to feel. And no matter if I didn't fully hate myself, it was hard to love yourself when no one else did. When no one had ever called you beautiful.

Except Micah.

I knew Cameron and Everett would say it too.

But I didn't know if I believed it. If I ever would.

A dark blue silk caught my eye, hanging among the rows of lace. It was a simple, short, babydoll nightgown. Covering enough that it soothed my anxiety, and revealing enough—with lace at the hem and baring a sheer, plunging neckline—that it wouldn't simply be seen as pajamas.

I closed my eyes when I pulled it off the hanger. There were even matching panties draped with it.

Breathe, Ocean. You can do this.

The skirt skimmed down my body, disguising my stomach and the worst of my stretch marks. They were going to see them anyway on my thighs and arms, but those were less visible.

This showed more of my arms than I was usually comfortable with. Laura's voice telling me I shouldn't wear anything sleeveless or strapless echoed in my head, but I pushed it away.

They chose me.

They wanted me.

I did look cute. Now I just had to...

Fuck.

Grabbing some lip balm, I put it on and didn't let myself look in the mirror again. If I was going to do this, I needed to do it. Trinity was in my head cheering me on.

After we got home from Nestled we ate dinner, and then I escaped to take a shower. Now, with my hair damp and curling, I was going to find them. Cameron said they'd either still be in the kitchen or back in the TV room.

This place was so big I still felt like I needed a map to get around it, but I knew how to get back to the kitchen. But they weren't in there. My bare feet padded on the stone tile as I made my way through it and to the TV room. Their voices sounded low through the air, and then a laugh. Again, I was jealous of how comfortable they were.

I paused outside the room, but only for a moment, because if it was more than a moment, then I'd run back to my room and hide and forget this whole idea ever existed in the first place.

Still, my toes curled under themselves as I walked in. I toyed with the edge of the skirt. Nerves felt they were burning under my skin.

Breathe.

Everett saw me first, eyes locking on me like the predator he reminded me of. He'd been speaking, and then he wasn't. Just staring at me. Micah, and finally Cameron turned to look at me.

No one spoke, the air thick with tension.

"Um, hi."

They still just stared at me. My face flushed, and the need to run rose up hard and fast.

"Sorry if I'm interrupting. I don't really know what I'm doing. I know I said this morning that I'm not really good at this, so I can go and—"

Cameron leapt up from his seat and crossed the space to me in three long strides. He sank to his knees in front of me, gripping my hips and pulling me closer. His face pressed into my stomach and the rest of him wrapped around me. "Don't you fucking go anywhere, sweetheart. Don't you dare."

My hands fell hesitantly to his shoulders, distracting me enough that I didn't notice Micah appearing beside me until his hand was tilting my face to his so he could kiss me. "You sure, princess?"

"If you are. I don't want to force you."

"Force us?" Everett asked. "Ocean, the only thing you need to tell us is if we're going to your bedroom or one of ours."

I swore my heart skipped a beat. "One of yours," I said. My room still didn't feel like mine, and having all three of them in my space like that felt more vulnerable than I was ready for. I would get there, but I still needed time.

"Dibs," Cameron said, rising to his feet and lifting me off mine.

Gasping, I pushed against his shoulders. "Cameron."

"What?"

"You can't carry me."

He growled, those green eyes pinning me with a stare even as he did *not* stop moving and didn't put me down. Instead, he scooped his arms further under my legs and braced them against his hips. "I beg to differ. I seem to be carrying you just fine."

Panic rolled through me. What if he dropped me? I would never live that down and then they would see the truth, and—

We walked through a door and into a warm, masculine space. He set me down on the bed. Slowly. With intention, showing me that he could carry me if he wanted to.

"Did I scare you?" he asked.

"I don't want you to hurt yourself carrying me."

Cameron's face was inches from mine. That playful energy still danced in his eyes, but this wasn't a joke. "Do I look hurt to you?"

"No, but—"

"I can and will throw you over my shoulder, wife. Would you like a demonstration?"

All the breath went out of my chest. "I'm good."

He smirked. "Later, then."

A hand touched my shoulder, and I nearly jumped out of my skin. Everett was now behind me on the bed. He chuckled softly before pulling me backwards and lying down beside me, a hand around my waist. "You're nervous, little nymph?"

Nervous was a fucking understatement. And it wasn't because of them. It was everyone else. Their judgment. My previous experiences. All of it clanged around in my head like a bad dream I couldn't get away from. "Yes," I finally said, though that single word wasn't enough to contain all of it.

Micah skimmed his hands up my legs, cleverly placing himself between them. "I designed this, you know."

"What?"

He leaned down, mouth brushing the silk over my stomach. "This nightgown you're wearing. It's our brand, and I'm the one who designed it. And now I'm thinking I need to design more just for you. The Ocean Collection. Or The Princess Collection. Worldwide best-sellers already."

"I don't—" a whine slipped out of me, and I closed my eyes. I hated that I was panicking when this was something I wanted. Something I'd started. But all I saw was their laughter later. Felt the horror of just being a bet. Of just being a fetish.

The softness of almonds surrounded me. Amaretto and almond frosting. "Take a breath for me, wife," Everett whispered.

I did.

"Again, please."

I obeyed again. Then I opened my eyes to his blue ones. "There you are." But he was looking through me. Seeing the struggle I wanted no one to see. He didn't look away from me. "Cam, run a bath."

"I don't need a bath. I just showered."

The steel in his eyes left no room for argument. So I didn't look away even as I felt Cameron's weight leave the bed, and Micah's hands still grazing my thighs.

"We're getting in the bath together," Everett said. "A place we can all be naked without being sexual, and you're going to tell us what's going through that gorgeous brain of yours. Understood?"

"I'm fine. Promise."

His growl tightened everything, and he lowered his voice. "Don't lie to me, Ocean. We didn't let you get away with it for the corset, and we're not going to do it with this. Because a few minutes ago you came to us and were ready. You wanted us."

I fought the emotion in my chest. "I still do."

"That's why we don't want you panicking," Micah said. "If you're ready. If you're really not, there's nothing wrong with that."

"And don't even think about telling me you're *not* panicking right now. Do *not* lie again." Everett's voice was nearly a growl.

I froze, my brain shuttering. Don't lie, or else. So much rested in the words unsaid. Punishment. Of course. I needed to figure out what their rules were, and quickly. They were kind, but there was only so far I could push them.

"Ocean." I focused on Micah's face. He had me sitting up. When did that happen? His hands were on either side of my face. "Where did you go, princess?"

"I'm right here."

"Your body is here, but your mind isn't. What happened?"

I shook my head, but he didn't let me, keeping me close and kissing me. Hard. The kiss brought me back. It slammed into me along with the taste of chocolate and caramel. Micah's tongue ran along mine. I moaned into his mouth. This was what I wanted. More of that. I didn't know how to ask and I didn't know how to get out of my own head long enough to just let it happen.

"Bath's ready," Cameron called.

156

He was naked in the doorway to the bathroom. *Fully* naked. And walking toward me with determined steps, like I couldn't see his cock and how thick it was between his legs. "Over the shoulder or normal? Your choice."

The image of me thrown over his shoulder made me shudder. "Normal. But I can walk to the tub."

"Nonsense." Cameron picked me up again. "I don't get to have my hands on you if you walk all on your own."

Bathtub was an understatement. This tub was practically big enough to be a pool. Well, not quite. But it was huge and deep and had all the jets and bubbles. My bathroom had one too. It was more than big enough for the four of us, and already filled with water and bubbles.

Cameron carried me into the water with the lingerie still on, delicious heat enveloping us both. "I can't remember the last time I took a bath," I whispered. "I love them."

"Then why don't you take them?"

My cheeks flushed. "Most bathtubs aren't big enough for me. It's not fun when you're half out of the water."

He sat down with me on his lap. This was deep enough that the water came nearly to my shoulders. "How's this?"

"This is good."

Splashing echoed behind me, and then hands on my shoulders. "I'm sorry, Ocean," Everett said. "Was it what I said?"

"It's fine. I don't know why I had that reaction." Frustration broke through. Now that we weren't in the bed and I was surrounded by warmth and *them* I felt safer. I also felt embarrassed and silly. "I don't know why I have *any* of these reactions. I've had a good life. I wasn't abused. I shouldn't be..." My hands dripped water as I gestured helplessly. "Whatever this is."

Everett pulled me from Cameron, settling me across his lap. He also was very naked. The way his chest lined up with my back let me feel everything. I shuddered, this time in a good way.

"I'm a cranky bastard," he said. "These two will back me up on that. I don't like people in general, and I often speak before I think."

Weaving our hands together, he crossed my own arms over each other so I was holding myself while he held me too. "Um, that's good to know, I guess."

He laughed and kissed just below my ear. "What I mean to say is, I don't want you to lie to us. But I want the reason you don't lie to be because you trust us. And you *can* trust us. Not because you're afraid of us. I wasn't thinking when I said that, and I'm sorry." Everett squeezed me slowly, purring against my back. "Please forgive me, little nymph. I didn't mean to scare you."

"It shouldn't scare me," I said, huffing a breath with renewed frustration. "It's my... I don't know. My fucked up brain?" Then I shook my head. "This wasn't what you signed up for when you married me. You said you wanted a real marriage, but I understand not wanting that because my brain refuses to cooperate. I'm not afraid of you."

Micah stood in the center of the tub, bubbles melting across his chest. "I think I'll have to disagree with your assessment of never being abused, princess."

"They never hit me."

"Just because someone didn't lay hands on you doesn't mean it wasn't abuse. And I would say what they did with that fucking corset is just as bad. Not to mention the way they speak about you. *To* you. In front of other people. And all we did was sign up to marry you. There weren't any other conditions."

I looked at the swirling surface of the water, moving with the invisible jets and creating currents that tickled my skin.

"Come here," Micah said.

Everett released me so I could go to him. Slowly, Micah peeled the wet nightgown over my head and tossed it away. It didn't feel strange to be in the tub with them like this. Because they couldn't completely see me with the bubbles. It was safer.

"I know you're not going to want to," he said. "But I'd like you to tell us about your other experiences."

"Why?"

Dragging his fingers up my sides, Micah didn't flinch away from the heavy curves in my body. Didn't emphasize them either. He was simply touching me. "Because you're my wife. And I don't want my wife thinking about someone else while I'm inside her. Especially if that person caused her pain."

I smiled in spite of myself. "I'm not sure if that's sweet or possessive."

"Both."

They had a point, and maybe if they knew they wouldn't judge me for my fear. Besides, I already knew they weren't going to let it go. I *did* want this. Want them. And if this helped? I wasn't sure if it would, but I'd try anything at this point. I was so *tired* of being afraid.

"Um..." Just fucking say it, Ocean. Spit it out. "The person who took my virginity did it for a bet. I didn't find out until afterward. His friends bet him he wouldn't fuck the fat girl. And I was so enamored of him and the fact that someone like him would be interested in someone like me that I didn't stop to question why."

Micah had gone still, and where I could see Cameron in the corner of my eye, his face was pure rage. So I kept going, needing to get it all out quickly.

"The other one lasted longer, but it wasn't me he really liked. He just liked big girls. He didn't care about *me*, he cared about the fact that I could get him off. And it's always like that. Taking a photo with a group of people and men not wanting to stand next to me because they don't want to be seen with the fat girl. Laughing because Isolde and Trinity would insist that I be sent drinks too when we're out together." I sighed. "It's just the way it is. That's why I have a hard time believing that you actually... *want* me."

Before they could say anything, I kept going. "I do want you. I do want to trust you. I want to be with you while we're together and enjoy it. But my mind keeps preparing for afterward when the good thing turns to more pain. I'm sorry."

"I could kill anyone who's made you feel like that," Micah said quietly. "How can we show you? That we want you?"

I lowered my eyes. "Just don't laugh at me after."

"Fucking never." Cameron pulled me away from Micah and spun me against the edge of the tub. "I'll make you laugh until you're crying, sweetheart. But I'll never laugh at your expense. As for everything else? I love your body. I love that you're soft where we're hard. You smooth our edges and are a cushion where we're rocks. Anyone would be crazy to think you're anything but beautiful. And yes," he whispered, lowering his mouth to mine. "I am attracted to women like you. We all are. But I promise we didn't choose you because you checked a box for what we wanted in a body. We met *you*. Were attracted to *you*. Chose *you*."

An arm snaked around my waist, and this time when Everett pulled me onto his lap, I was facing him. He arranged my knees on either side of his hips, and the hard length of him pressed against me. My eyes went wide, and he smiled. That ruthless, feral smile. "I certainly hope that feels like I want you, nymph."

"Yes."

He pulled me closer, brushing a kiss across my lips. A whisper, and vulnerability in his eyes I already knew him well enough to understand didn't appear often. "You never said if you forgive me. The last thing I want you to be is scared of me. Everyone else can be scared of me, and they should be. But never you."

"I forgive you," I said the second before he kissed me. And not just kissed me. *Devoured* me.

One hand slid into my hair and gripped it, tilting my face deeper. He tasted so good, I wanted to devour him right back.

Everett's other hand was low, slipping over my skin and downward. He nipped at my lips as he pulled back. "I would very much like to touch you."

I smiled. "You weren't already?"

He squeezed my hip and smirked. "I like when you come out to play."

159

"I'm still nervous."

"That's okay," Micah said from behind me. "We can work with that. Remember?"

"Yeah."

Everett brushed his fingers along the edge of the underwear I still wore. "If we weren't in the tub I'd be tempted to tear these off you. But I want to make sure you're ready."

My whole body flushed. Moving to get them off pushed my breasts directly into his face, and my body everywhere else. He didn't let me go far, molding me to him wherever possible, even after I managed to get the scrap of fabric off and toss it with the nightgown on the bathroom floor.

"Do you want to know the plan?" He asked.

"There's a plan?"

Cameron chuckled. "Everett always has a plan."

Those same fingers were still moving over my hip, but now without fabric as a barrier, it emphasized that I was naked, and that I could feel his cock pressed against my thigh. I was breathless when I spoke. "What's the plan?"

"The plan is to make my wife come." His voice was low. "With my fingers. Then again, on one of our tongues. And after you're pleasured and relaxed, I plan on taking you back to bed for the rest of it."

"The rest of it?" I gasped as he moved his hand, easing it between my thighs. My nerves flared to life, aware of everything. The roundness of my body and just how much of me there was, but Everett had no trouble finding exactly what he wanted. His thumb brushed over my clit. Barely there. Just a touch, and yet it felt like a live wire.

Hands lifted the damp ends of my hair off my neck, and a kiss warmed the skin there. "Whether you believe it or not, sweetheart, we want you. And *the rest of it* means us showing you exactly that."

Everett lifted one of my breasts out of the water and lifted it to his mouth. His eyes flicked to mine as my nipple disappeared between his lips. It was the hottest thing I'd ever seen. My mind went blank. Every thought narrowed to the pleasure spiraling outward from his tongue.

"You know what's excellent about where Everett is sitting?" Micah asked. He lounged next to us, watching us with a gaze full of heat.

I shook my head. Words were beyond me at the moment.

"The jets."

Beneath me, Everett shifted, pushing his thighs—and therefore mine —wide. Water from the jet rose straight into me. Exactly where my clit met his fingers. Oh. *Oh.*

Releasing my breast, he pulled my mouth back to his, now toying with my clit as the jet gave me delicious, familiar pressure.

I was pretty sure every woman had gotten off like this at some point, whether in a hot tub or a shower head. There was something about the unrelenting insistence of those streams of water that helped. It dug deep and let you work yourself into it.

"Did you have this planned too?"

The corners of his mouth turned up. "Cam is right. I always have a plan."

"Fuck." My hips jerked into his hand, and I had to close my eyes because that position was so much better.

Everett circled my clit one more time before he moved his fingers, curling his hand around the stream of water and lower—

He slipped inside me, fingers curling and seeking, gentle and insistent. And holy *shit*. That tiny spot they made toys for. The kind of toys I *loved*. He found that spot and brushed against it, making my hips jerk all over again.

I dropped my face to his neck with a moan. The scent of him made it all so much better. Deceptively soft until you caught the nuances. Pistachio swirled and was followed by the comfort of his almond. But sweet. Almost like almond frosting.

"Ride the water, little nymph," he said. "Make yourself feel good on the outside, and I'll help from the inside." A harder thrust from his fingers that sent my eyes rolling back in my head, and my hips moving. I did what he said, chasing the pressure, moving my hips over that jet, and every time I moved, he moved, at once matching and colliding with me.

I clung to Everett's shoulders, face still buried in his neck. The nerves had dissipated, my body now past the point of caring about anything but chasing that elusive pleasure. Honestly, I couldn't remember the last time I'd orgasmed. I'd been so busy there hadn't been time to care, or I didn't want to be reminded of what I couldn't have.

It came up so quickly I almost missed it. Stealthy but strong, I shuddered through it, hips still moving and trying to drag out that pleasure. It was almost too much now, that stream of water, but it was also *so* good.

Everett gripped my hair and dragged my mouth to his again. This wasn't a chaste kiss. His mouth opened mine, tongue claiming me just as thoroughly as his fingers just had.

"Now I have an entirely different reason to like baths," I whispered.

"I have a feeling I'm going to want to take them more often," he whispered, slowly easing his fingers out of me. And then he was moving me, and I was nearly dizzy as he placed me over the edge of the tub. "Now, for the next part."

"Everett." I pushed up, and a hand on my back kept me where I was. My hands were on the floor, and my ass was now above the water. "What are you doing?"

"Not me," he said. "And we're doing exactly what we promised."

I didn't have time to think about the position I was in or how it looked, because more hands were on me. Then lips. Then tongue.

And oh. *Fuck.*

Fig 25. Honeysuckle

Meaning: Bonds of love; Devoted affection;
Generous affection; Lasting pleasure

MICAH

*T*he taste of my wife's pussy was pure heaven. Her scent put me on the floor, but burying my face between her thighs was transcendence. I could stay here forever, feasting on her and on the gasps she let out in time with my tongue.

She didn't like being in this position. I could tell. Because she thought it wasn't flattering. Or that we were going to see the way her lush body folded against the tub and suddenly be repulsed. I wished there was a way to show her it was never going to fucking happen.

Once she knew we were her Alphas, and once we bonded her, she would be able to feel it. I hated that she didn't know, but I also understood that she wouldn't believe us if we told her. She barely believed I wanted to have my mouth on her, let alone a commitment for life.

She was already sweet, the water not having washed away all of her first orgasm. I wanted another one. I craved the feeling of her finding pleasure.

"Fuck, that's hot," Cameron said. He stood to the side, stroking his cock. On purpose. Ocean could look and just see him and how hard he was. For her. It was all for her, and wouldn't ever be for anyone else.

Without a doubt, we would have ended up here. As soon as we'd seen Ocean across that ballroom, we'd been enamored. Scenting her and realizing she was *ours* was like winning the goddamn lottery. Nothing could ever compare to that. But we would be here. With her. Either way.

On some level, all three of us knew we were going to make her our wife.

I licked upward, using my tongue to well and truly fuck my wife before curving it back around her clit and listening to her moan. Feeling when she shifted back into me, begging for more and when she relaxed like I was going easy on her.

My smile couldn't be stopped, and I hoped she felt it. I wasn't going easy on her. I was finding out what she liked so I could never go easy on her again. The three of us wanted her mindless with pleasure. Because pleasure was the way through. For her to understand that she was it, and we wanted her. Pleasure and tenderness.

I wanted this, but I wanted those sweet laughs and smiles too. To take all that pain she'd pushed aside and show her it was over now.

And at the moment, she was holding back.

Pulling away, I bit her ass. She yelped, and I smoothed the bite with my tongue. "You're tensing up."

"I feel—"

Her words stopped when I sucked her clit between my teeth, grazing it. It was swollen from her orgasm and my mouth. But we could do better than that. "The only thing you need to feel is my mouth," I lowered my voice and spoke into her skin so she felt the words everywhere. "Now let me taste your pleasure, princess."

I unleashed myself, focusing on those little movements I noticed she'd liked. Her hips moved backwards, silently begging for more, and I was more than happy to give it to her. Fucking thrilled when she groaned, fresh sweetness seeping across my tongue.

Fuck me. I would never have enough. There would never be a time when I wasn't addicted to my Omega's scent and taste. My wife's flavor.

Soon I'd have her ride my face so I could fuck her with my tongue properly and drown me with every climax I gave her.

Cameron stepped out of the tub and held out a hand to her. "The only reason I'm not picking you up right now is because I know it makes you nervous, and I don't want you to worry about either of us slipping on the tile."

She took his hand, but didn't move yet. Her whole body still moved while she caught her breath from the orgasm. "Could I have a towel? I don't want to make a mess on your bed."

He went to his knees in front of her so their faces were level. "So you don't make a mess or we don't look at you?" I couldn't see her face, but I saw the way she stiffened. "Because if I'm doing it right, you're going to make a mess in my bed either way, sweetheart."

"Bubbles," she said quietly. "I want to wipe off the bubbles."

Cameron winked. "Then I'll help you."

Our Omega let him help her up and out of the tub. I couldn't help but watch those same bubbles slide down her body. Over those dimples just above her ass and downward. It probably wasn't normal to crave licking the water from someone's skin, but I wanted to with Ocean. Every part of her.

Faint red marks still existed from the boning of those fucking corsets they made her wear, the bandages still at the top of her back. I had to push the thoughts aside, because it wasn't the time for me to fall into the pit of rage those marks sent me to.

The pale gray towel Cameron used wasn't big enough. I made a mental note to get towels that could wrap all the way around her. Envelop her, so she could be as an Omega was supposed to be.

Hell, along with the lingerie collection, we could do a bed and bath collection with the new Firefly launch. I'd never thought about the size of bath towels before, but then again, I'd never *had* to. Appropriate sizes didn't end with clothing. I needed to integrate that into everything.

I should have thought of that without seeing it firsthand. We kept our clothing available for all sizes, so it made sense.

Thankfully, Ocean wasn't focused on the size of the towel, but on the way Cameron was drying her off. Taking his time, kissing what he dried until the tan of her skin turned pink with attention.

"No more mess," he murmured to her.

With Cameron standing in front of her, staring, she began to wilt. He didn't let it happen, grabbing her hand and pulling her into the bedroom while Everett and I scrambled to dry ourselves and follow.

But I stopped in the doorway to watch. Our wife was still nervous, in spite of everything. I didn't want to overwhelm her again.

Cameron rearranged the bed, stacking pillows together against the headboard. Pulling back the blankets and making it perfect. "There."

I watched Ocean's toes and fingers curl and release in little motions that were louder than words.

My gut told me *now*. I approached Ocean from behind and slid my hands around her ribs. "What's wrong, princess?"

"No—" She caught herself before she could dismiss whatever it was. That was good. Pulling one long breath in, she let it out and relaxed back into me. "I just want to be like everyone else. Able to fall into bed without having to rearrange things just because I'm..."

Pulling her head to the side, I kissed her neck. "I promise, wife, none of us will have a problem bending you over the nearest available surface to take you hard and fast."

Her breath hitched, so I went a step further, purring and stepping her forward, closer to the bed and Cameron. "In every other aspect of our lives, we work to make our bodies comfortable. Clothes, sheets, temperature. Why should it be different for sex? We want you to be comfortable, and taking a minute to rearrange some pillows so you feel good isn't going to make us want to fuck you less."

Sex wasn't one-size-fits-all any more than most clothing. And yes, there were things we would do differently because of Ocean's size. That didn't bother me. I wanted her to feel good, and us to feel good. Nothing else came into it, especially other people's opinions or their favorite sex positions.

Cameron grinned and snagged her hand, pulling her out of my arms. She was off balance, and he caught her, spinning them so she landed on her back, right on the pillows with his body on top of hers. "That's better," he whispered before he kissed her. "Now you're all mine."

"For the moment," Everett said.

Our wife was flushed, eyes wide, dark hair spread across the pillow in a little starburst. Cameron fit himself against her and held there. Even feet away, I felt the self-control he had to use in order to stop. "Are you going to let me fuck you, sweetheart?"

She nodded.

"I need to hear you say yes, wife."

Wetting her lips, she whispered the word. "Yes."

Fig 26. Tulip
(Also: Lale, Pot of Gold)
Meaning: Absolute romance; a declaration of
love; A lover's heart darkened by the heart of
passion; Perfect lover; Sensuality
Meaning (Purple): Eternal love
Meaning (Pink): My perfect lover
Meaning (Orange): I am fascinated by you
Meaning (Red): Irresistible love; Undying love

OCEAN

*C*ameron slid into me with one long, hard thrust. I had to close my eyes. Holy shit. Of the three, he was the thickest, and it had been a long time since I'd been with anything other than a battery operated boyfriend.

Plus, let's be real. The external toys did the job just fine and were a lot less work most of the time. My dildos were gathering dust in whatever box they were still in from the move, and they'd been there for a while.

But there was nothing that felt like this. The heat of being filled and the weight of someone being *with* you. When someone looked at you the way Cameron looked at me now. I didn't think I'd ever been looked at like that. Like I was the center of his world.

Even if it was only this moment, it opened something in my chest.

"Fuck, Ocean," he groaned, dropping his lips to mine at the same time he lifted my thigh around his waist so he could press deeper. "As much as I want to take you for hours, you feel too good."

I was still too overwhelmed by the feel of him to speak. All I could do was wrap my arms around his neck and pull him closer. Kiss him. Every move he made felt good, and I didn't give a shit how long he lasted. I was already blissed out from the two orgasms they managed to wring out of me in the bath. Having another one? Probably not on the table. I was a one and done orgasm girl, even though my nickname was O.

"Talk to me, wife," he whispered. "Tell me what you like."

"I like it all." It was an honest answer, because every part of him—of *them*—touching me was incredible.

Cameron slowed down, searching my face. Then that playful light came into his eyes, and I swore his scent grew stronger. "If you won't tell me, then I'll just have to figure it out."

I laughed, and it cracked something in the air. The tension singing that still hovered. The seriousness and carefulness we were all moving with. It didn't have to be so serious, and I felt like I took my first breath after holding it forever. "I *do* like it all. But I also don't know enough to tell you what I like."

"Mmm," he pushed in so slowly it was almost painful. "So we get to experiment with you. Show you everything. I like that."

"You're not the only one." Micah laid down next to me, turning my face away from Cam to kiss me. Hard and deep, and *oh*—

He still tasted like *me*. I didn't know why the two of us together was so incredible, but I fucking loved it. The sound that came out of me, low and desperate, Cameron cursed and drove home.

Pleasure raced through me, the speed and the friction lighting me up. Cameron stretched me the way a toy never had. The new sensation building deep inside me was delicious. I'd never had this before. Never had an orgasm from this kind of sex. It was deeper. Larger and more... everywhere.

I couldn't keep my breath, the newness of the sensation racing up and through and out before I could even hold onto it. My gasps spilled through as I clung to the shimmers of it, letting them sparkle through my brain. Holy shit.

"I think our wife likes it hard and fast." Everett had gone to a knee beside the bed and watched me with that intensity I didn't dare trust. He took my hand and kissed the back of it, turned it over and kissed the point of my pulse, never taking his gaze away from mine. "Look at him, little nymph," he said.

Something about it made me smile as I looked back at Cam. Took in all of him. Raised my other leg to curl around his hips as best I could. Run one hand through his hair. Sink into the sensation of aftershocks and pleasure floating around me in a golden haze.

Dropping his face to my neck, Cameron moaned, thrusting deep and shuddering, knot locking into place so perfectly it made light flash behind my eyes. It might have been the hottest sound I'd ever heard, and I needed more. I pulled his face to mine, wanting to taste that sound. Needing it.

Cameron smiled through our kiss, but he didn't stop kissing me. "The way you hug my knot is fucking perfect."

"I've never had that," I smiled, unable to stop touching him. Face, shoulders, hair. Wherever I could reach. "An orgasm from actual sex. Hell, the fact that I had three is a miracle."

Shock froze Cameron's face, and then he was kissing me again, this time harder, rolling with me to the side, forcing Micah out of the way. "You shouldn't tell me things like that, sweetheart. If you start telling us we're taking firsts, we're going to get more possessive than we already are."

I pressed my lips together to suppress my grin. "Is that a bad thing?"

Heat lined my back as Everett slid onto the bed behind me. "If you're prepared for us to growl at any man who looks at you and want to keep you in the house so you're only ours, then no, it's not a bad thing."

He kissed my shoulder, and I loved that. Casual touches. The little things. They meant just as much as sex. Anyone could want to touch someone for sex. To get off. But just touching? Because you could? I didn't take that for granted. Especially as he slid his palm down my ribs. "You won't have to worry about the first one," I said. "And the second one won't be a problem. I like being home."

"And I like you calling this place your home," Micah said.

I rested my head on the pillows and closed my eyes, comfortable and spent and cozy. But most of all, not feeling awkward anymore. There was no chance my anxiety wouldn't rear its head again. But they hadn't laughed. They were still here.

"I'm going to point out the attention you get, little nymph. If not to show you how much you're wanted, to show you how I'm staking my claim."

As we rested, breathing in the comfortable silence, Cameron's knot loosened, and we eased apart. He wrapped himself around me, his whole body pressing into mine. "I could fuck you all over again," he whispered in my ear. "Never have enough."

For a long moment, I closed my eyes and basked in the feeling of those words. Let myself relax into his hold. Just breathe in lemon zest and powdered sugar. Savor the warmth of his skin on mine.

"What happens now?" I murmured, tired, but not enough to sleep. Not yet, at least.

"Whatever you want, princess. Food and more fucking? I'll take that option any time."

A laugh fell out of me, more like a giggle. I couldn't quite believe I was in bed with three of the hottest Alphas I'd ever encountered. My *husbands*.

Cameron laughed with me. "You like that idea?"

I nodded.

"Good," Everett sighed. "Because as much as we don't want to, we have to go into the office tomorrow. We have to sign the paperwork with Frank and a few other things. But trust me when I say we'll be rushing through it."

Something in my chest warmed. "That's okay. If that greenhouse gets set up tomorrow," I said, "I'll have Sally bring over some of the hybrids I've been working on. I need to check on them."

"Hybrid flowers?"

"Yeah. I'm not great at getting the outcome I want yet, but I'm working on it."

Everett sank his fingers into my hair and combed through the damp tangles, gently pulling with his fist close to my scalp. That felt so fucking good. "Don't stop that."

"Good to know." He chuckled. "And I'm sure the flowers are gorgeous."

There was no reason for that to make me blush, other than the simple trust and belief that I'd rarely had from anyone other than Trinity and Isolde.

"Tell me, wife," Everett used the grip on my hair to tilt me back into him. "What would you like? Food first? Or..."

"Or?"

He lifted my leg backward over his, settling his cock directly between my legs. The length of him pressed against me, and something cold. "You have a piercing?"

"Is that another first?" he asked.

"Yes."

"Then I think anything else can wait, don't you?" Everett scraped his teeth over my neck, making me gasp. He rocked his hips, driving the tip of his cock—and that piercing—directly into my clit.

"Yes," I breathed the word. "Yes."

A low, rough purr sprang to life as he kissed my neck and shoulder, long and slow. "Good girl."

Then his cock was thrusting deep, and there was no way to think of anything else as he took me.

Fig 27. Chrysanthemum
(Also: Mums, Flower of Life)
Meaning: A heart left to desolation

OCEAN

*S*oft comfort clung to me as I woke. The ridiculously butter-soft blankets on Cameron's bed. Somehow I hadn't yet managed to spend the night in my own bed, but if they weren't this kind of blanket we were switching them out with this kind because I could burrow into these and live here forever.

I curled a little deeper and heard a distinct *crinkle*.

Pulling the blanket down from over my head, I blinked away the morning light. I was alone in bed, but there was a note resting next to me.

COME TO THE KITCHEN FOR BREAKFAST WHEN YOU'RE READY. TAKE YOUR TIME. WE MIGHT HAVE TO GO TO THE OFFICE, BUT WE'RE THE BOSSES. WE'LL WAIT FOR YOU FIRST.

My whole body turned pink, and I buried myself beneath the blankets again, giving into the instinct to kick my feet and just *wiggle* with happiness.

There was too much of it, and it just had to come out until I flopped back on the pillows with a smile so big it hurt.

Everett had taken me entirely differently. Steady and slowly, but with brutal intention. It might have been slow, but it wasn't soft. Every thrust of that piercing had fireworks flashing in my mind, and now every girl I'd ever listened to rave about dick piercings made total sense.

By that time I *was* tired enough to sleep. They woke me up to eat at some point before Micah fucked me back to sleep again. I was sore, but in a good way. Like I'd spent all day moving plants around in the greenhouse.

I needed something to wear. The nightgown wasn't on the bathroom floor anymore, and I still wasn't confident enough to walk through the whole house naked yet. On top of the fact that I didn't know if there was staff here today. Was Ruby here?

The blanket was too big to take with me. But... *there*. Across the room there was a chair with a throw blanket. Good enough. I wrapped it beneath my arms like a towel and nearly bumped into Cameron on my way out the door.

He smiled, catching me by the shoulders. "Morning." When he kissed me, he tasted like mint.

"Morning. I'll give your blanket back. Promise."

"I want it back for you to use it like this. It looks far better on you than it ever did on my chair. But you could have borrowed one of my shirts. Or let us see you naked."

I tightened the blanket. "I didn't want to terrify the staff, and none of your shirts would fit me."

"Hmm. I'll be rectifying that. I want you to have something with my scent."

Desire and longing flashed through me like lightning. I wanted that *so much*. To be on a phone call with my friends and have their hoodies wrapped around me like it was nothing. To have them *want* their scent on my skin as much as I wanted it there.

Cam leaned down and kissed me. "Based on your perfume, you like the idea."

"Like would be a bit of an understatement."

"Then you'll have it. Soon." He winked. "And I'll make sure the staff are never home when we are, if it means you walking around naked, wife."

I screwed up my face trying not to smile and failed completely. "I don't know if I'm ready for that, but I will take it under advisement, husband."

"Call me husband again and you're never making it to breakfast."

Hitching the blanket up under my arms, I sprinted down the hall toward my room, followed by his laughter.

Ruby had done an amazing job in the closet. Even the things that weren't hanging were easy to find. I didn't think I was *going* anywhere today, so I kept myself comfortable. But I still avoided my more ratty lounge clothes. And it had absolutely nothing to do with the fact that I wanted to look cute for the Alphas I would see in the kitchen.

Not a single thing.

I grabbed my phone, noting that I had far too many messages. Then again, I hadn't even thought about looking for the past couple of days. They would keep for a bit longer. After everyone left for work, I'd have more than enough time to answer messages and explore the house.

The kitchen was bright and welcoming in the morning light. The windows over the side of the estate showed more magnolia trees that painted shadows on the floor, moving with the summer breeze.

Cameron was already back from his room, sitting at the large booth-like table in the breakfast nook. It wasn't really fair for him to look that good. He could be in a coffee ad, sitting like that with a tablet in front of him and a suit that fit him like a glove.

"There's hot water on the stove if you'd like some tea, coffee in the machine, and all of that." He gestured to the baskets on the island, full of fruit, muffins, and other things like croissants. There was a whole rack of different tea bags, sugar and honey, and a quick peek in the fridge showed creamer.

Tea sounded perfect this morning.

Spotting a blueberry muffin, I grabbed it. My favorite. I sat at the small table in the breakfast nook overlooking the trees and beyond. I could just barely see the beach from this angle. I liked this space. It seemed far too casual for this grand house. And peaceful.

Cameron reached across the table and squeezed my hand while he read whatever was on his tablet.

Everett came into the kitchen and smiled at me. In his work suit, he was so much sharper than the Alpha he turned into with me. I very much understood what he said yesterday. People would be afraid of him, and I liked that. There was something entrancing about being the one who could tame the beast and calm the monster.

"Morning," I murmured.

"Morning, wife." That little smile that was only for me appeared.

He poured coffee and made himself some toast before he grabbed a pear. It was interesting to see them fending for themselves. I assumed men as rich as them wouldn't do anything as simple as cooking, but I hadn't seen any staff in the house so far.

I nearly moaned at the first bite of the blueberry muffin. Holy shit, it was incredible. So far, all the food here was.

Everett didn't bother to sit, standing at the island with his coffee and toast. It seemed strange, the easy domestic feeling. As if this were all normal. Like we did it every day.

Warmth spread through my chest at that thought. I was going to make every morning and domestic moment count this year.

Micah strode in and went straight to the coffee machine. He sighed. "I'm sorry I can't stay. I wasn't planning on going in until our meeting with Frank, but Gregory seemed to think his thoughts on the designs for the new men's line couldn't wait till the afternoon, and I'd rather not spend the day getting yelled at, so off I go."

Cameron chuckled. "Good luck with that."

With a growl, Micah looked up. "Which one of you assholes took the last blueberry muffin? You know how I feel about that."

Cold dread swept through me, and I wasn't hearing the Alphas in front of me. I was hearing Frank's voice. *We've had this discussion, Ocean. You don't take something if there's nothing left of it for anyone else. It's selfish, rude, and you don't need it anyway.*

I should have thought about that. This was their house first, and I needed to make sure they had what they needed. But I also didn't want to lie. "Um, it wasn't them. It was me."

Cameron gave me a wink. "He'll punish you for it later."

I couldn't feel my fingers, and my heart pounded in my ears. "I'm sorry. I didn't know. It won't happen again." I pushed the muffin to the edge of the table. "I only took one bite." I twisted my hands together in my lap, focusing on a knot in the wood of the table.

This wasn't the reaction I wanted to have. Somewhere outside of myself I knew that I was currently trapped in my own mind, but it didn't make it any easier to get out.

My whole focus narrowed to the steam rising from my tea. A shadow from the blowing branches of the magnolia tree outside. The small chip in the nail polish on my thumb.

The silence around me was deafening. I was being crushed beneath it. "I should have asked. I'm sorry."

A presence suddenly stood beside me, and the scent of chocolate and caramel. The darker part of his scent was strong, the caramel smelling like someone had left it cooking too long. Nearly burned. "Ocean?" Micah asked quietly.

I couldn't look at him and see the anger there. "I know you're running late. Take it, please."

"I don't give a damn if I'm running late. Nothing takes precedence over my wife."

I did look up at him then, and there was no anger on his face. At least none that was directed toward me. He crouched down next to me and took my twisted hands in one of his. Loosened them. Relaxed them.

"I'm sorry I frightened you," he said softly. "These assholes, much as I love them, have a habit of stealing the last muffins I like because they know it winds me up. They've been doing it for years." Lifting his other hand, he brushed a hair back behind my ear and let his hand linger, thumb brushing along my jaw. "You don't have to ask permission to eat anything here. Ever. And despite what Cam said, we would never *punish* you for this. Not unless it was a game—something we all agreed to and enjoyed.

"We would never punish you for anything, princess. You're our wife, not something we own."

I gripped his hand, unable to let go of the fear lodged in my chest. Micah leaned in and kissed my forehead, squeezing my hands back. "Come on. Take a breath with me, all right?"

He inhaled deeply, and I followed him. When I let it out, I felt a little bit better. Barely. He smiled. "I'm glad I know you like them. I'll have an ally against these two."

I couldn't quite laugh, but I managed a small smile.

"Can I hug you?" he asked.

After I nodded, he pulled me up out of the seat and into his arms. He wrapped me up so tightly, one hand holding my head against his chest and his purr, that I couldn't help but relax. "I'm sorry," I whispered, my mouth dry. "I know you wouldn't. I swear I know. I don't think that."

Micah kissed my hair. "I'm glad you know. I'm sorry I can't stay. And I'm so sorry you've ever had to feel like this."

I said nothing more, my mind unable to stray from thoughts I didn't want, shame overwhelming me. After last night and breaking through that anxiety, I felt like I'd just stumbled back ten steps. But the way Micah held me, his purr vibrating beneath my ear, had me breathing deeper and my shoulders relaxing.

He kissed my hair again. "You mentioned you might work on your hybrids today? If Sally can bring them to you?" I nodded into his shirt. "When I get home, I'd love to see them if they're here." Pulling back, he kissed me—for real this time. "Eat that entire muffin, wife. It makes you taste like blueberries. And I'll be thinking about you the whole day."

Then he was gone with his to-go coffee out the door, leaving me reeling.

Cam leaned across the table and moved my tea closer to him, and then the muffin. He tilted his head next to him, silently asking me to come next to him. I did, heart still pounding from the sudden adrenaline.

As soon as I sat down he put his arm around me and pulled me to him. I leaned my head on his shoulder because it felt natural to do it. Like my head was made to rest there as he purred and scrolled through what looked like emails with his other hand.

"Will you tell us what caused that?"

I shrugged. "They didn't like when I took anything that was the last thing."

"*They?*" Everett asked.

Keeping my head on Cam's shoulder, I turned to see Rett where he leaned heavily on the kitchen island. "You can't kill him. We still need him."

His smile sent chills down my spine in the best way. "Killing him isn't the only thing I can do. And I'll be damned if he and Laura get away with treating you like this for so long with no consequences."

"I shouldn't like it when you say things like that."

"Oh?" He came around the island and stood beside the bench, looking down at me. "And why not?"

"I don't want to hurt anyone."

Everett held out a hand, and I took it, letting him lift me to my feet. In another movement he spun me and pressed me back into the island. His eyes were dark as he brushed his lips over mine. "You don't have to hurt anyone, little nymph. That's my job."

"Don't do it on my account."

"I protect what's mine," he growled. "And I absolutely will if I have to."

Until now, I never knew how much I needed those words. To *feel* protected. To feel like I was *worth* protecting. It was another realization —how unsafe I'd felt even though I hadn't consciously understood it.

My husband cupped my face and kissed me. "I promise not to kill him... today. And I promise not to do anything that will jeopardize your agreement with him. But I don't promise not to hurt him if I can. Because hurting *you*? It's fucking unacceptable."

All I could do was stare at him. What could I possibly say to that?

Cameron stood and gathered his tablet. "We should probably go and make sure Micah doesn't lose his mind before we have to sign these papers." He moved Everett aside to kiss me quickly. "The people from Nestled will be here at noon to build the nest. You don't have to deal with them at all if you don't want to. Marcela, the housekeeper, already knows everything. The wedding pictures should be published today too, so if you need anything, you call us, okay?"

"Okay."

With a sigh, Everett took another step back from me. "I don't want to leave you after that."

"I'll be fine," I said with a smile. And I would. Because of them and the way they *did* made me feel safe.

"Even if you don't need us, you can call us," Cam whispered. "We'll be back as soon as we can."

I watched them leave the kitchen, and Cameron turned back at the last second. "Don't forget to eat your muffin. Make yourself sweeter, so later we can eat yours."

They were gone before they saw my mouth drop open and my face flush red with embarrassment and arousal. But I ate every crumb of that fucking muffin.

Fig 28. Gladiolus
(Also: Sword Lily)
Meaning: Flower of the gladiators;
Give me a break; Integrity; Ready armed;
Strength; You pierce my heart

EVERETT

$\mathcal{T}$he office was quiet. Not unusual for a Monday morning. Our employees got their work done, and as long as they did, we didn't care how much time they spent in the office. Want to spend more time at home and therefore be more efficient? Be my guest.

But Micah's assistant Josie sat outside his office at her desk. Cameron made it to the door first. "He free, Jos?"

"It's been quiet for a few minutes, so I assume he's off the phone with Gregory."

"How'd that go?" I asked.

She smirked. "Nothing a stiff Monday morning drink can't fix."

Perfect.

Micah was hunched over his desk when the door opened, scribbling with a stylus on his tablet. The mockups for the men's line were there. "Don't break the stylus," I said.

"I might do it just to spite Gregory," he said. "I'll buy a new one."

Cameron sat in one of the chairs and observed our packmate with amusement. "He had thoughts?"

"Not good ones. He thinks the designs are too avant garde for men to wear, and I whole-heartedly disagree. With the way trends are going, by the time this collection comes out next year, this is the kind of thing everyone will want. I'm not going to let someone with a stick up his ass and an old-fashioned sense of style fuck that up."

"Good."

Micah looked up suddenly, like he hadn't even realized he was talking. It happened sometimes.

"Shit. Sorry."

"No, I like it," I said. "Take no shit."

He sighed and closed down the program. "Yeah. I won't. But he's going to be a pain in my ass about it."

Gregory was one of our marketing people, and he was damn good at his job. But he also had no qualms about voicing his opinions when he thought our products were on the wrong track. Still, when a decision was made, he executed it, like he would with this.

"Is Ocean okay?" he asked quietly. "I haven't been able to stop thinking about it."

"She's okay. Though the last place I want to be is here," I admitted.

Cam put his hands behind his head and stared out the window. "We should take her on a honeymoon. I know it wasn't part of the plans because it was all so fast, but getting her away from here? Where it's just the four of us? I want that. And it might help get her away from those instincts."

I looked at him. "When did you start having *good* ideas?"

"When you started smiling." He smirked.

"Dick."

One eyebrow raised. "You started it."

"Photos and story are out," Micah said. He stared down at his phone, scrolling.

It took only seconds for me to find it and start smiling. Because of the short timeline, we'd had the photographer provide the photos directly to our reporter of choice, but we would get them soon. And plaster them all over the fucking house.

She looked beautiful in every photo. Glowing, even though we now knew she'd been in agony. I wanted to take more photos with her happy and comfortable. But still, she had found some peace somewhere, and I would savor these pictures because they were the first time we made her ours.

The rest would come later.

"Story looks good," Cameron said. "And just glancing at my little notification numbers, we're already being tagged. We should grab something and post it."

"On every account," I added. We'd already instructed our social teams for Zenith and the other brands to post about it, but we would too.

I found the picture I wanted and posted it with a short caption, tagging Ocean as I did so, hoping it would be one of the first notifications she saw.

Deep satisfaction rolled through me. Perfect. I wanted the entire world to know that Ocean belonged to us. She was ours, and no one was going to fuck with that.

My little nymph might think I was joking when I told her how I meant to protect her, but I wasn't. There were lines I hadn't crossed and didn't plan to, but I already knew there was no line I wouldn't cross to protect my Omega if I needed to. That included her aunt and uncle.

I would do what I had to.

And I couldn't wait to see her and tell her how delicious she looked in every single one of these photos. "I do *not* want to be here today," I said with a laugh.

"We'll get back to her as soon as we can—" Micah's eyes drifted past me to the door, then sharpened. "Joseph. Come to offer your congratulations, I hope?"

I kept my face neutral as I turned to face him. His expression was hard and unreadable. "I didn't think you would move this fast."

"Is that a problem?" Sliding my hands into my pockets, I strolled to the wall and leaned against it, the picture of ease. "This was, after all, what you wanted. You threatened our legacy and livelihood in order to force us into marriage. Don't tell me you're not happy that we complied with your... request?"

We all knew the board's blackmail wasn't a request.

"We assumed you would take some time to find a wife," Joseph was pretending he didn't care, but he did. Our suspicious were right. There was more to this than he was letting on. "Build up the image and the anticipation in order to help change your image. Not drop photos from a secret wedding like an atomic bomb."

"Have you seen the photos?" Cam asked mildly. "There were plenty of people there. Clearly, it wasn't a secret. So sorry your invitation got lost in the mail. I think I have an extra copy floating around here somewhere. They were beautiful. Blue and silver." He paused, thinking, and looked at Micah. "Well, not fully blue. This delightful shade of bluish purple our wife loves. What would you say it is? Tanzanite?"

Micah shrugged. "I'd say it's more of a periwinkle."

"Hmm, maybe."

Joseph huffed out a breath. "Are you done talking about fucking colors?"

"Are you done pretending any of this was actually about us getting married?" I shot back. "Because I'm still waiting for the real reason for this whole failed coup you planned."

His face turned red. "Preventing you from running this company into the ground because of your image isn't a fucking coup. You—"

"No, no." I pushed off the wall and took a step forward. "We already established why your accusations have no place in reality. You know I'm not a patient man, so we're not going to go through all of it again. So you can either congratulate us on our wedding and get the fuck out, or you can tell me the truth.

"I can think of only a couple of reasons why you'd do this, and none of them have to do with the press or wanting us to settle down. So do you want to talk about those?"

He stood there, silent, so I kept going.

"Maybe you don't like where Zenith is headed. We're expanding in a direction you don't approve of, and you're already in too deep to get out without looking weak or like there was a scandal you were dismissed for. So maybe you thought the best way was to take us down and make *us* look like the bad guy." I stepped around him slowly, in a circle, making sure he felt like the prey he was. "But that doesn't make sense, since Zenith is the most valuable of its kind in the market, and I know exactly how over inflated your salary is."

"Congratulations." He gritted the word through his teeth. "On your wedding."

"Or maybe," I continued, "someone came to you with an offer. Get our company to suffer some losses in order to make us vulnerable to a hostile takeover. With your shares and all that notice, you'd stand to make more money than you'd ever seen in your life, and they'd give you a new position. So you and the board planned your little ambush, and now it's only been a week, everything you thought would happen has crumbled into dust, and you're furious." I stopped in front of him. "Am I getting close?"

If looks could kill, I would be lifeless on the floor. "Or maybe I care about this company and everyone in it, and don't want to see it run into the ground by your recklessness."

I tilted my head. "Okay, and what would that be? And you don't get to say we were reckless being photographed dancing, fully clothed, with a woman more than three years ago. You're going to have to do better than that."

Joseph's jaw flexed, but he didn't say anything. And in this moment, I was glad that Micah and Cam always had my back. Because I could say what I was about to without consulting them, and they would stand by my side.

"Here's what's going to happen, Joseph. We've decided to take our wife on a honeymoon at the end of the week. Don't know how long that will take, so we'll, of course, be available if we need to be. But when we come back, I want to know what your answer is. I want the truth, and I want your reasons. If you don't give me those, Zenith Incorporated will be looking for a new Chairman of the Board. Am I understood?"

For a second I thought he might hit me, and there was part of me that dared him to do it just so I could throw him out on his ass. He didn't.

Pity.

"You lost. Whatever your goal was, it didn't work. Make peace with that while we're away, and you let me know whether I need to hire a headhunter." I clapped him on the shoulder. "You're dismissed."

The shock on his face was a beautiful thing. He sputtered like he was finally going to say something before he turned and stormed out of Micah's office at full speed, nearly knocking Josie over where she was bringing a carrier full of to-go coffee cups.

"Damn," Cameron said. "I wish I'd recorded that, because that was fucking glorious."

Micah smirked too, but was still tense. "Are you sure humiliating him was the way to go?"

"His plan was to humiliate us. If you're going to execute a plan, you should make sure you're ready for it to come back on you. Besides, I'm frankly sick of his shit. I hope he doesn't tell us so we have a reason to get rid of him and bring in someone who doesn't fight us every step of the way."

The success we had wasn't accidental. It was because we knew how to run a business while also caring about the people it employed and those it affected as much or more than profits. Amazing what human decency could do. But as many boards were, they were looking at the bottom line. Joseph came highly recommended when we'd brought him on after going public, but he was also a barrier to most of our ideas, and we'd had to force him into too many things. It might be time for a change regardless of his decision.

"I can't say I disagree." Micah stroked a hand down his face. "But we should still be careful. He had the whole board with him, and even though we won this round, it doesn't mean they won't have something else up their sleeve."

"Yeah. And we need more information." I sent a text to Aiden asking for the details. If there was something to find, he would find it. "As for Frank, I hope you know I'm planning to hold him to every sticky little thing in the contract."

"I'm looking forward to that." Cam rubbed his hands together. "He should be here now, right?"

"Josie?" Micah called. "Is Frank McCabe in the building yet?"

The Beta poked her head through the door. "Yes. Oren called to let me know he's in the conference room on Mr. DuPont's floor."

"Call the legal team and have them meet us there, please." Micah waited until she retreated to point at me. "You can't kill him."

"I promised Ocean I wouldn't. Today."

He shrugged. "Good enough."

Cameron leapt to his feet and nearly skipped out the door. "Time to go see dear old uncle-in-law."

"Please call him that," Micah yelled after him. "He'll hate that."

"Precisely."

I shook my head and followed. This was going to be interesting.

Fig 29. American Mountain Ash
Meaning: With me you are safe

OCEAN

*I*t was a beautiful day outside. The greenhouse wouldn't be ready until later in the evening, so I told Sally to hold off. No point in disturbing the plants if they had nowhere to go. I had time.

Instead, I explored the mansion. Marcela found me turned around and introduced herself before pointing me in the right direction. She was older and sweet. At the same time, I could see an underlying sternness that was needed to run a place like this and possibly stand up to my husbands when they deserved it.

That made me smile.

They probably needed someone to stand up to them from time to time. In a playful way. The thought that I could be that person filled me with anxiety, but not the bad kind. Because I knew that these Alphas wouldn't hurt me. I knew it deeper than my own name. I knew before the wedding too, but my fear had still been there. Now? Living with them and *seeing* them? They were safe.

I was safe.

The mansion had a gym and a small pool. No need for a gigantic one when the ocean was right outside. They had offices which looked like they were used regularly. Formal rooms like the Caruso Estate had, but this house was far less sprawling.

I liked the layout. There was a large courtyard in the center, drenched in sunlight, with grass, a fountain, and a tiled portion where you could sit and enjoy the sun without truly leaving the house. It was there that the greenhouse was being built, in the grassy section with the other plants.

That they wanted to build me one at all lit up that place in my chest that seemed to brighten whenever I was around them.

Even though I couldn't work directly with my plants, and I didn't want to see the nest until it was done, I still had work I needed to do for some clients. So I gathered my things and sat beneath an umbrella on the back terrace, looking out at the water.

Until my phone started buzzing so much it felt like the vibrations were constant. What the hell?

My screen was filled with notifications. Texts from Isolde and Rin, but also from people I hadn't heard from in *years*. Tags on *Entendre*'s social media accounts and mine.

Oh.

I clicked on the link Trinity sent me to the article that announced our marriage to the world.

THE DUPONT PACK MARRIES CALDWELL HEIR

A laugh escaped me. Laura and Frank would *hate* that. Good.

Our favorite billionaires have tied the knot! In a small but luxurious ceremony this past Saturday, the Duponts said 'I do,' to their Omega. Ocean Elise Correa Caldwell, daughter of the late Caldwell dynasty.

Their Omega. I loved that. If only it were true.

The rest of the article was fine. Not much substance, touching on all the business under their corporation. They mentioned my business and more about my parents, but it was fine. And the pictures were...

Some of them were beautiful. All of them were beautiful. But it didn't make it easier to look at photos of me. The way I felt in my body and the way my body appeared didn't always match up. Even when I felt gorgeous, a photo of me at the wrong angle could ruin everything. Even the memory.

Most of these were good. A couple weren't great, but the majority I could look at without cringing, which was a relief. But there was one picture that stopped me in my tracks. It raised the hairs on my arms.

I remembered the moment. Right at the beginning of taking all the pictures. I'd felt so free and so happy, and the smile on my face proved that. Cameron had his arm around my waist. Micah stood on my other side, and Everett was behind him, staring at me. They all looked at me, locked in with matching smiles on their faces, and we all looked so fucking happy it leaked from the picture.

I saved it to my phone. That was one I would keep.

The end of the article came, and I scrolled down without thinking. Fuck. I knew this might happen, but knowing it and seeing it in front of your eyes was brutal.

That cow landed them? Must be for her money.

Well, no. They had more money than I'd ever dream of having. Even after I got my trust and the estate passed to me, my parents' money didn't hold a candle.

There's no way this is fucking real. Not with a person who looks like that.

I think it's sweet. Everyone deserves love. Hope she gets her shit together though and makes herself match her husbands.

I closed the article and shook my head, heavy uneasiness resting on my chest. It was fine. Those strangers didn't know me, and they had no idea of the real circumstances. It wasn't anything I hadn't dealt with before. But...

This would be on a global scale. I didn't think I'd realized how big it all would be.

Since I hadn't posted anything to my socials, the comments weren't on a post about the wedding, they were flooding my other pictures. Commenting on my body.

But there was another tag too. From Everett. From all of them, actually, but I clicked on Everett's post. It was a picture I hadn't seen yet. Of us during the ceremony and the moment he kissed me. Even in the photo, you could tell the kiss wasn't chaste. He had me pressed up against his body, and I didn't even remember that happening. All I remembered was that the kiss had been everything I wanted and needed, and this picture showed it.

The caption was two words.

My wife.

I didn't bother to look at the comment on the post. They would be bad or good, but it didn't matter. All that mattered was the post itself.

Should I post a picture on mine?

Hmm. I wasn't a celebrity. I had some followers, but mostly just friends and acquaintances. Still, I was being tagged over and over again, and comments were coming in. If they were going to comment on my socials anyway, it would be easier to do it on a post that was actually relevant.

So I found the picture I'd just saved and uploaded it, following Everett's lead.

My husbands.

There wasn't much more to say.

Cam had posted him feeding me a bit of cake, and Micah chose the moment he put his ring on my finger. All of them were great.

The door to the house opened and Ruby came outside. I hadn't seen her yet. "Hey, you're here."

"I'm here. Do you need anything?"

"I'm good for now. What do they have you doing here?"

She laughed. "Nothing except helping you."

I stared. "What?"

With a shrug, she smiled. "They asked if I'd be willing to come with you, and I said yes. They're paying me more than Frank and Laura ever did, and all I have to do is make sure you're comfortable and have whatever you need. So consider me at your beck and call."

"Wow."

She suddenly looked unsure. "If that's okay with you."

"Yeah," I said. "I mean, you know me. I'm pretty low key, so you might be bored."

Approaching the table, she gave me a look. We'd known each other long enough that we were casual with each other. "You've been low key because you've been forced to be low key, Ocean." I began to protest, and she held out a hand. "I don't think your true personality is super high maintenance, but there's nothing wrong with asking for things. Especially when that's my job. I'm happy to help with whatever you need. Whether it's copying something for *Entendre* or grabbing you a bottle of water."

I stared at her. "And you're... okay with that?"

Back at the Caldwell Estate she'd been a catchall employee. She'd assisted the housekeeper and did what needed to be done, acting as Laura's right-hand, kind of like she was describing.

Ruby was older than me. She hadn't known my mother for long, but she'd just started working for our family when she passed.

"Yes," she said, "I'm fine with it."

"So if I told you to make sure my towels were warm?"

Ruby smirked. "I'd say I don't have to because you have a towel warmer in your bathroom already, and the cleaning staff load it when they do laundry."

"*What?* Where? I took a shower already."

"I'll show you whenever you want. It looks like one of the cabinets, so I'm not shocked you missed it. This place is like a candy land of all the best things. I'm pretty sure there's a switch to make the floor in your bathroom heated too. Oh, and those are in *both* of your bathrooms."

The regular bathroom and the one in the hallway to the nest.

This was on a whole new level. I'd always been wealthy, but there was wealthy and then there was whatever the hell this was. Where there was a greenhouse being built in a day and an entire nest assembled just for me.

"How's the nest coming?"

"Good. I think it will be done in an hour or so."

That would be nice. I couldn't wait to see it and curl up in it. A nest. A *real* one. "Thank you. I don't need anything else right now." She turned to walk away, and I had the thought. "Ruby?"

She turned back.

"Why did you stay? Working for Frank and Laura."

"Your aunt didn't turn into a poisonous bitch after your mother died. She was always like that, just muted. Your mom passing simply let her out of her cage. And though," she shook her head and looked away, "though I couldn't do nearly enough to protect you from her, I couldn't leave you there with them alone."

194

Awe and dread flowed into me in equal measure. "You stayed for me?"

"I tried to be the barrier for you as much as I could. It worked better when you were younger. Once you were an adult, I couldn't make excuses in the same way. I'm sorry for that."

I shoved everything in my hands onto the table and went to her, pulling her into a hug. "It is absolutely not your fault. I never knew that's why you were there, and for whatever you did, thank you."

"I'll never understand the choices your parents made," she said quietly. "Keeping you with Frank and Laura for so long. I doubt they imagined being gone so soon. But she wouldn't have wanted you to be alone."

Closing my eyes, I hugged her tighter. "Thank you." When we broke apart, I laughed. "I wish I'd known. I would have told you to get the hell out of there and save yourself."

"Which is why I stayed," she said, putting a hand on my shoulder. "And I'll stay as long as you want me to. Your husbands are very generous. My husband and I are grateful."

Ruby was a Beta. I'd met her husband a handful of times, and he was a good man. She deserved that. "I appreciate it. And if you're still here, I guess let me know when the nest is done. Otherwise I'll be here doing some work."

"I'm going to unpack some more of your things. They're almost done."

My mouth dropped open. "Have you been doing that all day?"

"Maybe."

"Ruby."

"Have fun with your flowers." She slipped away before I could scold her. But honestly, it was nice to have someone who had my back. And I hated packing and unpacking. I needed to thank my husbands when they got home for getting her to come with me.

My phone still buzzed when I sat back down. I would need to change the settings on all my notifications if it was going to be like this. I hadn't thought that it would get this much attention. Sure, the guys were famous because of their wealth, but they weren't the kind of people who were followed. Not often, at least, according to Trinity.

There was that guy at brunch, but nothing else.

The phone rang. "Hello?"

"Is this Ocean Caldwell?"

Something about the man's voice on the other end of the line made me pause. "Who's asking?"

"This is Gary Hampton with the Sunset City Standard. I'm looking for Ocean to ask for a comment on her recent marriage to the DuPont pack."

Shit. I hadn't asked them what to say or how to handle this. "No comment."

I hung up before he could say anything else, staring at the notifications filling up my screen. I tried not to absorb them, but it was hard not to. So many of them looked negative. Angry emojis and vomiting faces. Some seemed okay. Others talked about my parents.

Before I could second guess my thinking, I called Trinity. She answered quickly. "Hello, my beautiful friend. Are you calling to tell me I can do an exclusive with you and your pack for the magazine? Those photos are fucking stunning, by the way."

"I was actually hoping you might give me some tips on how to dodge calls from reporters. Just got one from Sunset City Standard, and if they're calling, there will be more. My phone is overflowing with notifications, and it's overwhelming."

"Yeah." I practically heard her wince. "If it makes you feel better, I genuinely didn't think the news would hit this hard. But with how beautiful the photos are, and you four being fucking adorable, it's taking off like a rocket."

Sighing, I ran a hand through my hair. "Not helpful, Rin."

"Right. Well, your Alphas probably have someone in place for everything related to Public Relations already. You just have to talk to them, and they'll help. Probably get a different number that's private so you only take calls from the people you give it to. And for the love of god, don't go on social media for a few days."

"Too late. I don't even know where to start with that."

In the background, I heard papers shuffling on her desk. "Whatever they're saying, O, it's bullshit."

"I know." And I did know. But like everything else, it would creep in at the edges. "And I guess I'll talk to the guys about a thing for the magazine."

"I wasn't serious about that. You're going to get enough attention right now. If you ever want to do one? You know I'm game. I'll make it all about you and your flower business and we'll show the entire world what a badass you are. But until then, just try to hunker down and enjoy your pack."

"Husbands," I mumbled. "They're not my Pack. You know this has a clock on it."

"We'll see. And it's only been a couple of days. *Way* too early to be worrying about a clock."

"Probably right."

"I'm so sorry I have to go," she said. "Text our group chat about lunch?"

I nodded. "Will do."

There was already a voicemail, but I didn't listen to it. I navigated back to their posts. Cam's comment section was a mess.

196

My stomach twisted. It was a strange kind of duality, knowing the comments meant nothing, and yet feeling the weight of them. These people didn't know me, or Micah, Rett, and Cam. But they still felt like they could judge me in the same way that Laura had. In the same way most people did. And it was...

It was exhausting.

That's what it was. I knew they didn't matter, and it was easy to say that. But I was so tired knowing that even with friends who loved me, husbands who would protect me, and even employees who had my back, to the world I was still only one thing: fat.

For most everyone, that's all I would ever be.

A fat girl who landed men she didn't deserve. A fat woman whose size was her fault from eating everything in sight. Someone on their way to death with diabetes, because no one could be fat and healthy at the same time. A person who needed to be grateful for any and all attention because it was all she'd ever get.

I hadn't noticed how long I'd been scrolling through the comments on all our posts when Ruby came back out. "They're done and cleared out. So you can see it whenever you're ready."

"Thank you, Ruby."

"You okay?"

"Yeah." I didn't know how to voice what I was feeling, and what I needed was to be in a place that felt safe. "Thank you."

She didn't push it and let me gather my things and head inside alone.

My room was different. Ruby had unpacked things, and now my familiar trinkets were all over the space, making it seem more homey. I still wanted to redecorate a little, but this felt good.

The sliding door to the nest was open, and I crept down the hallway toward it. All the cushions that had been white were now in the jewel tones of blue and purple I'd chosen. There were a couple pops of jade and vibrant pink, but mostly the blues.

Shimmering lights now lined the ceiling, and a quick exploration found a little remote that controlled them. Piles of blankets in the same color scheme sat ready for me to arrange. Silky throw pillows. And in the glassed in area, the crystal light catchers I'd chosen, casting rainbows around the space.

It was beautiful.

Something in my chest settled.

Yeah. I needed this.

I left my phone on the dresser in my closet, where I couldn't hear the incessant buzzing or be tempted to go down the rabbit hole of criticism that was the entire fucking internet.

Following pure instinct, I grabbed a pretty night dress that Ashley had picked out in a deep, forest green. It had no right being so comfortable. I needed to send her a bouquet of flowers after what she'd gone through with Laura.

The pile of blankets held one I couldn't stop thinking about. A purple that matched the stone in my ring, but light enough that it was meant for comfort and not heat. I crawled into the cushions in the glassed in space and arranged pillows around me until I was entirely ensconced.

I watched the waves as the sun continued to fall toward the horizon.

Safe.

Fig 30. Majoram
Meaning: Blushes; Comfort;
Consolation; Joy; Love

CAMERON

$\mathscr{F}$rank McCabe could get fucked.

Talk about the longest deal signing in the history of doing business. It shouldn't have even taken an hour, and it had taken more than four. I swore, every time I called him 'uncle-in-law,' he found one more way to drag it out.

Or he just wanted to be really fucking thorough.

All of us were tired and cranky now, desperately wanting to be with our Omega and not the man who'd made her life a living hell for who knew how many years.

I called her, hoping to hear her sweet, husky voice. It rang out, going to her voicemail. At the moment I was holding the large, soft sweatshirt I'd had Josie get, so Ocean could have something of mine to wear that smelled like me. The idea of her wrapped in my scent did things to me. Like make me hard in the middle of the office.

The call went to voicemail.

"Ocean?" Micah asked.

"She didn't answer."

"If she's in the greenhouse, she might not have her phone," he said.

Right. That would make sense, but something told me it wasn't that.

Everett smiled down at his phone. He'd been doing it at regular intervals. But then again, so had I. When I saw what our wife had posted, I could barely think about anything else.

"So where are we going for the honeymoon?" I asked.

It had just been an idea when I floated it, but now we were going. If the way Everett handed Joseph his ass hadn't made me smile, his declaration about the honeymoon would have.

Everett shrugged. "Maybe somewhere in Europa? I figured we'd ask her where she wanted to go. But I have some ideas. I need to make some calls about them."

"Cryptic bastard."

He didn't even look up as he lifted his middle finger toward me. I laughed and looked back at my phone. The comment caught my eye, because it was gaining replies.

Of course he's feeding her cake. Makes sense. Probably ate the whole thing herself.

For fuck's sake.

"Woah," Micah looked at me, and I realized I was growling, holding my phone so tightly it felt like it might snap. "What is it?"

"Someone whose neck I want to snap making a comment about my picture with Ocean." I swiped on my phone to open an email. "I'm letting the socials team know and making sure they're on top of any negativity. I swear to fuck if I see any actual outlets commenting on Ocean's size or implying that she's somehow not worthy of us, I will lose it."

Micah's face went slack. "Fuck."

It was my turn to be confused.

"We warned her the story was coming out today," he said. "But we haven't added her to the socials team yet. Ocean doesn't have anyone managing things for her. No wonder she doesn't have her phone."

Dread speared through me. It had been one of the things I meant to do today, and we got derailed by Joseph, and then by Frank. I'd known there would be negativity, and I meant to make sure there were people making sure to delete the comments when they saw them.

Normally, we didn't care what people said. They could give us shit and we wouldn't touch anything. Why interfere? But now? The thought of letting people berate *my* Omega was absolutely unacceptable. Not in the spaces we controlled.

"Fuck." I echoed Micah's sentiment and closed my eyes. This was on me. It was my job to make sure she would be protected through this, and I hadn't.

"I'm getting her a new phone," Everett said, not looking up. His face was hard. "It'll be at the house in the morning."

Seeing my face, Micah lifted his phone to his ear. His conversation made it clear he was speaking to our personal public relations manager, telling them we needed help tamping down on the comments on our socials. If Ocean wanted help with hers, we would give it in a heartbeat.

Someone would come at us for censoring people, and to that, I'd do exactly what Everett did and give them the middle finger.

"I—" The words wouldn't come, and I shook my head. "I fucked up."

Micah came to me and put a hand on my shoulder. "It will be all right. We all knew this would happen, even Ocean. Let's just get home to her and make sure she's okay."

"Yeah." I kept a hold on the hoodie, trying to infuse it with scent as quickly as possible.

It took way too long for us to get home, worry swirling in my gut. I headed straight for my room, nearly tearing off my suit. Changing was my first priority, because as soon as I found Ocean, I wasn't leaving her side.

I didn't bother with a shirt, but kept her new hoodie with me as I started looking. Marcela was in the kitchen, finishing up for the day. "Mr. DuPont."

Shaking my head, I smiled at her. All three of us had begged her to call us by our first names for years, but she never did. "Have you seen my wife?"

"Not since this morning."

"Thank you."

One glance into the courtyard told me she wasn't in the new greenhouse. Not in the TV room. The others had the same plan as I did, appearing in casual clothes as I made my way to Ocean's room. "Nothing yet. Maybe she's in the nest."

Micah nodded. "That's what I'm betting."

The door to the nest was open, and she was there. I knew as soon as I stepped into the hallway. My Omega's scent was fresh and strong. So sweet. And yet there was a darker undertone to it. One that I'd smelled before.

The nest looked incredible, but she wasn't in the inside portion.

She was curled up in the glass porch, surrounded by cushions and blankets, just resting, looking out at her namesake. Her expression was blank, and I hoped it was because she was relaxed and not because she was devastated.

"Hey, Sweetheart."

Her eyes met mine. Blank. A hole opened in my chest.

"How do you like your nest?"

"It's beautiful," she murmured.

I leaned against the door. "Can I join you?"

A single, slow nod. The others hung back. In sight, but not crowding her. We'd fucked up today. Protecting her from the press and public opinion should have been our priority. Should have been *my* priority.

Easing myself down next to her, I pulled her close and inhaled. God, she smelled so fucking good, even with that thread of worrying darkness. "I brought you something."

She pulled the hoodie out of my hands and buried her face in it. "This is for me?"

"It's for you, sweetheart. Any time you need me to freshen the scent, let me know."

A small smile, and she held it closer. But she still looked and *felt* subdued. I moved, slowly sliding and arm beneath her so I could pull her closer. "I missed you. Called you a little earlier."

"My phone is in the closet."

I winced. "Yeah. I thought you might have left it. I'm so sorry, Ocean. It's my fault." There were plenty of reasons I could say as to why it fell off my radar. Joseph, Frank, being distracted by the photos themselves, but none of those made it better. "I'm sorry," I said again.

She sighed, snuggled into me, and closed her eyes. "It's okay. I mean, it's not *okay*, what they're saying, but I get it."

"Everett ordered you a new phone. We can change your number, and we'll make sure you have someone to help with your accounts if you want that."

"It's not like I didn't know," she said. "I just wasn't expecting it to be that big, which was silly, I guess. And I need to know what you want me to say."

I felt their presence behind me as they came closer. "What do you mean, little nymph?"

"I answered the phone before I thought about it, and it was a reporter wanting me to comment on our marriage. I just said no comment, but is there something else you'd like me to say about it?"

"You can say whatever you want about it," Micah slipped past all of us and sat down on Ocean's other side. "I don't recommend it, simply because the more you feed the beast, the hungrier it gets. Creatures can't survive when they're starving."

My Omega laughed, leaning on me, and I felt her relax. I released my purr and enjoyed the further melting of her body into mine. "That's the best description of the press I've ever heard."

"It's true."

Tilting her face up, I searched her eyes. "Are you okay?" No need to clarify what I meant.

"I think so. It doesn't *hurt*. Not in the way some of the things Frank and Laura did would hurt. It's just the knowledge that I'll always be that for most people." She put her hand on her chest. "It feels heavy. Hard to explain."

"No, I get it," Everett said. "It's beyond your control, so you can't do anything to stop it, but you're still aware of it. The scope of everything."

"Yeah."

With that, Ocean wrapped an arm around my ribs and pressed her forehead to my chest. An Omega seeking the safety of her Alpha, even if she had no idea how fucking true it was. I locked eyes with Micah and smiled. There was nothing in the world like the high of an Omega trusting you enough to let go.

"Do you have any events or bookings for *Entendre* in the next few weeks, little nymph?" Everett asked. "Anything urgent?"

"No." Her voice was muffled. "Just normal arrangements. Up until now, I've only taken one big event at a time so the staff isn't overwhelmed, since I'm limited in what I can do."

Everett frowned, and I knew what he was thinking. What the hell was she bound by that wouldn't let a fully grown adult run a business? The trust made sense, even if the provisions weren't traditional. But this?

"Would you mind if I looked at the documents for your trust, Ocean?" he asked.

She shrugged. "Sure. Not like it will change anything."

"I'd like to understand it better. I don't think I knew how... extensive it is."

The frustration in her tone was clear. "If you manage to understand it, feel free to let me know. I've been trying to figure it out since I turned twenty-one."

"But you're okay with us seeing them?"

She nodded, and I shifted us so she was lying across my chest. Ocean looked up at Rett. "Why?"

"We want to take you on a honeymoon," I whispered, never letting my purr stop. "Thought we'd leave on Friday."

She laughed, the sound bright and bubbly, like she was coming back to herself. The selfish part of me loved that we could help her do that. "A honeymoon? For a fake marriage? That's funny."

Micah leaned forward and spanked her silk-covered ass playfully, following it up with a kiss. "Keep calling our marriage fake, princess. See what happens. I'll have to take you into the nest and show you how real it is."

Wiggling from the sting, Ocean pushed herself upright and glared at him. But there was no weight to the glare, and he grinned at her. "Fine. But you know what I mean," she said. "We didn't do this to go on a honeymoon. We did it to help you and your company."

"Humor us. Where would you want to go? Anywhere you can think of or have wanted to."

Ocean bit her lower lip, and I wanted to catch it between *my* teeth. Just being near her soothed something deep and primal within me. Yet I wanted more. I needed to be inside her again as soon as humanly possible. Take my turn tasting her.

"Grecia," she finally said. "Everything there looks so beautiful. All the ruins and everything. Flowers are my first love, but I love ancient history too. I've always wanted to go."

Everett moved, kneeling in front of her, bracketing her legs with his. "Then, other than not believing its necessary, do you have any objections?"

"To going on a honeymoon?" Her cheeks deepened with a delicious shade of pink. "No. No objections."

Every part of me craved knowing what had made her blush. And what I could do to make it happen again.

"Then we'll go," he said, slowly leaning in to kiss her. "We leave on Friday. The only thing you have to do is make sure your employees can take care of things while you're gone."

"Clothes?"

"Ruby will pack them, and we'll let her know if we need anything special. And if there's anything you want from your current wardrobe, let her know. If you need anything, I'm sure there are clothing stores in Grecia."

"Probably not many that fit me."

Her statement was a reflex. She hadn't even thought about it, and it was said without any pain. That's how ingrained it was. Something many people would never have to think about, and many others lived with every day.

Everett didn't let it slide. "You're with us, little nymph. If we can't find something, we'll pay someone to sew something for you, we'll do it in a heartbeat. But we have stores everywhere. You don't have to worry about that." He kissed her, stealing away whatever words were on her lips.

"I'll call Geneva in the morning," Micah said. "She'll get it settled."

Ocean looked over at him, and Everett kept kissing her skin. Cheek, temple, jaw, neck. "I like her. She was really nice during the wedding planning."

"That woman can plan anything. She'll have things booked before we can even tell her what we want, and she's right more than half the time." Reaching out, I stole her from Everett and pushed her down on the pillows. "But I think that's enough planning, for now. I need to make up for my fuck up today, and the only thing I've been able to think about all day is tasting you."

There. There was the blush I craved.

And a hesitance I was determined to chase away. "Any objections to this, wife?"

She shook her head no.

My hands glided up her thighs, and there was absolutely nothing underneath this sinful nightgown. "Did you wear nothing underneath on purpose?"

"I wasn't thinking," she said. "Just trying to snuggle up."

"Well then." I settled between her thighs with a grin. "I vote for thinking less. If it leaves you bare like this. Now close your eyes, because I did promise to eat your muffin."

Ocean obeyed, closing her eyes, and I dove deep and tasted heaven.

Fig 31. Prairie Gentian
(Also: Lisianthus, Texas Bluebell)
Meaning: Outgoing nature

OCEAN

*T*he line for Cream Dream, Clarity Coast premiere x-rated waffle store, was long. But it was all right, because Trinity was late, so it gave her a little time to get here.

Isolde's pack was here too, dutifully waiting in line farther back so we could have time together. "You know I wouldn't mind if they were waiting with us, right?"

She laughed and glanced back at them. "I know. But let's be honest, if they were standing next to me I would be distracted, and they would be doing their best to distract me. Not that they're not still trying to do that through our bonds."

My gaze fell on the now-healed bites on her neck and shoulders, bared by her tank top. "What's it like?"

"Overwhelming," she admitted. "But at the same time, it's incredible. Because you never have to guess the truth of what anyone is feeling. It's there in your chest. It doesn't make it easier if you fight, but it does help clear things up faster?"

I nudged her shoulder with mine. "Fighting already?"

"Honestly? No. But we're still feeling our way around each other, and even the guys have to get used to feeling everything too. They can butt heads, but they make up fast."

Longing welled up inside. I wanted that. The closeness and the simple knowledge that you belonged together. No matter what. Alphas and Omegas could bond even if they weren't scent matched, but it wasn't a guarantee in the same way a match was.

"You're really lucky."

Isolde put her arm around my shoulders. "I am, aren't I? But I'm not the only one who can say that anymore."

There was a push and pull inside of me. There was no way to believe I was only a convenience for my husbands. Not anymore. And not simply because they treated me better than almost everyone in my life. I believed they cared. But that didn't mean it was forever. The reality was we'd agreed to a year.

Not even a week and I was already dreading it ending. The truth was, I had a desperate desire to grab this honeymoon with both hands and sink into them and their affection, but I was still terrified.

"Can I ask you something?"

Isolde looked over at me. "Of course."

"When you finally made your choice to go to them and take that chance—"

"You mean when you and Rin bullied me into it?"

"Yeah. That." I laughed, swallowing. "Were you scared?"

209

She blew out a breath. "Fucking terrified. Because I thought it was going to end and I didn't want to fall in love and go through that pain all over again when they left. Thank fuck it worked out better."

I nodded. That was exactly what I felt. "So you'd do it again?"

There was a shift in Isolde's eyes to one of understanding. "Yes. I would. And I think you should. Even if it doesn't work out, take the happiness. Because looking back, even if everything had ended, knowing them and loving them would have been worth it."

"I feel like it will break me," I finally admitted. "They're so great, and so much—" The words cut off, and I shook my head. "After everything else, I feel like loving them and losing them will break me in a way I can't come back from."

"Hi, hi, hi." Trinity ran up to us. Her platinum hair was frazzled and wild, the sun glinting off the hand-chain bracelets she nearly always wore. "I'm sorry. This time it wasn't work, and *fuck*." She heaved in a breath. "I need people to stop getting surprise married, okay?"

Isolde and I stared at her. "Who's getting married now?"

"My dad." She rolled her eyes. "He decided to just throw it out there while we were meeting for a quick lunch. Like it was just another list of things on his to-do list and not an atomic bomb."

I laughed. Not at her, but at the expression. "Honestly, I'm not shocked, Rin."

Rin's Beta father was a free spirit. He was always jetting off on adventures with half of a plan and even less of an idea. That he would get married again, and quickly, seemed fully in line with his character.

"I'm not either." She rolled her eyes. "But I'd still like people to stop springing weddings on me."

"When is it?" Isolde asked.

"I don't know. Hopefully not for a couple of months. I just need things to take a breather for a minute."

"Well," I said, "if I'm in town, then you know I'll be there."

Trinity froze and looked at me with suspicion. "Why wouldn't you be in town?"

I gave in and released my smile. "They're taking me on a honeymoon, leaving this Friday. I've told them they don't have to, but they want to, and I'm going to let them. Even though I'm terrified."

"*Fuck. Yes.*" She pulled me into a hug, jumping up and down. "This is going to be *so* good, O. You deserve it. Let those Alphas pamper the fuck out of you. And fuck the luxury into you. Either way, this is *glorious*. Don't even think about my father's wedding."

The thing about Trinity was she never hid her enthusiasm for anything, and it was contagious. It all seemed so simple when she said it like this, and it made me relax into the idea. "Thank you."

"I expect pictures. And at least one souvenir."

"I can do that."

She stared at me for a long moment, making sure I was serious before she grinned. "Good."

Isolde touched me on the shoulder while Rin dug in her bag. "We won't let you break, O. I promise. Do this for yourself, okay?"

My breath shook, but I nodded. "Okay."

Trinity pulled out her little glucose monitor and pricked a finger to test her blood sugar. It beeped, and she swore under her breath before tossing it back in her purse and slipping the used test strip into the nearby trash can.

"What's up?"

She scrunched up her nose. "Sugars are high today. So I'll get something, but save it for later. I've been really good lately. I don't want to push it too high for no reason."

Fair. Trinity took care of her diabetes ruthlessly so that she could still live normally, be healthy, and have the treats everyone else had without damaging herself. Even if she cursed it sometimes.

A group exited the shop up ahead, letting the line move closer. The same group passed us, girls with cock waffles dripping with white and dark chocolate. The sight never got less funny. One of the reasons we loved coming here. That, and the waffles were excellent.

One of them looked at me and stopped. Then she came right over with a bright smile on her face. "You're that girl, right?"

"I, um," I swallowed. "I don't know. Who do you think I am?"

"You're that girl who married the DuPonts." She fanned herself. "They're so fucking hot."

Tension gathered in my chest. "Yeah. That's me."

She grinned. "I knew it."

Some other people looked over at us, because she wasn't exactly being subtle. But no one seemed to catch on. Small favors.

Was this something I had to worry about now? I didn't think I needed to, even with the press attention. Most of my life I'd been invisible. People didn't look at you when you were my size. Their eyes slid over you to your more attractive friends. To someone more interesting or less offensive to look at.

Being noticed was different.

One of her friends who overheard stepped up next to her and looked at me. She didn't have nearly the same joyous, happy look as her friend. "Why are you here?"

Isolde took the question for me with a laugh and jerked her thumb over her shoulder at Cream Dream. "We love the waffles, same as you, it seems."

The girl frowned, flipping her gaze between me and the store behind me. "Don't you think you should skip it?"

Rin's head snapped over so fast I thought she might break her neck. She stepped in front of me, but she didn't even get anything out before the first girl's mouth dropped in shock. "Connie, what the fuck?"

"What? You said it yourself. She just married some of the hottest Alphas on the planet. Seems like she's the only one getting the good part of the deal."

My friends and girl number one weren't the only ones staring at her in horror. The entire group looked at their friend like she just grew a second head.

"Listen," Trinity said, stepping forward. "First—"

I put a hand on her arm and shook my head. "It's not worth it, Rin. This is probably how it's going to be now."

"Doesn't mean I'm going to sit by and take it. Neither should you."

Smiling sadly, I just shrugged. "If I fought every person who thought that, I'd never get anything done."

The new phone Everett ordered for me arrived this morning. Before they left for work, they sat in the kitchen with me, on the phone with a new public relations woman, Clara, they hired specifically for me. We made new, safer passwords for my accounts that only the five of us would have, and she would do the work of cleaning up the spaces we had control over.

I hadn't thought it was worth the effort, but one look from Everett made me think otherwise. After that, we turned off my notifications, and an invisible weight slid off my shoulders. Until that moment, it hadn't struck me just how heavy that weight was.

It was going to happen. I couldn't stop that unless I became an entirely different person, and that, I couldn't do. My whole life had been a parade of diets and trying to fight my body's inclination to be large. I was healthy. Healthier than plenty of people in my life. My body was just big, and a few years ago I finally stopped doing things that were only going to make me miserable and focused on only that: my health. If that was okay, then I could make peace with the rest of it.

Or at least, I could try. I wasn't quite there yet.

The first girl who approached me looked at her friend with a face full of disgust. "Yeah, that's not okay. Find your own way home. You're not riding in my car if you're going to get that attitude all over my leather seats."

The incredulous expression on Connie's face was priceless. "You're going to strand me here because I'm telling the truth?"

If it's the truth, then why did they marry me in the first place? I wanted to ask out loud, but I didn't. Over the last few days they'd drummed it into me enough. They wanted me. It didn't mean they wanted me *forever*, but they did want me. They chose me.

"No." The girl snorted. "I'm stranding you 'cause you're a bitch, and

I'm not going to be friends with someone like that." She came to me and smiled. "I'm sorry about that. I thought your wedding photos were beautiful, and I hope you guys are really happy."

"Thank you."

She glanced at Connie one last time as she returned to the group of women. "Bye, bitch."

I almost felt bad for the way Connie wilted as the people who had been her friends left.

Almost.

The line moved forward again, and even though there were more curious glances toward us, it didn't spiral out of control. Thankfully.

"Look at that. I didn't even have to get my hands dirty," Trinity said.

"It's good to know not everyone thinks they're slumming it with me," I whispered.

Isolde looped her arm through mine. "I would say the majority don't. The assholes just have a bad habit of being the loudest people in the room."

"Truth," Rin said. "There are half a dozen examples I could give you from work alone."

"Everything okay, princess?"

That voice didn't belong to my Alpha. It belonged to Isolde's Beta, Cade, who frankly should be an Alpha with the presence he had. The two of us shared a look at the nickname. Now that I understood what it meant to be called that, her blush made total sense.

"Yeah," she said, separating from me long enough to lean into his side and accept the kiss on her temple. "Someone being a bitch to Ocean, but thankfully, the bitch's friends took care of it."

Cade looked at me. "You all right?"

"I'll be fine."

He looked at me the way Everett looked at me. Like he saw too much and wasn't quite ready to accept the answer. But he nodded before turning back to Isolde. One of his hands gripped her hair as he kissed her. Soft and slow and...

I knew what that felt like now.

"Enjoy your waffle, princess. The five of us decided we need some studio time later."

My friend gasped softly. "Really?"

"What do you think about that?"

She smiled up at him like he was the only thing in the world, and he did the same. It was beautiful. Her hands curled into his t-shirt. "Yes, Sir."

Cade flicked her nose playfully before he whispered something in her ear neither Rin nor I could hear. But by the way Isolde turned redder than her hair, it wasn't meant for us.

Retreating back to her pack, he left us alone.

"You good?" I asked with a laugh.

"Yup." Her voice was hoarse. "Fine."

Trinity leaned on me with a heavy sigh. "Promise you won't leave me even though you both are in the middle of your happily ever afters."

I didn't protest and say it wasn't going to happen. Because, for the moment, I was going to ignore my fear. In three days we were going on our honeymoon, and I was going to fucking enjoy it.

"Only for the honeymoon," I said. "Then I'll be back."

"Perfect. Now, you should order two waffles just to spite that woman, and you need to tell us everything."

I glanced between my friends. "Everything?"

"Everything," Isolde confirmed. "As much as you're comfortable with."

Making sure no one else in line could hear me, I told them everything.

Mostly.

Fig 32. Laburnum
(Also: Golden Chain, Golden Rain)
Meaning: Forsaken; Pensive beauty

*M*y heart was in my throat as the car pulled up to the Caldwell mansion. My home. Or it used to be. Even when the estate fully passed to me, I wasn't sure I would want to come back and live here.

Yes, there were good memories of me and Mom, and a few of Dad, but there were more bad ones. Even pulling up felt like the world was darkening, even though the sky was crystal clear and blue.

My husbands had been so busy I'd barely seen them, getting ready to take time off for the honeymoon. There was a product launch soon, so they were putting things in place to run smoothly.

I told them we didn't have to go if it meant they had to work so hard, but they insisted. The downside was they hadn't fucked me since that night in the nest porch.

They'd been getting home late, usually after I'd already gone to bed. And yes, the blankets were the same as the ones on Cameron's bed, and I couldn't get enough.

I might have gone to sleep by myself, but I didn't wake up that way. Each morning I woke up with an Alpha wrapped around me, and each morning they purred and held me until we were both ready to leave the bed.

"I cannot wait until we get you out of here," Micah had whispered this morning. "Haven't had enough of you."

I smiled. "I'm right here."

"I know." He groaned. "And the truth is, if any of us let go, we won't leave the house. We won't leave for the honeymoon. We'll just be here, naked, the whole time."

"I'll be honest, that doesn't sound like a bad thing."

"Only a few more hours," he whispered into my neck. "Just a few, and then we're off."

"To Grecia?"

They'd been cagey and mysterious about where we were going. Not that I minded. I hadn't really gone anywhere, and wherever they wanted was fine with me.

Micah narrowed his eyes, but he grinned. "Yes. Not at first, though. We have a couple of other stops."

"That's fine."

"I hope you don't mind. There will be a couple of work related things on the trip, but I promise they'll be fun."

I laughed. "You're the owners of one of the world's biggest clothing companies. I didn't think you could just disappear for a few days with no consequences, even if you guys are working yourselves to the bone."

"The only bone I want to be working is the one in my pants," he said. "And I will. Later." Reluctantly, he sat up.

"Tell me another favorite," I said suddenly. I still didn't know enough about them, and I wanted to know everything. "Other than blueberry muffins."

"And you?"

My cheeks flushed. "Yeah."

"My favorite color is green. A rich, dark green that would look fucking stunning on you, princess. Like that nightgown the other day." He came around and sat on the bed next to me, taking one of my hands.

I loved the tattoos on his forearms. One side had a map, topical lines that outlined the forest where he and his brothers used to play, it morphed into other things that were personal to him. A line of braided ribbons for one of his mothers, line art of an open book, and other hidden secrets. The other side was more colorful, realistic swirls of paint that seemed almost three dimensional. Like chunky oil paint, which I learned was his chosen medium for his own art.

"Anything else you want to know?" he asked.

"Everything."

"Everything, huh?" His smile was soft. "You already know I have brothers. A family that's almost too big, actually. I'm glad that Everett handles the business side of things because I'd much rather hide in my designs than look at a sheet of numbers. Classical music is my favorite. Old movies too. I love living at the beach but visiting the mountains, and muffins are pretty much the only blueberry thing I like. How's that?"

"It's a good start."

Micah leaned down and brushed his lips over mine. "I'll think of more, but I want those same answers in return."

"Okay." I sat up with him. "I'm going over to the Caldwell mansion today, just for a bit. I want to check on the rest of my flowers before I leave. Sally's been doing it, but I'll feel better if I see them myself."

His face darkened. "You'll take a driver?"

"Yeah."

"Good." He sighed. "I'd rather you not go over there alone."

I slipped off the bed and headed to the closet. "I'll be fine. Promise. If I'm lucky they won't even know I'm there. In and out. Like a fat ninja." Following me, he growled low. I raised an eyebrow. "What?"

Micah studied me, assessing. "Just checking."

"For?"

"Whether my wife is talking down about herself. Which isn't allowed."

My smile was real this time. "I wasn't."

"And that's the only reason I'm not spanking you."

A strange feeling flowed through me. It wasn't a bad one. The words didn't trigger any fear or memories. Only curiosity. "Guess you'll have to save that for later," I said, breathless.

He'd cursed before kissing me hard and leaving my room. Now, as I stared up at the house I'd called home for most of my life, the memories I held with them were the reason I could do this by myself. Barely married a week, and they were already helping me.

Isabel opened the door before I could ring the bell. "Hello, dear."

"Hi."

"Do they know you're coming?"

I shook my head. "I'm just here to check on my flowers. Have they given Sally a hard time about it?"

"No, she's stayed out of their way."

That was good. "I won't be long. They're here though?"

"Yes. Don't worry, I won't tell them." She winked at me.

"Thanks, Isabel."

The greenhouse was tucked outside in the garden. Mom loved more than just flowers, so she'd turned a portion of the estate into a beautiful grove. Her refuge away from the hard research she did, and later, from her illness. It was one of my favorite places in the world.

Right now, with the sun bright, the greenhouse looked like a sparkling jewel in the middle of a sea of green. And after using the fingerprint lock, I was relieved to breathe in the delicious scent of the air and see that all the flowers that remained here were thriving. Sally knew what she was doing.

I didn't deserve her. Especially since she was willing to still take care of the flowers while we were gone. Both here and at the DuPont estate. There wasn't enough time to move the rest of them before we left tonight.

Humming to myself, I pulled on a pair of gloves and sank into my routine of watering those that needed it, checking the plants that might need trimming, and taking a look at the hybrid flowers I'd been working on. They were still sprouts without blooms. But by the time we came back they might be ready.

It didn't take as long as normal, because so many plants had been moved to the transitional greenhouse in our courtyard. The ones that were left here were more delicate. Either older, more settled plants that I'd been monitoring for a long time, or a few of the hybrids that I didn't want to risk an atmosphere change while they developed.

When we built a permanent greenhouse at the DuPont Estate, I would move them then.

My smile couldn't be stopped by the time I was done. I hadn't even realized how much I missed spending time here. But also the knowledge that I was leaving and going back to safety and happiness.

Unfortunately, inside the greenhouse was where the happiness ended. Laura stood at the entrance to the house with her arms crossed, glaring at me as I came back. "Why are you here?"

I rolled my eyes. "That's not a real question when you know the answer."

"Your uncle wants to speak with you."

"Can it wait? I need to get back."

"No, it can't." She walked away, fully expecting me to follow. I could simply leave, but given we were flying out of the country tonight, I didn't want either of them to come to our house furious and give Ruby or Marcela any trouble. Besides, there wasn't anything they could do to me now. They married me off, and if they did anything, my husbands would ruin them.

So I followed her.

I missed the light hallways of the DuPont mansion. Everything felt so dark here. It hadn't when Mom was alive. That came later. Laura's taste in decoration was as bad as the rest of her.

My uncle looked up from his desk when we came in. "Ah, Ocean. I need to know the internal quarterly profits for Zenith Incorporated for the last few years, and a breakdown of each of their subsidiaries."

I stared at him. "Excuse me?"

"I told you when we made this deal that you were going to help us take their company for our own. Time to start holding up that part of the bargain."

"It's barely been a week. They're not going to show me internal financial documents, and me asking for them will be a huge red flag." Not that I would ever do it. I knew exactly what I signed, and like I told Laura on my wedding day, I was well aware of my obligations. Which were nothing.

"Find a way. We need those numbers."

"What for?"

Laura snorted. "You don't need to know that."

"Actually I do. You're asking me to perform corporate espionage, which is a crime. So I expect you to tell me what you need the numbers for."

Frank didn't even look up. "Get the numbers first. Then I'll tell you."

"You'll have to wait. We're leaving tonight."

Laura's head snapped in my direction. "What?"

"We're going on our honeymoon. Europa. A few places, though they haven't told me all the stops."

"Your *honeymoon*? You can't be serious."

I stared her down, loving the fact that she had no power. "If you'd like to call my husbands and ask, you can. And like I said before, I need to get back."

Frank sighed, sounding bored. "Fine. When you're back, I want those numbers."

Saying nothing, I turned and left. He had cameras in there, and like hell was I agreeing to that. I never did, and I never would. He could try to force it, but there was nothing he could really do. Starve from the lack of information for all I cared.

Isabel greeted a man coming in the door as I was leaving, and I gave her a wave as I slid into the car. My phone buzzed.

EVERETT

We finished early and have everything ready. Have Jon drive you straight to the airport.

OCEAN

What if I need something from home?

EVERETT

Do you? Ruby said she packed everything you could possibly need.

I'd planned a plane outfit, but I didn't *need* it. I hadn't stayed in the greenhouse long enough to need a shower, and getting out of here faster sounded incredible.

OCEAN

I guess not.

EVERETT

See you soon, little nymph.

Fig 33. Bleeding Heart

(Also: Butterfly Banners, Dutchman's
Britches, Eardrops, Lyre Flower,
Soldier's Cap, Squirrel Corn)
Meaning: Fly with me; Love

OCEAN

$\mathcal{I}$ wasn't sure why I thought we were going to the normal airport to get on a plane. In my head I'd thought we would fly first class in those cool little pods you could shut and sleep in.

What I hadn't imagined—though I should have—was the scene straight out of a movie as Jon pulled the car up on the tarmac near a sleek private jet. "You're sure this is the right place?"

Jon didn't even have to answer, because Everett stepped out of the plane and came down the stairs. But the driver chuckled. "Looks like it."

"Thank you, Jon."

"Have a good trip, Mrs. DuPont."

My breath went short. That wasn't my legal name, but every time I heard it, a little thrill went through me. Because it was an acknowledgment that I belonged here with them. "I will."

Everett smiled. Easy, casual, and just for me. He held out a hand and pulled me in when I took it, kissing me hello. "Ready to go, nymph?"

"I thought we were going to the real airport."

He laughed. "This is a real airport."

I swatted his arm as he guided me toward the stairs. "You know what I mean. I expected first class. Not a private jet."

"Sorry to disappoint."

"I'm not, I—"

We stepped through the door, and... wow. It was gorgeous. All white leather and dark wood, plush chairs outfitted with seatbelts, and what looked like a bedroom in the back. A woman in a uniform poured glasses of champagne in a kitchen area.

Cameron stepped out of the bedroom with a grin. His sleeves were rolled up, hair tousled like he'd been running his hands through it. "There you are."

"Here I am." I sounded awed, and I was. This couldn't possibly be my life. "Where's Micah?"

"Taking a call in the back. He's almost done."

Pulling me down into one of the seats, Cam kissed me. "Now that we're off the clock and we have nothing but time, I'll be kissing you every chance I get. And more."

"Champagne?"

I managed to take my eyes off my husband and look at the attendant smiling down at me. Cameron took one off the tray and handed another one to me. "Thank you, Anna."

He sipped his glass while Everett sat across from us. "Don't get her drunk too soon, Cam."

"I'm not getting drunk," I said, a laugh bubbling up out of me. "Do

223

I lose points if I say I'm not the biggest fan of champagne? Or at least not champagne on its own?"

Turning my face toward his, Cam kissed me. Full and deep and real, his lemon scent mixing with the bite of champagne. "You already have all the points, sweetheart. You can never lose them. And no. Of course not. What would you like?"

"I love the weird mimosas."

"Weird mimosas?"

"Our, Isolde's, Trinity's and mine, favorite brunch place has this amazing mango mimosa. Those, and the peach ones. Though those are technically called Bellinis."

Everett smiled at me. "Anna?" He called. The attendant appeared. "Would you mind turning my wife's champagne into a Bellini, please?"

"Of course, sir." She took the glass from me.

"I don't think we have mango juice, but I'll make sure we have it next time."

Micah appeared, leaning down to kiss the top of my head before heading to the cockpit and speaking a few words. "Buckle up," he said, sitting with Everett. "We're off."

"Where are we going first?"

"A surprise."

I pouted. "Still?"

Anna appeared with my Bellini, distracting me. Now *that* was good. "Thank you."

"How were your aunt and uncle?" Everett asked, far too casually.

"Fine."

He raised an eyebrow, and all I did was take another sip of the drink. Anna disappeared, and Micah stood to help buckle me in. "I can do it."

"Then I wouldn't get to touch you. Or look you in the eye and see if you're lying."

"It's not important. I promise."

He gripped my chin with infinite gentleness and made me look at him. "Everything is important when it comes to you."

Throwing back the rest of the drink, I gave him a look that made him laugh. "Frank really doesn't like the three of you."

"We could have told you that," Cam said. "I doubt his new nickname helps."

"Nickname?"

"Uncle-in-law." He grabbed my hand and kissed the back of it. "He hates it."

I couldn't laugh with his lips so close to my skin. The plane started to move, and all I could think about was that he was so close and we couldn't do anything while the plane was taking off.

"He's trying to screw you over, but I don't know how?"

"Not surprising," Everett said. "He'll have a hard time."

I swallowed. "When he told me about the marriage and offered me the deal, he told me that I was going to help him take over your company from the inside out. But the papers he made me sign didn't say anything about information, and I was never planning on helping him. I swear."

Everett leaned forward on his knees, eyes glinting with interest. "Now that's fascinating. He wanted to use you? What did he ask for?"

"Just numbers of everything for the last couple of years. He wouldn't tell me what they're for. Do you know?"

He shook his head. "I don't. But that actually helps us, nymph, thank you."

"You're not angry?"

Cam looked at me. "Why would we be angry?"

"For even talking to them about it. For pretending like I might help so they would leave me alone."

We started down the runway, the plane picking up speed and launching into the air. My stomach hollowed out, and I ducked into Cam's side. The armrest on these chairs didn't move, big and cushy as they were, but he slid his arm around me as best he could. "You okay?"

"I don't fly much. Takeoff always makes me nervous."

"We've got you," he said, purring. "You're safe, I promise."

No one said anything else until we were well into the air and finally leveling out. A small chime sounded overhead, and they relaxed. Everett unbuckled his seatbelt and came straight to me. "To answer your previous question, little nymph, no, we're not angry. In fact, it's perfect. Because now you can help us, if you want. We would never force you. But there's definitely something going on with Frank, and possibly a man we work with named Joseph. So knowing he wants numbers gives us a little clue. Thank you."

I blew out a breath. Relief I didn't know I needed soothing over me like cool water. "Okay."

He tugged me up and over to the seats on the other side of the plane —the ones that were more like couches and distinctly *didn't* have armrests—and cuddled me into his side. "Micah mentioned wanting favorites."

"I want anything," I admitted. "We're married, and I want to know about you."

"Only child. My favorite color is black. The only artistic talent I have is because these assholes dragged me to a few drawing classes back in college. And my favorite sex position is you beneath me with your legs over my shoulders."

I gasped. That wasn't a way he'd fucked me. Yet.

"You like the sound of that?"

"Yes. But..."

225

Biting my lip, I glanced toward the front of the plane. "The pilot. Anna. They'll hear everything."

"They get paid more than enough money to see nothing, not to mention the NDA they signed."

I didn't doubt it. If there was one thing I knew, it was that the DuPonts paid their people well. But the idea of being heard like that terrified me. I was only just learning how to accept them wanting me. Doing it in front of strangers made something climb up my throat and choke me.

"Take a breath, little nymph."

Air filled my lungs. I hadn't even realized that I'd stopped breathing.

"I miss you," I whispered. "And I do want you."

"But you're not ready for people to hear you have sex?"

I gave him a look that made him chuckle. "I'm still getting used to the idea of *having* sex at all."

"We're hoping you get very used to it. Especially on your honeymoon. I want to know everything you like and everything you want to try. But if you don't want us to make you scream in the air, I won't."

Suppressing a laugh, I leaned into his shoulder. "Don't hate me."

"I could never hate you, little nymph." Then he smirked. "I'll warm you up to the idea, and by the time we're flying home, you'll be ready for the mile high club."

Somehow, I didn't doubt at all that it was true.

Fig 34. Hibiscus
(Also: Queen of Tropical Flowers,
Shoe Flower)
Meaning: Delicate beauty;
Peace and happiness; Rare beauty

*B*lindfolds on my wife were distracting.

I wanted her to be blindfolded for an entirely different reason, and I fully planned on using them in the future. For the moment, I couldn't strip my gorgeous Omega naked and worship her body, even though I was tempted.

She reached out her hands, hesitantly stepping forward, and Cameron caught her. "Are we almost there? I hate feeling like I'm going to trip over something."

"We're not going to let you fall, sweetheart," Cam said. "But yes. We're almost there. I think you're going to love it."

In front of us, the glass doors to the catwalk slid open, and the fresh scent of flowers washed over all four of us. Not just flowers, but over-powering *freshness* and sweetness that encompassed the millions of flowers currently in the building that was, literally, the size of a small country.

Ocean froze and inhaled, mouth parting in shock. "Where are we?"

"Ready to see?"

"Yes."

Cameron kissed her hair. "Take a look."

She pulled down the blindfold and gasped, eyes going wide. "We're in *Almere*? You brought me to Almere?"

Without waiting for confirmation, she darted out onto the catwalk above the warehouse floor, looking down at the flowers being moved by the staff in giant shelves and carts organized for the auction.

The Royal Flower Auction in Almere was the biggest flower auction in the world. Millions of flowers moved through here daily, and even I was impressed by the solid fields of flowers laid out below us.

Everett had the idea to bring her here to see it. There wasn't much we could do except walk around and take in the flowers, peek into the room where the brokers were bidding against each other for the flowers —which was more tame than I'd imagined since most of it happened digitally.

"I'm a bit disappointed the auction isn't people hurling flowers at each other like papers at the stock exchange," I said. "But yes, we're in Almere."

The joy on Ocean's face was palpable. We hadn't seen her look like this before. Pure, unbridled happiness. That was the expression I wanted on her face for the rest of her life. If I could make it happen, I would.

"There's so many," she whispered. "It's so beautiful."

Below us, the scene was like a patchwork quilt of flowers. Squares of different colors arranged and rearranged. I could recognize some, like the roses, but there were many I didn't.

Everett trailed behind us, watching everything with sharp eyes. We had Ocean blindfolded since we got off the plane because this wasn't far from the private airport. There had been photographers waiting for us.

The press was something we dealt with, and we would deal with it. But we weren't going to let them steal Ocean's joy by following us inside. So he was on guard.

I pressed my body into hers against the railing. "What do you want to see, princess?"

"Everything."

Laughing, I brushed her hair away from her cheek and leaned around to kiss it. Just like when she wanted to know about me. "Everything, huh?"

"Mhmm."

"Then we have just the person for that." I pulled her away from the railing and gestured to the tall woman who now approached us. She was a Beta who smiled, and whose light accent lilted. "Welcome to the Royal Flower Auction. You are Ocean?"

"That's me."

"Are you ready for your tour?"

Ocean looked up at me with wide eyes. "Really?"

There wasn't a chance in hell I could resist leaning down to kiss her. "Really. We'll be right behind you. Don't slow down on our account. See what you want to see and take all the time you want."

Her cheeks turned pink, and she smiled. "Okay."

She followed the guide, and the rest of us slowed our pace. Cameron shook his head. "She's so fucking adorable. Well done, Rett."

Everett smiled, but it didn't meet his eyes as we followed our wife, happily chatting with the tour guide. "Aiden texted. Nothing concrete yet. I asked him to add Frank to his list of things to investigate with connections. But we're at that point, so I need to ask you both."

Cam and I looked at him, and I frowned. "Already?"

"It makes sense. If they're looking to take down a company the size of ours, especially not voluntarily, they need to be careful about it. And we do too, but in my opinion, if we get the information, no matter how, it's to our benefit."

I sighed. He meant that the means employed to get what we needed might not be legal anymore. If it came to an actual legal settlement, what we found wouldn't be usable. But... "I say yes, with the usual limits. If we know it exists, we can get it legally if we need it. But I'd rather know how they're trying to screw us. Especially since Ocean is involved now. Not directly, but because we married her. I don't think Joseph wanted us to marry her."

Tilting his head, Cameron's brow furrowed. "You think he had his own candidate?"

"Maybe. If we'd gone to the board and told them 'okay, yes, we'll do it,' then I don't know if they would have just left us to our own devices, given us a timeline, or possibly offered someone they knew as an option."

We turned down a different catwalk, still trailing Ocean. Everett shook his head. "I'm not sure how that would help them. Unless they'd planned to do what Frank is trying to do to Ocean and force that person to provide information. Which, for the record? Violates one part of our agreement with him. If we can prove it."

"I hope that's true," I said. "But in the end, what we really need to know is *why* they were so desperate."

The three of us met while we were in college, and in that way that packs formed, we were drawn to each other. We knew as soon as we met that we were it. There wasn't a question or hesitation. And everything else as far as the company was a bit of skill and a lot of luck. Everett was the business mind, and I was the designer. Cam was the architect behind the *feel* of our brands. He understood people in ways neither Rett nor I did.

Though we were ruthless in going after what we wanted, we didn't want to step on people to do it. Every employee was paid what they were worth or more. Happy employees did more for a company than shiny profit reports ever could. And yes, because we had success, we had enemies. But we didn't make them on purpose.

Even with Frank, though we hated him for what he'd done to our wife, we made the deal fair. Well, mostly fair.

The point was, there were plenty who would love to see us screwed over, or help someone screw us over. But why now and in the last decade? "Why *now*?"

"That's the question, isn't it?" Everett asked.

If we hadn't been so taken with Ocean and the wedding we would have dived into all of this sooner. I didn't regret a single second. But if someone was coming for us, and therefore our wife, it needed to be dealt with.

"Not to mention—" Rett stopped mid-sentence like he'd remembered something.

"What?" Cameron asked.

Everett pulled out his phone and typed something quickly. "Nothing. Well, nothing yet. Just a thought. I'll let you know."

I watched him carefully. If Everett thought something but didn't want to say it until he was sure, it had the potential to be explosive. "Please do."

We trusted each other implicitly and always had. There wasn't anything we wouldn't do for each other, and now, for Ocean.

Like I'd called her name. She looked over her shoulder at us and smiled. It lit up the whole damn room.

I touched Everett's arm. "Everyone's asleep on our side of the world. Let's catch up with our wife."

He smirked and put away his phone. "Don't mind if I do."

Fig 35. Balsam
(Also: Bang seed, Jewelweed,
Pop Weed, Snapweed, Touch-Me-Not)
Meaning: Ardent love; Impatience;
Waiting is difficult for me to do

OCEAN

I'd never seen so many flowers in my life, and I was a fucking florist. The flower auction was exactly as cool and overwhelming as I imagined it would be. And by the time we were finished and piling into the back of a sleek black car, I was exhausted. There'd been some sleep on the plane, but it was still a total time shift.

Curling myself toward Cameron and leaning my head on his shoulder, I closed my eyes. "Where now?"

"Venisi," he said. "It's only an hour by car, and we'll be there for a couple of days. And if you're okay with it—"

"I'm okay with pretty much anything," I said through a yawn.

He laughed quietly. "Good to know, sweetheart. We were going to come here next month for the Extasis product launch. We have a big party, a bunch of celebrities come for the exposure. Red carpet, the whole thing. Since we wanted to bring you here anyway, we thought, why not? We moved it to tonight, but we don't have to go if you don't want to."

Extasis. Their sex toy company. I already had several toys from their line, but I wasn't going to tell them that. At least not until we got home and they saw them firsthand.

My eyes widened. "You're taking me to a sex toy party?"

A low growl came from across the car. "We're taking you to a party *about* sex toys. No one will be using them at the party," Everett said. "Nobody gets to see that but us."

My whole body sizzled with heat. I hadn't meant that, but the possessiveness in Everett not wanting to share me with anyone else made me feel things.

"You were okay with people hearing me," I teased.

His eyes blazed with heat. "Hearing? Fine. Let them listen to me make my wife come. But if they take even one look—"

I smirked. "You'll kill them?"

"You're getting to know me so well."

Shaking my head, I leaned on Cam's shoulder. "Did we pack things for this kind of party?"

"We have people who will meet us with clothes."

"Even for me?"

Cameron turned my face to his. He smiled, but his eyes were serious. "Did you think we wouldn't include you in that? Of course, sweetheart."

The fact that it was a *given*. I sighed and nuzzled further into his shoulder. Then I froze. "This will be the first time we're in public together. Are you sure you want it to be at a sex toy party?"

235

"I very much want it to be that," Micah said. "I don't think there's anything better than showing the world how much we love our wife. And that we can use *any* way to pleasure her."

I was glad the divider was up between us and the driver, because the air was suddenly flooded with my perfume. Cameron pulled me in, holding me. "Sleep, wife. Take a nap before we ravish you in the car and the driver hears us too. We'll be there soon."

How the fuck was I supposed to sleep now when they'd put that vision in my head? But Cam's purr soaked through me, relaxing me so quickly that I slipped under, savoring the sound.

"Wake up, princess."

I opened my eyes to fresh air brushing my cheeks. The door to the car was open, and Micah held his hand out for mine. It hadn't been that long, but fuck, that was a good nap. I supposed jet lag would do that to you.

As soon as I stepped out of the car I forgot all about sleep. The surrounding city was old and beautiful. Cobblestone stretched behind us with tall buildings that looked like they were older than the world, and in front of us spread water that led into the canals of Venisi. An older city that was built on the water, with bridges everywhere and boats with men who would sing to you as you rode.

A boat waited for us, but it was a regular, motorized kind, to get across the substantial water between us and the sea-soaked portion of the city.

Gray clouds pooled in the sky, threatening rain, but it was beautiful and moody and I felt a profound sense of peace. "It's beautiful."

"Yes. It is."

I looked at Micah and found his eyes looking nowhere near the view. They were entirely focused on me. Just me.

He laced our fingers together and gently tugged me toward the boat, Cam, and Rett. "Come on."

Micah held me against the railings as we rode, the spray from the water misting us both. It was a little foggy, the ancient buildings appearing like ghosts out of the air.

The atmosphere was at once eerie and soothing, though that seemed impossible.

As we entered the canals and grew closer to the center, more people walked along the canals. There was press everywhere. Bright lights and a red carpet. "That's where we're going?"

"Close," Micah said. "We're in the hotel behind it."

We pulled up minutes later to a set of stone steps, brightly lit, music playing, and uniformed employees who rushed down to grab our bags and help us out of the boat.

I didn't speak the language, but my head snapped up when Everett spoke fluently. He smirked when he saw me and pulled me to his side. "What's that look?"

"That's just... really hot."

He laughed and kissed me. Not just kissed me, but *kissed* me. In front of all the employees, the people milling around the lobby, and anyone passing by. Everett kissed me like he was going to lay me out on the floor and fuck me right here, and I couldn't bring myself to care about anything other than his lips on mine.

The blended scent of us sharpened. "Fuck," he murmured. "We should have planned the party for tomorrow."

"Lesson learned," I whispered.

"You're exactly right, little nymph. No more parties. We'll only stay home with you from now on."

"*No.*" I smacked his arm. "That's not what I meant."

He shrugged. "But it's what I heard."

I startled as I saw someone taking photos of us together. "Is that all right?"

Everett glared at the photographer, but sighed. "No, it's not. But with the launch, there's not much we can do except get upstairs."

It took me a second to realize it was the same photographer who'd found me at brunch. He'd come all the way here? Since this was a giant launch it was public knowledge. Still, it felt strange to be followed across the world.

None of them seemed worried about our bags, and we were in the tiniest elevator I'd ever seen going to the top floor. It was so small I was pressed up against every one of them, and they took advantage of it. I was drunk on the way they touched me, hands roaming under my shirt and dipping into the waistband of my pants.

"Okay," I finally managed, inhaling them. "I'm starting to agree with no parties."

The elevator doors opened to bustling chaos. There was no hallway. We simply stepped into a luxurious suite filled with people. Racks of clothing and bright mirrors and lights. It reminded me of Ellie's wedding and the time Trinity hired a makeup artist for Isolde.

A woman with wild, curly hair ran up to us. "Good, you're here. Miss Caldwell, we need to get started on your makeup and make sure your dress is to your liking."

"I—"

Everett stepped forward and brought me with him. "We need a moment with our wife. She'll be right back."

They surrounded me on all sides and swept me into the bedroom. Fuck, that was an incredible bed. Huge, it took up half the space, tucked into the walls. No space around the edges. Just a giant place to cuddle and sleep.

The windows were arched, looking over one of the canals. Late afternoon sun finally peeked through the clouds and began turning the water to a beautiful teal. This place was beautiful. Everything with them was beautiful.

"I'm sorry, princess," Micah turned me toward him, Everett stepping in behind me with his hands on my hips. "I didn't realize how chaotic this would be."

I smiled at him. "Why are you sorry?"

"Because this is our honeymoon. This is for you and all of us. And I hate that you might be overwhelmed, and the fact that I can't pin you to the bed right this fucking second."

My laugh bubbled in my chest. Not at him, and possibly because I was still sleepy, but because it was sweet. Looping my arms around his neck, I pulled his lips to mine. The words begging to come out had been a long time coming, but the vulnerability still made my stomach twist with nerves. "I've been hiding for a long time. Because almost everyone in my life— hell, everyone in the *world*, told me I wasn't worth seeing. You've never said that. Not once. All three of you make me feel..."

I shook my head, not able to fully describe how they offered me strength I never knew I had. "Does being seen and photographed and witnessed make me nervous? Yes. I won't pretend it doesn't. Because the world doesn't want to see me. But if you're willing to have me with you while the world sees all of us, then I'm willing to do it."

My breath wavered, the rest of it coming out in a shaky wave. I didn't truly own the confidence of those words, but for them, I wanted to try. They would protect me, and I never knew how much I'd needed it.

"You're incredible," Cam murmured, while he kissed my hair from beside me. Rett squeezed my hips, and Micah stared at me with both awe and pride.

"After tonight," he said, "we're all yours and only yours. Promise. And fuck yes, I want you by my side, princess. I want the entire damn world to see my wife. Our Omega."

I shoved away any dark thoughts about timing and how long we would last. And I opened my mouth to say something that was entirely forgotten when I saw a steamer trunk on the floor near the bed. It wasn't an antique. It was a royal purple color with gold embellishments. "What is that?"

"It's a set of everything from the Extasis launch." Cameron strode over and heaved the lid open, displaying it with a dramatic gesture.

"Holy crap."

It was like a sex store in a box, and everything was that matching purple and gold, looking slick and gorgeous. Anything you could ever want, from the intimidating wand vibrator on the very top of the box to the dildos I spotted peeking out of the bottom.

"See something you like, sweetheart?" Cameron whispered the words in my ear. "Because you, me, and some of these toys seem like a dream come true."

I looked at him and said nothing, just letting the images spin out of control in my mind. Him and me, tangled, and him using whatever he wanted. A shudder worked its way through me, and Cameron grinned. "Unless you haven't used any toys?"

The look I gave him had him laughing. "I'm thirty and up until now have been chronically single. What do you think?"

"I think I like your sassy side, sweetheart. But now I need to know if you have any of *our* toys at home."

"No comment."

The softest growl rolled through the air, echoed three times. "I knew it." Then I was in his arms. "I'm not sure you understand what the thought of you and our toys does to me. Like you were ours before we even knew you."

Something about the way he said that—

A knock on the door, and the same woman pushed the door open a fraction. "I sincerely apologize, sirs, but we're running short on time."

I smirked up at Cameron. "I said no comment. Who knows what the truth is?"

Releasing me, he slid his hands into his pockets and stared at me with unbridled heat. "I'll get it out of you later."

"We'll see."

Those green eyes went dark, like a night forest and a hunter within them. "Yes, we will."

I followed the woman back to the main room, an entirely different set of nerves and anticipation now in my gut.

Fig 36. Hoary Stock
(Also: Ten Week Stock)
Meaning: Bonds of affection; Lasting beauty;
You'll always be beautiful to me

OCEAN

I didn't know how celebrities did it. No one told you how fucking *bright* those lights on the red carpet were. Because holy shit, it felt like my eyes were filled with rainbows because of the lights and all the flashes.

The dress they put me in fit perfectly. Purple, just like the collection, but trending towards violet. A deep neckline showed almost too much cleavage, but with the stunning underwear set they gave me, I was supported, and nothing hurt.

Makeup and hair and dressing was a whirlwind. Now I knew why the woman—I never managed to catch her name—had been panicked. Everything took longer than I thought it would. But as soon as I was ready, I was being swept downstairs with my husbands in tuxedos.

If I hadn't already known what they looked like naked, I would say it should be their daily wardrobe. Because it came second, but it was a *close* fucking second.

What I'd thought was a red carpet was actually a purple carpet, and I was surrounded by famous people. *Literally* famous people. An actress named Clarissa waved at us. Or rather, she waved at my husbands.

I found myself stepping closer to Cameron and taking his hand. He took it a step further and put his arm fully around my waist. I felt his smile as he kissed my temple. It was almost our turn on the carpet. "Jealous, wife?"

"No," I lied. "I know you had a life before me."

Cameras clicked in our direction as he bent to speak in my ear. Chills rose on my skin and my eyes fluttered closed. It wasn't fair how simply being close to them could make me feel like this. The scent of lemons and sugar curled around me like a physical embrace. "I like you jealous. I want you as possessive as the three of us feel. As for Clarissa, she did some modeling campaigns for *Cheria*. That's all we know her from. Nothing more."

Pleasure and relief swirled down my spine, and I stood straighter. "Good."

He laughed quietly.

We were stepping on the carpet when I panicked. "I don't know how to pose."

"You don't have to pose, princess. You're perfect."

Unease rose under my skin, knowing that the pictures very well might not be perfect. But it would be okay. I was who I was, and whether or not a picture was flattering didn't matter to who I was or how they felt about me. They'd already seen all of me.

Micah took my hand and kissed the back of it. A wave of *light* crashed over us with all the flashes. "Ready?"

"No?"

"We've got you," Cam said.

It was only a few feet of distance, but it felt like a mile. The noise was now a physical force, questions being hurled at all sides. This was more than a product launch, I realized. It was a press event of all kinds. A way for the rich and famous to see and be seen and also to advertise for the brand. *All* their brands. Since myself and others were wearing their clothes.

Maybe next time I could design the flowers.

I stopped that thought in its tracks.

"Cameron," someone shouted. A male voice. "You're on your honeymoon?"

"Almost. First, we have to spend the evening with all of you."

A female voice now. "How is marriage treating the DuPont pack?"

In response, Micah lifted my hand to kiss it again, making me smile. The wave of light in response didn't even bother me while I was looking at him. "Very well," he said. "It's going very well."

We moved down the carpet, being asked various things. There were a few questions I caught wind of that weren't kind, and I just as swiftly saw Everett mark them, and I saw someone pulled out by security.

Turning, I reached for his hand, taking a turn with him next to me. "You don't have to kick out everyone who has a mean question."

"Watch me, little nymph."

I tried to squash the smile and failed. "Don't alienate someone who could be good for your business."

Everett snorted inelegantly and glared in the direction the reporter had been taken. "Fuck them. There's not a reporter in the world that can break our business. We don't need them, and I won't tolerate bullies. Or assholes. Every single one of our companies tries to be inclusive. Why should there be reporters here who don't value that?"

Tears blurred my eyes, and I blinked them away. Not only so the cameras didn't see, but so I didn't ruin the beautiful makeup I had on. Rett's face softened. "Are you all right?"

I swallowed. "It's just nice to hear someone say those things and actually mean them. It's not just words with you."

"Never just words." His gaze strayed downward to the way my breasts pushed against the gown, nearly touching his chest. "Have I mentioned how fucking incredible you look?"

"No."

"You do. Micah has the right idea, wanting to design a whole collection for you."

"*Everett.* The three of you have barely been seen with women in the past. Is it because you have a fat girl fetish?"

My husband's head snapped up so fast there were gasps. In a single breath he went from my husband to the predator that had built a worldwide empire. I felt the visceral rage that built under his skin.

Cameron and Micah were with him, searching the crowd for the source of the question. But they kept their rage leashed. Barely.

Everett growled. "Where is he? I'm going to beat him into the ground."

I grabbed his hand and squeezed. "Everett. Look at me." He didn't. "Husband?"

That word got through and he looked down, anger pouring through his gaze. "Don't attack him. Kick him out if you want, but don't touch him. I need you for the rest of the honeymoon, not in a Venisian jail."

One long, harsh breath out through his nose, and he closed his eyes before pulling me closer, gluing me to his side with an arm. "Fine," he muttered, inhaling me. "I'll murder him later."

"No murdering," I teased him.

"Yet."

I just shook my head with a smile. The way he jumped to my defense sent delicious heat shivering along my bones. I loved it, but I also told the truth: I didn't want him to hurt anyone and I didn't want him in jail.

At the end of the carpet there was a reporter with a camera and a microphone. Her dress sparkled in the lights. "Is this normal?"

Rett sounded closer to normal when he spoke. "Is what normal?"

"All of this. It's brilliant, don't get me wrong. But this isn't a movie premiere. All the press and interviews for a sex toy company seems... I don't know."

One side of his mouth pulled up into a grin. "Yes and no. We host events like this when we can because they work. People love wearing things they've seen on famous people, and they love the idea of using the same toys as their celebrity crushes. We've never done one for Extasis, but there's an added benefit to this one."

"What's that?"

"You."

I flushed. "Why me?"

"The whole reason our board wanted us to marry is because they, incorrectly, think we have a branding problem and aren't family friendly enough. So while having this now was convenient for the honeymoon, it's also a big *fuck you* to them. Having our first public appearance with our wife be for a brand that's all about pleasure."

The word *pleasure* rolled off his tongue and made promises that spoke of silk and darkness and shared breaths.

"You're a bit devious."

"You have no idea, little nymph."

243

He pulled me around so I was standing in the middle of the three of them in front of the camera and the lights.

Cameron leaned in and whispered, "Her name is Layla."

"Finally," the reporter said with a laugh. "I think we've all been waiting for this moment tonight. The DuPont pack. Our creators of the hour. Without you, none of us would be here. Congratulations on the launch of the new Extasis line."

Cam was the one who spoke. "Thank you so much. We're happy to be here celebrating with everyone."

"And of course, we can't ignore the news. You're recently married. Congratulations again. And welcome." Her eyes fell on me. "Are you wearing your husbands' designs, Ocean?"

"Thank you," I said, nerves making my voice sound smaller than I wanted it to. "And yes, I am. It's part of the larger *Caesura* collection. My wedding dress was *Caesura* as well."

Micah leaned forward and smirked at me. "She's wearing *Cheria* too, but that's only for us to see."

My face must have turned a cherry red, because Cameron kissed my cheek with a low chuckle.

"Now, I have to ask," Layla said. "There's been a lot of press coverage talking about how this is an unconventional match. There are even rumors that your wedding was hiding a scandal. This is a chance to clear that up. Are the rumors true? What do you say to people who question your relationship?"

"There's no scandal or secret," Everett said. "I know that won't be enough for most of the press, but it's true. They'll keep digging, but there's nothing to find. As for your other question, we're not even going to dignify it with a response. It's offensive, both to us and to our wife."

I froze, but tried to make it seem like the question didn't bother me. "Careful," I faked a laugh and put a hand on Everett's arm. "He's been kicking people out left and right for questions like that."

He smiled down at me. This time, the smile was sharp. The ruthless Alpha who would stop at nothing.

The reporter tilted her head and narrowed her eyes. "But surely you understand the questions? You three are— excuse me, *were*, one of the world's most eligible packs. You've been connected with many women and Omegas over the years, and now you're off the market." The way she let the words hang made the unsaid words read. They were off the market with a nobody, and someone who looked like me.

Should I say something? I wanted to, but at the same time, defending myself against something like that would feel shallow. Like I was desperate.

But I didn't have to. Everett took a small step forward. "Ocean Elise Correa Caldwell is our Omega and our wife. That's the only statement we'll make on the matter." He turned me to him and kissed me the way he'd kissed me in the hotel lobby earlier. Unashamed and deep. His tongue tangled with mine to the point of indecency, showing the world in no uncertain terms what he thought of their questions.

He stole my breath. Owned it. Gave it back before he stole it all over again.

"Thank you, Layla. Enjoy the rest of the event." I heard Micah say it from outside myself. Because everything in me is still wrapped up in Everett.

He pulled me away and into the entrance of the venue, which was still the hotel, just entered a different way into a big ballroom decorated in purple and gold. Fabric dripped down the walls in sumptuous columns, and the lights were low. It gave the room a sensual glow. Light music pulsed beneath the hum of the crowd.

Cocktail tables dotted the space, and waiters circulated with drinks and finger foods. It was everything Laura wanted the Caldwell Gala to be but had never quite gotten right.

The atmosphere was so much lighter in here, despite the darkness of the room. Because we were out of the sight of the press, and everyone was suddenly being more themselves.

Cam and Micah wandered further into the party, but I glanced up at Everett, who still had me glued to his side. "How's my lipstick?"

"Not ruined enough for me."

A soft whine rose from me, and I wasn't sure if it was anxiety or arousal. I felt both. "Rett."

"Fuck, I love the way you say my name, little nymph." But he stopped and looked at me, running his thumb below my lower lip. That single movement didn't have any right to be as hot as it was. "Good as new."

"Thank you. Not just for the lipstick."

I felt more than heard his purr beneath the noise of the room. "If I have anything to say about it, that woman will not report on any more of our events. That was more than inappropriate, and I'm sure whichever outlet she's with, I can't remember, will agree with me."

The sleeves of his tuxedo did little to hide the muscles beneath as I smoothed my hands down his arms. "Promise me one thing."

"Anything."

"Don't get her fired."

He raised an eyebrow at me. "Why not?"

"Because she's not wrong. People are asking those questions. And even if she shouldn't have asked them to *us*, it's still her job."

Everett shook his head slowly, but that tiny smile was still there. "You're too kind, little nymph. Most of these people don't deserve it."

"Please?"

"Anything for my Omega," he murmured, kissing my forehead.

I whined again, craving that nameless feeling I had whenever they claimed me as theirs.

"Now," he said, turning me toward the room, and where Cameron and Micah waited. "I have some people I want to meet our wife."

Fig 37. Aegean Wallflower
(Also: Gillyflower, Goldlack, Revenelle, Violacciocca)
Meaning: Bliss; Bonds of affection;
Enduring beauty; Natural beauty

CAMERON

*T*here were few things I loved more than watching Ocean come out of her shell. Because that shell didn't belong to her. It had been forced on her. Needed to protect the gentle, soft-hearted person she was.

But as she let it drop away, her sweetness drew people to her. She was funny and clever, and even though she wasn't outspoken, she was charming everyone at the party. I watched her from a small distance while she spoke with Clarissa Winters. The actress she'd been jealous of. Now it seemed they were fast friends.

The three of us had seen some looks at Ocean, from a distance, and I marked those people in my head if I knew them. It wasn't *only* about protecting my Omega. It was that people who would judge her purely based on appearance weren't the kind of people we wanted to associate with.

I didn't understand the stigma to begin with, considering I loved Ocean's body and the way it curved. The way it hugged me. Moved with me. Its softness.

Fuck, I needed to stop that train of thought or I was going to cut the party short with her.

Well...

Glancing at my phone, I looked at the time. It had been a couple of hours. More than enough time to have mingled. If Ocean was game, there was a whole trunk of toys waiting for us back in our suite. Micah and Everett could keep the party going and entertain the guests.

If I didn't have my hands on her soon, I was going to go mad. I kept getting little flickers of her scent through the room. Like fireworks in my senses, drawing my gaze always back to her. Each time I caught even the slightest breath, my reaction was the same.

Mine.

She was mine.

My wife.

My Omega.

My forever.

Clarissa put a hand on Ocean's shoulder as her date approached, and she gave a little wave. Good. They were leaving. This was my chance while she was alone. Before someone else could be charmed by her.

I wrapped my arms around her from behind. "How are you, sweetheart?"

"I'm good. A little tired, but good."

"Too tired for me to take you back to the suite and how much I can make you moan with my tongue?"

She froze, then melted, a wave of sharp perfume enveloping us. "No, I'm not too tired for that."

"Good." I spun her in my arms. "Because as beautiful as this dress is, it currently deserves to be in a pile on the floor."

Ocean smiled, her entire face lighting up. "I'm going to tell Micah you said that."

"In this case, even though he's proud of his work, I think Micah would agree with me."

I loved the way her arms slid around me and locked behind my lower back. The fact that she was holding me in public and not looking at anyone else or worrying about what anyone might think, I was so fucking proud of her.

"Are they coming too?"

Giving her a subtle wink, I smirked. "I thought we'd let them keep rubbing shoulders with everyone at the party so I can steal you away for myself. Trust me," I whispered. "They'll be so jealous later they'll take it out on you. In only good ways."

Narrowing her eyes, she stared at me, expression feisty. Like she was deciding whether I was telling the truth. "They won't be mad?"

There was no way to stop myself from kissing her. Thank fuck the room was loud enough to swallow her whimper, because I knew she wouldn't want anyone to hear her. "No, sweetheart. They won't be mad. Just like I won't be mad when they steal you away from me."

Her blush was so pretty. "Okay."

"Okay."

Before anyone else could approach us, I grabbed her hand and ducked for the interior entrance to the hotel. No need to go outside and face the press again. She'd already been an absolute badass today, and now she deserved a reward.

The suite was completely empty now, except for our bags. It was beautiful, but I only had eyes for her. "I'm tempted to tear the dress off you."

Ocean gasped. "Don't do that. It's too pretty for that."

I laughed, but obliged, spinning her and unzipping the back when we reached the door to the bedroom, leaving her only in the lace underwear beneath, and her high heels. The lace was the same rich color as the gown, and it complemented her tan skin. Made it richer. Fuck.

Part of me wanted to do an entire marketing campaign with her and all the photos of her in lace because she was so beautiful, and the other, possessive part of me didn't want anyone but the three of us to see her ever again because she was *ours*.

Backing her to the enormous bed, I pressed her back until she was beneath me in nothing but lace while I was still fully dressed. We would be skin on skin soon enough. First, I needed my fill.

The last time I'd tasted her was now *days* ago, and that was too long.

"You have a favorite toy, wife?"

"Why?"

I hooked my fingers in the waistband of her underwear and drew them down her legs. "Because I want you to think about what I might use on you. As soon as you come all over my tongue."

"We don't have to use those."

Chuckling, I sank to my knees at the edge of them. "We might as well. Since I had them delivered to the room for all of us."

"Really?" Her breathy voice floated to me. I couldn't see her face now. "I thought it was like, something all the guests received."

"They got something. But they didn't get *everything*."

That was enough talking. I slid my hands up her thighs and consumed my wife. The little gasp for breath told me everything. She wasn't used to owning her pleasure or allowing it to show, but that didn't mean she didn't feel it.

However long it took for her to bloom into the curiosity she had and let her personality shine as much during sex as it did during everything else, I didn't care. Because there was literally no better taste on earth than her.

So many layers to her scent and flavor, and it all made sense. In the days leading up to the wedding, when all I wanted was to be closer to her, I looked up orchids. They could smell like anything from sugar to lemons to chocolate to that pure, sweet floral that was in its own league entirely. And every lick into her was another unfurling petal of her, overwhelming my senses.

I needed more. Gripping her hips, I slid my shoulders beneath her legs and pulled her closer, burying my face in her pussy. She liked when I traced her clit with my tongue and then added suction, so I did it until her hips were lifting off the bed and she was *dripping*. All for me.

My groan wrenched out of me as I fucked her with my tongue, unwilling to miss a single drop that could be mine. "I love it when your cunt weeps for me," I whispered the words against her skin. "I need to have you above me so I can just drink from you."

The only response I got was a moan, and I smiled. Her hands fisted in the silky comforter, thighs beginning to shake with her effort to keep them still. Because she was still worried.

"Let go, sweetheart."

I felt her shudder, and then I tasted her orgasm. Drank it down. Didn't release her until her hips were writhing in the aftermath. All I wanted was more.

More, more, more.

Making sure she was supported on the bed, I stripped my tuxedo off while she watched with dazed, pleasured eyes. "Careful, wife. I might get used to you looking at me like that."

"You look like that." She gestured, her arm falling limply to the bed. "Bet your ass I'm going to look at you."

I laughed before bracing myself above her and stripping her of the last of the lace. "You think of your favorite?"

"Depends on what you're planning for it," she said. Ocean's eyes sparkled with fire that I never wanted to leave her eyes.

"I'll let you guess," I said, kissing her softly. "But choose, or I'll choose for you and have you at my mercy."

Her pupils, already blown wide with pleasure, grew more. The tremble in her breath was like a melody. Every little sign she gave me, I was beginning to read like sheet music, and I was happy to be the conductor.

She swallowed. "You choose."

I winked. "You got it, sweetheart."

Fig 38. Avocado

(Also: Alligator Pear, Butter Fruit,
Testicle Tree, Wild Pear)
Meaning: Love; Romance; Sexual Romance

OCEAN

*M*y husband observed the treasure chest of toys with a playful gaze. And I was happy to watch. Because all of him on display, cock hard and ready, muscles shadowed in the dim light like a damn painting? It was a masterpiece.

Not to mention I needed a minute to catch my breath.

I wanted to know what he would choose for us and not think about it. Of course I had my favorites, but being at his mercy made heat flash through me in ways I wasn't entirely familiar with.

"There's so many things in here," he mused, as if he and the others hadn't designed everything in the trunk. "We'll eventually get through all of them."

"Tonight?" I stared at him.

A sinful smirk crossed his lips. "As much as I wish, we might have to save some fun for the others."

Pushing myself up on my elbows, I watched him retrieve something small and place it at the edge of the bed, and then pick up a rectangular box from the chest and turn away, hiding it from me. All that did was give me a view of his glorious ass, which I wasn't complaining about.

Anxiety gripped my chest, the insecurity washing up like a wave. I took slow breaths through it. This incredible Alpha had just been on his knees for me, eating me like he was a dying man and I was his last meal. I didn't need to question whether he wanted me. But seeing him like this, so confident and stark, drew the comparisons between us in my mind.

I didn't doubt them, but I also didn't know if I would ever feel completely at ease in my own skin. But seeing the way they looked at me helped more than they could ever know.

"What did you pick?"

Cameron tossed the toy onto the bed faster than I could see it and caged himself on top of me before dragging me up the bed with him. He moved me so easily. I was already where he wanted me to go before the worry hit my brain, and that alone was enough to have arousal pouring over me like honey.

Big girls didn't get manhandled. Big girls were grateful anyone wanted them at all. Big girls didn't get the same things, like being fucked up against walls or carried. With them, they seemed determined to give me everything, and it didn't seem like a hardship.

"I picked a couple of things. First one I know you'll like." He stared at my lips, seemingly entranced. "Because I know how much you like it when I suck your clit."

My mouth dropped open, making him laugh. Cam kissed me,

tangling our tongues and sucking on mine like he was giving an illustration. "Embarrassed, sweetheart?"

"I— I don't know. I'm just not used to anyone saying things like that out loud."

"Well, I'll say it. We'll all say it. Because I like it as much as you like it. The only thing I like more than that while my mouth is between your legs is dipping my tongue inside you. Fucking you with it. That's where you're the sweetest."

I caught his shoulders, loving the way his body settled on mine. My favorite type of weight. "I haven't tasted any of you."

His eyebrows rose. "You want that?"

Biting my lip, I nodded. His scent was already everywhere around me. Seeping into my senses and my skin. And I wanted him *everywhere*. On my tongue, so I could have one more sense simply be aware of him.

"I'll make sure to remember. Maybe I'll have you sit on my face while you taste my cock."

I snorted. "And crush you?"

Cam leaned down and sucked one nipple into his mouth, making me arch toward him. It felt like so much more than a simple touch. One breast and then the other until I couldn't even keep my eyes open.

"You wouldn't crush me. But even if you did, being smothered by your pussy would be my favorite way to die." His smile told me he was teasing me. "But right now, back to your love of suction."

Leaning back, he retrieved the toy, and it was familiar. I had a similar one. A small, palmable vibrator that sucked at the same time. It was *delicious*.

"I like that look. I'm guessing I chose well. For that one." He guided my thighs apart with his knees and stayed there, reaching for the other thing. And I froze because I honestly had no idea what I was looking at.

"What is that?"

The shape of it was vaguely dick-like, but the clear toy had wavy ridges on it. And little bumps in between those ridges. I'd never seen anything like it.

Cameron leaned over me and brought it closer, the movement bringing his cock right against my entrance, so fucking close to where I needed him to be.

"This, wife, is a cock sleeve."

I stared at it. "A what now?"

He smirked. "We have a bunch of them. Different patterns and colors. Some are thicker than others. Some vibrate. I thought this one would be fun to try. It goes over my cock and makes me thicker, not to mention the texture makes everything feel *different*."

All I could do was look. Now it made sense, but I'd never heard of such a thing, let alone thought about what that would be like.

Cameron ran the side of it over my lips, letting me feel the rippling waves and the small bumps. Goosebumps chased themselves over my skin, bringing my nipples to further hardness and new wetness gathering between my thighs.

"What do you say?" His voice was low. "Want to try it?"

"Yeah."

That slow smile was deadly. Like he knew I'd say yes, but wanted to hear me say it. That smile would devour me whole and make me love every second. "Good."

Sitting back, Cameron fisted his cock, stroking it a few times before fitting himself to the sleeve. A low, feral sound came out of him as he worked it down his shaft. "It feels just as good for us," he whispered, voice straining. "We made sure of that."

Cam was already the thickest of my three husbands. Watching him slowly fucking the sleeve onto his cock was turning me into a living inferno. I'd be rubbing my thighs together if he didn't have me spread on either side of his knees. Trapping me open while he fucked himself in order to fuck *me*.

My body convulsed with need. He was so close, and I needed him. "Cam."

"Such an eager Omega."

"*Please.*"

"Almost there," he groaned, finally pushing the last of his cock into the clear silicone. There was a hole at the tip, and it was short enough not to impede the swelling of his knot. But I wasn't thinking about those things as he pressed the head of his cock into me.

Oh, *fuck*.

He was so much thicker already, and it was enough to have my eyes rolling back.

Slow, even thrusts had him working his way into me like it was the first time. Every ridge and ribbon and bump, I felt. Pressing into me in a hundred ways and all of them were incredible. It was like Everett's piercing, but *everywhere*.

The sleeve made him so thick it was hard to breathe.

"You okay, sweetheart?"

There were no words. How was I supposed to be capable of speech when he was filling me up like this? I could barely think, let alone pretend I was coherent.

Taking my mouth in a kiss, Cameron moved. Rocking his hips and setting off a hundred thousand fireworks in my body and brain. Holy. Actual. Shit.

It was too much. Not enough. I was going to fall into oblivion with this feeling and he hadn't even started yet.

With my eyes closed and my ears filled with my own heartbeat, I hadn't even noticed him pick up the little suction toy. Or the way he'd lifted himself up so he could nestle it against my clit.

"*Fuck*." I gasped the word. Vibration and suction started at the same time, Cameron still fucking me. I'd never used this kind of toy with anything else. The combination of him and the sleeve and the toy sent white light shooting behind my eyes. "Cameron." His name was a whimper. "Alpha."

He smiled with that same easy grace, keeping his pace slow and thorough. Harder now as my body adjusted. All the way in, all the way out, his hips pushing the toy just a little harder into my clit each time, and he fucking knew it.

"You gonna fall apart for me, sweetheart?"

I was. And it was terrifying. Because on the other side of this orgasm, it felt like falling into nothing. Into the unknown. This wasn't three Alphas taking care of their wife. This was him and me. And I knew —I *knew*—that these moments with each of them would absolutely ruin me.

The pleasure spun through me, coiling in my favorite way. That infinite falling sensation just before the orgasm that *almost* felt better. Where you were so close and so far away and you never wanted it to stop. I was trying to hold on to it. The friction of the textured sleeve cock stretching me and hitting deep, and the suction lapping at my clit.

My muscles strained as I held on, clinging to the fraying rope that was my self control.

"Hmmm." Cameron dropped his mouth to my neck. "Naughty Omega, holding on when I'm trying to make you come. You like denial?"

I shook my head. "No."

"You're fighting awfully hard." His hips moved again, forcing the vibrator—which he already held tight against me—closer.

"I—" Dizzy delirium overtook me. "I don't know how to say it."

"Just say it. Whisper it if you have to."

My arms wrapped around his neck and I pulled his ear close, embracing the terror of putting voice to something I'd never said before. Not even sure I fully understood. My breath shook, my control fraying and every moment pulling me deeper. "I like drowning in it. Those moments before you fall. Not like edging. No backing off completely. Just making it last as long as possible. I've gotten good at it."

Cameron groaned, kissing my skin and never stopping moving, though he'd slowed, torturing us both and keeping me on that precipice. "And when you finally come, do you give in? Or do you hold out until you can't hold on and your body gives you no choice?"

A strangled moan was all that made it. It was right there, and I held it back. "The second one."

Lips brushed mine. Once. Twice. A third time. "You want me to make that choice, wife?"

I nodded desperately, and the surrender into his care and trust almost sent me over the edge. Even if it had, it didn't matter, because Cameron moved. Driving into me hard and deep, clicking up the intensity of the vibrator so there wasn't a way for me to resist.

Pleasure came down from the sky like a solid sheet of rain, and for an eternal moment I thought it *would* drown me. I would die of this orgasm because I couldn't breathe couldn't move couldn't think—

Air seared into my lungs on a ragged cry as the tide broke, shattering through me like the finale of a fireworks show. There weren't words, but I was speaking. Voice carried on every shuddering wave.

Cameron tossed the little toy aside, gently pulling out of me. The sleeve on his cock glistened with my arousal, and I missed the fullness of him with it. I missed *him*. I needed him.

"Wait."

His mouth smirked, but everything about him was laced with fire. Alpha. "I'll be right back."

I caught my breath, chest heaving, unable to move my body because it had turned to jelly. I wasn't an Omega anymore. I was a puddle. Cameron had liquefied me.

He was in the chest again, and I didn't bother to look. Whatever he chose, I knew it would be good. More than good. Fucking explosive. After those two orgasms, I could fall into a coma for a full day, if not for the fact that I needed more of him like I needed the oxygen I was inhaling.

Needed his knot more than life.

A small sound drew my attention, and then the dipping of Cameron's weight on the mattress. He settled between my legs, filling me again with ease. He filled me so perfectly it made me ache. Even without this sleeve lining him and making him bigger, he was perfect. This was more.

He watched where our bodies were connected, utterly entranced. "I love seeing you stretched open like this, wife. All because of me. Your cunt is greedy, sucking my cock in even with the sleeve on." Then he chuckled. "I'd better be careful so you don't love the sleeve more than me."

"That won't happen."

"You're so sure?"

"Yeah."

He dropped over me, hands on either side of my head, cock so deep his balls pressed against me. "Good. Because as much as I like fucking you with toys, I like fucking you without them just as much. I like feeling this greedy pussy skin on skin and every little shudder and gasp.

And while we're going to try every fucking toy I can get my hands on, I'll never have enough of you.

"I can't promise there won't be times where I just bend you over because I need you so fucking badly." He punctuated the last two words with hard, savage thrusts. "I plan on claiming you in every way possible. Pulling you out of your shell. Getting you to show us every naughty, depraved inch of you and teach you things you didn't even know you wanted. Got it?"

"Yes."

Cameron grabbed my wrists and pinned them to the bed, thrusting again and rolling his hips so I lit up with pleasure like a fucking Christmas tree. "Do you understand, *Omega*?"

I sank into the instinctual surrender. "Yes, Alpha."

He brushed his lips over mine, not quite kissing me. "Now I'm going to ruin you."

He pushed away, reached, and then I saw what he'd brought with him.

The wand vibrator, a cord draping off the bed to where I assumed it was plugged into the wall. "Ready for this?" One eyebrow rose like a dare.

"I've never used one." I swore it sounded like I'd run a hundred miles.

"Don't worry," he said, pushing the broad head of it directly against my clit. "I'm not going to make you pass out from orgasms this time."

This time.

No more warning. The vibrator thrummed to life and Cameron released everything he'd been holding back. No more slow and steady. This was hard and fast—almost brutal, and it was everything.

There was no control and no way to hold myself in that space we'd talked about. I didn't care. Cameron's cock and the wand shoved me off a cliff into ecstasy. I couldn't see, only feel. I might have screamed, but I couldn't hear enough to tell. The party might be able to hear me.

I came crashing back into my body, gasping. And he didn't stop. Past the orgasm and further, chasing his own pleasure and holding that wand exactly where it was.

The next orgasm crashed into me on the heels of the first. It barely felt like the first one had stopped. I squeezed down on Cameron, and the sleeve on his cock made that feel so fucking different. The shapes and textures pulled out more desperation. Was I even on the same plane anymore?

No one had ever made me feel like this. I didn't know it was *possible*. I faded into the afterglow, though Cam didn't stop fucking me. Using the wand to pull every last shudder from me.

Too much, too much, too much.

Perfection.

Sultry heat rose from somewhere so deep I didn't understand it. It filled the crevices inside me and offered me a different kind of pleasure.

Cam's eyes closed, every muscle tight, every movement sharp and jerky. He was close, but I was closer. That rich, dark heat was rising and I couldn't stop it. It flowed up and up and up—

My husband came with a shout, burying his knot inside me and shuddering. That sleeve was locked inside me too, along with this knot, pressing every divine button. It pushed against the invisible places only an Alpha could reach and gave me one last push. And he pushed with the wand, too. Hard.

Heat on heat and heat pouring out of me. Dripping over my thighs and Cameron's cock. His knot. My whole body shook, and it didn't stop. It was a *release* in a different way, easing me down, bringing me back to earth.

A cracking sound came, jarring, and the vibrations cut off suddenly. It didn't matter. We were both done, trying to find our place in the world all over again.

Cameron set the wand aside, staring at me in awe. It was only after I took a few breaths that I realized that heat was real. Wetness soaked both of us, dripping down onto the bed.

"Oh my god." Horror struck deep and true. "Please tell me I didn't just pee on you, because I won't come back from that."

The smile on my husband's face was blinding. He leaned down and cupped my face, kissing me. "You didn't. But you did squirt all over me, and it might have been the sexiest thing I've ever witnessed."

I stared at him, and he chuckled again before lowering his weight slowly onto me. "I didn't know I could do that."

"I'm fucking glad I know. That's going to happen again. I'm making sure we have waterproof sex blankets for the nest and all the bedrooms by the time we get home."

"But," I breathed, "how?"

Cameron moved his lips over my skin slowly, like he was taking me in. Cheeks, jaw, lips, neck. "I'm not an expert. And from the little I do know, it seems very individual. But with you? I'm guessing I pushed your body so far it had no choice but to release everything."

I didn't hate the sensation. Not at all. But—

"Did I ruin the bed?"

"Doubtful. But we'll have someone come change the sheets."

Covering my face with my hands, I groaned. "That's going to be so embarrassing."

"Why?" Cam laughed when he saw my expression. He moved so one hand slid behind my head, massaging my scalp with his fingers. "I promise you, whatever you think is embarrassing, most hotel staff have

261

seen worse than a post-sex bed. Especially at events like this one. You know us crazy rich people. We go wild."

Jealousy flared so fast it stole my breath. "Anything I should know about?"

"We've never been part of the wild ones, but I've heard stories. And I think any of us would be happy to recreate them with you if you want."

Slow, soothing motions of his fingers relaxed that instinct, along with his purr. "Are you purring to try to change the subject?"

"No. I'm purring because I have my beautiful Omega underneath me, hugging my knot so well it makes me feral. If anything, I want to encourage that possessive streak you pretend you don't have."

"I don't like being jealous."

He smiled, and there was something behind it, but he didn't say it.

"What's a crazy story you heard?"

"Some kind of sex party turned into a food fight. They ordered sundaes to... you know, have fun with. I heard there was whipped cream and chocolate sauce on the ceiling. Something about the curtains being ruined. So a little wet spot is nothing." Then he frowned. "Speaking of crazy."

He reached down to the side and held up the wand. When he pressed the button, nothing happened. It looked like the head was too loose now. Clearly, the toy was dead.

A giggle slipped out. "I'm not the only one you pushed too hard."

"Maybe." He stared at the toy, still shining with me. "It's brand new, so it shouldn't have broken."

"Things happen."

"Things do happen," he agreed. Cameron's knot eased, and he kissed me slowly before moving. He inched out of me, letting my body release the sleeve slowly so it wasn't as jarring. "Come on."

He didn't waste time, and didn't let me protest as he took me into the shower and washed us both before wrapping me in what had to be the softest robe I'd ever felt and bringing me to one of the plush couches to cuddle with me in his own robe.

Even when he called down to have someone from the hotel come, his hands were on me.

"I have questions," he said after he hung up.

"Questions?"

"That feeling you like. What made you figure that out? Did you get good at it because you thought you could only come once before you were done?"

I leaned further into him, thinking about it. "Maybe a little. But I actually love the feeling. It's different than the orgasm. It's in a different *place*. Lives deep in my gut and my chest and my bones. Then it explodes."

"What else are you hiding in there?"

Sleep was starting to cling to the edges of my vision. It had been a long day, and I was still jet lagged. But I didn't want to fall asleep yet. "What do you mean?"

"While that might not be edging, it's in the same realm. Any other kinks we have yet to discover? And to be clear, this isn't a bad thing."

I shook my head. "No."

Cam gave me a look, and I sighed. "I mean, there might be some, but if there is I either don't know it or don't know how to say it. It's hard to focus on kinks or even think about them when you can't even get someone to have sex with you."

With one easy movement, Cameron grabbed my legs and pulled them across his lap, bringing us close. "Well, if you think of any, I want to know."

The door to the suite opened, and I hid my face in Cam's shoulder so I didn't have to see whoever was here to clean up my mess. I'd already admitted to one thing, and more was overwhelming. "One thing at a time," I whispered. "Please."

"Can do, sweetheart. But we're still going to work our way through that box. I'm having another one sent to our next hotel. Including a new wand. And the other kinds of cock sleeves if you want to try them."

Hell yes, I did. If this was what trying new things was like, I would happily try anything with him.

"By the way," I whispered, "you were right."

"About what?"

I pressed my lips together and smiled into his skin. "I do have Extasis toys."

"I knew it." The words were victorious, but all I could do was feel his purr and relax into the soothing rumble. He said something I didn't hear. Because by the time the bedroom was clean, I was already asleep.

Fig 39. Poppy

Meaning: Dreaminess; Eternal sleep; Fantastic
extravagance; Imagination; Oblivion
Meaning (Red): Pleasure
Meaning (White): Consolation; Dreams; Peace

OCEAN

I groaned softly as I came to consciousness. After the orgasms and the jetlag, it was the kind of sleep where you woke and felt like you'd been in a fairytale that lasted a hundred years. Like dark tendrils of sleep still clung to your body trying to drag you down.

Cam had taken me to bed, but I barely remembered it. What I felt now was multiple bodies around mine. Including someone laying on me, arm slung across my legs, head on my ass.

Moving slowly, I peeked over my shoulder and found Everett there. The fuzzy robe I was still wrapped in had been pushed up around my waist, baring my skin. He was naked too, aside from his watch, the symbols tattooed along his spine stretching down his naked back.

Even though I'd been careful, he moved too, one hand squeezing my upper thigh to tell me he was awake.

"Are you using my ass as a pillow?"

A low, dark chuckle. "I love your ass. Is there a reason I shouldn't?" He grazed a bite over my skin. "It was too tempting, little nymph."

He pulled me down to him, away from the pillows and where my hands were still tangled with Cam's. "If you hadn't been dead to the world, I would have shown you."

"I don't remember you coming back."

"You were very *very* asleep. And given the broken toy, I can guess why." Everett kissed me before I could flush with embarrassment. "I'm jealous," he whispered.

"You absolutely should be," Cam said. "Fucking glorious is what it was. Ocean—"

"*Cam.*"

Soft laughter, and I felt the mattress move before his face appeared above mine, nearly pushing Rett out of the way. "You want to keep that a secret, sweetheart? They're going to find out eventually. Even if I have to give them a demonstration."

"Now you have to tell us," Everett said, eyes gleaming.

"If it's that you've agreed to be the star of our next lingerie campaign, then I whole-heartedly agree," Micah said from across the bed. "I'm already designing the collection in my head, princess."

I rolled so I could bury my face in the comforter. "You're all the worst."

Keeping his arms around me, Everett laughed quietly as he kissed my hair. "And you're adorable when you're embarrassed. I love teasing you. But I hope you know that's all it is."

I did know that. It was the reason I wasn't falling apart. Because it wasn't something they meant to tear me into pieces. If anything, their teasing was building me up into things I wasn't ready for. "I know."

He stroked my hair until I stopped hiding my face, peeking up at him. "What's your secret, nymph?"

"I don't think I can say it."

Everett's gaze rose to where Cam sat.

"Ocean squirted all over me while I was using the wand on her, and despite the toy breaking, I can't wait to make her do it again." He sounded so fucking *casual*.

"Fucking hell," Everett growled, the sound morphing into a purr. "I can't believe I was buttering up celebrities and missed that."

"They had to change the bed," I murmured. "Mortifying."

His eyes hardened. "Did they say something? Tell me if they did."

"No." I shook my head. "But they would obviously know."

Soft sounds drew my gaze toward the bedroom door, startling me. Cam kissed my forehead where he looked at me upside down. "Breakfast."

Everett playfully glared at me when I made him let me up, but he did let me, staring at where I fixed the robe. Everything in his gaze told me he'd eat *me* for breakfast. But I was hungry for actual food, and the rest would absolutely come later.

The elevator door was closing as I pushed the bedroom door open. A gorgeous spread of food lay waiting on a table by the windows over-looking the canal, including a giant basket of blueberry muffins and *only* blueberry muffins.

Micah must have asked them for them specifically. I made coffee before taking the muffin and some butter over to the windows. The morning was bright and cheery, the aqua of the water so much more vibrant than it had been when we arrived. This city was beautiful.

If we were not leaving for Grecia, I would ask to stay here and explore. Hopefully we could come back.

For the first time, thoughts of the future didn't fill me with fear, but with hope. Every sign and signal told me they did not necessarily see an end, and even though it was still fast, I found myself hoping it was real and not them merely being kind to their temporary wife.

Boats filled with locals and tourists cut through the water, the latter with cameras pointed at every possible angle. There were even those long black boats tilting to the side and their owners, dressed to the nines, pushing their charges along with poles that reached the bottom of the canals.

Micah came out of the bedroom with a smile. He was dressed, but casually. It still shocked me to see them in clothes like 'normal' people. "What will the press do when they see you in a t-shirt?" I asked.

"Hopefully ask me where I got it, and then I can plug the new

Firefly men's line." He smirked before noting the blueberry muffin in my hand and then the basket of them with no other kinds. "Are they good?"

I moaned in response. It was, quite possibly, the best muffin I'd ever had. And I had no idea whether it was because it was actually good, or because we were in Venisi and I was sparklingly happy so everything would taste good.

He was in the middle of making his own coffee when Cameron came out and started looking at everything. Then he burst out laughing. "Well, they certainly worked fast. I wonder how many papers they had to pulp to print that headline."

"What?"

I hadn't noticed the stack of papers next to the food. Cam brought one over with his coffee and eggs, setting it on the chair beside me. The picture was me. Or rather, Everett kissing the hell out of me while the others looked on, smiling.

BILLIONAIRES RUIN BED WITH NEW WIFE

A quick glance at the article told me there was a vague quote from a 'hotel insider,' followed by a discussion of the event and Everett's declaration about me being their Omega. But I couldn't stop staring at the headline. "Oh my god."

Cam was still smiling in amusement, but his eyes were careful as he reached one hand for mine. "Are you all right?"

"I—" Closing my mouth, I swallowed. "I'm honestly not sure. I'm fine, but shocked, and... why do they even care? Is being with me really that shocking?"

I hadn't realized the source of the hurt until I said it out loud. Because still, after all of this, was them being with a fat woman really the end of the world?

"Hardly," Micah said. "It's just the newness of it, princess. We don't go many places. When we do, it draws attention even if we wished it didn't. The fact that we're boldly offering ourselves to the press with the wedding and now this is an anomaly. The media loves anything that's new and different."

Everett stood in the doorway, glowering. "Though the hotel needs to keep a better leash on their staff if they ever want our business again."

I smiled at that. He would absolutely follow through on the threat. "It's a beautiful hotel."

"There are plenty of beautiful hotels in Venisi, little nymph. We'll find one whose staff doesn't race to reveal its guest's secrets."

The fact that they were acting so normal about it made me feel better. One thing I noticed—the picture was... incredible. The angle it was taken from captured Everett's tongue as it slipped into my mouth. It showed the way my fingers had instinctively gripped the lapels of his tuxedo and the way his fingers curled around the back of my neck.

My dress looked good, and even though the picture was from the side, I didn't feel like it had turned me into a whale. I couldn't remember the last time I'd felt comfortable with a picture fully from the side. But my size didn't matter. What mattered was the look on my face.

Bliss.

The look on his face, too. Like he was lost in me. Micah and Cameron watching with proud smiles. It was a great picture. Finally, I looked back at Cam. "I'm good. I like the picture, and even though I'm not really looking forward to seeing what other people have to say about it, I don't mind."

"It's an incredible picture. And if any of the bullshit gets past Clara, let us know."

"I will."

Everett extended his hand to me. "Last day of hurrying on other people's schedules, wife. We need to get to the plane. But once we're on it and on the way to Grecia, we're all free."

Grecia. Excitement bubbled up in my chest. I wanted to wander streets that were ancient and see ruins that had stood for a thousand years. The fact that it was happening at all was incredible. With them? I shuddered.

"How much time do I have?"

"We'll leave as soon as you're ready."

I left the robe behind in the kitchen, racing to dress.

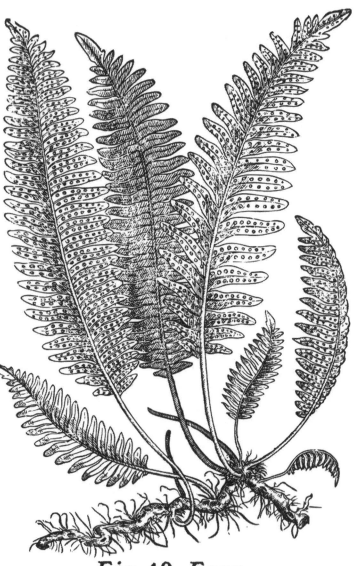

Fig 40. Fern
(Also: Devil's Brushes)
Meaning: Confusion; Wealth

EVERETT

$\mathcal{I}$ watched my wife explore the penthouse of the hotel with an enthusiasm I'd never seen from her. She was *giddy*. Looking in the closets and drawers, exclaiming at all the things she's found.

"There's makeup in here," she gasped from one of the bathrooms. "Like literal, actual *makeup*. It even looks like it might match my skin tone. It's not pale. What fucking magic is this?"

The magic was that this was a five-star hotel. On the coast of the capital city of Grecia, Thenos, with a view of the ocean on one side and a city—complete with the mountaintop ruins in the center—on the other. Though we hadn't been here in years, they knew who we were and did whatever they could to make our stay pleasant. Including getting makeup for our wife, her colors supplied by the makeup artist we'd used for the Extasis event.

A squeal of joy came from the direction of the pseudo-nest in the corner of the top floor suite. I locked eyes with Cameron, unable to contain my smile. Her joy was contagious, and I wanted more of it. All of it.

But Micah knelt in front of the trunk of sex toys Cameron had delivered, frowning. The wand that Micah and I had found broken beside the bed in Venisi was in his hand. "If you pushed that hard, I'm not surprised it broke."

Cam shook his head. "That's the thing. I wasn't pushing that hard. The reason it pushed Ocean over the edge like that is because she was already so blissed out. I ate her out and used this one first." He pointed to the small toy that curled in a swirling shape but used suction and vibration. "It was because her body was so overloaded. I didn't even have it on the highest setting. I might have tried that if it hadn't died."

Now Micah was following his gaze, his expression changing to the one he wore when he dove into a design problem. "More than died. It looked like it had cracked."

"Yeah." Cam nodded, setting the toy on the bed. "The head was like... dangling."

I crossed to him and picked the wand up. We'd seen all the toys before during development and when the designs were approved. This felt different. Lighter than I remembered.

"What the hell?" Cameron muttered, looking at his phone. "Something is wrong."

"What?"

He shook his head, scrolling through something. "I decided to look, just to see. There's already reviews coming in for the new line. It's not

271

just a fluke, the toys are breaking. So far, lots of anger and disappointment. Saying that things feel cheaper than they have in the past. I need to call Trish." Our head of marketing.

"I just thought when I picked this up that it was lighter than I remembered."

Micah took it from me, eyebrows rising. "Agreed. That feels way lighter."

Ocean walked past from where she'd been, heading into the suite's spacious kitchen, clearly on a mission.

If the launch was floundering it needed to be addressed, but this was also our honeymoon. Our wife wouldn't mind if we had to take care of things. She understood. But I wasn't going to let her joy suffer because of this.

"I'm going to take her to the ruins," I said, nodding to Cameron. "Just the two of us. It'll give you a chance to talk to Trish and get ahead of this in any way you can. And—"

"And I'm going to figure out why the hell it feels like the whole body of this is made from heavy plastic and not metal," Micah said.

While he didn't directly design the machines, he was still in charge of their appearance. And he worked closely with the specialists and engineers to create the products. He would know what needed to be asked. Their expertise was more needed here than mine.

Plus, I was selfish.

I wanted to spend time with my wife. Bask in the glow that she gave off simply because she was happy. She was so excited to see the ruins, and though we couldn't see them all today, it was a good start.

"That's a good idea," Cameron said. "I want to go with you, but..."

But a poor launch, especially because of product dissatisfaction, could do irreparable damage to the brand and spread like an infection. No one had to say it out loud. We prided ourselves on being luxury. Especially with Extasis. Yes, our products were expensive, but they were also the best. If people didn't value that reputation? It would crumble into nothing.

Something tingled at the back of my mind, but it was fuzzy. Like a camera that was blurry. An image I was getting, but wasn't quite seeing clearly.

"We'll leave you to it."

I found my wife out on the balcony facing the water that shared her name. The wind off the sea blew her hair back and she closed her eyes, letting the sun warm her skin.

Trapping her against the balcony, I whispered in her ear. "Trying to get back to the water, little nymph?"

"Not yet."

"Not yet." I hummed into her neck. "That's good for me. At least until I get you into the pool later."

She looked over at it. "It's incredible."

The pool was an infinity pool, the edges appearing to fall off into nothing and reflecting the city and ruins back at us.

"Will you be terribly disappointed if I'm the one to take you to the ruins today?"

Ocean turned in my arms. "What do you mean?"

"Is it okay if it's just the two of us?"

I saw the panic enter her eyes. "Is something wrong?"

Sighing, I grabbed her hips and pressed my body into hers. "Business none of us want to deal with. I swear to you when we promised you this trip, we didn't envision it like this."

"It's been pretty great so far. But no, I don't mind if it's the two of us." Her smile turned shy. "I like having time with each of you."

"Do you need anything?"

She wore a flowing white dress that looked like she stepped out of a history book. Her skin looked even darker against the bright fabric, and with the sun shining off her hair... *fuck* she was beautiful.

"Sunscreen. We're going to be in the sun for a while."

"Definitely."

"Okay. Be right back."

I watched her walk away, thoroughly enjoying the way her hips moved and the swish of her long skirt. When was her heat? I needed to find a way to ask without making her think the question was strange, because I was dying to tell her everything.

She was better.

She was *blossoming*.

As soon as her heat revealed who and what we were, I wanted to sink my teeth into her neck and bind myself to her forever. I would have done it that night at the gala if I'd thought she would have believed us and welcomed it.

Finally, I felt the confidence she hid because other people were assholes and made her feel lesser. She was starting to believe us when we told her the truth. That she was beautiful. Hopefully she heard the words we didn't say just as clearly.

That we loved her.

Because I did.

I loved my Omega like nothing I'd ever loved before. Not even Micah and Cameron, though they were my pack and part of my soul in the same way she was. Ocean was the *center* of my soul. She was the center of theirs too. The center of us. We were a triangle and rotated around her like she was the sun and we were the planets.

273

We just needed to be able to fucking tell her.

Shaking my head of the thoughts so I didn't blurt everything out the minute I saw her again, I followed her inside and called for the car. Time to show my wife how beautiful the world was, and the lengths we'd go to just for her.

Fig 41. Smilax
(Also: Bamboo Briar; Sarsaparilla)
Meaning: Loveliness; Lovely; Mythology

OCEAN

y legs bounced in the car, excitement pinging around inside me like a pinball going too fast. We were here. We were *here,* and we were going to see the ancient ruins I'd dreamed about since I was little.

None of it seemed real. Except there was an Alpha next to me, holding my hand on his thigh and rubbing his thumb over the back of my mine and he was *very* real. Which meant I was actually here.

Olive trees line the hills, leaves fluttering in the breeze off the sea. The pale bottoms of their leaves make all that fluttering look like glitter. I opened the car window, and the mild temperature seeped through the air, the fresh scent swirling and melding with Everett's pistachio and almond.

Everett lifted my hand to his lips, kissing the back of it. When I looked at him, those blue eyes searched mine, and he smiled softly. So much more softly than he did with anyone else other than Cam and Micah.

My stomach did a flip.

"I want you to look like this all the time."

"Should I buy stock in sundresses?"

He smiled and shook his head. "I love your dress, but that's not what I mean. You look happy. You *feel* happy."

A shiver of nerves ran along my skin as I bit my lip and took a risk. "I am happy."

Not caring that this wasn't a car with a separation from the driver, Rett pulled me and turned my body so I was draped across his lap and we were chest to chest. "What can we do to keep you this happy, even after we go home?" He cradled me with one arm, using the other to drift his knuckles over my cheek. "Anything."

Keep me.

The words were on the tip of my tongue, and I held them back. We were in a different place now, but the bone-deep terror of it all falling apart still clung to me. I would talk to them, but together, and not today when everything was so beautiful.

"What's going on in there, little nymph?"

"I'm not little," I whispered, just like I had the first time he called me that.

His eyes crinkled at the corners as he smiled. "And I love exactly what you are. But I'm going to keep saying it anyway. Unless you hate it."

I shook my head, breath short in my chest. I didn't hate it. *Definitely* didn't hate it. And he'd just said he loved me. He didn't mean it that way, but I still grabbed onto that little memory and tucked it into the corner of my heart for later.

"Are you going to tell me what will make you happy?"

"I'll think about it."

Everett raised an eyebrow like he didn't believe I needed time. He was right. I didn't. But he smiled. "I will ask again." It was a promise.

The car stopped, and Everett helped me out. There was a crowd of people in front of wrought-iron gates. Which wasn't surprising, considering the ruins were the most popular tourist destination in the city. But we weren't close yet, and no one was being let in past the gates. "Are the ruins closed?"

"Not for us."

Our driver helped us maneuver through the crowd, and Everett showed his phone to the guard at the gate, who let us through. A couple of other people tried to follow, but they were kept back.

Stone paths wound up the hill through all the olive trees, and we were the only people walking those same paths. "Everett, what is going on? Shouldn't this place be *packed* with people?"

He grinned. "Not today."

"Why?"

Weaving our fingers together, he guided us to the larger of the paths in front of us. "Because we wanted you to experience this in the best way possible. Any pictures you wanted. As much time as you wanted. Wherever." He glanced at his phone again. "Looks like there's seven different ruins here. Do you know where you want to start?"

I stared at him before turning back to look at the gate and the crowd behind us. "Did you buy us an hour by ourselves?" The tickets I'd seen were based on time so people could flow in and out of the ruins without them getting overcrowded.

"We bought the whole day."

For a solid second I swore the world went quiet, including my heart. "The whole day?"

"The whole day, little nymph. It's just us."

My jaw dropped, making him laugh. "They let you do that? You *wanted* to do that?"

One arm came around my hips as we kept going up the hill. "There's nothing I wouldn't do for you, Ocean." Then, quieter, "You're our Omega."

My mind still doesn't want to accept the fact that this was entirely for us. Not us, for *me*. This was a fucking national landmark. Scratch that, it was one of the most famous places in the entire world, and they bought out the day so I could see it the way no one else will really get to.

Tears pricked my eyes, and that same sense of happiness flooded my veins. It wasn't about the fact that they'd spent their money. That was incredible, and I wasn't foolish enough to think it didn't matter. It was a fucking privilege to be married to a pack so wealthy. But it wasn't about that, it was that they'd thought about it. They thought about what I'd want and what would make it special, and made a plan.

It wasn't just throwing money at me or substituting that for a connection or an experience. He was here with me. Invested *with* me.

"I thought maybe we'd go over there first." Everett showed me the map on his phone of the far side of the complex with a big, pillared temple. A monument to an old god of fire. "Work our way back here to the main event."

The main hill that rose to our right held the most famous temples and the ruins scattered around the bottom.

"Yes."

He pointed to a small cart resting by the abandoned ticket stand, like it was waiting just for us. "Let's go."

I felt like I was on top of the fucking world. We'd seen almost everything, and now I was on top of a rock near the base of the main attraction, looking at a view of the city that went on for miles. The sea sparkled in the distance, the sun burning down with gorgeous clarity.

I'd had to reapply sunscreen twice, with my husband's very enthusiastic help, but it was that or get burned. I had no plans to spend the rest of my honeymoon nursing a sunburn, so I made sure of it.

Every moment here felt soaked in history, and there was a kind of peace in knowing I was walking the paths so many had walked before. Especially since we were alone. It was so much easier to imagine it as it once was. With the olive trees in full bloom and people journeying to the temples with the flowers they needed to offer, among other things.

History was what brought on my love of flowers in the first place. They were in all the stories, and unlike everything else, I could see them and imagine. Pomegranate flowers and anemone. Apple blossoms and crocuses. Daffodils, also known as Narcissus. And as soon as I realized all the flowers had hidden meanings, I was a goner.

When I turned from the view, Everett was waiting near the stairs, watching me. I swore he'd been watching me more than everything around us, and I didn't hate it.

"Ready?"

"Ready."

More than ready. Excitement tingled at my fingertips. Because this was the best part. Everything was great, but this is what you really came to see.

We walked past the theatres where worshippers had celebrated and spilled wine while watching the gods come to save them at the last second, and up the sun-soaked stairs into the pillars that made me feel small.

The top of the mountain spread out in front of us, the biggest temple right there. *Right there.*

"It's incredible."

"It really is," Everett said.

Statues of beautiful women lined one of the smaller temples. Or the same woman. The goddess this entire place was dedicated to. More than one temple for more than one aspect of who she was.

All I could do was look around me and feel a sense of fucking awe. It was gorgeous and overwhelming, and there was a nameless swell of emotion in my chest. The crux of being in a place that was once the center of everything and somehow felt like it was *still* the center of everything. Like my life was narrowed to this moment, and it all spiraled outward from here.

"Thank you for bringing me here," I whispered.

"Any time, little nymph."

I smiled as we walked toward the entrance of the largest temple. "I think the nymphs probably stayed closer to the water."

Everett nodded. "You're right. While you're here I should call you my goddess."

A laugh burst out of me, but he didn't look like he was remotely joking. "Everett."

"Ocean."

I shook my head, rolling my eyes with a smile, and he didn't move. Suddenly, he swept his arms beneath my legs and scooped me off the ground. "What are you doing?" My voice was a desperate gasp as he climbed the steps to the temple and *inside it.*

Where we were very much not allowed to be.

"*Everett.*" I hissed his name. "We're not supposed to be in here."

He smirked. "Too bad there's no one here to tell us that."

"But—"

"We'll be careful, goddess," he whispered, lips brushing my temple.

I was too shocked to protest about him carrying me. It didn't feel like he was struggling, though he had to be. I swallowed, wiggling a little to see if he'd let me down.

"Afraid I'll drop you?"

"No. Just don't want you to throw your back out or something."

My husband scoffed. "I'm not that old. And contrary to what you believe about yourself, the world doesn't end if I carry you for a little while."

"Everett."

He set me down on an ancient stone that I realized was the altar. I was sitting on the goddess's altar in the middle of the temple. Holy. Fucking. Shit.

Literally holy, some would say.

If my mind hadn't been going in a hundred directions, I might have laughed.

"I will tell you this until you believe it, Omega." He tilted my face up to his. The way he was silhouetted by the afternoon sun made him look like a god, and in this moment, I was his willing sacrifice.

"I do not give a damn what you weigh. I don't care that you're not thin. I don't care that you're not light as a feather. And maybe when I'm old and gray, there will be a time when I can't carry you. If that time comes, then we'll figure it out. But in the meantime, I can, and *will,* whenever I damn well please. Who cares if you're not as small as others? That's never what I wanted nor what I asked for."

"Rett—"

He sank to his knees in front of me, hands dragging down my legs along with his movement. "I know, baby. I know that the world and your family have made you believe the shape of your body makes you less worthy, but it isn't fucking true. Just because they're assholes who don't appreciate your curves doesn't mean your husbands don't." Hands ran up beneath my skirt and the inside of my thighs. Everett ran his nose along my bare knee and inhaled like I'd been made just for him.

Those same hands gripped my thighs, fingers digging into them deliciously and hauling them apart so he knelt between them. There was no way to speak.

"I love how soft you are. I like seeing my fingers press into your skin like your body wants to mold to my will. I love the motion of everything. The ripples in your body while I fuck you."

My breath went short. He hadn't fucked me in long days. Nearly since that first night we all shared.

"Because every ripple means I'm the one causing them. And eventually they'll mean pleasure for both of us." A sly smile crossed his lips. "Should I keep going and tell you how much I fantasize about watching your tits bounce and swing while one of the others takes you from behind and I watch? Or taste them?"

"Everett." This time his name was more a moan than anything else.

"Today this is *your* temple, Ocean Caldwell, and we're not leaving until you've been worshipped like the goddess you are."

My Alpha surged off his knees, capturing my lips with his and taking them without mercy and without restraint. He had me up and turned around before I could draw a full breath, pulling my dress off my shoulders and letting it pool at my feet like I truly was a sacrifice.

An offering.

He shoved the underwear off my hips and let my bra fall. "I've never been more tempted to burn clothing as this underwear, little nymph. Purely so I know you're naked underneath this dress."

But the words were nearly forgotten as he touched me. Every single part of me. Wrapped his body around mine and caressed. Squeezed. Held my breasts in his hands and weighed them with a groan. Kissed my neck, leaving my skin burned with the scruff of his beard behind.

Everett placed his hand in the center of my back and pressed until I bent at the waist, my breasts scraping the stone altar once more.

Then he fell to his knees and worshipped.

Fig 42. Cowslip
(Also: Mad Violets, Shooting Stars)
Meaning: Divinity; Divine beauty;
You are my divinity

OCEAN

*E*verett consumed me like a starving man. It was the first time his mouth had touched me, and he held nothing back. The way his hands gripped my hips and ass, *feasting*.

There was nothing but him. No doubts and no more hesitation. Only him.

Alpha.

And me.

Omega.

I shuddered, pleasure sweeping up over me in a wave that had my fingers gripping ancient stone and offering prayers I didn't remember knowing.

Everett groaned with me, fucking me with his tongue through that pleasure and leaving me spent, but not alone. He'd barely stepped away for seconds when I felt the relief of his skin on mine, the curve of his cock entering and his piercing finding the spot that made the very air sing.

His hands came down on mine on the altar, pinning me in place. I was so full of him and trapped by him in the most carnal way possible. Teeth scraped over the point of my pulse with a delicious threat. An Alpha teasing an Omega with the bite that meant forever.

"You see what you do to me?" he growled in my ear. "You turn me into a madman, Ocean. Not just anyone. *You*. *Your* body." He thrust me into the altar, emphasizing the hardness of his body and the softness of mine. "Your scent. *Fuck*."

I whined, the sound desperate. All I wanted was more of him, because this was everything. It was a sacrifice of a sort. Offering my fears and insecurities and letting them untangle from my soul while Everett fucked them out of me.

They wouldn't go away. They were twisted too deeply for that. But I felt the shift. A loosening of a knot so deep I'd never been able to reach it. And maybe I never would have. Maybe it was too far on my own. Someone had to hold on to me and let me know they would pull me back before I fell.

That was what it took to touch that knot of pain and shame and everything else.

Someone else finding beauty in the things the rest of the world had painted with black and rot.

Three someones.

Everett's piercing hit me deep, and I came. It felt like a breath of mountain air. Like waking up and feeling whole.

"On the altar, goddess."

If I was a goddess, then he *was* the god he'd looked like before. He knelt above me, staring down where I was wrecked and ruined and perfect.

I hadn't quite made it to my back, and he didn't care, lifting a leg over his shoulder to plunge into me once more. This time deeper.

"Holy shit." I tried to hold on and barely could.

Everett's body slapped against mine, every punishing thrust bottoming out inside me. I could do nothing but take it.

Be worshipped.

His eyes devoured me as he took me, showing me exactly what he meant when he told me he liked the way my body moved. There was no shame in this. No embarrassment. Not when my husband's eyes looked like they glowed with the fire of the gods themselves and he'd set the world ablaze with it if he could just keep looking at me.

"One more," he breathed, muscles straining. Sweat lined his body and made him shine in the sun.

He was utterly fucking glorious.

"One more before I offer you my knot, goddess."

Everett moved, flipping me the rest of the way to my back and letting a hand fall to my throat while the other curled my leg around his body to keep me close. And he didn't stop, didn't stop, *didn't stop.*

I held onto his forearm like it was a lifeline. My eyes fluttered closed, and I surrendered to the rising pleasure beneath my skin and the feeling of being the center of someone's world. At the center of the ancient world.

Something raw and primal opened within at being taken like an offering and worshipped like a deity. Yielding power and gaining peace. The orgasm that swam behind my eyes would kill me. I was sure of it. Tear me apart from myself and I wouldn't come back the same.

Relief dropped over me.

Good.

Everett's voice was nothing but a breath in my ear. "Come for me, goddess."

I did.

My screams bounced off the ruins, coming back in shattered echoes. Pure pleasure. Golden, shining, perfect.

My body bowed off the altar into his. Pleasure and pressure. So much I couldn't breathe. It was too much. I was going to pass out because it kept fucking building.

How did it keep building?

Rett came too, his own cries joining mine, knot swelling inside me so fast it shocked us both. He couldn't stop moving, and neither could I, aftershocks still driving us to thrust against each other and savor those electric ripples that followed being knotted and claimed.

We stared at each other until we could breathe normally. I didn't remember when he'd released my throat, but those strong arms braced above my shoulders now, stretching his lean body above mine. Pressed it into me.

Finally, when we could breathe without gasping, he smiled before he kissed me.

"Did you have this planned?" I asked.

"No, actually."

"Really?"

"Really."

I stroked my hands over his shoulders, enjoying the feeling of his knot, and the way his piercing was still pressed exactly where I needed it because of it. "Then what made you—"

"Made me want to fuck my wife?"

Rolling my eyes, I scraped my nails along his ribs purely to see the spark in his eyes. "Made you want to fuck your wife by breaking probably a *lot* of laws."

"You laughed when I called you a goddess," he said simply.

I frowned. "Why would that be the thing that did it?"

"Because it's not about the nickname."

My hands kept traveling because I couldn't stop touching him. "I don't understand."

"Your default is self-deprecation," Everett said quietly. "And it's not always bad. We all do it as a joke. But it's not a joke for you, little nymph. I see it in your eyes. You believe those things, and I hate it. One day I hope I can call you a goddess and have you understand that I'm not saying it because it's silly. Or think that you're less deserving of it than another woman simply because you were born with a body that's bigger than others.

"And what better way to show you that I believe the words I'm saying than illustrating them in the place where a goddess was once worshipped?" His gaze dropped to my mouth.

I had no idea what to say. Fresh tears glossed over my eyes as he kissed me. Thoroughly.

"I'm sorry this world is cruel to you, Ocean. But any time it is, let me remind you how worthy you are."

A laugh hiccuped through a sob. "Keep saying things like that and I'll be a mess."

"I'll happily clean up your mess with my tongue."

I swatted him on the arm before he kissed me again.

And kissed me and kissed me and kissed me until his knot eased and we came apart, though I didn't want to.

Everett didn't let me put my underwear back on, wanting me naked beneath the dress, and it felt right. He tossed them in a trash can on the way back down the hill, making me laugh.

His hand never strayed from mine as we left. We didn't speak. We didn't have to.

I understood now why people came to this place and offered things. No matter if the gods these ancient people worshipped were real, it wasn't about that. It was about the offering. Walking up to an altar as one person and walking away as another.

Before and after.

Closing my eyes, I rooted the sensation in my mind and my memory. My husbands would never let me go back to *before*.

Just like them. There would always be a before and an after, and I could never go back.

Fig 43. Oregano
(Also: Herb of magic)
Meaning: Soothing; Will banish sadness

MICAH

$\mathcal{I}$ woke to the sound of gasping. Ocean sat straight up in bed next to me, chest heaving, staring into the darkness of our hotel room.

"Ocean?"

She startled, looking over at me.

Moonlight drenched the room, and I could see her just enough to make her already dark eyes look nearly black. And she was panicked.

"Are you okay?"

She laid back down slowly, curling toward me. "I think so."

We were in the center of the bed, the others asleep farther away. I pulled her in and tucked her head beneath my chin before arranging the blankets over us once more.

"Just a bad dream," she murmured.

I stroked my hand over her hair and watched the way the faint moonlight shone off of it. The world was made of shades of blue at the moment, and my wife was no exception. I loved the thought of painting her with nothing but those shades that reminded me of her name.

"Want to talk about it?"

She shook her head where it rested in the crook of my shoulder. "I'm better now. I don't get them that often."

Quietly, I began to purr. Not enough to wake the others. Just enough for her to feel and relax into me. Which she did.

When she and Rett had returned from the ruins, they'd found me knee deep in charcoal sketches of anything and everything. Because drawing was the way I could process my thoughts. I couldn't just sit and let them run, and while I'd been digging through the problems with the launch, I'd needed to *think*.

But I hadn't realized how long I'd been doing that, and my eyes were burning when Rett came into the office in the penthouse and dragged me out to go to bed.

My hands still had dark stains on them.

"Then tell me what it was," I whispered. "Please. I want to know."

One of her hands slid over my ribs to my back, holding me closer. A soft sound came from her. She was already nearly asleep once more, but she spoke, voice soft and drowsy. "You weren't there."

My purr faltered for a second before I caught it and brought it back. Emotion flooded my chest. Not some kind of terrible monster or even a nightmare about her aunt and uncle. Not about being mistreated or chased or any of the normal things you would think of for a bad dream.

Just us not being there.

Fuck.

I pulled her more tightly against me. She didn't know yet what we were to her. And though our Omega thought she was hiding it, I saw when she froze thinking about the future. The doubt.

Soon, she would be ready to hear and understand that we weren't going anywhere, and we never would. This was all for her. Every step of this journey had been because of her.

Us not being there was her nightmare.

I felt the same. If I woke in the morning and she wasn't in bed with us, and we found out she was simply *gone*? I couldn't even let the thoughts fully enter because it was so devastating.

Ocean's fear was the last thing I ever wanted. But if this was her fear, I was grateful. It meant she was letting us in. It meant she was starting to believe the things we told her.

I kissed her hair and pulled the blanket further up over both of us. "We're not going anywhere, princess. I promise."

"You're lucky I love the three of you," Raina said. She fixed us with an unimpressed stare through the screen of the tablet. "With anyone else, I would have flipped off the phone and said fuck you till morning."

"Hello to you too," Cameron said with a grin.

She rolled her eyes, clearly already in a robe and pajamas. Her Omega made tea in the background. "What's going on?"

"Believe me, it's the last thing we want to be dealing with right now. But we need you to do some digging and it needs to be kept quiet. It'll be much harder to do while we're out of the country."

I took a pen off the desk and began sketching to keep my thoughts clear. The view of Ocean last night. Dark shadows curving over her, away from where the dim moonlight shone.

When we got back home, I was going to paint it.

Glancing over her shoulder, Raina stood and left her kitchen and closed her office door behind her. "What's going on?"

"Something's wrong with the Extasis launch," Cameron said. "We saw the toys while we were at the party here, and they're not what they should be. They're breaking. They feel cheap. Check the reviews. We're getting slammed."

I dragged a hand over my face, still chasing sleep away since it was early. "We tried to look into it yesterday, but everything shows that it's fine from my end. All the design specs I send over. Everything from the technical team all checks out. But it's not correct."

Raina looked at my packmate. "You're very quiet, Everett."

"There's not much to say."

Tilting her head, Raina studied us. "You think this is part of it? Why the board forced your hand?"

"I don't know." Rett ran a hand through his hair. "I want to say yes, but throwing out an accusation like that isn't going to get us anywhere. And so far, our resources haven't found anything."

Meaning Aiden. The hacker hadn't found any evidence of wrong-doing from any of the board. Which meant that they were being excruciatingly careful, or we were wrong.

"Which is why we'd like you to dig around. If they're doing something, it has to be analog," Everett said. "Or buried so deep our guy wouldn't know the difference. If it is them, I still don't pretend to know why."

Raina's eyes sparked.

"You have a thought?" I asked.

"Maybe."

Cam chuckled. "Care to enlighten us?"

"I'll get back to you. You're right. Throwing accusations won't get us anywhere, and I'd rather come to you with a complete theory than random musings."

Everett sighed and nodded. "We appreciate this, Raina. Cam put some measures in place to curb the bad press. Free replacements for anything broken. A statement saying we're investigating a possible production error. Making sure it doesn't spiral too badly before we can get to the bottom of it."

"Sounds good. I'll start looking at it tomorrow. Try not to let this distract you too much from your vacation. All of you deserve it."

"We'll try," I said.

She winked. "Enjoy your Omega. Now I'm going to bed so I can enjoy mine."

There was no goodbye before the call ended. Cameron laughed. "Bye, then."

It was early morning here, but it was late night back home. I didn't blame her. *Our* Omega still slept in the giant bed, tangled up in the sheets. In a few minutes, we would wake her for the massages we had scheduled at the hotel spa.

But first, "Ocean had a bad dream last night. You didn't wake up, but I did."

"Is she all right?"

I nodded. "She went to sleep right away, but when I asked her what the dream was, she said 'you weren't there.' She was already fading, so I don't know if she'll remember saying that, but I wanted you to know."

The same thoughts I'd had crossed their faces. We would never be glad about her being afraid, but we were infinitely glad that something had shifted.

"I'm not sure I can wait for her to go into heat," Rett said. "I nearly told her yesterday."

"Let's wait until after the trip, and figure out what the hell is going on with this." I gestured to the tablet. "Because once we do tell her, and she knows, we won't want to come up for air."

"Damn right." Cameron smirked. "I promised her we'd use every toy in the trunk. I suppose I can share that with you two."

"Generous, thanks." I laughed.

Everett tapped his phone and looked at the time. "Our appointments are soon."

I glanced down at the little sketch I'd made and smiled as I set it aside. "Then let's go wake up our wife."

Fig 44. Fuchsia
(Also: Lady's Ear-Drop)
Meaning: Taste

OCEAN

*F*or a spa that was underground, this place was surprisingly airy. Water cascaded down one rocky wall in a faux waterfall, and gentle music flowed through the air. The atmosphere was calm and quiet as we sat on couches and waited.

The three of them woke me up not long ago, wrapping me in the robe I currently had on, telling me we had spa appointments we needed to get to.

Up until this point, I hadn't known how much I needed to see my husbands in bathrobes. I'd seen Cam, but the three of them together made me hold back giggles. It wasn't fair for them to look this hot while wearing terrycloth, for fuck's sake.

Everett was filling out some paperwork on a small tablet, and Micah used a napkin to clean what was left of his art mess from yesterday off his fingers. Actually, it looked like there might be more of it than before. Had he sketched this morning? I liked seeing it there. He disappeared into his art the way I disappeared into my flowers.

Catching me staring, he smiled. No words were necessary. He held me last night after I'd dreamt that I woke up and these past weeks were a dream. Nothing had happened, and I was still under Frank and Laura's thumb.

I didn't think I'd ever experienced the type of panic and horror I felt in those false moments. And Micah chased away that fear in seconds.

A beautiful woman with dark hair approached us. "Are you finished?" she asked Everett.

"Yes."

"Perfect." Double checking the paperwork, she glanced at me. Her voice held a light accent. "We're almost ready for you, Miss Ocean."

"A female masseuse, please," Everett said. I raised my eyebrows, and he shrugged. "I don't want another man's hands on my wife."

"I'm sure he would be professional," I said, even as the employee hid her smile before retreating to the reception desk.

Everett helped me up off the couch. "Professional or not. I don't want you naked with another man. Doesn't matter if he's an Alpha, Beta, or Omega. Only us."

I tried to make a sassy face and failed, because the possessiveness spread warmth through me. I liked it far more than I should.

A different woman came out from the entrance to the spa. She was blond, beautiful, and even the bland scrubs she wore didn't hide her body. Her accent matched the others. "Micah?" she called. "You'll be with me today."

The air filled with a growl, and it took me long seconds to realize it was coming from me. *I* was the one growling, and my husbands were all staring at me.

Cameron and Everett grinned. Micah's face was careful as he stepped close. "Princess?"

I had to force the growl to stop. "If I have to have a woman for my service, then you need a male masseuse." Then, lower. "I don't want her touching you."

They were *mine* and if they were going to be possessive, then I was going to be possessive right the fuck back. The thought of Micah on a table with that woman spreading oil and whatever else on his skin made rage creep up beneath my skin.

Micah broke out into a smile and pulled me against his side. "You're absolutely right."

My fear and anger gave way instantly, my instincts soothed. He rubbed my back through the robe. "Sorry," I whispered.

"Never be sorry for that, princess."

Everett was already explaining at the desk. I was sure this wasn't the first time a pack's instincts had come out to play. Massages were intimate, and there was some relief in knowing I wasn't isolated in my reaction.

"I'm sure she's very nice," I said. "And professional."

Micah turned me to him and took his time threading his fingers through my hair and brushing it back off my forehead. "I'm not just agreeing to make you happy, Ocean. I would also be more comfortable. The only hands I truly want on me are yours."

"Okay."

He hugged me, tucking my face into the softness of his robe and purring until my masseuse came for me. A dark-haired woman. Not the blonde one from before. She probably *was* nice, but getting a massage from the person I just *growled* at was an awkward experience I could live without.

That being said, the massage was incredible. I needed to do this more often. Places I hadn't even known were tight felt better. It felt like my shoulders had dropped by inches.

"I'll take you to the recovery room," my masseuse said. "When you're ready."

I groaned. "There's a recovery room?"

"Yes." A soft laugh. "Most feel like you do after their service, and need it."

The room itself was filled with soft chaises and filmy curtains separating them. Snacks and drinks lined a long table, and misters filled with fresh scents made the air pleasantly damp.

Cozy and dim, it was almost like a nest without all the trimmings.

I was the only one in the room at the moment. So I got a cup of water and a plate with some dates and nuts before lounging back on one of the chairs. This might be heaven. It certainly felt that way.

The door opened a few minutes later and a man in scrubs gestured Micah into the room. He smiled when he saw me. "How was yours?"

"Amazing."

"I'm glad."

"Was he... okay?" I asked. "I didn't make it awkward, did I?"

Micah got his own glass of water and some of the chocolate snacks and the dates—which were incredible—before joining me. "No, princess. If you hadn't said something, I would have."

"Really?"

"Really." He sat on my chair, stretching out with me. It wasn't big enough for both of us, but he didn't let that stop him, pulling one of my legs over his. "That's better."

The oil they used for the massages made him smell impossibly *better*. Like it had brought every little bit of the chocolate and caramel to the surface. It made the snacks sitting on the table beside us entirely unappealing. But he was.

Micah watched me carefully in that way he had. He never said more than he had to, and when he did speak, he'd already thought about the words.

"What are you thinking?" I asked him.

"Colors. Your colors."

"My colors?"

He slid his hand over my shoulder, but beneath my robe. "Your skin, hair, and eyes. No matter what light I see them in, they're beautiful. I want to paint you in all the shades of blue from last night." Micah's smile was faint, but his eyes kept traveling over my face like he was trying to memorize me. "Ocean blues."

Need punched through me.

Earlier, before the massages, my instincts had raced to the surface, and they were still there. I was relaxed, he was so close, and even though he hadn't been touched by any woman but me, my Omega still felt the need to stake her claim.

I pulled Micah's robe apart, exposing his chest. "Do you think anyone else but Cam and Rett are going to come in here?"

"I don't know. Why?"

Dropping my mouth to his skin, I followed my instincts, because I needed to touch him and taste him and if I didn't, I was going to lose it.

More. I needed more. This wasn't my heat—they felt different. But sometimes instincts came out of nowhere, and it hurt to fight them.

The robe was in the way. I pushed it off his hips, drawing a path downward with my mouth and tongue. He tasted slightly spicy from the oil with the underlying flavor of him.

My knees hit the tile floor, and he sat up, facing me, and his cock was *right there*. Curving upward, begging me to do what I'd wanted to for a long time now.

"Princess." He placed a hand around the side of my neck, using his thumb to tilt my chin up so I couldn't look away from him. Which was good because his cock was distracting and my mouth watered with the need for it. "Are you sure you want it like this?"

I blinked. All I wanted was him in my mouth. Right now. "What?"

He smiled, eyes warming. "I'll never say no to having your mouth on me. I'd be lying if I said I hadn't thought about it. But your entire life you've been made to feel less than what you are. The sight of you on your knees makes me rock hard, but if anything about being there brings back those memories, or if *you* ever think I wanted you on your knees for that reason, I'll never let you kneel. There are other ways."

Other ways. Those words painted images in my mind as effectively as if Micah were the one painting them. I wanted those other ways. Maybe Cam was right, and I wanted more things than I realized. Maybe learning what it was like to be wanted unlocked more desires.

But no. Not today. I wanted to be right where I was. "I'm sure."

And it needed to happen *now*.

I didn't think any more, leaning forward and taking the tip of him between my lips. Thank fuck for instincts, because I'd never done this before. The other experiences I'd told them about hadn't involved oral in either direction. We hadn't gotten that far.

My eyes fluttered closed because he tasted just like I imagined. *Better* than I imagined. Melted chocolate and buttery caramel. That flavor would only get sharper, and I wanted it.

More of him. I needed more of him.

Micah groaned softly, a hand landing on my hair. But he did nothing other than remind me he was there. Part of me wanted to ask him to show me what he wanted, but the desperation zinging along my spine didn't have time for that.

Later. I would ask him later.

I moved my lips down the side of his shaft, using my tongue until I'd touched every part of him. Nervous energy tingled in my fingertips when I reached his balls. Was this okay? Would he—

"*Fuck.*"

He swore the second my lips touched his skin there.

"Ocean." It sounded like he was barely holding himself back from taking control, and that sent power surging through me. Micah tasted darker here. Addictive.

Sinking into the lust and power, I took his balls completely into my mouth and moaned. I'd waited too long to do this. The only thing that would stop the craving was his pleasure on my tongue.

Moving back to the tip, I sank onto him. There was no way to take all of him in my mouth. Not without practice, at least. But I did what I could, even when my eyes watered and I didn't think I could go further. I *needed* it.

I barely registered the sound of the door opening. Everett's voice was firm. "This room is off limits until we're finished."

Had someone seen me? I didn't care. Not while I was drowning in Micah and wanted him to come. I wasn't Ocean at the moment. I was only an Omega, and I was *desperate*.

Hands peeled the robe from my shoulders, and warmth lined my back. "This is a sight to walk in on, sweetheart," Cameron whispered in my ear.

"Don't stop me."

"I'm not going to stop you. I'm going to help you."

I dove back onto Micah's cock, now savoring the slide of him on my tongue. He felt different now. The angle was harder for me to take and somehow making me want more.

He'd stood up.

Micah now towered over me, looking down with dark fire in his eyes. My gaze slid up every ridge of muscle and the way his arms flexed with need. One corner of his mouth lifted, telling me absolutely everything.

Such a tiny movement didn't have any right to be so *fucking hot*.

Fingers wove into my hair and took control of my movements. But not Micah. Cameron. His voice was low and dangerous. "You told me in Venisi you wanted to taste all of us."

I whined, barely moving my mouth away. "I need it."

"You want to taste *all* of us? Right now?"

Cameron was pressed against me, but I felt the way he'd turned. The way his hand was moving near my hip, stroking his cock in quick, firm strokes.

All of them.

Together.

What had been heat turned into an inferno. Perfume exploded in a cloud around me, and between my thighs I was so wet I might leave remnants on the tile. But I didn't do anything about it. The only thing that would put out the fire was them and the need to claim them after others—no matter who—had touched them.

I nodded, unable to speak with my mouth full. So fucking full.

"You don't have to think about anything, sweetheart. We see how much you need it."

Another whine, my body shaking with it.

Cameron guided me further onto Micah's cock, and I took more than I had before. I let go, and I loved letting go. There was beauty in knowing that they would take care of it. Take care of *me*. Even while I was doing something for them, they had me.

It was the reason I could be on my knees without fear. The reason I wasn't thinking about the way my naked body looked from above or in the awkward position of kneeling. They were safe.

"You're going to let him fuck your mouth until he comes all over your tongue." Cameron murmured the words into my neck, still holding my head where he wanted it, still stroking his cock. Everett was somewhere behind us. I heard the sounds of his pleasure too.

"And when he does, you're going to let that taste you want so badly coat every part of your mouth, and you're going to keep it open, understand?"

I closed my eyes. Brutal arousal had its fist closing around my ribs. It was hard to breathe, and all I wanted was for this sensation and the feeling of them to suffocate me.

"Understand, wife? You keep your mouth open so Rett and I can come between those fuckable lips of yours, and then you'll be tasting all of us together."

A shudder rolled through my whole body. I didn't need to tell him I understood. That was crystal fucking clear.

"Look at me, princess."

I managed to open my eyes and look up at Micah. He took my face in his hands, and something surged. The control he'd wanted and given to me because he knew I needed it. I gave it back willingly, and nothing had ever felt so right.

He took my mouth. Hard, fast, and deep. I didn't know how long it took and I didn't care because the feeling of him fucking me was everything.

"There," he groaned. "There it is."

Micah pulled back and spilled into my mouth. I reached for him and held on because if I didn't hold on to something, I was going to give in and swallow him because he tasted so fucking good and it was all I wanted.

New fingers gripped the top of my hair, turning me. Everett. He barely put his cock to my lips before he came, shuddering. Oh, fuck. I needed—

The richness of him. His almond was the strongest, spinning together with Micah and calming something in me. It was almost perfect.

Almost.

Why was this what I needed?

Fuck the questions and anything else that told me I shouldn't want this. I shoved them aside with any judgment and doubt. Who gave a shit? No one else was here but the four of us, and we were all that mattered.

Cam stepped in front of me and smirked, pressing the head of his cock against my lower lip. He closed his eyes, hips jerking as he came. His cum mixed with theirs, adding the sharpness of lemons and that elusive hint of sugar.

"Swallow us, wife."

I did, without hesitation.

It was the three of them, but so much more than that together. My Omega preened with the knowledge that she'd done that. She'd made them come and taken it all.

Micah lifted my chin once more and ran his thumb along my lip. He quirked an eyebrow with an amused smile. "Feel better?"

"I don't know what came over me."

Slowly, Everett helped me back into the robe before lifting me to my feet. "We don't always have to know. And instincts or not, your mouth is a fucking miracle."

"You haven't even been inside it yet."

He tied the sash of the robe and tugged me into his still-naked body. "*Yet*, being the key part of that sentence."

I swallowed again. The flavor of my husbands still sat heavy on my tongue. It seemed impossible for them to taste so good, or to want to get down on my knees just to have them do it all over again.

Cameron noticed my blush and took my hand, spinning me under his arm with a grin. "Don't go shy on us, sweetheart. That was incredible."

"Not shy, just weird."

He laughed. "Weird?"

"Yeah." I cleared my throat. "That might be the best thing I've ever tasted."

Still slowly dancing me around the room, Cameron started to purr. They all did. "I'm not sure I can tell you how much my Alpha loves that. But I still don't know why it's weird."

"Because I can't *tell* people that," I said, breaking into laughter. "If someone asks me my favorite flavor, I can't just tell them it's my husband's cum." My voice wavered on the last word, and I blushed over my entire body. The embarrassment made sweat begin to gather. I wasn't ashamed of it, and yet I'd been so trained to be embarrassed by everything to do with pleasure and *me* that I couldn't help it.

Everett stole me away from Cam and kissed me. The way he loved to kiss me. Consuming me so deeply I didn't know up from down. Open mouths, tangling tongues, and my every breath belonging to him. "You can tell people whatever you want, little nymph. I would happily tell people that my favorite thing to eat is my wife's pussy. The only reason I haven't is because I don't want you to murder me in my sleep."

"I wouldn't murder you." I smacked his arm.

"No? Then I'm finding the nearest reporter."

"*No.*"

He smirked before unlocking the door. "Our favorites will be just for us then."

My breathing eased. I didn't want them to shout it to the world, but I liked knowing I was their favorite too. "Just for us."

Fig 45. Amaryllis
(Also: Belladonna Lily, Naked Lady, Oxblood Lily)
Meaning: Radiant beauty; Sparkling

OCEAN

I leaned against the edge of the pool, looking out over seeming infinity to the ocean as the sun set. I held my phone well away from the water as the video call connected.

Rin appeared, hair wild, papers spread around her on her couch. She looked exhausted, but her face brightened when she saw me. "Oh my god, hi."

"Hey."

"Are you literally in the pool right now?"

"Not just a pool." I angled the camera so she could see both sides. "An infinity pool."

"You're such a lucky bitch."

"I am, aren't I?"

She looked at me and narrowed her eyes. "What, no protest? No minimizing? Who are you and what have you done with Ocean?"

Laughing, I shook my head. "I'm still me. Just... enjoying all of this."

"You better be. You deserve all of it. And you're glowing. Marriage looks fucking fantastic on you."

It was good that my husbands were still inside the penthouse, because they'd puff up at that idea. Not that I minded them *puffing up*. I was already looking forward to the next time that happened.

"Thank you."

Rin moved a stack of papers to the side with a heavy sigh. There was a weight clinging to her that normally wasn't there. Trinity often covered up any heaviness she had with energy and positivity, which could get her into trouble.

"You okay?"

She glanced toward where she had her phone propped up. "Of course. Why?"

"I don't know. You just seem... down."

A smile that wasn't real. "Just a lot happening at work. You know how it is. And I'm still drowning in all of it because Tracy left behind so much when she died. It's just a lot."

I watched her as she uncapped a highlighter with her mouth and marked something before scribbling with a pen she held in her other fingers. "Okay. As long as you're taking care of yourself."

Her smile, though small, was real this time. "I'm fine, O. You know me. I'm always fine."

"Bullshit."

The screen split and Isolde appeared, out of breath and smiling. "Hi. Hi. Sorry. I'd left my phone up here in the house. Joel called down to Cade."

"Did you just run up the cliff?"

"Yup." She collapsed on the couch. "Terrible idea. Zero out of ten, do not recommend. I need to actually start working out again if I'm going to do that."

Rin looked at the camera and deadpanned. "Please don't throw up where O and I can see it."

"I'm not going to throw up. How's Grecia?"

"Beautiful." I flipped the camera to the horizon so they could see the fading glory of the oranges and purples. We had plenty of beautiful sunsets in Clarity, but there was something about being here, on the other side of the world, that made this one feel different. "I'm never leaving."

Isolde pouted. "That's only acceptable if we can come visit."

"Please do. I'm sure they would send their plane for you. It's more than big enough for your entire pack and Rin."

Grinning, Iz turned over on the couch and leaned her phone somewhere, propping her face up on her hands. "I love this for you. So it's going well?"

"You could say that."

"I already told her she's glowing. And I'm guessing it's from all the vitamin D. I do *not* mean the sun."

My mouth dropped open, and my friends started laughing. I cleared my throat. "I don't know what you mean."

"Yes, you do." Isolde rolled her eyes. "And I'm proud of you. How long are you guys going to be there for?"

Looking over my shoulder, I spotted the three of them gathered around their tablet. They'd been working on something in small bursts, and I'd caught the worry on their faces. As much as I wanted to stay here with them forever, they couldn't just disappear for weeks on end.

"I don't know. They probably can't be gone *that* long, but I'm along for the ride." I looked at Rin. "How are the wedding preparations going?"

"Ugh. Don't get me started. They're fine, but it's Dad. He's doing his off the wall thing. I swear he wouldn't be able to find his own shoes if his housekeeper didn't know where they were, and the wedding is no different."

Trinity's father was a photographer. A famous one at that. But he was also a free spirit, and not always in a good way. If he wanted to go somewhere or do something, he went and did it with very little consideration for anyone else. Trinity included.

I knew it hurt her, but there wasn't much we could do.

"When is it?"

"No idea. They haven't picked a date. I'll let you know, though."

A hand entered Isolde's frame and popped a chocolate in her mouth. She tried not to laugh and failed. "Go away, I'm talking."

"Sure about that, little flower?"

I raised an eyebrow. "Do you need to go?"

"No." She glared playfully off camera. "He can have patience."

"I'm nothing but patience. You know that."

Isolde flushed as Rowan leaned into the frame briefly and kissed her hair. "Let me know when you're finished."

"You both are going to abandon me for dick appointments, aren't you?" Trinity grumbled.

"Not yet."

She snapped her fingers. "While I have you, O. Think you could convince your delicious husbands to comment on the Extasis thing for me?"

I frowned. "What Extasis thing?"

"You don't know? I figured they'd be all over it. The new launch is tanking in a big way. Lots of product issues. They're doing a great job with damage control, but unfortunately they can't control the narrative completely."

Product issues. Was that why the wand broke that night? I'd thought it was because Cam had fully released himself, but maybe not. "I'm sure they're aware, but they've been trying to work as little as possible."

"As they should." Isolde nodded and pointed. "Speaking of?"

In the camera that showed my face, I saw Micah coming out from the penthouse in swim trunks and nothing else. The sunlight was fading, painting him with glimmering orange light.

Trinity groaned. "So unfair. But go have fun, O. We'll see you when you get back, okay?"

I couldn't help but smile. "I'll text you guys later, okay?"

"Have fun." Isolde stuck out her tongue right before I ended the call. And a moment later, water swirled with movement and the heat of a body lined my back. "Was I interrupting?"

"Nothing that won't keep."

Micah plucked my phone from my hand and took it to the safe side of the pool so it wouldn't get wet before returning. He turned me back to the lingering sunset and wrapped me in his arms.

"Is everything okay?"

His chin rested on top of my head and he purred. "Of course. Why wouldn't it be?"

"Trinity mentioned the launch isn't going well and the media isn't great."

Micah sighed. "That's true. We're doing what we can to get to the bottom of it. It's a bit frustrating. But these things happen. Not everything goes according to plan."

"Is that why you and Cam stayed here for the ruins?"

"Mmhmm." He hummed the sound in my ear. "Sorry about that."

I turned in his arms and looped mine around his neck. "Don't be. Everett and I had a good time."

He smirked. "I heard."

Leaning on his chest, I listened to his purr. The sex was amazing, and I loved it. But this too. Just existing in someone else's presence, knowing they were there for you and no one else.

I didn't know how long I'd wanted that, but I did. Desperately. I wasn't going to let the moment pass. We stayed like that until darkness fully arrived.

"Perfect," Micah whispered.

"What?"

Against my temple, his mouth curled into a smile. "Besides you?"

My stomach did a little flip.

"Turn around. I wanted you to see this."

I did, confused. It was the ocean. Unless there was a storm, or the moon, after dark there wasn't much to see.

All along the shore, the water was *glowing*. Bright blue. It came in with the waves, disappearing briefly before appearing again. "What is that?"

"Bioluminescence. Disturbed by the movement of the water."

It was so beautiful. All I wanted to do was touch it. "Can we see closer?"

Micah took my hand and pulled me out of the pool. Our robes were on and sandals were on our feet in seconds. I almost stumbled being pulled behind him, but he didn't let me fall.

None of them would.

"The beach is probably going to be filled with people looking at it," I said.

"Not this beach."

On the ground floor, Micah took a different path out of the hotel and down to the sand. High stone walls cradled the path before flaring outward into a massive chunk of the beach that was blocked off on both sides and entirely deserted. "Is this a private beach?"

"Just for the penthouse."

I shook my head, grinning. "The three of you never do anything by halves, do you?"

"Never."

Up close, the blue in the waves was vibrant and neon. Every wave was a new burst of color. There were tiny bits of green and purple. Almost like the aurora had fallen to earth and come to life in the water.

I tossed my robe and sandals onto the sand and waded in. The ocean was warm, and the minute my feet touched the water, it glowed around

310

them. I leaned down and ran my fingers through it to watch the way the light followed it.

"Look."

Micah came with me, lifting a handful of water up. It glowed in his hand, remaining lit instead of fading. He poured it from one hand over the other. As the water fell, it left a glow behind. Fading, but it stayed for a moment.

"Wow."

This was... incredible.

"I meant what I said this morning," Micah said. "When we get home, I'm painting you."

The darkness meant he couldn't see the heat in my cheeks.

"But that doesn't mean I can't paint you right now."

"What do you mean?"

Another handful of water. This time gently poured over my shoulder. The glow of it reflected in Micah's eyes. "Ocean blues."

What he meant clicked. Paint me. With this. Right now. I opened my mouth, and he didn't let me speak, closing the distance and kissing me. Gathering me up and saying everything he could without words. He was quiet, my husband, but he knew how to *speak*.

"Will you let me paint you, Ocean?"

Both our voices were barely a breath. "Yes."

He curved his fingers into the straps of my bathing suit and pulled them down my shoulders. "I need my whole canvas."

No protests from me. We were entirely alone anyway.

"If I'm naked, you are too," I whispered. I wanted to watch him.

I caught the curve of his smile in the scarce light. "Yes, ma'am."

If this was the way he undressed me, I wanted him to do it more often. With slow, careful attention. Touching the skin he revealed and kissing places I didn't think had ever had a mouth on them. Until I was bare beneath the stars and rising moon, and he was too.

He dragged a handful of glowing water up my side and let it drip. I couldn't help but look down at it, entranced by the way tendrils of light clung to my skin. And another handful that he let fall over my breasts. "Can I take pictures while I paint you?"

I glanced at the pile of our clothes. His phone was on top. I hadn't even realized he brought it with him. "Only for you, right?"

"Only for me," he murmured. "And Cam and Everett."

"Okay."

He kissed me slowly. "Something tells me I'm going to want to paint this too, and I don't want to do it from memory."

I laughed, breathless, as he lifted me off my feet and took me to the sand, right in the middle of the shallow waves of the rising tide. There was something luxurious about being naked on the beach and the feel of the water *everywhere*. Especially when every wave was a wash of crystal light.

"You can't only paint me," I told him. "You have lots of other things to design and paint."

"The design teams have been begging me to let some things drop off my plate. Maybe now's the time I do, and only make paintings of you." Micah ran a wet hand through my hair and leaned over me so I could see his eyes even in the darkness. Stretched out beside me so the water washed over us together.

"Micah—"

"I haven't had nearly enough time to savor you, princess." He tangled our legs so I couldn't escape. Not that I wanted to. "I know I get caught in my own head."

I smiled at that. He did. But I understood it. Because I did it too. I'd be looking at an arrangement of flowers or imagining one, and when I came back to myself, I'd have been staring at the wall for an hour watching a movie in my own mind.

"But I promise you that when I'm with you, I'm with you. Nothing else is in my head."

"I've never doubted that." It was the truth. He was softer than Cameron and Everett. Softer didn't mean less powerful. He was simply quieter. When he was passionate about something, it meant everything. I would never forget his face on our wedding night when he discovered how much pain I'd been in. It was like it had been *his* pain.

He'd taken care of me ever since. Always making sure I was okay. Always checking to see what I needed. I loved him for it, and I hoped he loved doing it. Because it was clear to me it wasn't only because of the corset, Frank, or even Laura. Taking care of people was part of who he was at his core.

"I'm glad," he said. "But I'm telling you because I don't want you to think I have better things to do right now. The only thing in front of me is you. And I plan on taking every advantage."

He shifted so he was over me, pressing me into the sand, fully skin on skin. I reveled in the feeling of being surrounded by him and the ocean and all the pretty blues. The waves reached my waist now, but I felt them creeping upward.

When he sat back, I couldn't quite see his eyes anymore, but I felt them. "You're already a masterpiece, princess. But I'm going to make you *my* masterpiece too."

He did.

Micah painted my skin with glowing handprints and filigree designs. He used the waves to spatter me with starlight and turn it into swirls. There were pictures, but I stopped worrying about them, and just enjoyed him and the waves and the stars above me.

As the moon rose higher and the sky turned brighter, I could see more of him. Everything above the water was lined with silver, everything below lined with blue.

If someone had told me a month ago that I'd be lying on a beach, naked, with my excruciatingly hot husband, and letting him take fully nude pictures of me, I would have laughed in that person's face. But here I was. And all I wanted was for this to last. The peace and safety I felt, because I knew that Micah only wanted to make me beautiful. And it didn't matter what anyone else thought.

"Come here."

He helped me to my feet and pulled me deeper into the water. Deeper, until the water was around my breasts, making them float. The first time I ever went skinny dipping, it was a horrifying and comical realization that boobs floated. Now, every movement laced them with that electric glow, and Micah couldn't keep his eyes off them.

Even when he lifted me, and wrapped my legs around him. I didn't mind this. No worries and no weight. Just the two of us and no words needed.

I wasn't sure if he kissed me or I kissed him, only that we were kissing each other and if we kept going like this, I would never need air. Micah kissed differently than my other husbands. He kissed me *slowly*. Pulled my tongue into his mouth so he could explore every part of mine. Stole my breath and gave me back his. Deepened it until I wasn't sure where we separated or which way was up from down.

Micah held me to him, never letting me back off or ease up, just kissing me like he would do it until the world ended. And maybe a bit longer, even then.

It felt like he was memorizing every part of me. If my husband wanted to make me in sculpture, he would be able to do it from memory by the time the night was over.

I gasped when we finally broke apart. I leaned my head against his, hauling in breath even though I would rather be breathing everything that was this man.

This Alpha.

"Are you all right?"

"I'm so good." I managed a laugh. Down below my ass, I felt his cock, hard. I teased him. "Are *you* all right?"

"I've been thinking about your mouth all fucking day."

"Really?"

He laughed low, sparking heat deep in my gut. "Absolutely. The fantasies I have, Ocean."

"What are they?"

"Hmm, I don't know if you're ready for them."

I tilted my head and frowned. "Why?"

"We don't want to scare you."

"You think I'm that easily scared?"

A grin, and he turned us in the water so I was looking out over the horizon and toward the moon. "Maybe not. But there's no way to describe how much we want. How deep it goes. I won't pretend I'm not obsessed, and I won't deny that I want to *consume* you. Until your soul knows nothing else but the three of us."

There were a lot of things in my life I was afraid of. Pain. Humiliation. Abandonment. Heartbreak. But right now? With them? With Micah? I wasn't. "I'm not afraid of that."

He hummed into my skin. "Telling you all my fantasies would take all night."

"Just one then."

"I want to fuck your mouth underwater. Train you first so you can take all of my cock and then have you sink beneath the surface and take me all the way down. Let me fuck you until you're desperate for breath. And do it all over again until you taste me."

Even though we were in the water, I was wet.

"And I'll give you one more," he whispered. "Because my fantasies can be dark and dirty and raw. But they're also sweet and soft. I want to wake you up early before dawn and take you to the nest porch. Make love to you slowly while we watch the sun rise. And hold you while you fall back asleep with my name on your lips."

My heart did a flip in my chest. I could envision exactly what he meant, and I wanted all of it. Everything.

We were kissing again, this time driven by need and desire. My thoughts kept clinging to me. I needed to know before I begged him to fuck me. "This morning. Was it okay?"

He jerked back to look at me. "You had doubts?"

I bit my lip. "I mean, yes and no. It was my first time, so…"

Micah froze, a growl rolling out of his chest at the same time his arms locked harder around me. "Are you telling me the first cock you had in your mouth was mine?"

Shivers ran over my skin at his tone. Everything tightened. "The first to cum in my mouth, too."

A low sound in his throat. "Remember what we said about firsts? It turns us into savages, princess."

"There are still plenty you can have."

"You want to be pinned to the sand with my cock? Is that it?"

I smirked. "I kind of assumed that was going to happen either way."

"What are your other firsts?"

Nipping at his lips, I wrapped my arms fully around his shoulders. It was safe to tease him and drive him wild, because he was safe. "Guess."

He squeezed my ass and moved his fingers until he brushed my hole. "Has anyone had you here?"

"No one."

His face dropped into my neck with a groan. He lifted me higher and tilted me against him, and suddenly his cock was pressed right where his fingers had been. Daring. Testing. Beautifully terrifying.

"If you don't want me to fuck your ass right this second, tell me. I won't be disappointed. I'm more than happy to fuck your tight little cunt over and over again. But you need to tell me no. Right now."

I shook my head. "I'm not telling you no."

Micah stumbled to the shallows with me, locking my legs around his waist. My back hit the sand. This time we were both fully in the waves, the glowing water brushing my hair and neck. Every splash clung to him and me, painting us with what felt like magic. Like this moment was *more.*

He guided my legs up and back, pressing his cock in, jaw clenched like he was holding himself back from ravaging me completely. "Relax, princess."

The command in his tone held no room for argument. An Alpha commanding an Omega to obey, and I wanted it. Relished the way my body softened and let him in. I thought it might hurt, but it didn't. Omegas were made for Alphas in every way. Even though I'd never done this, my body was ready.

Eager.

Watching Micah move, working himself into me inch by inch, luminous waves splashing against his ribs... I understood the desire to paint the image and capture it forever.

Pleasure swirled, but it was different. Deeper. Everything bloomed in a way that was familiar, but I'd never felt anything like it. I could imagine feeling Everett's piercing here and loving it. I could imagine two of them—

Micah threw one leg over his shoulder so a hand was free. And *fuck,* he used it. "I think you need more, princess."

Water surged around our hips, drowning us and his hand as he slid two fingers inside me. Full of his cock and now his fingers... it was like Cam and the cock sleeve. So thick it was impossible and delightful and lighting my nerves up brighter than the luminescent water. Yet, without needing to say it, I knew I could take more if they asked.

My Omega wanted this again and more. Now that she knew what was possible, she wanted *everything.*

Thrusting his hand and hips together, Micah released that part of him he'd been holding back. The darker, brooding piece of his Alpha that hid beneath the art and his occasional silence. That sliver of himself that wanted to hold me beneath the waves for his pleasure and give in to the darkness.

And at the same time, he was still the man that wanted to caress me simply to see me blush. To hold me through my nightmares. He was a contradiction that made sense. And he was mine.

Micah's thumb circled my clit.

That was all it took.

The subtle pleasure that had grown from newness slammed into me like a tidal wave. Hard and fast, gone like a firework, but there.

My husband wasn't finished.

Another thing to tell Cameron. I loved that space before the orgasm where it felt like drowning in desperate pleasure. But I loved the space after it too. Being fucked because they hadn't had enough of me yet, or knowing they'd taken the time to push me over the edge first. It felt *good*.

I hadn't known I loved it until now.

Even if I didn't have another orgasm, I loved this. Pleasure and warmth in my chest and the beauty of Micah staring down at me like he'd crawled out of the sea specifically to take my ass and make it his.

"Princess," he said. The next words were lost in the water. The waves were nearly covering me now, and I didn't fucking care.

In the next second he pulled out of me and groaned. His orgasm splashed on my skin, painting me in an entirely different way before that, too, was washed away. Micah went stiff, working his cock until every last drop was squeezed out.

And then—

Oh *fuck*.

Micah dropped to the sand, burying his head between my legs even as the water covered his head. What he wanted, he was giving me. Every part of me was sensitive. So fucking sensitive from being fucked elsewhere but barely touched. The water pushing and pulling and dragging added to the overload.

He needed to breathe, didn't he?

My husband needed to breathe, but he didn't breathe. Licking, sucking, swirling, and all the way around again until I was grabbing his hair and holding him there out of desperation because I was so fucking *close* but he was going to drown.

Those two fingers slid back into me, joined by a third, and Micah knew exactly where to thrust to finish me.

My cries were lost in the sound of the wind and waves, the heat of my orgasm mixing with the tides, and still he didn't fucking breathe until I was done and collapsed and shuddering with every flick of his tongue.

Only then did he crawl up my body with wild light in his eyes. "Mine."

I tasted both of us on his lips.

"I thought you were going to drown."

"Never. Because if I drowned I could never do that again, and I plan to."

"Fuck me on the beach?" I raised an eyebrow.

"Pretty much anywhere, but yes, definitely the beach. The one by our house hasn't been christened yet. We'll have to take care of that."

I laughed, still out of breath, and yelped when a glowing wave briefly covered my face. "Painting me, fucking on the beach, sunrise sex. It sounds like we have a lot of things to do once we get home."

Micah kissed me on the nose before rescuing me from the next surge. "You have no idea, princess."

Fig 46. Atlas Flower
(Also: Fairy Fans; Red Ribbons; Silk Flower)
Meaning: Charming; Enthusiasm;
The variety of your conversation delights me

OCEAN

J snuggled down into the plush couch and glanced out the
windows. The sun was setting once more. It was sad, because
we were going home tomorrow, but at the same time, I was glad to be
going back.

My husbands needed to get back to deal with the fallout of the
Extasis launch. On a call earlier today Raina said she had something for
them, but because of the sensitivity, she was hesitant to share it without
being in person.

I had a few events coming up I needed to prepare for, and I wanted
to see the progress my hybrids had made. But just because I was happy to
be going home didn't mean the last few days hadn't been pure bliss.
They had.

There was the sex, and working the way through the toys like Cam
had promised. But it wasn't *only* that.

They took me all over the city. To more and different ruins—no sex
this time. Restaurants where we were photographed, and a gorgeous
symphony with the temple mountain lit up in the background.

Pictures of us were still everywhere.

That photographer that had been following me was annoyingly
persistent as well. Wherever we went, he was there. He was obnoxious,
but since he wasn't doing anything illegal, we did our best to ignore him.

A picture even surfaced of Everett and I *post* ruins. The comments
were still awful, though when I looked, I saw more good ones than had
been there before.

Amazingly, I didn't care. Focusing on them and no one else allowed
me to breathe and let go of those fears.

Micah sketched on his tablet across from me, and Cameron had his
arm slung around my shoulder as he read a book. Everett was on his
laptop, probably answering emails. The silence was easy and
comfortable.

And in that comfort, I wanted to get to know my husbands more. I
knew them. The way they fucked and the way their moods changed. The
different kinds of smiles. I now knew that Cameron was an endless abyss
when it came to eating pasta and Everett, though you would never guess
it, went wild for anything sweet. Bonus if there was any kind of ice
cream involved.

I learned the way Micah saw colors before anything else, and his
favorite shades were jewel tones.

But I wanted more than that. History and family. The kinds of
things I would have learned if we had courted and dated and not gotten
married because of a contract.

Well, it was still a contract, even if it didn't feel like it anymore. I needed to remember that. Hard to do when it felt like they were everything I'd been missing. Still, I wasn't going to focus on it. I was grabbing onto this temporary happiness with everything I had.

"I want to play a game," I whispered.

Everett looked up from his screen. "What did you have in mind?"

"Twenty questions. Also known as a way I get to ask you whatever I want."

Tossing his book to the side, Cameron chuckled. "I have a better idea. How about truth or dare? You still get to ask questions, but it's more fun."

"But you'll all pick dare and not answer anything." I pouted.

He nuzzled into my neck. "Maybe we make the rules that we pick truth and *you* pick dare."

"Are you going to tell me that you won't just dare me to do something sexual that will derail the game completely?"

Cameron's grin turned hungry. "We'll go first. So you'll get at least three questions. But no, I don't promise that."

I rolled my eyes, but I was smiling. "Fine. You first."

"What do you want to know?"

"Tell me how the three of you met?" Micah smothered a laugh, and Everett looked like he was holding one back. I looked at them. "What?"

"I think it's actually better if Cameron *doesn't* tell this story, little nymph."

Cam scoffed and used the arm around my shoulders to pull me into his lap. I stiffened, the instinct of not wanting to be too heavy rising hard and fast. I usually sat next to them. Not *on* them. If I was on their lap I straddled or laid across it. Not placing all of my weight directly on their legs.

"Don't be ridiculous," he said. "I was doing a marketing presentation for a product we made for a marketing class. A waterproof phone case. So we had to test it. These two were interested in it after I finished the demonstration, and we just clicked."

"Okay," Micah said. "Now can I tell the real version?"

I tried to move, but Cameron held me fast as he sighed. "Fine."

Micah looked at me and smirked. "He was doing a demonstration for his product. But what he's leaving out is that it was at a frat party, he was nearly blackout drunk, and his idea of a demonstration was filming him jumping off the roof of the frat house into the pool with his phone in the case."

My jaw dropped open, and I twisted so I could see his face. "Is that true?"

He shrugged, but there was a smile in his eyes. "They're exaggerating."

"Are we?" Everett turned his laptop around. A video was on the screen. Small, shaky, and grainy, but there was music and college kids drinking around a pool. And suddenly, there, on top of the two-story house, was a younger Cameron. Shirtless and in swim trunks. "HERE WE GO, BITCHES."

I burst out laughing and clapped a hand over my mouth.

The Cameron on screen leapt, doing a somersault in the air before landing feet first in the water. There was a momentary silence from the crowd before he surfaced and crowed with victory. The crowd followed suit, and he climbed out of the pool with the biggest smile on his face.

He stumbled to whoever held the camera and held up his phone in the case. Showed it working. Clearly he was *very* drunk, swaying on his feet, but he pulled up what looked like a logo.

A thousand-watt smile straight at the camera. "Good as new, no matter what you do."

The video ended, and I couldn't stop staring. "Holy crap."

"No matter what these dickheads say, that worked. We sold out of our entire stock when we put out the video."

Everett laughed. "And Cameron DuPont, marketer extraordinaire, was born."

"But that still doesn't tell me how you met."

I tried to move again, and Cameron slid his arm around my waist. "Stop trying to get off my lap, sweetheart." My mouth opened, and he kept speaking. "And if the next words out of your mouth are about crushing me, I'm going to go get those leather cuffs we haven't tried yet, put them on you, and the only getting off you'll do will be as you sit on my face."

Desire poured over me, and now I was squirming for a different reason. But I closed my mouth. That was exactly what I'd been about to say.

"We were at the party," Micah said. "Saw the stunt, and when we ran into him later, congratulated him. We felt the pack bond click in. Thank fuck he remembered enough of the night to remember us."

"You guys had already met and formed the pack?"

"In a manner of speaking," Everett said. "Though I was a business major and not marketing, I had to take that same class and we created a product. We decided on a coloring book based on the college itself, and we needed an artist." He shook his head. "I got volun*told* I was going to be the one to find them. So I went to the art department and ran into Micah nearly tearing his hair out over a piece he was working on. But his style was exactly what we needed."

I looked between them. "And that's when you knew?"

"Yes and no." Micah this time. "We felt the beginnings of bond, and were pretty sure it was one, but it didn't *fully* snap into place until Cam."

The thought of them in college made me smile. "Are there any other videos I should see?"

"No," Cameron said at the same time as Everett said, "absolutely."

Behind me, Cam grumbled something inaudible before he kissed my neck. "I think that's more than enough for a dare."

"No," I moved off his lap on purpose this time. "That was all your question. I want more."

"Greedy?" He asked with a smirk, knowing exactly what I was remembering. He called my body greedy, and for them? It absolutely was.

He reached for me and I danced out of his reach. He would get me eventually. But I was going to play the game. "Okay, Rett. I know Micah has siblings, but I don't know about your family."

Setting the laptop aside, he leaned forward on his elbows. He was wearing a t-shirt, so all that did was make his biceps strain against the fabric of his shirt and put his forearms on display. The dark rings on one forearm and the opposite bicep were visible when they usually weren't, and I loved them.

"My biological mother has passed," he said. "But my biological father is alive, along with one additional father and mother. One older sister."

I stopped to think, and my eyes went wide. "I... they've never met me. All the stuff they've seen about me—"

Everett reached out with a hand. "They don't think anything bad about you, little nymph. We let them know we were getting married. All our families."

Cameron smiled. "Beta parents here, only child, and Micah comes from one of the biggest packs I know."

"They're happy for us," Micah said softly. "But they understand why meeting you right away couldn't happen."

I took a breath slowly, pushing down the instinctual nerves and fear. "Do you want me to meet them?"

"Of course, princess." Micah caught me by the waistband of my jeans and pulled, spilling me into the overstuffed armchair beside him. The tablet he'd been working on had a drawing program open, and beside it was... one of the photos he'd taken on the beach.

We'd been so exhausted when we came back upstairs I'd forgotten about them until just now. I looked ethereal. Eyes closed, head tilted back, hair wet and wild across my face while a glowing wave struck my stomach, but stopped just before Micah's glowing handprint right over my heart.

"Wow."

"Here." He took the tablet and opened the album with the rest of them. There were so *many*. More than I realized he'd taken. And they really were pretty. I looked pretty.

Maybe Trinity and Isolde were right and I actually could do a boudoir photo shoot and look good while doing it. Or maybe it was because it was Micah who was taking the photos, but I couldn't stop staring at them.

"Do you like them?"

All I could do was nod.

"You've got one more question, sweetheart," Cameron said. "Make it a good one."

"What if I have more than that?"

He chuckled. "We're not going anywhere. You can ask us questions any time."

As Micah turned the tablet off and set it to the side, I snuggled into him. For the first time, I really felt like it might be true.

"Why did you choose art?"

He took my hand and turned it palm up, tracing the lines with his fingers. "Cam's right. I come from a big family. And believe it or not, they're all a lot more like Cameron. Loud," he smiled. "Boisterous, outgoing. I'm none of those things."

"You're not exactly shy."

"No, but in comparison, when you're in a pack that has six people, and you're one of four kids, it can be a stark difference. Everyone was always talking, and honestly, it started with writing. If I couldn't get a word in, I would write down what I needed and hand someone a note." He laughed and lifted my palm to his lips. "Then I started doodling with those notes. It just... grew from there."

I liked picturing a young Micah holed up in a corner with a sketchpad while the rest of his family created chaos around him. The image was so true to who he was. "I'm glad."

"All right." Cameron slapped his thighs as he stood. "Your turn for a dare. But I'll give you the chance to earn one more question."

"What's the catch?" I narrowed my eyes. My husband was already grinning, preparing to play.

"Make it to the bedroom before I catch you."

I was out of the chair before he finished speaking, sprinting for the bedroom with him right on my heels. But I didn't run as fast as I could, because I wanted him to catch me.

And he did.

Fig 47. Angel's Trumpet
(Also: Ghost Flower, Hell's Bells, Sorcerer's Herb)
Meaning: Deceitfulness; Disguise; Suspicion

CAMERON

*G*oing back to work after a full week of relaxing and having the best sex of my life wasn't putting me in a good mood. I would rather be home with Ocean, doing anything else than wading through the PR mess that was the Extasis launch. The team had gotten ahead of it. Mostly. A wave of returns and promises to do whatever we could to make the problems right went a long way.

But it didn't solve the source of the problem.

Everett texted me.

EVERETT

My office. Raina needs us.

Fuck. I hoped she'd gotten to the bottom of everything. My gut was unsettled with the worry of it. The three of us put everything into Zenith, and we did everything with intention. Yes, bad things happened, but this was still our hard work. I wouldn't pretend it didn't hurt to miss the mark or have people saying the things they were.

CAMERON

On my way.

"I'm in Rett's office if you need me," I said to Oren. "But don't need me. This is important."

"This is about what Raina was doing?"

I stopped and turned around. Frowning. "How do you know about that?"

"She came and asked me to find and print a bunch of your correspondence about Extasis. She could ask IT for those emails anyway, so I didn't think much of it. But she wanted them printed." He raised an eyebrow. "I'm not naïve, nor am I blind. Something's going on, and you're trying to find out what and why."

I took a deep breath. Oren was trustworthy. Everyone who worked directly with us or beneath us was. The very fact that they had made it into that circle was testament enough. "Any ideas?"

"Yeah. But I'll wait until you talk to Raina. She probably has a bigger picture. But I'll try not to need you."

He threw me a cocky grin before I left.

Everett was texting someone when I walked in, and Micah was on his tablet going through some designs.

"Any word from Aiden?" I asked.

"Thought we'd call him when we were finished with Raina."

It was odd not to hear from the man for so long. He was usually very prompt, but if Everett had heard something while we were on the honeymoon, he hadn't mentioned it.

Raina approached a minute later, her assistant following with three large binders filled with paper. She nodded when he set them on Everett's desk. "You can go."

When her assistant shut the door, Raina locked it behind him. I grinned. "I know we're irresistible, Raina, but remember, we're married now."

She didn't rise to the teasing bait like I expected, and that was the most frightening thing of all. Raina was always one for a joke and served it back to me on a regular basis.

"Sit down, Cam."

Even Everett looked shaken. "What the fuck is going on?"

"A lot more than I expected or hoped, unfortunately. Honestly, it's a good thing that the launch went poorly. If it hadn't, we might not have found this in time, and wouldn't have been able to pull it back."

None of us spoke. She had the floor.

"The factories producing the Extasis toys were given the appropriate schematics. Everything they needed as normal. But the materials weren't the same. Everything was swapped out for cheaper options before production even started."

"What?" Micah's voice was deadly. Design was his corner, and he took pride in it, including choosing materials specifically for both luxury and endurance. With clothing as well as our toys. "How the fuck did that happen?"

Raina sighed and sat back in her chair. "I'll give you all three guesses, but if you need more than one, you don't deserve your offices."

"Joseph?" Everett ground out.

"One and the same. He was fucking careful though. *Really* careful. Going to the trouble of printing out all the designs and making notes by hand before going to the team and asking them to make those changes on the way to production." She held out a hand. "Don't worry, they won't tip him off. I made sure everyone I spoke to signed an NDA that would eviscerate their lives before I left the room. But as long as they talked, I let them keep their jobs."

"We might not be able to keep that promise," I said. From a public relations perspective, at least one head needed to roll. Maybe several. Joseph's, certainly, but if they had knowingly helped them—

"They had no reason to question the Chairman of the Board. He was using your names and saying you'd approved the changes. Among all the other proof, is sworn and signed statements from everyone I spoke to. As far as I can tell, no one was intentionally trying to sabotage anything. They were simply misled. More than one of them was horrified, because they've seen what's happening. Your employees care about their work as much as you do."

Her faint smile made me feel better. When we started Zenith, the one thing we vowed never to do was compromise. Not on what we needed, not on cost, not on having a healthy work environment.

"But Extasis isn't the only problem. He's starting to do it with the other lines as well. Swapping out our more expensive fabrics with ones that are less expensive. Taking a cashmere, for example, and swapping in a blend that would appear the same to most consumers but would cost half the price."

I pulled out my phone and started typing. "I haven't seen any reviews like that. Where are we getting hit?"

This time, when Raina smiled, it was vicious. "That's because he hasn't managed to do it yet. He's only starting. Want to know how?"

Everett growled. Truly growled. Rage poured off him like a physical thing. He planted his hands on his desk and rose out of his chair. "If it's Frank fucking McCabe—"

"Ding ding ding, we have a winner." Raina let the sarcasm drip.

Part of our deal with Frank involved utilizing McCabe fabrics as one of our larger suppliers. We'd already been using them in a much smaller capacity. Bringing them in to cover most of our fabric needs would infuse his company with money, which would keep it alive. But this?

"Why?" Micah asked. "I don't see the plan in this."

Everett settled his elbows on the desk. "Let me take a guess, Raina, and you tell me if I'm right."

She smirked and crossed her arms. "Go for it."

"The shareholders were annoyed by the last few quarters having *even* profits instead of *growing* profits, so they went to Joseph to see what the 'problem' was, and did some threatening."

"Correct."

Everett shook his head. We'd known about the even profits, but it hardly mattered. They were *good* profits. Incredible ones. Only fools thought profits could go up infinitely. Now that Firefly clothing was under our umbrella, we'd get a bump.

"And instead of coming to us with those threats, he decided he'd try to make more profit for the company by cheapening the materials. He didn't come to us because he knew that we would say no without a second thought."

"Yes."

His brow furrowed. "But I'll confess, I don't understand forcing the marriage. Were the other board members involved?"

"Not that I can tell, but you can thank your man for that. He sent me half of this after we spoke on the phone."

"Our man?" I asked.

327

Raina raised an eyebrow. "The hacker."

"For fuck's sake." Micah scrubbed a hand over his face. "Why wouldn't he tell us that?"

"No idea. But as far as I can tell, the McCabe Fabrics thing is new. He approached Frank *after* the offer. I don't have proof, but I suspect he intended the marriage, and a very public search for a wife, to distract you and engage you in a PR crisis so he would have more time before you noticed. There's no way that this *never* would have been found, and he knew that. My best guess is that the marriage scheme was a distraction to weaken you. He really did want to remove you if he could, but you moved too fast."

I shook my head. "Fuck."

"Yup. But it's an easy fix," she said. "The Extasis production has already been corrected, and I'll let you take care of the rest of that, Cam."

Everett chuckled. "You might need a promotion, Raina. This is far more than the scope of what we asked, and I can't thank you enough."

"I'll keep that in my back pocket." She winked and stood. "Let me know the plan and when you're going to hand Joseph his ass. I want to see it."

I nodded. "Sure thing."

She left us alone, and for a long minute we didn't do anything but stare at each other. Finally, Micah spoke, putting voice to everything we were thinking. "What the fuck."

"Pretty much sums it up."

Everett sighed. "I'm still convinced there's one other element to this. Because the swapping of materials could be written off as a mistake or an accident when he got caught. Yes, forcing us to marry was a distraction, but he would need a bigger reason than concealing this scheme."

I looked at him carefully as he picked up one of the binders. "You think it's like you said before? He was prepping for a hostile takeover?"

"That's the only thing I can think of. If he weakens us, or the board followed through on their threat to resign. Combining that with the production issues, the shareholders would start to bail, driving the price down, and someone would start buying."

"How do we prove that?" Micah asked.

"We don't have to," Everett said. "We have more than enough here to remove him. And I have half a mind to replace the entire board along with him." Then he smiled. The kind of smile that made people absolutely terrified of him. "Not to mention, despite the four hours of hell he dragged us through, I don't think Frank quite understands the agreement he signed if he thinks he can get away with it."

I watched him flip through the binders Raina brought until he smiled. "We don't have quite enough to void the deal with him, since he can claim that Joseph misled him, just like the production line, but we will."

Pulling out his phone, he called a number, set his phone on the desk, and put it on speaker. A deep, accented voice answered. "Hello?"

"Want to explain to me why you took everything to my employee instead of directly to me?"

Aiden laughed. "She was already digging around it. Figured I'd save you both some time. Besides, you deserved to enjoy your honeymoon."

The three of us shook our heads. We'd met Aiden in college when he was an exchange student from Albion, an island nation just off the coast of Europa, and to this day we'd never met anyone quite like him. Fucking brilliant and terrifying. He knew way too much, and it was good he was on our side.

"Well," Everett said, "we appreciate it."

"I'm sending you the other documents you asked for now. The ones about your wife."

I frowned, and Everett mouthed the word "*Trust.*"

"Thank you. We need one more thing from you, but I can't ask you."

Another chuckle. "That's a pity. If you can, let me know."

"I haven't had a chance to review everything yet. There's a lot here. But it seems like you had to look at a new family connection. Our wife's uncle."

That was Everett setting up deniability. He'd already asked Aiden to look into Frank in connection to this. He knew who the asshole was. But he'd been looking into the problem with Extasis, not Frank specifically.

Leaning forward, I stared at the phone like I was able to see through it. "I did see that. Congratulations. Becoming a monopoly one company at a time."

"Fuck off," Micah said with a laugh.

I swore I *felt* Aiden shrugging. "Can't fuck off if it's the truth."

"I hope he understands what he got into with us," Everett said. "It would indeed, be a *pity* if he thought he was untouchable and decided to do things which might get him in trouble."

"Mmm. Yes. That would be a shame. People can get in over their heads so easily nowadays."

Everett smirked. "Anyway, thanks again. Send us your invoice for the work."

"I'll make sure to double it."

The line went dead.

Everett closed the binder and put it back. "We should have what we need soon enough."

"It won't be legal."

"We don't need it to be. We can get Frank to admit it, I'm sure. And once he does, it doesn't matter. If he doesn't, our lawyers can get what we need legally."

Micah spun his stylus back and forth through his fingers. "You asked him for Ocean's trust documents?"

"Before the honeymoon."

"Why? She said we could have them."

Turning to his monitor, Everett pulled up his email. We hadn't had a chance to talk about this in all the frenzy. "Because even though she agreed to let us look at them, I knew Frank wouldn't give them to us, and I didn't want Ocean to worry about it. Have you ever heard of a trust fund that pays out at thirty-five? Or gives the trustees complete control over someone's finances? That's not a trust, and I don't *trust* Frank and Laura at all."

A text chimed on my phone. Our combined text thread with Ocean.

OCEAN

My uncle wants to talk to me so I'm heading over to the Caldwell mansion if I'm not home when you get there.

Maybe it was the discussion of her trust, or maybe it was because I was falling in love with my wife, but I couldn't quite explain the fear in my chest. Her uncle had already tried to force her hand into being a spy for him. The more deeply involved he got with Joseph, the more desperate he would be.

We knew he was involved now, but we didn't know how deeply, and that was terrifying. We had no idea what Joseph had told him or what kind of agreements he'd made, but Frank held no love for his niece. He'd already hurt her, if not physically. If she refused him, which she would, how far would he go to make her agree?

Everett and Micah were already on their feet. Even if nothing happened, Ocean wasn't alone anymore. She didn't need to face that asshole by herself.

My instincts rose, telling me that my Omega needed me, and she needed me *now*.

We didn't stop.

Fig 48. Monkshood
(Also: Bear's Foot, Cupid's Car,
Helmet Flower, Leopard's Bane,
Thor's Hat, Wolf's Bane)
Meaning: Beware; Danger is near; Deceit;
allantry; Knight; Poisonous words; Treachery

OCEAN

---

*B*eing here was the last thing I wanted, but I figured it was better to get it out of the way. My guess was that Frank was going to ask about the information he'd demanded I get for him. Which I wasn't going to do. And I would tell him so.

I was jetlagged and a little worse for wear, but I felt good. When we arrived home yesterday, we did nothing. Absolutely nothing but turn on a movie and create a giant nest of blankets in the television room. I woke up in Everett's bed, though they'd already left with a note and a rose on the bedside table.

A red rose.

You didn't need to be an expert in Floriography to know what that meant.

They hadn't said those words to me, and I hadn't either. But I felt them in the way they looked at me and in every touch. More than that, I *believed* it.

And I was falling for them too.

There was no point in denying it or trying to hold myself back.

I was falling in love with my husbands. If I was really honest with myself, I was already there.

It was that realization that kept the smile on my face all day. While I worked in the new greenhouse and made a note of the flowers that still needed to be transferred from the Caldwell Estate, catching up with Sally, and generally making sure nothing was on fire.

Now, though, my smile fortified me as I walked into the house. I'd noticed it before when I visited, but the big house felt *dark*. It never felt that way before my mother died. Proof enough that people could influence the energy of a place. It wasn't inherently dark, it just felt that way.

Isabel let me in, and she was in shock. "Ocean, you look *wonderful*."

I paused. "Thank you?"

She laughed softly and placed a hand on my shoulder. "I meant you seem well. You're brighter, and it's been years since I've seen you smile like that."

It was sad that it was the truth. "I'm happy."

"Good. I'm glad."

"Is Frank in his study?"

She nodded. "Go on in."

I'd worn a bottle green dress today. Straps that clung to my shoulders but exposed some skin. It flounced around my knees. I mainly chose it because it was comfortable and pretty, but also because I knew it would drive my husbands wild as soon as they saw it. I looked forward to that part.

"Ocean?"

I turned and found my aunt staring at me from the entrance to the living room where she spent most of her time. Her face was frozen, like she didn't quite know what to do with me. "Hello."

"What are you doing here?"

"Frank wanted to talk to me, so I'm here."

Her nose turned up. "Well, it's about time we have some progress on that front. I see the only real thing you've been doing is making progress on your waistline."

I rolled my eyes. "Is that really what you're going with? It's getting boring."

"I can't help it if it's the truth."

"If you don't have anything else to say, I'm not speaking to you."

I turned, and she grabbed me by the arm and turned me back. "Just because you got married to Alphas desperate enough to take you doesn't mean you get to be rude to me. And you've never once wanted to hear the hard things, Ocean. Believe it or not, I've always tried to *help* you."

"Yeah. Okay."

"Most people go on vacation to Europa and *lose weight*."

"Most people give a shit when you talk. I guess we'll both have to be disappointed."

I looked at her, not feeling anything. The words simply fell to the wayside without digging their claws into me. Because I knew better now. I had Alphas who craved me just the way I was and never let me forget it. They didn't reduce my value to numbers on a scale or the circumference of my waist.

She was still gaping at me when I turned and left her there, continuing to my uncle's office. My foolish heart hoped I'd stunned her enough that she wouldn't follow. Or she would, and I would give her more.

Fuck, this felt incredible. *Freeing*. More like myself than I'd been in this house since...

Since mom died.

I knocked softly on the door before opening it. "Frank?"

He sat behind his desk, glasses on his face, glancing between the papers on his desk and whatever was on his monitor. I couldn't remember a time when I'd come to this office and found him actually working. Most of the time he preferred the illusion that he didn't need to work. Fake it till you make it. Pretend everything was light and easy.

But he still hadn't noticed my presence.

"You wanted to talk to me?"

Frank looked up, startled. "Oh. Yes. Come in, Ocean."

I closed the door gently behind me.

"I need those numbers."

Walking over to where his fireplace was lit despite the summer heat, I looked around his study with fresh eyes. There were papers spread around one of the armchairs, like he was splitting his time between there and his desk. It was messy. Like he'd been in here for days.

I crossed my arms and gave him a look. "We had a discussion before I left on my honeymoon where I said I wouldn't be doing that."

"Now is not the time to toy with me or be a brat. I need those numbers, and you fucking agreed to get them for me. So you're going to follow through. I specifically told you I needed them *when you returned*."

"I never agreed to that."

Rage contorted his features. "Don't fucking play with me."

"I'm not. I never agreed to get anything for you. You informed me that you needed the numbers, and I walked out without saying anything. When you told me that I would have to get information for you the first time and I said 'sure,' I only said that to get the fuck out of your office. No papers had been signed, and I knew that whoever you'd set me up with wouldn't be dumb enough to let their fake wife near any confidential information."

He opened his mouth, and I surged ahead. "And if you're about to tell me that I signed a contract that agreed to it, check what you actually had me sign. Because it says *fuck all* about whatever corporate espionage bullshit you're trying to pull off on my husbands. It says I had to stay married for a year to get my trust. No more and no less."

Based on what my husbands had said about him, it seemed like Frank wasn't in the habit of fully reading and comprehending his contracts.

I thought he might pass out with the color he was turning. The drawer he ripped open nearly fell out of his desk. I'd never seen him so angry, and my gut twisted. My uncle wasn't a violent man that I knew of. But I'd also never pushed him this far.

Enough was enough.

Frank's hands shook as he looked at the contract we'd signed. A shiver of fear went through me and I forced it down.

"If, for some reason, you thought I would do it out of the kindness of my heart and because I'm your niece, I have some news for you. You and Laura have never treated me as anything more than a rock stuck in your shoe. So if you want me to help you, invent a fucking time machine."

He looked at me smoothly, anger cooling down into something harder and darker. "You think I couldn't do more? I could ruin whatever fantasy life you've created for yourself with the DuPonts and have you back here under my thumb in ten seconds."

"Then do it." I dared him. "Do it. Because I don't think it's true.

You might have my money and my home by the balls, but you do *not* have me. You will never have me again, and my husbands will tell you that themselves."

"Are you so sure?" From that same drawer, he pulled a large envelope and tossed it to me. "The DuPonts married you to solve their image problem. What do you think happens when a wave of press hits you like you've never seen? Feel free to keep them. I have copies."

My heart dropped. Inside the envelope were pictures, and I immediately knew who had taken them. The asshole photographer who wouldn't stop following us.

The picture on top was from that brunch with Trinity and Isolde, me taking a bite of cake. It was taken at an unflattering angle, almost intentionally.

The rest of the pictures were the same. From all over our honeymoon, all the photos bad. Taken from angles intended to make my body look horrific. Playing into every stereotype and harmful idea that clung to fat people—fat *women*—like glue.

I swallowed.

Knowing that I was worthy of living my life and finding love and being free despite the size of my body didn't erase the pain of these. Too many years of brainwashing and media telling me that I was *wrong* had done their damage. And yes. It would hurt to see these go to the media. But it wouldn't do anything to me or my husbands. I believed that now.

The fact that they were waiting for me and would be overjoyed to see me was the thing that allowed me to slip the photos back into the envelope and meet my uncle's eyes. "Go ahead. Do your worst. It's not anything I haven't already dealt with."

"Those aren't everything. I have more. I promise, Ocean, I can ruin you."

My body shook with adrenaline, but I held my ground. "The answer is still no."

Frank strode toward me. Pain cracked through my face, the force of the blow sending me reeling. The second blow was excruciating. I lost my balance and fell, photos flying out of the envelope in a twisted kind of rain.

He loomed over me, face poison. I'd never seen him like this. It was both rage and desperation. A dangerous combination. Terror clutched me with black claws. If he was willing to hit me now, when he never had before, I didn't know what he'd do or how far he'd go.

"I hope that got through to you, and you better fucking listen, Ocean. You are going to go home, you are going to fuck them into a coma, and you are going to get the information I need. Understood? I have made promises based on this information, and you. *Will. Fucking. Get. It.* Whether it's before or after I destroy your life is up to you." He straightened, looking down at me and straightening his shirt like the way he'd struck me had released what he needed. "I expect it in less than forty-eight hours, or all of you will pay the price."

Pain throbbed in my head and my cheek.

I wouldn't do that. Even if our marriage ended up being temporary, I wouldn't. I was falling in love with them, and I could take the punishment. I'd been taking it my whole fucking life. I wouldn't betray them. "No."

"No?" His voice was as cold as I'd ever heard it, and fear dropped through me. Frank was coming toward me again with his hand raised, and all I could do was panic. There was nowhere for me to go as I scrambled backward. If I could make it to my feet, maybe I could run—

The door flew open and Everett came striding through. His fist connected with Frank's jaw with a sickening thud. It knocked him away from me.

Micah was there, scooping me up and pulling me close, hands tracing my face where I'd been hit.

The growl in Everett's throat was feral. "If you ever lay a hand on my wife—my *Omega*—ever again, I will rip your tongue out of your fucking skull and make you choke on it before I kill you. Slowly."

Frank sneered. "You think you have any right—"

His back hit the mantle so fast it was a blur. "We have *every* right, you piece of fucking shit."

Cameron stood back with hands in the pockets of his slacks, his stillness terrifying. Rage pulsed off the three of them like a living thing.

But Everett was still the one speaking. His tone belonged to the Alpha who inspired fear, and I'd never been more grateful. "You will never speak to Ocean again. You will never look at her. You will never contact her in anyway unless she chooses to do so first. If I hear that you've mentioned her to anyone, they'll find your body beyond Clarity's coastal waters. In pieces. I'll do the chopping myself, and your hands will go first. They'll never know who did it. Do you understand me?"

I didn't even realize I was crying until Micah gently swiped the tears away, but I couldn't take my eyes off Everett and Frank.

My uncle was as pale as death. Micah turned and kept me behind him. His hand grasped mine. An Anchor. "We will be sending a team to gather every single thing of Ocean's left in this house. To dismantle the greenhouse and move it to our home. You won't resist this. Got it?"

"You can't just threaten me and think it will stand." Frank wiped blood from his lip where Everett split it.

"You want to test that theory?" Cameron snarled. "We know how many cameras you have in this house. We'll be taking this footage, including the footage of you assaulting our wife, with us when we go. Everett?"

One punch later, Frank was unconscious on the floor. My breath hiccupped, tears and panic flooding to the surface. My entire body shook despite Micah holding me once more.

"I told him no," I said, my voice breaking. "I wasn't going to do it. I told him no. I told him *no*."

"Shh," Micah breathed the sound into my hair. "We know, sweet girl. It never even crossed our minds."

All the fear I pressed down came up and burst out. The relief of them coming to save me, even when I hadn't known I needed it.

Micah kissed my forehead, clutching me to his chest before gently letting the others hold me. I needed all of them and couldn't stop holding on. Because if I let them go, I was afraid I'd melt.

Everett lifted my chin with a single finger. I didn't look at him, but he didn't let me look away. "We got here as soon as we could. Frank deserves everything that's coming to him and more. We'll explain once we're home and you feel safer. But you don't ever have to see him again." He kissed me once, and then again, harder. "We'll always protect you, Ocean. I'm sorry we didn't get here sooner."

I let my forehead fall to his chest and basked in the feeling of safety they gave me. Cameron lifted me off my feet. I went to protest, but he gave me a look that silenced me. "If you say anything about your body right now, on my ability to carry my Omega, I'll punish you." He winked as he said it, though there was still anger in his eyes. Directed elsewhere. Not at me.

Tucking my face closer to him, I fought against the throbbing pain and tried to breathe. Tears still leaked from my eyes, and I hurt, but they had me.

They came for me.

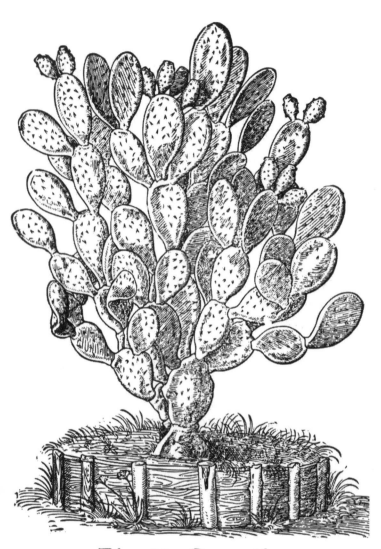

Fig 49. Opuntia
(Also: Prickly Pear; Paddle Cactus)
Meaning: I burn

OCEAN

*C*ameron didn't let go of me the entire ride home. But as soon as the door to the car opened, I didn't let him carry me again. It wasn't fast enough. "Nest," I mumbled as I moved, hoping they heard me. It was still bright outside, but the nest was dark and warm and everything I needed right now.

My instincts were high and my Omega needed my nest. Darkness and softness and soothing comfort. My face *hurt*. Everything hurt, and it shouldn't hurt, but I was sure with the adrenaline and fear, my body was overreacting.

The whiplash from being happy and confident to terrified and broken and back to safety had me reeling. I didn't know what to do with it. But I knew I needed my nest, and more than that, I needed to feel it on my skin.

This dress was too hot.

I pulled it over my head and tossed it to the side, reaching for a blanket in the pile of blankets and arranging it on the side of the nest. Where it belonged.

"Here, princess." A hand appeared in front of me with some pills, another with a glass of water. "Everett has an ice pack for your face."

I swallowed the pills and handed the glass back, ignoring the ice pack. That could come later. The nest wasn't finished, and I needed that more than I needed the relief. "After."

Low murmurs reached me from the edge of the nest, but nothing penetrated. The only thing that existed were the blankets and pillows. I found a shirt in the pile that smelled like pistachios and almonds. Like Everett. I whined, adding that to the circle I built.

Another soft, purple blanket, and another shirt. This one smelled like Cameron. I smiled and added it. A whole pile of their clothes waited when I finished with my pillows. *Perfect*.

If Omegas could purr, I would be. I needed clothes from my Alphas for my nest. Because they were mine.

Sweat beaded on my skin, and I shed my bra and underwear. Why was it so fucking *hot*? It was like they'd turned the heat in here up to eleven. And I could smell all three of them together. Like I had my nose buried in their necks instead of where they waited at the entrance to the nest, simply watching me.

Micah's suit jacket was closest to me. I crawled and pulled it to my nose, inhaling the scent of him. Chocolate but more than chocolate. Layers of cocoa and darkness that went all the way to the sweetness of white chocolate, laced through with the warm, contrasting caramel. Sometimes salty, sometimes not. So fucking good.

The shirt I found of Everett's was the same. I scented the delicate layers of his scent. Pistachio at every stage, from whole to crushed. Almond frosting and almond liqueur. It was so different and so *good*.

They were mine.

The words in my head echoed like a bell.

They were *mine*.

I whirled around to face them and found them all watching me with awe and so much love. I sat, unable to process. "What?"

Micah took a step, waiting until I nodded before coming in. He came straight to me and fell to his knees, but he was smiling as he placed the backs of his fingers against my forehead. "You're going into heat, Princess. Your instincts were out of control because of that asshole, and your Omega is responding the only way it knows how."

I just looked at him. "But... but... what? You—"

He took my face in my hands and kissed me. Hard. "Yes, wife. You're my Omega. You're *our* Omega. We knew the second we met you, and we couldn't even look at anyone else."

Everett and Cameron joined us in the nest, surrounding me with heat and scent and fuck it was so good.

They were mine.

My Alphas.

My scent matches.

And my whole world shattered.

All these weeks of them telling me they wanted me and that I was perfect. Of me being convinced they were falling for me while I was completely falling for them. And it wasn't real.

They hadn't picked me for me, they'd picked me because they'd scented me and our biology picked us to be together. Nothing more than that.

If they hadn't matched with me, would they have liked me? Would they have rather had someone small? I hated the fear that clawed up my throat, but there wasn't a way to banish it now that the truth was out.

I thought—

I swallowed and held back my sob. They didn't need to see how my entire world was falling apart. All I'd wanted was for it to be real. And now everything was gone like it never existed.

And that hurt so much worse.

"Oh. I see."

Everett growled, and then he was in front of me, tilting my face up to his. Pulling us closer. "If there's one thing I do for the rest of my life, it will be to make those shadows disappear from your eyes. They *don't belong there*. Understand me?"

Pain cracked through my chest. "Yes. I just..." I hated that tears came. I hated that this moment which was supposed to be joyful was nothing but sadness. I thought it had been true connection, and not a quirk of DNA. My heart cracked all over again. "I wanted it to be real."

His arm came around my body, gathering me up while the other one buried itself in my hair. "I don't think I ever told you when I first saw you. Did I?"

I was so still. Because if I moved I would want them, and I couldn't. Not when it hurt like this. "When I was dancing with that asshole, yeah."

"No," he said, voice low and dark. "No, I'd already seen you by then. We were on the balcony at that gala, dreading being there. Then I looked down and saw you by the windows in the ballroom, a glass of champagne in your hand. Dressed in that blue that reminds me of your name. The first words out of my mouth were '*who the fuck is that?*'"

It took me a few seconds through the raging heat and hormones in my brain to understand what he was telling me. That he'd seen me from all the way across the ballroom and *noticed*. Long before he could have scented me.

I looked up at him, and all I saw in his gaze was love.

Cameron and Micah crowded me from both sides. "It's true," Micah said. "You were so beautiful. We would have come to you even if that sorry excuse of an Alpha hadn't had his hands on you."

"You are our Omega," Everett murmured. "And I'm so fucking grateful that you are. But don't you dare think, even for a *second*, that it's the only reason we want you. I wanted you the second I laid eyes on you." His mouth quirked into a smile then. "You pulled me out of thoughts that usually drown me, little nymph. You've been in my mind every second since then. And I wanted you before I ever scented how fucking perfect you are."

My tears spilled over and I gave in, crying in relief. It felt silly for it to matter so much, but it did. It *did*. They wanted me for who I was and not what our bodies instructed us to do.

Everett kissed me softly, deepening his hold until he was devouring my mouth, consuming my lips and tongue. Everything glowed gold and fiery, the burn of heat returning in force now that my Omega understood that she was wanted. And loved.

"I'm sorry. I don't—" my sob cut off the words. "I don't know if I'll always believe it."

Cameron lined himself up with my back and eased me against him, taking the time to smooth his hands over every part of me he could reach. "Good thing we have the rest of our lives to convince you."

"What about the year?"

Micah nipped at my shoulder. "We were never going to let you go, Ocean. This was always what we wanted. You. Just you and always you." He laughed then. "Honestly, we pretty much invented the deal with your uncle so we could marry you. We were told we needed to marry, but we were going to fight it tooth and nail. Until you. We had no plans to do more business with Frank. Then we saw you and had to get closer. And when we scented you? We had to make you ours. It just happened to be perfect timing."

Tilting my head to the side, Cameron kissed the place where my neck met my shoulder. Licking my skin and dragging his lips up to my ear. "It's been delicious torture, knowing this and not being able to tell you."

"Why didn't you?" My voice had been reduced to nothing but breath.

Everett pulled me away from them and laid me out on the cushions, covering my body with his own. "We'd just rescued you from a man who'd fetishized you like an ass. Without a way to prove it to you, we didn't want to look like we were the same. And then we got to know you better." He drew his nose up the line of my cheek and nudged my head with his. "And we knew you weren't ready. You couldn't believe we would want someone like you, let alone wanting you for the rest of our fucking lives."

It would have been unthinkable. I wouldn't have believed them. Actually, I probably would have thought they were making fun of me on purpose.

Instead, they'd taken the time to show me how they felt. Backed up words with actions and proven over and over that I was who they wanted. I reached up so I was holding his face. "Please don't hate me for being relieved that you saw me before you scented me."

Everett grinned before he kissed me. "I could never hate you, little nymph. Not when I love you so fucking much."

I sobbed into the kiss, overwhelmed by finally hearing those words I wanted for so long. His purr echoed twice over, the nest full of it.

"And I understand why. I hope you feel it and know how deep it goes. I hope your heart aches a little bit less."

It did. So much. My breath hitched as I looked at him. Then Micah, and finally Cameron. "I love you." My words still shook. "It was the fact that you would be there for me that helped me stand up to him. I admitted to myself I was falling for you, but I think I've been there for a while."

Sudden heat took my breath away. And *pain*. Pain that wasn't connected to my bruised face or my healing heart. Pain that demanded attention and burned like a supernova had been shoved down my throat.

Knot.

I gasped, whining. Writhing against the pain. "Alpha," I begged. "Help."

Everett flipped me over on the cushions and thrust into me in one movement. It wasn't easy or gentle—it was exactly what I needed. Fiery heat flared through my bones. I'd never felt anything like this before.

Heats... I'd had a few now, but it was nothing in comparison. Those had been a gentle warm day compared to the inferno now crashing through me and consuming me from within.

I needed, needed, *needed*—

He settled himself with me, chest against my back, fingers entwined and locked against the cushions, legs pressed along mine.

My Alpha took me.

It was like a part of Everett had unlocked which hadn't been there before. Part of me too. He wasn't just my husband, he was my *Alpha*. Tied together by more than just need and want and love, but woven into each other in the deepest fabric of who we were.

Everett's teeth grazed my ear, gentled compared to the way he was fucking me, driving me into the velvet cushions with his cock. "You're *mine*, Ocean." I felt the growl in every single part of me.

"Mine. My nymph. My goddess. And I plan on worshipping you every single fucking day until there's not a doubt in your mind. I don't care if my knot never leaves your cunt again. You'll believe every good thing, every compliment."

My voice was muffled by velvet and blankets and their clothes, but it felt like my entire body was lined in starfire. Silvered and beautiful and *burning*.

His voice dropped to a harsh whisper as we both grew closer to the edge. "Eventually you will watch me drop to my knees for you and you'll welcome it because you understand your own fucking worth."

I came.

Pleasure exploded outward and then inward and I couldn't speak to tell him that even if that was ever true, it would also be true in reverse. That I would fall to my knees for him and them because they were my Alphas. They were the only ones that ever made me feel truly safe, and it was everything.

We would worship each other, and within that, we would find our own grace and peace and happiness.

He followed me into pleasure, knot swelling and adding another firework to the already burning flames of my heat and desire.

"Got it, little nymph?"

I laughed, breathlessly, melting into the cushions. "Got it. But—"

"But?" He growled playfully. "Do I need to fuck the lesson into you again?"

A whine burst out of me. It wasn't the lesson, it was him. Them. I moved on his knot, trying to make it press deeper. I understood, I just needed more. It was like I was thirsty and no amount of water would get rid of the sensation. "More."

Everett purred in my ear. "I see. We can do that, little nymph."

He pulled me up on all fours, stroking my body while he did so. But it was the cock suddenly in front of me that had me distracted. Cameron's thickness, the rich lemon scent of him so much stronger now that I was in heat and now that I understood he was *mine*.

My Alpha smirked, full of that wicked confidence that told me he was prepared to ruin me, and he would have the best time of his life while he did it. "This what you need, sweetheart?"

Yes.

His cock between my lips made my eyes roll back in my head. He tasted so good. Citrus sharpness and candy sweetness. A lollipop I never wanted to stop licking. And I did lick him. From the crown of him, down the thickness of his shaft and lower. The more of him I tasted, the easier it was to breathe.

I took as much of him in my mouth as I could, but I didn't get far. He was too thick and I had no idea what I was doing. Cameron didn't care. He groaned and framed my face with his hands, not taking full control, but keeping me steady. His hips moved, pumping deeper like he couldn't help it, and I loved that.

It was me. *I* was the one making him lose command of his body.

"Fucking hell, sweetheart. I would have taken your mouth before if I'd known it would feel like this."

My Omega shivered with the praise.

"A miracle is what it is." Micah's voice was beside me. So close, and yet I couldn't turn my head to see him while my mouth was full of Cameron. What was he—

Everett's knot released me, and he pressed a kiss to the center of my back before pulling free. I moaned, mourning the loss of him. The sudden emptiness was *hungry*. A void so rich and dark and reaching that it needed to be filled and never stop.

I lunged down onto Cameron's cock, savoring him, nearly choking on him. Fingers grasped my hair at the same time I was moved. Micah slid under my body and guided me down onto his cock. The relief was palpable. They were giving me what I needed. More knots. More Alpha. More pleasure.

"Suck slowly," Cameron said. I looked up at him and loved seeing him towering there, muscles flexing and tightening as he tried to keep a grip on his pleasure. "Take whatever you need from me while he fucks you, baby. And when Micah knots you, I'll give you what we both need."

The word *both* was a promise and a purr.

My eyes fluttered closed, and I sucked harder but slower, reveling in the texture of him on my tongue and the seeping sweetness that told me his cock was just as ready for me as I was for him.

"Put your hands on my shoulders, Ocean." From somewhere outside myself, I heard Micah's command and tried to obey. He was underneath me, holding me while he eased in.

We'd never done it like this, with me on top of him. In that place outside of my heat brain, I knew that this made me nervous. But it was impossible to be nervous when I was stuffed to the brim and out of my mind.

Micah's curve felt different like this. Fingers gripped my ass, holding me in place, and he let himself go. Hard and fast, plunging into me with a pace that would break me.

Oh, how I wanted to be broken.

I couldn't even use my mouth. Frozen. Taking what they gave me and slipping into the clouded place where there was nothing but heat and light. Time didn't exist here. Only the interval between one brutal thrust and the next. The space between novas. The sweet, grinding friction that lifted me up and dropped me into free fall like a roller coaster.

I had no control. Pleasure seized my body and rendered me helpless. I bucked and writhed and rode Micah's cock until I felt his knot—his glorious fucking knot—fill that aching place that always needed to be filled.

Sweet lemon sugar flowed over my tongue. It would be so easy to become addicted to them, and I wasn't resisting it. I wanted to know them so deeply it would change me at a cellular level.

Cameron kissed my forehead and then my lips, my cheeks. "You're doing so good, sweetheart."

The burning had banked. I was full of a knot and had the flavor of Alpha on my tongue. For the moment, I could breathe. But I didn't want to sleep yet.

Micah moved to lean against the edge of the nest, and I snuggled down on top of him, my head on his shoulder. "How do you feel, princess?" He stroked my spine slowly, and one of the others draped a silky blanket over the two of us.

How did I feel? Ravenous and needy. Sleepy and spent. But instead I went for the core of everything. The truth.

"Happy."

I dozed off to the sound of his purr beneath my ear.

Fig 50. Primrose
Meaning: Eternal love; Feminine Energy;
I can't live without you; Obsessive love;
Pleasure; Satisfaction

EVERETT

*W*e waited for a long time before daring to speak. Ocean was dozing, not quite under while she sprawled across Micah's chest. The way she clung to him was both precious and heartbreaking, because we knew how much she'd wanted everything we had to give and didn't believe she could ever have it.

My soul was so much lighter now that she knew what we were to her and we could be honest. This had never been fake. It had always been real, and she was ours. Forever.

Our phones sat outside the nest where we'd stripped our clothes off in order to give them to her. My suit pants poked out from behind a pillow next to Micah's boxer briefs, and the sight made me smile. Even when she hadn't known, she *knew*. So deep in her own instincts that she hadn't stopped to question why she was building her nest with our clothes.

I crept to the door and retrieved my phone. "I'll take care of things," I said quietly.

"Give me mine," Cameron said. "I was going to have some things brought over. I'll get on it."

"What things?"

A slow smile crossed his face. "Prototypes that aren't going to fucking break. I told them I needed them, but had planned in the next couple of days. I'll just get them here now."

I chuckled and tossed him his phone.

"And I'm getting someone over to the Caldwell Estate to get everything," he said. "The sooner the better."

"There can't be much left," Micah said. "I thought we had everything brought over."

Cameron shrugged. "Call it an instinct. Aside from that greenhouse, which I know means a lot to her, I'm betting there's either some things Ocean left behind because she assumed she'd be living there again, or something Frank and Laura want to throw at her, either to be hurtful or wash their hands of her. Regardless, I want them to understand that we don't make idle threats."

"No arguments from me. Just be careful of the flowers. Don't move those without talking to her."

Cameron nodded.

I sent a message to my assistant and told them what had happened, and to let the other assistants know to cover everything for a few more days. Despite what had caused Ocean's unexpected heat, this was perfect timing. Since we'd just come back, there weren't any real meetings scheduled. We could take whatever time we needed.

I texted Raina.

Ocean went into heat. We'll be out for a few days. Don't worry, you'll still be a part of the takedown. Keep an eye on things?

RAINA

Will do. Have fun.

Straight and to the point, like Raina always was. We owed her more than we could ever repay, though I had an idea about that. It needed to be discussed after the heat.

I let Marcella know so there would be food we didn't need to prepare. Also food that was easily portable. I was glad the nest had been completed, so it was ready for this. If she'd doubted us on top of not feeling her place of safety...

The sight of her doubt already made my heart hurt. But that might have broken me completely.

Micah's hand came up behind Ocean's head, holding her to him as he shifted a touch more upright. She didn't move. "She's out," he said softly.

"I know we were already going to take action against Frank, but I'm going to have a hard time not—" I huffed a breath. They'd heard my threats when I was in the middle of punching him.

My Omega's face was still fucking red from where he'd *hit* her.

"You're not the only one," Cameron said. We'd stopped on the way out of the house and taken the security footage with the help of Frank's housekeeper. She didn't hold much loyalty to them, which was another strike against him. But we held all the proof we needed to show why my hitting him was justified.

Actually, that was something Raina should know.

EVERETT

Frank hit Ocean. I knocked him out and we got her out of there, but can you let legal know in case he tries to do something? We have video footage.

RAINA

Are you serious?

EVERETT

Very.

It looked like she was typing and deleting for about a minute.

As much as I would like to say otherwise, I'm glad you kept it to just that. I'll make sure legal knows. If you can get the footage to us that would be great.

Oren will have it.

"Send the footage to Oren," I said. "So Raina can get ahead of me punching the shit out of him with legal."

There wasn't a leg to stand on. He'd physically assaulted our wife. And if that wasn't enough, she was our Omega. The instincts to protect an Omega—especially a scent matched Omega—outweighed almost everything else.

"Fuck." I shook my head. "I don't want to think about what he would have done."

When I'd burst into the room he had her in a corner, her scent reeking with rotten terror. I'd seen red. We'd already been delayed by Laura, who declared we couldn't just barge into her house. Micah picked her up and moved her out of our way. She was probably still sputtering in shock when we left.

Good riddance.

"If the stuff with the business wasn't enough, which we now have proof of on the video along with whatever he said to her, then assaulting her is more than enough to exercise the morality clause," Micah said.

Our agreement with him had protections. Of course it did. We weren't foolish. A man like Frank would always try to take more than he was given.

We held the majority stake of his company now, and though he thought he could get out of it, it was over. I would bet good money Frank had promised Joseph the numbers he was pressuring Ocean to get. And if he didn't provide them, Joseph had set him up to take the fall. If I was right, Aiden, and then our lawyers, would prove it.

"You didn't have a chance to look at the trust," Cameron said.

"Not yet. And I won't until after the heat. I won't be able to think about anything properly. And if they pulled something shady while all of our instincts are at their highest?"

"Agreed. It's a good idea to wait." Micah let his hand sweep down her back once more. Then he paused. "Now that she knows. Do you think she'd want to?"

He didn't need to clarify what he meant. Bonding. I'd wanted to bite her the instant I scented her, and I knew they were with me. "I do," I said. "But we'll see if she's ready for that."

Our poor Omega was still overwhelmed by the reality of our loving her. Bonding to us for life was a huge decision no matter what. For now, the fact that she was our wife and ours was enough. But the minute she

351

said the word, I would sink my teeth into her and meld our souls. Make her mine forever.

"We should all probably eat something," Cam said.

Marcella hadn't answered yet, which was fine. It was past her daily hours, and we didn't force her to answer things when she was off duty. There was more than enough food in the house for the four of us.

"Let's grab something," I said to him.

We needed pants, just in case one of the staff was here. Which was why it was good that we'd designed all our bedrooms in the same wing. It was generally off limits outside of specific times to be cleaned.

Cam ran a hand through his hair and leaned on the kitchen island. "Not how I expected to end the day."

"Definitely not. But I wouldn't have it any other way."

I spotted a banana and smiled. We needed more, but that would be perfect. Especially after our wedding night. There was a muffin too, and that would be enough, with some water. With the amount of fucking we were doing, there would definitely be more time for snacks later.

"No," Cam said before laughing. "Me either. But damn, my head is still spinning."

"I know the feeling."

We inhaled some food and grabbed some for Micah before his phone chimed. "Toys are here."

"Excellent." Watching Ocean with toys on our honeymoon had been entrancing. Now that she was ours and knew it? I hoped she would release every last inhibition.

I retreated to the nest. Even Ocean's bedroom was soaked in the syrupy sweetness of her heat perfume. It made my mouth water. I would need an entirely different kind of snack soon. And when I stepped inside, her eyes were open. Sleepy, but open. She hadn't been asleep long, but with how intense her heat had it, that wasn't entirely unexpected.

"Hello, little nymph."

She smiled and pressed her head into Micah's chest. "Hi."

"I brought you some food. Micah too. Need to keep your strength up for all the fucking."

Ocean's cheeks turned a delectable shade of pink, darkening her skin further. I set the food down and Micah helped move Ocean over to me, so she was curled against my side and he could eat.

She tried to sit up, but I didn't let her.

"I can eat by myself."

I held in my laugh and kissed her forehead. "You're barely keeping yourself awake, nymph."

She grumbled but didn't protest more. I peeled the banana, and when I held it up to her, she giggled. "Still like watching me eat bananas?"

"Always, wife."

Ocean ate the banana one bite at a time, never taking her eyes off mine. It was only my Alpha instinct to make sure my Omega in heat was fed and protected that prevented me from stealing kisses and making her arousal surge all over again. As it was, I felt her skin warming and her perfume swirled around us.

"I also brought you a muffin. Do you want it?"

"Not right now."

Micah was already on it. He took the muffin and the peel away, exiting the nest briefly. After drinking some water, my Omega burrowed into my side beneath the blankets, but didn't stay still. She curled in on herself and moaned and sighed. "I'm not used to this."

"What's that?"

"This kind of heat." Climbing up my body, she pushed her face into my neck, seeking my scent. "It's not like this. Ever. But I can't stop."

Slowly releasing my purr, I held her and let her explore. Whatever she needed, I would give her. "You don't need to stop. But everything happened so fast, we wanted to ask you."

"What?"

"Is there anything you don't want us to do? Our instincts are driving us just as hard as yours, baby. So if we let go it might not be soft or gentle. We want all of you, hard and fast. I want to pin you down and take what's mine and make you come so hard you pass out. So if there's something you don't want? Tell us now."

She kept breathing me in, thinking for a second. "Anything we've already done is fine. Ask me for something new. But other than pain, I can't think of anything I don't want."

"No pain. You've had more than enough pain. All I want to do is make you feel good."

Her lips found mine, at once desperate and soft. She whined. "I can't believe I'm about to say this out loud."

"Say what?"

Barely a whisper against my lips. "Can I have a different kind of banana?"

I'd been half-hard since before I fucked her the first time. Not anymore. My instincts raced to the surface to meet hers and made me rock hard. Gripping the back of her hair, I tilted her face back so I could see her. Kiss her. Tease her briefly. "How can I say no to that when you asked so nicely?"

Her tiny whimper made all the remaining blood I had flow south. Fuck, I loved the sight of her desperation. All for us. I kissed her slowly before I released her.

"Lie down, Omega. Let me feed you."

Fig 51. Iris
(Also: Sword Flag)
Meaning: Fire; Flame; I am burning with love;
I burn

OCEAN

*I*n life, there are things you imagined and never believed you'd do. Like the things you watched in porn. It might be hot, but you'd either never do that thing, or it wouldn't be nearly as sexy as you imagined.

Lying on the floor of the nest, arching my back, and allowing my Alpha to push his cock straight into my throat was easily one of the hottest things I'd ever done. And I'd seen my fair share of those videos. No one told me it could feel like *this*.

Like even though he was above me, feeding me his cock, I was the one who held all the power.

Everett's piercing was cold and heavy in my mouth. Strange when it pressed deeper, but I didn't have the same resistance. Heat pulsed in my veins like a living thing, opening me up in every way possible. I wanted all of him. Every single inch.

He was the longest and straightest of my husbands. So he slid in and in and in, and when I felt the skin of his stomach meet my lips, he let out a growl that had my body gushing with slick and arousal and my cunt clenching for a knot because it was *empty*.

"Starting without us?" Cam's voice reached me from somewhere else. I couldn't speak—couldn't even breathe—while Everett held me like this. Captive by his cock, captivated by the rest of him. He tasted incredible. And like he'd promised me moments ago, Everett didn't hold back.

Gripping my hair until it tangled in his fingers, he angled my head just enough to fuck me harder. Using my mouth like he was fucking me elsewhere.

Someone knocked my legs apart with their knees, and then I felt Cameron's thickness pressing into my core. My body was so ready and so wet that he slipped in almost too fast. That rare kind of delicious pain followed—the kind that was an ache while your body adjusted to something it loved. Not the pain I'd been talking about with Rett.

"Shit, sweetheart." He laughed. "Look at you. Spread out like dessert for the three of us."

A mouth fell on my breast. Lips and tongue, adding to everything that was gathering in my center like a cannon ready to explode.

Everett pulled back and let me breathe, but not for long. I didn't care. At this moment I wanted him more than I wanted air. I fell deeper into the trance of the heat, knowing I was safe to let go and just experience the pleasure they offered with no consequences.

Between my legs, Cam moved, taking me with a slow and easy rhythm. "Should we show them how you squirt, sweetheart?"

There was no time to say yes or no. The familiar buzz of the wand pressed against my clit, and all that banked pleasure burst outward in a wave. Like he'd reached inside with those vibrations and pulled it out of me. I had no voice as they took me. Back and forth, one cock and then the other. Over and over while I bathed in bliss.

"Your throat is strangling me, Omega," Everett said, voice rasping as he pulled back. "So fucking close."

I had no conscious thoughts. Micah was still tasting my skin anywhere he could reach. From my breasts to my stomach and stretch marks. Everywhere. And all I wanted was more. I opened my mouth, stuck out my tongue, and watched my Alpha's eyes go black with feral need.

Everett plunged into my throat and took me. Brutally. Forcefully. I loved it. His grunts echoed through my body and built on the vibrations that were bringing me back up to that strange place *beyond* pleasure where I would soak them.

"I'm—" Rett pulled back and came, spilling himself across my breasts. God, I loved the sound of my husbands moaning. There wasn't a hotter sound in the world than a man's pleasure like that. "Some day I'm going to knot this pretty little mouth," he growled.

I'd never even *thought* about that. The image of being trapped to his cock while fucked rolled over me, and that deep inferno erupted. My orgasm soaked the two of us, going everywhere, and then there was a mouth and tongue there, helping me along. Micah. Drinking my orgasm like a man dying of thirst.

"Do we think you could make her squirt again?"

A deep laugh that licked along my clit with his tongue. "If we do, you need to taste it. Our wife is so fucking sweet."

I shuddered, opening my eyes to the three of them watching me with hunger. Wrecked and covered in my cum and theirs, I'd never been more at home or at peace.

Pain wracked my lower body. *Fuck.* "Knot," I gasped. "Please. I need it."

"Let's save the squirting," Everett said. "I have a better idea."

Cameron released me, and he hadn't come. His cock still dripped with me, even as Everett rolled me on top of him and took his place. His already-swollen knot pressed against my entrance, and it was too big.

"Rett." I braced my hands on his chest. "You can't."

His slow smirk had me dripping down on him with need. "You sure about that?"

I wasn't sure. This was my heat, and I was able to do things I'd never dreamed about. His knot was *right there* and I needed it. Releasing a breath, I sank onto him, feeling the stretch, until he slipped into me, locking me in and making me complete.

My breath came in short, sipped gasps. I left nail marks on his chest. "I— I don't know how."

"Your cunt was made for me, that's how. No matter what state it's in, you can take me."

Lips warmed my shoulder. "The question is, can you take another one?" Cam slid his hands down my hips and spread my ass wide. "Two of us at once?"

"Make that three." Micah stepped closer, cock bobbing in line with my mouth.

All three of my Alphas at the same time. Inside me.

Yes yes yes yes yes.

Wetness poured over my ass. I didn't know where Cam had gotten the lube, but if he had a wand, he must have brought everything. Which meant he planned to play with me the whole heat.

I couldn't stop the smile on my face or the happy tears in my eyes. They were mine.

Mine. Mine. Mine.

The head of Cam's cock pressed against my ass. I hadn't thought about how thick he was, and I was already knotted to Everett. "It might be too much."

"You think so, sweetheart?" His lips brushed my ear, breath making my skin tingle. "I think you can take it."

"Can I? You're too thick."

He laughed, and the others followed, and then he was pressing inside me. "Thank you for the compliment, wife, but I think I'm just thick enough." He growled his whisper, punctuated with the movement of his hips. "And I know you can. My Omega's perfect ass will take this fat cock all the way in and let me fuck it until I fill it up with my cum and knot you against your other Alpha so you're absolutely *helpless* with pleasure."

"Cameron."

"Say my name again," he growled. "Right now."

I shook with the power of his command. "Cameron."

With a driving thrust, he pushed in. Enough to make me feel like I was breaking in the best way. Filled more than I ever thought possible, and there was still more of him.

"Everett made a mess of you, didn't he?" Micah asked, running a finger through the cum on my skin and lifting it to my lips. Painting them with the flavor of almonds. "Seems a waste not to clean it up." He lifted my breasts in his hands. Higher and higher, until I could almost reach them.

I never thought this would be a reason to be glad my breasts were large. But hell, there were all kinds of things I hadn't thought about right now. The taste of Everett made me shudder, even from my skin.

His hands gripped my hips hard enough to bruise. "Keep licking me off you, and I'm going to have to fuck you again, little nymph. Knot or no knot."

I met his gaze, daring him to do it, and licked the last of him up.

"There." Cam pushed once more, and he was fully seated inside me. So full I couldn't quite breathe. If it felt like this, I was fully okay with not breathing. Just give me this *wholeness* I felt in the center of my soul.

"Good girl," Cameron whispered into my skin. "Our perfect Omega."

They rocked their hips together and my eyes rolled back. "You're teasing," I whined. "I can't. *I can't.*"

"When you're ready, open your mouth for Micah, and be ready. Because we won't stop when you do. No more teasing."

I was ready. I was fucking *ready*.

Closing my eyes, I opened my mouth.

Everett's fading knot pressed inside me where bright sparkling, crackling ecstasy lived. Friction from the two of them fucking in and out. So close and so full and I was already overloaded in every sense I couldn't take more. Right?

The orgasm slammed into me all at once. My whole body. Someone had connected me directly to a power line. I should have been glowing. Molten and hot and melting. Drinking chocolate and scenting lemon sugar.

One moment I was coming, and the next I was coming again, one into the next. I was too far gone to have *one*. I was made of only pleasure now.

I didn't know how long they fucked me before they came. I only knew what it felt like when they buried themselves to the hilt over and over. The sounds of their effort and our bodies coming together. The scent and the taste of Micah as he held my lips against his swollen knot so I didn't miss a drop. The unreal heat of Cameron finishing and filling me and Everett's knot stretching me once more.

I couldn't support myself anymore. My body was limp and soft and finally felt satisfied. For the moment. They caught me before I collapsed on Everett's chest, purring as they turned me between them.

True sleep found me before I could say anything else. But I was thinking words of love.

Fig 52. Alstroemeria
(Also: Lily of the Incas, Parrot Lily,
Peruvian Princess)
Meaning: Powerful bond

OCEAN

"*We* talked about this. I'm going to crush you."

"Then crush me, Ocean. I don't fucking care." Cameron yanked my hips downward so my pussy was directly over his mouth so he could devour me. Micah had my hands behind my back so I had no leverage to move.

"I don't want to kill you," I moaned. My head fell back on Micah's shoulder, and he laughed, but I heard the exhaustion. We were all spent.

Cam's only response was to suck my clit between his lips and tease it exactly the way I liked. I was already on the edge, thanks to the last of his toys. One last one I'd never tried, and I hadn't picked because I had no idea what it did.

The clear plastic that looked like an oxygen mask sealed over my pussy and created suction so hard that everything swelled. And now, my swollen clit and cunt were twice as sensitive to his tongue. His lips. His fucking *teeth*.

He scraped them over the top of my clit just hard enough to make me fall apart. Shudder and gasp. Sweet torture. My heats had never been this long, and every time I came it was better and worse and I would never have enough.

"Everett, hand me that."

The suction toy. With vibration. It went against my clit and Cameron fucked me with his tongue. I panted, trying to speak and unable to get a word out.

Micah kept my wrists in one of his, using his other arm to pin me to his chest. "One more, princess. Give us one more."

I shook my head. It wasn't possible. The pleasure was too sharp and too big and there wasn't anywhere to go from here.

"One more."

"It's too good for more."

Everett caught my face and kissed me the way only he kissed me. Hard and deep and all-consuming. Micah licked my neck and bit down just enough to make me feel it, and I exploded.

Rich warmth that sank through me and made me squirt, which was Cameron's favorite. Everett swallowed my scream and kept me close, kissing me through the pleasure and into the relief and coolness following the orgasm.

Coolness.

I shook, body weak. The shift from fire to ice was jarring, sweat cooling on my skin. Everett felt the difference and looked at me. I melted into him. "I'm done. It's over. It's over."

His smile was blinding. Kissing me again, he moved me, pulling me off Cam's face and bundling me into a corner of the nest with a soft purple blanket.

He brushed the hair off my face. "You okay?"

"I think so. I'm cold now."

Tucking himself in behind me, outside the blanket, he offered me his warmth and his purr. Cameron was next, laying his head on my hip. Micah pulled my blanketed feet into his lap, and for long minutes, we just rested.

"I need to sleep for like a week," I said quietly. The heat lasted three days, and they were the most intense days I'd ever experienced. Incredible and life-changing as much as exhausting. "And at the same time, I don't want it to be over."

"Me either, princess."

They were *mine*.

Now that my head was clear and hormones weren't wreaking havoc on my system, I could fully process it. They were my Alphas. Scent matched.

That last moment with Micah biting me sprang to mind. I wanted that. But real. I wanted them to bite me so I belonged to them in every way possible. Not just marriage and not just scent matching. Forever.

"What are you thinking?" Micah asked.

I shook my head, clearing it. "What?"

"I've never seen that expression before, and your scent turned as sweet as honey. What were you thinking about?"

A blush overtook my body. I looked away, and Cameron caught it. He smiled, but there was a little sadness with it. "You can trust us with anything, sweetheart. Promise."

"I know." My throat was thick with emotion, partly because coming down from heats was a delicate balancing act of getting back to normal, partly because I was nervous and happy and scared and a hundred other things at once.

The idea of asking them terrified me, but it had to be now, because I would regret it forever if I didn't. I swallowed. "Can I ask you something?"

Everett kissed just below my ear. "Anything."

I shifted so he could see my face. Cam's head was now in my lap, and I didn't mind at all. It felt right to be all connected like this.

But I couldn't get the words out.

Micah came around and sat next to us. He turned my face to his, offering that softness and safety that was all him. "What's wrong, princess?"

Tears flooded my eyes. "I'm scared."

One hand gently cupped my cheek, thumb brushing away the tear that spilled over. "Why are you scared?"

There weren't words for it. Just that huge nameless *fear* that rose up and blocked all the sound. The fear of rejection, even though I knew—*I knew*—they were mine. It wasn't logical or rational. But I couldn't stop the terror of what it would be like to come this far and have them say no.

All I could do was shake my head.

Micah's other hand rose so he held my face before he kissed me softly. "We love you," he whispered. "No matter what it is, we've got you."

I clung to his arms, my tears spilling over as I held onto him and the feeling of them. It was stronger and deeper than the fear, even if the latter was all I could hear in my head. "Would you—" I sucked in a watery breath. "Would you bite me?"

Silence reigned. It was too quiet, and the fear took hold of me with icy fingers digging into my ribs. But when I looked up, daring to know what their reaction was, Micah's gaze was filled with awe. "Are you sure?"

"If you don't want to—" I couldn't tell them it was okay, because I wouldn't be okay.

"Ocean." Everett pulled me so my back was cradled to his chest, his purr so fucking strong it wrapped me in comfort. "I wanted to bite you that night at the Gala. If there'd been any way, I would have. I've wanted to bite you every fucking day, because there's nothing I want more than to feel every part of you, and for you to finally understand how real and deep this is."

I shuddered in relief, sagging in his hold and bowing my head. Micah lifted it. "If you think my asking if you're sure meant I don't want this, then let me make myself clear. Biting you is the highest honor I'll ever have. You're my wife and my Omega." His hand curled into my hair. "The only reason I asked if you're sure is because I want *you* to be sure. Especially right after your heat. Never doubt that if you're ready, I'm yours."

Cameron climbed over me, taking me down onto the cushions. If the blanket wasn't trapped between us, he'd nearly be inside me again. His face was uncharacteristically serious. "There's nothing funny about this, Ocean. No jokes. No teasing. I love you. You're mine, and I want you. Do you want me to bite you, sweetheart?"

My heart skipped a beat, and I nodded. Before he could ask me for the words, I told him the truth. "Yes. More than anything."

He didn't hesitate.

Cam tilted my neck to the side and bit me. Right where my neck met my shoulder, for the entire world to see.

The brief pain melted into sweetness and light. Cameron's bond in my chest. It tasted like him. Sharp and zingy and citrus. All his playful teasing and the darker side of his dominance. And all the love in the world. So much love it stole my breath. I felt everything.

I had to kiss him. *Needed* to kiss him. He met me halfway, consuming each other.

The joy coming through our bond made me laugh when he pulled away. He was grinning. "No take backs now."

"Never."

Deep inside, I felt that the only reason he was releasing me was because he wanted the others with us in these bonds. Feeling him and the truth of everything was a balm to my soul. There was no wondering and no questions. Just simple clarity.

It felt like I could *breathe*.

"Any preference?" Micah asked, raking his gaze over my body.

"No." It was the truth. He could bite me anywhere. It didn't matter where, as long as I was his. His face turned into a smirk, and he rolled me over, ripping the blanket away to expose my ass. Low—where it was nearly leg and *not* ass—I felt the softest of kisses before he bit down.

The bond that wove between us was so different from the first, and yet it was familiar. Like I already knew, the bond was softer than Cam's. Rich and dark and deep, but no less loving.

Micah felt like those moments in Grecia when I'd woken from my nightmares. The steady presence that made the darkness less frightening. Warm arms and soft kisses and just as much love. The sweetness and salt of his scent.

I laughed then. "My ass?"

"One of my favorite parts of you." I heard his smile as he kissed up my spine. "One of many."

Everett rolled me back over, searching my face. "Ready, little nymph?"

I nodded.

He bent his head and bit high along my ribcage. The third bond snapped taut between us, completing everything. The *sincerity* flowing from Everett leveled my soul to the ground. When he said he loved me, it was an understatement. When he called me a goddess, he truly believed it.

And beneath that, I felt the reason he'd bitten me where he had. Because he wanted his bite to be on a part of me that I might not always love. One of my soft places. Where he could remind me how much he loved all of me, just as I was.

Then he was kissing me and I fell into the feeling of him. Wild and dangerous. He was a threat to anything that wanted to harm what was his. Protecting me—protecting his pack and his Omega was the only thing that mattered to him. End of story.

His nutty sweetness layered with my other Alphas, resonating together in a way that was utterly complete.

"Do you believe us?"

"Yes."

Everett kissed my forehead, and we breathed together. Feeling their emotions was so overwhelming, but in a good way. Now I understood what Isolde meant when she described it. There weren't words for it until you had the experience.

A laugh burst out. "Fuck, that's strange," Cam said. "Feeling them through you, sweetheart."

Rett laughed into my skin. "I know. It's all going to be different now."

"What do we do?"

"Besides shouting to the entire fucking world that you're ours?" Everett asked. "Whatever you want, Ocean."

Their joy at feeling *my* joy nearly had me crying the way it layered one on top of the other and back again.

There was such peace now, knowing we had time. No more clock counting down in the back of my head. No more worries. "I think... I want a shower," I finally said. "Then I would kill for some pizza."

"Pizza it is." Cameron winked before tackling me with kisses. All of us were laughing.

It was going to take us forever to leave this nest.

Fig 53. Sesame
Meaning: Purge; Reveal

MICAH

*T*he glass panels of Ocean's greenhouse—the *real* one—sparkled in the sun where we were having it set up on the side of the house. Cameron already had contractors working on securing the property more than it already was.

Sure, we had security, but when we lived here alone, we weren't as worried about ourselves. Now we had Ocean, and there was no way in hell we were going to let anything happen to her. We wanted her to be able to go anywhere on our property without fear. Which meant better fences, cameras, and guards, though we would do our best to make sure they were invisible.

My Omega's happy brightness sang in my chest. She was out back with her friends, sharing what happened and having a good time while what little remained of her belongings were delivered. We'd been sure to hire people who would take the utmost care with her remaining plants, with her approval.

I couldn't wait to see her in her own environment like this.

"Sir?" Marcella's voice came from the house's side door.

"Yes, Marcella?"

The number of times we'd asked her to call us by our given names was probably in the thousands, but she still called us sir. It was a joke now, and she laughed as I gave her a look. Still, her face was serious.

"Mrs. McCabe is here. I didn't want to leave her standing outside, but she's in the foyer."

"Did she say why she's here?"

"She wants to see... Mrs. Caldwell?" She smiled. "I'm not sure what she would like to be called."

I hadn't asked, but I looked forward to the inevitable blush on my wife's cheeks when I did. Reminding her of who and what we were had a tendency to do that, since believing it was all new to her. "I'll ask her and let you know. Or you can ask if you see her first. But I'll take care of Laura, thank you."

With one backward glance at the workers, I headed into the house. I was the best one to deal with this. Because, of the three of us, I would probably come out unscathed. Though if Laura decided she wanted to play with me, she wouldn't like the consequences.

Ocean's aunt stood looking around the foyer in a severe green suit, her hair pulled back into a style far too tight for her face. She often wore it like that, and it was none of my business. Though, in my designer's opinion, the number of styling mistakes she made regularly was mind-boggling.

A pair of workers carried an older wooden trunk through the front door. Not many of Ocean's possessions had been left, but there were a few things of her mother's she'd asked us for. Laura's face twisted as she watched the trunk pass, in disgust, not any sort of grief. "That needs to go back to the Caldwell Estate," she said. "Right now."

The men stopped, and I stepped into view. "No, it doesn't. Carry on, please."

Laura spun toward me. All the disgust she showed before was gone, but there was anger she couldn't hide.

"Hello, Laura. We didn't expect you."

"I'm here to see my niece."

"That won't be happening, but if you need something, I'm happy to help you."

Her eyes narrowed a fraction, and I noticed her fingers twitch, like she was itching to smack me across the face. The feeling was mutual, and I couldn't remember ever wanting to hit a woman. "I need to ask her why the hell our house is being *emptied* and brought here. She's taking things that don't belong to her, and it's unacceptable."

Sliding my hands into my pockets, I approached, keeping an eye on the movers. The chest seemed to have been the last thing. "From my understanding, the few things which were retrieved today either belonged to Ocean or her mother. Is that incorrect?"

"She needs to ask before she takes things. Like that chest. Like all the jewelry. Like my sister's fucking *portrait*."

I tilted my head and watched her. Growing up the way I had, with so many people in my pack, I was good at watching people. It had been helpful over the years. Laura was good at hiding the truth about what she was feeling, masking it with anger and other negative emotions.

"Your husband was informed that we would be taking everything Ocean considered hers," I told her. "After he physically assaulted her. If you have an issue with what was taken, bring it up with him."

"Why go to all the trouble? She'll just have to move it back when you finally kick her to the curb after your agreement is up."

I allowed myself to smirk. Little did she know. I wasn't going to tell her. No, I wanted to be there when Ocean delivered the news that we weren't ever going to kick her to the curb. She was ours forever, and there wasn't any changing it.

My phone buzzed in my pocket. A reminder. "Like I said, you'll have to speak to Frank if you have an issue. My wife is busy and has no interest in speaking to you." I gestured to the door. "But I'll let her know you stopped by."

"I'm not leaving until I speak to her."

"You will, or I'll have you removed."

Laura stared at me. "You can't be serious."

I smiled, trying to stifle my true, genuine laughter. "I am entirely serious. For some reason you seem to think you still have a claim on Ocean's time and control over her life. You do not. Now get the hell out of our house, Laura."

She stood there, and I silently begged her to try to fight back. I would happily watch our brand new full-time security escort her off the property. But she seemed to sense my eagerness and left. Good riddance, though I was sure it wouldn't be the last time we saw her.

My phone buzzed again. I needed to get to Everett's office. Aiden was set to call us with what he found. I hoped it would be enough for us to take care of things, or start to.

Everett's face was frustrated when I walked into his office. "You're glaring at that screen so hard it's going to crack."

"I wish it would," he muttered.

"Why?"

He let out a long sigh and leaned back in the chair. "The trust is legal. It's fucking absurd, and the grossest overreach of control I've ever seen in any kind of these, but it's legal."

I frowned. "That's not fun, but what does it matter? She'll get everything in a year because of her contract with Frank."

"Will she?" He looked at me and tapped his fingers on the arm of his chair. "There's a good chance we're about to destroy McCabe fabrics, or restructure it so thoroughly Frank doesn't know what hit him. Once his company is gone, he won't want to sign anything over to Ocean. I know they have a contract, but I could see a good lawyer having a chance to overturn it."

"Because their contract was entirely based on a deal that won't exist anymore?"

"Exactly."

I scrubbed my hand over my face. "Okay, let's say that happens. And Ocean has to wait five years before it pays out. She won't need money." We had more than enough money for lifetimes.

"There are accounts they can't touch, thankfully," Everett said. "Rather, there's ones they're not *supposed* to touch. At this point I put nothing past him. But that's not the problem."

"Let me guess," Cameron said from behind me. He stood in the doorway. "The level of control they have over her finances is legally dictated by the trust, meaning it doesn't matter if she's married to us. They hold that control until the trust pays out?"

Everett's jaw was tight, but he nodded.

"Are you fucking kidding me?"

"I wish I was," he said. "Now you know why I want to punch the monitor."

Dropping into one of the chairs, I shook my head. "It doesn't really make sense, does it."

"How so?"

"You said it yourself. It's not the normal structure for a trust. Of all the things Ocean has told us, she's never said anything bad about her parents." She hadn't told us much, but the few times she'd mentioned her mother, the memories seemed happy. They stood out because they were some of the few memories she had that weren't laced with pain.

"The thought did cross my mind." Cam leaned on the back of the other chair. "Why the hell would they set it up this way? If there was some strange family tradition or a purpose to it, is there a way to find out? What about the will?"

Everett reached behind him, grabbed a folder, and handed it across to us. "I wondered that. The will is very brief. It leaves everything, in trust, to Ocean. But it defers to the details of the trust itself for the rules. There's nothing in there that changes anything."

"So, theoretically, if they're ignoring the fact that they're not supposed to touch certain accounts, what's stopping Frank and Laura from rearranging all the finances and the estate itself underneath their company so that Ocean is left with nothing?"

"Until recently, not a damn thing. Until we bought the company. Which explains why Frank is desperate. Which is good for us, because he's not thinking clearly and making mistakes."

I leaned forward, elbows on knees. "You're going to have to walk me through it."

"Frank thought he had plenty of time to fuck Ocean over on the trust, so he hadn't bothered yet. But the company was in trouble, and even Ocean's money wouldn't be enough to save it, and what he'd have to do would take too long. Especially if he wanted to keep it under the radar.

"Then we entered the picture. I'm assuming Joseph was the one to leak the Firefly deal to him, with his plan for alternate materials already in mind. But he didn't tell him about that until after we offered the deal."

Things started to come together in my brain. "So when we made Ocean a part of the deal, he saw an opportunity to do more than one thing? Sabotage us with Frank's involvement, and use Ocean to spy on us, probably because Frank declared he had something on Ocean."

Cam swore under his breath and Everett nodded once. "He made the deal with us to save McCabe Fabrics and used the trust to get Ocean on board. But realized after that he wouldn't be able to rearrange her trust without us noticing, especially in a year. Which gave him even more motivation to say yes to Joseph's proposal. He needed McCabe Fabrics to be more profitable, but he also needed more profit to offset what he believes he's losing by giving Ocean what's actually hers."

I rubbed my forehead with the heel of my hand. "That's a bit of a mind fuck."

"Tell me about it," Cam said.

On the desk, Everett's phone lit up. He put it on speaker. "Aiden?"

"The one and only. You're lucky I can make time in my busy schedule." His tone was laced with both charm and sarcasm.

"Still the cheeky asshole, huh?" I asked.

"Well, first, it's arsehole, but yes. And you'll find your paper trail in your inboxes. More than enough to do what you need."

I opened the email that appeared and started to scroll. There they were. Emails between Frank and Joseph's personal account—one the Zenith IT department couldn't access. It was everything we feared. Frank was all too happy to sabotage and lower the quality of his fabrics. Because he'd already been doing it for years in an attempt at solvency.

Everett swore. "We owe you one."

"Actually you don't for that, because you pay me handsomely. But for this? This you might owe me one for."

Another email appeared, and I opened it. The documents were older, clearly scanned in, and grainy. But there was no doubt about what they said.

I looked up, and my packmates met my gaze. "Holy shit."

Fig 54. Tarragon
(Also: Dragon Herb, Fuzzy Weed,
Green Dragon, King of Herbs,
Snakefoot)
Meaning: Horror; Permanence;
Shocking occurrence

OCEAN

"*I* love your house, Iz," Trinity said. "And god knows I love your parent's estate, but this is *nice*."

We sat on the back terrace behind the house, lounging in the afternoon breeze. The umbrella over the table wasn't doing that much good, but I savored the bit of shade. Especially since I was wearing a light cardigan. I would take it off soon, but I wanted to reveal my bite when we were comfortable and not in the doorway.

Isolde laughed and rolled her eyes. Her own bites were on display with her strapless top. Four of them. Her Beta had her bite on his neck. They were gently faded now, and you wouldn't immediately see them if you weren't looking.

My skin was darker. Would Cameron's bite be paler when it healed? Right now it was still obvious, and I didn't mind one fucking bit.

"So have you recovered? You dropped off the planet for a bit there. Jetlag must have been a bitch." Trinity raised her glass.

"You could say I'm recovered, yeah."

In my chest, my husband's emotions hovered gently. All three of them felt like they were concentrating in different ways. The fact that I could feel them all was simply my favorite thing.

"Why do I feel like that's leading to a story?"

I sipped my drink. Marcella made us some of the best margaritas I'd ever had. This one was strawberry, but I wanted to taste the watermelon one she'd offered. "Because it is." Clearing my throat, I told them about Frank and what had happened.

Trinity grabbed her phone. "I can still ruin his ass, O. Let me at him."

"Pretty sure my husbands are already on it, but that's not the real story."

"*That's* not the real story?"

I shook my head and pulled the cardigan away from my bite. Their gazes fell to my neck, and they both went still.

"Wait," Isolde said. "Really?"

"Really. They're mine. Scent matched. That night at the gala they saw me and wanted to approach me, and when they did... they scented me." I couldn't stop my smile. "They invented the marriage in order to get close to me."

Both my friend's mouths hung open, staring at me.

"Please say something."

"Oh my god, *congratulations*!" Isolde was out of her chair and hugging me, laughing. "I can't believe it."

"Me either," I said honestly.

It still hadn't fully sunk in that this was real and not some sort of desperate fever dream that I made up.

Trinity was still in her seat, and I caught the look on her face. Pain. Tears glossed her eyes, and she blinked them away before she stood and leaned over to hug me. "I'm so happy for you."

"Are you okay?"

"What do you mean, I'm fine?"

Standing out of my chair, I continued to hug her. "It's okay if you're not, Rin."

"I am so *fucking* happy for you," she said. "Of anyone, you deserve this."

The way she clung to me told me everything. She *was* happy for me. And sad, too. Because it wasn't her. And now both of her best friends had packs while she was alone.

"You know that just because I'm bonded now doesn't mean anything changes?"

She laughed and stepped away, swiping at her cheeks. "I know. And I'm holding you bitches to it."

"*Oh*," Isolde went to her purse slung on the back of her chair. "That reminds me, Rin. I have something for you. Courtesy of Rowan."

She handed Trinity a small, square box, and the three of us burst into laughter. Isolde's Alpha Rowan made candy. Well, he made cannabis treats, and some of them happened to be chocolate, though he made the regular, non-high kind too.

"Which kind are they?"

Isolde smirked. "Both. The fun ones are stamped with stars."

"Noted. Thank you." She looked at me and grabbed her glass. "Now, I'm toasting to you, O. Congratulations, and I'm looking forward to getting to know your guys better now that they're not going anywhere. And," she took a sip of her drink, "As the final single friend, I'm going to need more details about how this happened. *All* of it."

I let my smile creep over my face. "Fine. But first, I need to tell you what happened in a temple in Grecia."

"*What?*"

Laughing, I took a long drink. "You're going to love this one."

A couple hours and several drinks later, I waved to my friends as they were driven away by one of the DuPont drivers. I didn't know all their names yet. I needed to learn them. Since this was my home now, they were also my staff.

"Have a good time?" Micah asked, snaking an arm around my waist.

I leaned back into him, loving how I could *feel* his enjoyment of touching me. That my scent was intoxicating to him. I was just tipsy enough that I wanted to lean back into him and just... be. "Yeah. We had a good time."

"They're happy?"

"Mhmm. I think it was a little harder for Rin, but I don't blame her. She's feeling a little left behind, and she already deals with enough of that. But she is happy for us. Be prepared. She'll probably grill you when she sees you next."

His purr rumbled against my back, soft laughter in my ear. "I think we can handle it."

We closed the door, and he kept his arm around me. "Come with me."

"Where are we going?"

"The kitchen. For food."

I made a face. "I'm not that hungry."

"Still."

It was then that I caught the undercurrent of worry in his emotions, and the others felt the same. "Is everything okay?"

"Yes," he said. When he took my hand and pulled me with him, he squeezed it. "Absolutely. But we need to talk to you about something."

"Everyone in the world loves that fucking sentence."

We were close enough to the kitchen that Cam burst out laughing. "Please keep the sass coming, sweetheart. I love it."

"Seriously though."

Everett patted the seat on the bench beside him. "Seriously. It's a good thing."

"Ooookay." I sat, and he tucked his arm around me before placing a paper folder in front of me. "What's this?"

"We have someone who..." Cameron shrugged. "We met him in college. His name is Aiden, and he works in what we'll call a gray area as far as information. He helps us when we need him to, and because of everything happening with the company, we asked him to look into something about your uncle."

I accepted the glass of water Micah handed me. "If you sat me down to tell me my uncle is involved in some shady shit, it's not like I didn't suspect that. It's not a huge surprise."

Everett pulled me in and kissed the side of my head. "No, I don't imagine so. But Aiden went a step further on this one. We didn't ask him to, but he found something you need to see."

Well, that sounded a bit dire. I opened the folder and started to read. Wait... what?

These were the documents for my trust. But... they weren't the ones I recognized. These said that I was meant to get everything when

377

I turned twenty-one. The trust made provision for my aunt and uncle in a small way, as a thank you for being my guardians, but nothing more.

And there weren't any restrictions listed. None of the money-managing bullshit I'd been dealing with. No qualifications for receiving it. Just turning twenty-one. Nerves lodged in the pit of my stomach. "Is this some kind of joke? Because if it is, it's not funny."

Micah took a slow breath and let it out. None of our bonds had any trace of joking, or even levity. "It's not a joke, princess."

I stared at the pages in front of me and read them again. And a third time. "I don't understand."

"We believe this is the real trust that your parents signed." Everett flipped to the last page and showed me the familiar signatures. They were my parents' signatures. I'd seen my trust paperwork more than once over the years, and I knew the signatures like the back of my hand. "Do you remember the first time you saw your trust?"

"No. I remember seeing it, but not exactly when. Everything was a bit of a whirlwind after mom died. All I knew for a while was that Frank and Laura were taking care of me. By the time I was in high school and starting to think about college, that's when I actually started asking questions. I didn't know any better."

Cameron reached across the table and captured my hand. "Of course not."

I shook my head. "How is this possible? Or legal? They changed it?"

"Possible?" Everett asked. "Aiden is diving deeper into that for us. Our best guess is that after everything was resolved with your mother's will, all the legal documents were handed over from her lawyer to Frank's. With you being so young, he fabricated the new papers, though we're still wondering about the signatures, since they match. As for it being legal? Absolutely fucking not."

"I just—" I slumped back in my seat and leaned on Everett. "If this is real, then…"

I couldn't even verbalize the primal rage that hovered on the edges of my consciousness. If it was true, then the last nine years were for nothing. All their control and the struggle to get *Entendre* off the ground when I had to *beg* them to allow me the money to get started. They barely gave me enough seed money to even buy the first round of flowers. But I'd been desperate enough to make it work, and so I'd made it work.

Every single painful comment and attack, all while they were living off money that was mine. And relishing it.

Keeping my breathing even, I closed the folder. "These aren't the originals. They won't do anything to fix it."

"No," Everett admitted. "But we're working on that."

I let my face drop into my hands. "Even Frank isn't foolish enough to keep copies of documents he's intentionally trying to bury."

Cameron smirked. "You're right. But we won't get them from him. Our best chance is if your mother's lawyer, or their firm, still has original copies. With clients like the Caldwells, I'm sure they keep everything they have. Your parents still have charitable foundations that are sustained and run, right?"

They did. And those wouldn't have been handed over to a new lawyer. Even when I was small and curious, Mom told me that they made sure to keep themselves out of it. To make sure no one had any questions about what was happening with the money. I hadn't understood what she meant, but now I did.

"If we can prove it, what do we do?"

"Well." The three of them were smiling, and Everett placed a different folder in front of me. "We didn't get a chance to tell you everything that happened, because we were a little busy wi—"

"Fucking you," Cameron said. "We were busy fucking you."

I sensed nothing but pride and pleasure from his place in my chest, followed by his thoughts spiraling somewhere dirty. "Cam."

"I don't know what you're talking about."

"Sure you don't." Beneath the table, I nudged his leg with my foot. Which backfired when he caught my ankle and held it captive.

Micah leaned on the table, suppressing his laughter. "*Anyway*. There's more to tell you about Frank and why the toys broke, all of it."

And they did. Every little detail of what had transpired. The things that led to our marriage, and the things our marriage had encouraged and allowed, as well as their theories about why Frank was suddenly desperate and making bolder moves than he had before.

When they finished, I downed the last of my water and stretched. "What a mess."

"More like a nest of snakes," Micah muttered.

"So what do we do?"

On the table, Everett wove our fingers together and held my hand. "*You* don't have to do anything, wife. Aiden is looking, as are our lawyers. But we're planning on taking everything they have from them, getting you your money so you can do whatever the hell you want with the Caldwell Estate and your inheritance, and leaving them all behind in the dust."

"That sounds nice." Not just getting what my parents wanted me to have, but being taken care of. Not having to take on the heavy burden of figuring it all out. I didn't have to do anything. I simply had to let them help me.

Cam rose and held out a hand to me. "There is one thing you can do though, if you want?"

He spun me under his arm before pulling me back. "Once everything is settled, we need to deliver this news all at once, so neither Joseph nor Frank has a chance to defend themselves or do any more lasting damage to either you or the company. So, we're going to call Geneva tomorrow." His grin was wicked. "Feel like designing some flowers for a party?"

Fig 55. Bird's-Foot Trefoil
(Also: Butter and Eggs, Deer Vetch, Eggs and Bacon)
Meaning: Retribution; Revenge

OCEAN

*T*he little flower in front of me wouldn't cooperate. In the long run it wouldn't matter, as no one was going to look at this little nigella blossom and single it out. But I was a little nervous, and fixing this flower was helping.

Guests would be here soon, and unlike the Caldwell Gala, I was looking forward to this one. The first party in my new home, and the party where we would make things right.

I'd chosen a theme of fire for the flowers, and of course, they had a deeper meaning that made me smile. Deep crimson roses for our love and passion. Red Petunias for anger and disdain. Orange lilies for revenge. Yellow celandine for legal matters and protection. The pale blue nigella, for the hottest part of the flame, meant embarrassment. Those flowers also had a different name which made me laugh—Jack In Prison. Appropriate.

And finally, young and pale sesame flowers which meant to purge something, or to reveal it.

Combined together the flowers looked like they were burning, and it was lovely. Something deep was satisfied by the fact that they were shouting condemnation without us having to say it out loud.

But of course, we would say it.

Cameron appeared in his tuxedo, and every thought of fixing the little errant flower flew right out of my head. He smiled, feeling that thought and returning it right back to me.

I wore a dress I'd owned forever and never worn before because I thought I couldn't pull it off. Floor length, off the shoulder, sparkling red fabric that skimmed down my body and hugged it in the right places. A light, gossamer train floated from the back of the shoulders. I was still fat, and this dress showed that, but the fear was no longer claws piercing my heart.

It was still there, but lessened. One day I hoped I wouldn't care what anyone thought of me. But in the meantime, I had Alphas who loved me and found me beautiful. Nothing else mattered.

The way my husband looked at me made it worth every ounce of nerves I had while putting this dress on. And watching Frank and Laura see me wearing it without shame, and seeing my now-healed mark, would be equally cathartic.

"Now I know why you wouldn't tell us what you were wearing," Cam murmured as he approached.

"I needed you to *not* tear it off me before we even made it to the party."

"You need to know that I'm taking that statement as full permission to tear it off you later." He made a little motion with his finger for me to twirl.

I laughed. "I'll happily let you *remove* it later. No destroying."

"Seems like I need to invest in more clothes I can destroy when it comes to you."

"Or," I slid my hands up his lapels and straightened his tie, "you can think of it as me presenting you with a pretty package for you to unwrap. *Slowly.*"

I used the word presenting on purpose. My own double entendre.

"Careful, sweetheart, or I'll have you presenting right in the middle of this ballroom."

"I don't think that's the kind of show we're trying to put on tonight."

Cam sighed and kissed me lightly, so as not to mess up my lipstick. "You're right. I'll have to suffer."

I was going to tell him he was looking forward to this gala as much as I was, but I was distracted by Micah and Everett coming in. Now I was surrounded by hotness, and I savored their attention on me.

"Your first guests are here," Micah said, but neither of them could stop looking at me.

I smirked as I passed them, going to meet Trinity and Isolde. They watched me leave, and the fire burning in all three of our bonds nearly had me perfuming.

"Holy shit, Ocean," Trinity gasped. "You look incredible."

"Thank you."

I twirled again just in time for Isolde to step inside and see me. Her pack followed her. "You're finally wearing it. *Fuck* yes."

Faking a curtsy, I pulled them both into a hug. "It honestly feels really good. And I can't wait for the rest of it."

"Oh, I am so ready for the show," Trinity said with a grin. "I can't wait."

Back in the ballroom, my husbands and Isolde's pack introduced themselves. I'd spoken about them on our honeymoon and over the last few days while we planned everything. It was good to see them mingling, because if I had my way, we would all be seeing a lot of each other.

Isolde nudged my shoulder with hers. "Happiness looks good on you, you know."

"Right back at you."

Even I could admit I looked different when I looked at myself in the mirror. Happiness and peace were the only things that had ever made me feel that way. And tonight, I hoped a taste of revenge would do the same.

I heard the front door open once more outside of the ballroom and smiled. "Here goes nothing."

The party was a complete success. Raina and her pack were here, along with other friends of my husbands. More people than I knew, but many of them I recognized from our wedding. It didn't matter because I was walking on clouds.

Until I saw Jason. The man who I'd danced with at the first gala. I would thank him for providing my husbands an easy entrance, but I now knew they were always going to come for me.

I approached him at the drinks table. "You're Jason, right?"

He grinned, full of arrogance. "I am. Nice to see you again, Ocean. You look fantastic. Change your mind about letting me take you home?"

The urge to roll my eyes was so strong it was painful. "I'm married now. And bonded. Surely you knew that if you came here?"

"Yeah, but..." he shrugged. "It's all for show, right?"

"It is very much not for show."

That only made him smile deeper. "I knew it."

"Knew what?"

"That you were a freak. You must have had something to trap them into this. Or they're the freaks, just like me. Or," he leaned closer. "You're lying, it is all for show, and your husbands are cheating on you with women they actually find attractive, in which case, I'm still *very* willing to take you home."

Rage filled me, both at the implication that I wasn't good enough, but also at the idea that they would do something like that.

My Alphas.

I needed to protect them at all costs. My instincts rose, and I was fully about to slap this man in the face—damn the consequences—when a voice spoke from next to me.

"My wife is too kind to put you in your place," Everett said. "But I will."

The man opened his mouth and closed it, looking like a fish. Everett closed the distance between us and placed a hand on my lower back before leaning in and kissing my temple. "You all right, little nymph?"

"I am now," I murmured.

"Good," he breathed. "That's good."

He turned back to the man, whose gaze was fastened on us like we were some sort of weird science experiment that had just blown his mind.

"It's Jason, right? Jason Marsh?"

"Yeah."

"Hmm." Everett's hand curled around my hip. "Well, Jason. While the rest of the world finds it entertaining to speculate about why my

385

pack and I married Ocean, we decidedly do not. So the next time I hear you suggest that my wife had to do something to trap us, that she's feeding a fetish, we're all cheating on her, or any of the *bullshit* I know you have already said tonight, let alone what you just said to her face, I will take everything you love and shred it into pieces so small you'll never find them before setting them on fire."

Jason swallowed while Everett took a smooth sip of his drink. Then he leaned in. "And once I'm finished with your business and all of your possessions, I'll come for you. Got it?"

"Got it." Jason's voice was dangerously close to a squeak.

"Now get the fuck out of our house."

The man didn't hesitate. From the look on his face, he was about to piss himself with fear. He might have if Everett had said anything else. I leaned into his arm. "You didn't have to completely terrify him."

"Oh, yes I did. Even if he weren't in *our* home talking shit about us, which is completely disrespectful, no one gets to talk about you that way without consequences."

I shivered, enjoying the possessiveness he showed. "But didn't you invite him?"

"We did," Everett confirmed. "So we could do exactly what I just did."

"Really?"

"Don't you remember?" he whispered. "I protect what's mine."

He was about to kiss me as I spotted my aunt and uncle entering the ballroom. Late. *Really* late. Not that it was a surprise. They hadn't even wanted to come after the threats Everett had leveled at them, but my pack insisted, leaning on the fact that they were business partners, and Frank, at the very least, was expected to be there.

My aunt would never leave my uncle to do an event alone. It wouldn't look right, and looks, as we knew, were everything to her.

I saw them as soon as they walked in, and they saw me. Everett stood nearby, and I felt his attention turn toward me. "Need help, little nymph?"

"I've got this part."

"Call us if you do. Ten minutes, all right?"

Right. Ten minutes. I could do that. I handed him what remained of my drink and headed over to them.

"Frank, Laura. Thank you for coming."

Laura's gaze fell on my neck, and her eyes went wide. Her mouth dropped open before she could check her reaction. I touched it. "Oh, right. Sorry I didn't tell you. It turns out the DuPont pack are my scent matches. I went into heat after my husbands rescued me." I looked my uncle in the eye. "From you."

I watched Frank's face go pale. "Congratulations?"

"Thank you. We're very happy."

He floundered, and I didn't waver. Part of me felt uncomfortable with *his* discomfort, and another part of me was relieved. I finally had some power. How many times had they both made me feel exactly like this? Tongue-tied, speechless, and with no way out.

"I suppose I should congratulate your... pack as well. Excuse me." He left so quickly, Laura was left gaping after him.

I looked at her. "If you have something to say about my appearance, now would be the time."

"Really? That's what you're going to do? You invited us, Ocean. We didn't come here to be attacked, and I won't stand by while you do it."

"Fine." I didn't need to stand there with her trading insults. What I really needed was to get her into the smaller salon off the ballroom. "While you're here, I found something you should see of my mother's."

"Really?"

"Yes. I discovered it not long after the rest of my things were delivered. She would want you to see it." I gestured toward the salon, and after an unsure look at me, she went. I met Micah's gaze across the room, and he nodded once. It was time.

We were the first ones in the room. Laura looked around in distaste. She'd always liked gaudier and more traditional design. Our home was far too light and sleek for her taste.

I thought it was perfect.

"Where is it?"

All the papers were spread on the coffee table. "There."

"Ah, there you are," Cameron said. My husbands entered the room with Frank in tow. Raina had been instructed to bring Joseph in later. One thing at a time.

Laura crossed her arms. "What is this, Ocean?"

"I didn't lie. Take a look." I glanced at my uncle. "Something of my mother's."

Huffing out a breath, she strode to the coffee table and started to look. Then, like Frank had earlier, she went pale. "Frank?"

He was at her side in a moment.

It was a strange sensation, watching someone's world fall apart. But I couldn't feel a shred of sympathy for them.

Aiden, the hacker, and my husbands'—*my*—lawyers figured out the entire paper trail. It was exactly like they'd suspected. After the trust had been passed over to Frank's lawyer, he'd been paid off to help them change it. The Caldwell family lawyer still had copies, dated well before my mother's death.

Hard to prove, since the originals had likely been destroyed.

Until my husbands threatened the lawyer with everything they had. Thanks to Aiden, it wasn't hard. Where one crime was, more usually followed, and the man had a laundry list of crimes to his name. Exposing any one of them would end his career, the firm he was a partner of, and his life's work.

We settled for his career and a signed confession.

My mother's lawyer signed a statement too. It said that he'd been present for this version of the trust and when it happened. There wasn't much more we needed.

"Where did you get this?" Frank asked. "This is absurd."

"No," I snapped. "What's absurd is the two of you using this as a way to control and abuse me. Not that it should have ever happened, but for nine years past when it should have fucking ended."

"*Abuse you?*" Laura looked like I'd struck her. "We only ever tried to do the best for you, Ocean. It's not our fault you refused the help. That you're lazy and entitled and unwilling to compromise."

"Compromise." I laughed. "That's funny."

Frank tossed the papers back on the table and shrugged. "You can't prove any of this. No ink tests or anything." His smile sickened me. "The real documents are long gone."

The doors to the salon opened, and Raina practically dragged a man through the door. "What the hell are you dragging me in here for?" he snarled.

"Ah, our final guest," Everett said. He was the first one of my husbands to speak.

"Wait," I said in sudden recognition. "*That's* Joseph?"

Everett looked at me. "You've met?"

"The day we left for the honeymoon. When I was at the Caldwell Estate. He came in right as I was leaving."

Joseph glared at me, silently. He didn't seem to know why he was here, but he wasn't happy about it. Everett pulled me against him and kissed my temple. "Thank you," he whispered. "Now there's a witness to their collusion."

"He looks like a weasel," I whispered back.

My husband suddenly had a coughing fit, and in my chest I felt how hard he was laughing. But he got it under control and stood taller, ready to finish this off. They'd agreed to let me handle the first bit, and I felt their pride. Now, I was happy to let them take the reins.

With a wave of a hand, our security closed the salon doors.

"What's going on, Everett?" Joseph asked.

"We know."

"Know *what*?"

Cameron chuckled. "Everything. You know you actually wove your own downfall by pushing us to marry? If you hadn't, you might have gotten further. But it was that decision that unraveled everything for you."

We didn't have the same scent canceller in here, and several scents were turning distinctly sour. Joseph still held on to his relaxed demeanor. "I have no idea what you're talking about."

Winking at me, Cameron slid his hands into his pockets and stepped forward. He'd asked permission for this, so I knew it was coming. "What I'm talking about is us finding our scent matched Omega. One of the many reasons we married so quickly. And then we went on our honeymoon, and in the course of usual *honeymoon* activities, one of our lovely Extasis toys broke.

"Now, we design products that are only the best, so that was unusual. Would you like me to continue?"

Frank sneered. "What the fuck does your sex life have to do with any of us?"

"We never said it had anything to do with you." Everett tilted his head. "But now that you've spoken up, we know your role in this as well if you'd like to get the confession over with."

"I'm leaving," Joseph said.

Micah sighed. "No, you're not."

The security guards at the door blocked Joseph's path. He growled, but they didn't move. I thought he might try to hit them. Given the demonstration I'd been given after they were hired, I kind of wanted to see him try.

"Let's get this over with," Everett said. "We know that you've been deliberately sabotaging Zenith Incorporated's products, and those of its subsidiaries, in order to make higher profits and get shareholders off your back. We know you went to Frank to continue this plan and use our marriage to Ocean to further weaken our position when your distraction plan didn't work. We know you wanted to take over Zenith and take it in an entirely different direction with a new set of investors. Along with one hell of a salary bump."

"You covered your tracks well," Cameron said. "I'll give you that. But not well enough."

"What are you going to do to me?" Joseph scoffed. "Nothing I did was illegal. Changing the materials of products isn't a crime. Nor are conversations about potential business maneuvers."

Micah came over to stand with me, slinging a casual arm around my shoulders. He seemed at ease, but inside I felt he was anything but. They were all taut as bowstrings, ready to snap if these men broke the wrong way. "You're right. Those things aren't crimes. But corporate espionage? That is a crime."

"She never gave us shit. Talking about something *isn't a crime*." Sweat shone on Joseph's forehead. Did he realize he'd just admitted it?

"Of course. But did you ever provide our internal numbers to people outside of Zenith in an attempt to sway them to your plan?"

Everett asked. But he wasn't really asking. We already knew the answer.

Micah stepped away from me to join Cam and Rett, the three of them staring down Joseph with a wall of raw Alpha power.

It was fucking hot.

"Here's what's about to happen. The Board of Directors is being informed of your crimes, with ample proof, as we speak. We are formally pressing charges against you for corporate espionage, among several other things. Your lawyers will tell you soon, I'm sure." Cameron smiled. All of them were enjoying this.

Hell, I was enjoying it too.

Joseph blinked. And again. He sputtered. "You can't just do this."

Everett cleared his throat. "According to the Zenith bylaws, if a member of the board is engaged in any criminal activity, they can be removed without a vote of the board, and the majority shareholders can appoint a replacement, effective immediately. This is the official notice of your removal."

One of our guards peeked out the door and nodded. Two uniformed police officers entered and approached Joseph. He lunged for the door, but they were faster. The whole party watched as he was walked out in cuffs, and behind us, Frank and Laura were edging toward the other doors.

Micah spun. "As for you. Your lawyer folded. Confidentiality doesn't cover these crimes. On top of the espionage, you're being charged with forgery, fraud, and assault. I'm sure there's a few other things in there too."

"Oh, for sure," Cam said with a laugh. "Too many to memorize. You know how it is."

Two more police officers came for my uncle, and he was too stunned to fight them or resist. On his face, there was utter defeat. It loosened something deep in my chest. Healed it. He made this bed, now he had to lie in it. It was possible he'd be buried in it.

They were halfway to the door with my uncle when Cameron called after them. "Oh, and there are people taking possession of the Caldwell Estate as we speak. It doesn't belong to you." Turning back to my aunt. "Any possessions will be delivered to you, Laura, as soon as you notify us of your new address."

My aunt, stricken though she was, melted in relief. "You're not charging me?"

"No," I said.

Straightening, she nodded once. "At least you've done one good thing. Thank you for recognizing that I was trying to help you."

The laugh came out of me so quickly I had to cover my mouth. She stared at me, and I kept laughing. It was so forceful tears came to my eyes. My voice was still shaking with it when I started to speak. "I'm not recognizing anything, Laura. The reason I'm choosing not to send you to prison for the rest of your life is that this is far, far worse."

She frowned. "What?"

"Did you hear them?" I asked. "You can't go back to the Caldwell Estate. And they might have skipped over this bit, but all the Caldwell accounts have been frozen until they can be transferred to my name. You have no home, and no money. But I'm sure you'll figure it out."

"I—"

"The *real* trust my mother made for me. *Your sister*. Has a little gift of money for you, as a thank you for taking care of me. Because I'm not like you, I'll make sure you get that. But nothing more."

I walked toward her, and I'd never felt more powerful. She was small in comparison. Relief shook along my limbs. My voice was low and even. "But the real reason I'm not sending you to prison isn't because I want to see you poor and homeless, Laura. It's because I know that me sending you to prison would be the last nail in the coffin of your bitterness. You'd use it to convince yourself that you were right. I'm just your fat, lazy, piece of shit niece who never appreciated anything and never did anything right. So I'm not sending you there. I'm letting you go free.

"You'll be living your life, whatever life you have left, without Frank. You'll have to scrape for what you have and go without, exactly like I had to while I was living under your care. And the humiliation of having to do something as menial as work for a living, knowing that you have to be grateful to me not being in prison, is ten times worse than locking you up where you can rot with your own thoughts and hate me."

For the first time, she truly looked afraid. Her eyes flicked past me to Frank. His head was bowed, and there was something like shame on his face, though I had no way of knowing whether it was real.

"Frank?" Her voice wavered. "What do I do?"

The officers began to read him his rights, walking him out through the ballroom.

"Frank, *what do I do*?" Her shriek echoed loudly.

"Whatever you do," Everett said, "do it somewhere else. You're not welcome in our home. Get out, don't come back, and pray you find somewhere to stay that doesn't put locks between you and your food."

She looked at me, eyes watery. Her hands wrung in front of her. "Ocean, please."

"Hold on to this feeling for later," I said. "So you know how helpless and furious I've felt since you took over my life. And understand, finally, that this is what it's like to be truly disposable."

Laura jerked back like I'd struck her. For one solitary moment, I saw desolation in her gaze. Then she stood perfectly straight and schooled her face before she strode out through the ballroom and didn't look back.

Cameron waved to the guests. "We'll be right out. Sorry for the interruption." He looked at the security. "Find Marcella and tell her to make sure the catering staff are circulating with food."

"Yes, sir."

The doors closed behind him, and we all blew out a collective breath.

"Fucking hell, princess," Micah said, breaking into a smile. "You were fucking incredible."

Power lined my body. I felt like I could jump over the ocean all the way back to Grecia on my own. And still, there was a tinge of pain. "I feel incredible. But is it normal to be a little sad too?"

Raina cleared her throat. I'd nearly forgotten she was there. "I think it's normal to grieve when these things happen. Even if the relationship was utter shit, it's still a break that needs to heal."

"Thank you," I whispered.

"Raina," Everett said. "We've talked about it, and if you accept, we are appointing you as Chairman of the Board of Zenith Incorporated, effective immediately."

She froze for a moment, shocked, then she smiled. It was the kind that Cameron had. Charming and cheeky. "Well, it's about time you noticed my worth."

All of us laughed, breaking the tension.

She shook their hands, and we all drifted back to the party. Everyone had questions, and the gossip was already circling. Isolde and Trinity were nearly feral, but I needed a moment.

"Are you all right, little nymph?"

"Yeah," I said. "I really am."

Our connections all rang with the relief and pride in each other and what we'd done.

"Then let's party," Cam said. "So I can rip this dress off you later."

We laughed and did exactly that.

Fig 56. Phlox
Meaning: Our souls are united

*M*y husbands were seeing the last of our guests out of the house when I went down to the water. Barefoot, still in my dress, it was the first time I'd stepped on the beach here. At *our* home.

A waxing moon shone just a touch of light onto the water, gilding it in silver. And though the sea was calm and rhythmic, I wasn't settled. My chest felt lighter than it had in years. I was finally free. I could do anything I wanted with my family's house and money. I never had to worry about a snide comment or a strange punishment again.

Yet I couldn't ignore the tiny ache of sadness in my chest. Not because of what I'd done—there wasn't a person in the world who would see the aftermath and think I wasn't justified. But because it had always been there. The ache of a child who'd lost her parents and desperately wanted love from the only people she had left.

Even after everything, there'd been a tiny part of me that hoped they would see me and show me that they'd cared. At all. That somehow I'd missed it, and they were telling the truth when they said they were trying to help me.

But it wasn't true, and that ache wasn't going to go away with the satisfaction of revenge. That ache was why I'd kept trying so hard for so long, despite knowing the truth I didn't really want to face. I *was* sad, but I was sad for my younger self, who didn't get what she needed. I was sad for all the lost time when I could have had the happiness I had now. Sad for everything that felt lost.

Still, if it hadn't happened this way, I might never have met my pack.

I felt them coming closer. Our bonds were still so new that even focusing on them in my chest was a shot of joy straight to the chest. Which they felt, and they lit up like a cluster of stars made just for me.

Micah reached me first, the scent of chocolate and caramel mixing with the scent of the sea. It reminded me of that night in Grecia—which I wouldn't mind repeating.

"I wish we had bioluminescence here," I said softly.

"I can look into it if you like."

I laughed and turned to wind my arms around his neck. "I love you for that, but let's not pollute the ocean with any invasive species just so we can have some glowy sex."

"Who says they're invasive? I'll check anyway. And if not, I'll build you a pool that glows."

"Or you can take me back to the real thing."

His lips brushed against mine. "That too."

The wind picked up as he kissed me, cool now that the sun had set. I shivered, not entirely from the breeze.

A second pair of hands touched my waist. Cam. "How do you feel?"

"Good." I hesitated, letting him feel it before the words. "Bittersweet, but free."

"That makes sense."

Sighing, I leaned back into him and let him spin me away from Micah. "It's overwhelming too. What I'll have to do to figure out the Estate's finances now that it's mine. How to take care of it or modify the house. Or find something to do with it. Something Mom would have wanted."

If my mother were still here, I had no doubt that the Caldwell mansion would have been turned into something else by now. Something for one of the many charities she donated to or something that helped the world. Something beautiful. I didn't know what it would be yet, but I wanted to do that.

"It's the same for you guys. All the work to undo the damage Joseph and Frank did. Both behind the scenes and publicly. Not to mention the money it will take."

"That doesn't matter," Everett said. His bowtie was gone, the first few buttons of his shirt undone and hair ruffled in the breeze. He was fucking stunning, and I felt through our bond that he thought the same thing about me.

"I know you have enough money to do it, and I know you're not worried about it. That doesn't make it right."

Rett smiled, but it was soft. Amused. He came to stand in front of me, using the moonlight to search my face before lifting his hand to my cheek. "That's not what I mean. I mean that it doesn't matter. All of it doesn't matter. Even if they'd succeeded and ruined us. Even if we were bankrupted and penniless because of the things they did, I wouldn't change a fucking thing." He moved to my face, dropping his forehead against mine. "Let them come again. Let them try to take everything. I would change *nothing*."

The depth of feeling swirling between us in the bond nearly sent me to my knees. And the others, now standing at my sides, surrounding me with warmth and love, felt the same.

"Why? If you could know what was coming, why wouldn't you change it?"

We were so close I could barely see it, but Everett smiled. "You," he whispered. "There is nothing I would not lose, no injury I would not take, and no price I would not pay in order to find you."

"You're ours," Cam turned me to him, thumb brushing over his bite at my neck. "Body and soul. But we know how close we came to never meeting you, sweetheart. We'll never forget it, and we'll never not be grateful for the things that brought us together. Even the bad ones."

My eyes filled with tears. Happy ones. Barely minutes ago I'd thought the same thing—that finding them and loving them made all the bad worthwhile, no matter what.

Micah turned me back to the ocean, tucking my back against his chest. He lifted my hand and kissed my wedding ring. "Everything in this world costs something. Money or time or sanity. And before you, there was nothing we couldn't have if we chose. Nothing that eclipsed all of it. Until you." My tears spilled over. I couldn't stop them, and Micah held me tighter. "You're priceless," he murmured.

Suddenly I was surrounded on all sides. All of them holding me together and me holding them back. My voice was muffled in Cam's shirt. "Warn a girl before you're going to make her cry."

They laughed, one by one starting to purr.

"I only ever want to make you cry happy tears," Cam said. Then he grinned. "Well, that, or you crying because we're drowning you in pleasure."

A snort came out of me, mixing with the tears, and I swatted at his arm. "We were having a moment, Cam."

"We're still having a moment, wife." He tilted my chin up. "We're going to have a million moments. Every moment we can with you. But," I felt the change in his bond. Both the heat and the joy as he traced his fingers along the top of my dress. "You did make me a promise."

"I did?"

"I believe you promised me I could unwrap you. *Slowly*."

My own smile appeared despite trying to hide it. "I don't remember promising any such thing."

"Then I'll just have to remind you."

He swept me off my feet and started toward the house. "*Wait*," I wiggled. "Put me down."

"Ocean—"

"I just want to say one more thing." My feet hit the sand, and I pulled them all close again, throat thick with emotion. "I love you. I love you and I never thought I would get to have this kind of love with anyone. And every bad thing, I'd do it all again for you. Every time."

Their words of love didn't have to be spoken. I felt them loud and clear. Micah's eyes were glassy. "No more bad things, Princess. Okay?"

"Okay."

My feet didn't touch the ground on the way to the nest. From now on, there would only be good things.

Fig 57. Baby's Breath
(Also: Love Chalk, Soap Wort)
Meaning: Everlasting love

EPILOGUE

OCEAN

ON THE DUPONT PACK'S ONE YEAR ANNIVERSARY

I stood in the middle of ancient ruins once more, staring at the men I loved, wearing my wedding dress with no corset in sight. They waited where the altar was, in tuxedos.

Just like the last time we'd visited, there was no one here. Not even an officiant. We didn't need one.

The last time we got married was for everyone else. This one was just for us.

But now, walking toward them, I couldn't keep it together. This last year had been a dream, and seeing them standing there like this drove it all home.

I wasn't alone. I saw and felt the same emotions from the three of them. We made it.

I couldn't keep my slow pace any longer, racing to meet them. It had been Everett's idea to do this here. Just the four of us. I loved it, and it gave me the chance to wear my wedding dress again. This time it was a million times more comfortable, and I was a million times more ready for them to take it off.

We would have a real wedding night this time.

Everett reached for me and spoke first. "I, Everett Shaw, take you, Ocean Elise Correa Caldwell, to be my wife and my Omega." He spoke the vows in one unbroken breath, with no hesitation.

Then Cameron, and finally Micah. When they were finished, they slid my rings back on my finger together.

It was my turn, and I wasn't going to make it. "I, Ocean Elise Correa Caldwell, take you to be my husbands and Alphas." My breath hitched, but I kept going, meaning the vows more now than I ever had. "As long as we all shall live."

I gave them their rings, and we didn't wait for anyone to pronounce us married. Nor did we need it. All that we needed was each other.

Micah took me in his arms and danced with me slowly in front of the altar. "I don't think we dance with you enough, wife."

"No?"

"No. We're going to do it more often."

I smiled. "I'm not going to argue with that."

Everett sighed. "I didn't think this through. With the photographer here I can't fuck you on this altar again."

Somewhere there was a hidden photographer making sure we had memories of this. "Can we do some real pictures?"

"No comment about the altar fucking? I'm shocked." His eyebrows rose. "Maybe I need to have these two block the view and give you a reminder."

"I'll never forget that moment," I told him. "But we all know you're going to want more than one round on the altar can give us. And there's a very nice bed waiting back at the hotel."

He grumbled as he signaled the photographer over, but was still smiling, and through our bond, I felt no disappointment. Only eagerness.

We took more photos than we could ever need before retreating to the car and the hotel. Cam was pulling off the lace cape before we could get into the bedroom. "Wait," I said, "I need to put something on."

He growled. "That defeats the purpose."

"Trust me." I danced away from his hold and into the closet. First, I still didn't want them to destroy the dress, and second, I'd managed to convince the design team at *Cheria* to help me.

Micah was designing a collection based around me. The Princess Collection. I'd told him a hundred times not to, but he didn't listen. So I asked for one of the designs. Just a prototype to wear for this moment.

The first time I seduced them I wore his designs, and I wanted this to be the same. Yet different. What I put on wasn't a babydoll dress, and it didn't hide anything. Instead, it was strappy and bared almost everything. A deep ocean blue that looked amazing on me. The ribbons of the bra and panties clung to my skin in the right places. I *felt* beautiful.

I still had moments of doubt and dread. No one was perfect. But with my husbands, I never had to fear. They wanted me in every way, all the time.

"All right." I pushed the door to the closet open. "I hope you like it."

Micah's mouth dropped open. All three of their bonds were laced with shock and hunger and heat. "Where did you get that?"

Letting my hips sway as I walked toward them, I grinned. "I might have made friends with Phoebe in your design department and begged her to make one for me. A test garment."

In one movement, he picked me up and tossed me on the bed, rolling me over to lick over his bite, just over my ass. "Fuck, I love you. You're going to have to model every single piece for me now. You know that, right?"

I arched up into him. "If it gets your jaw to drop like that again, absolutely."

Cameron laughed. "You're asking for it, sweetheart."

"Yes. I am. So fuck me, husbands."

"Don't have to tell me twice." Micah had already stripped and didn't bother to strip me. He simply moved his design to the side and thrust deep, keeping my face pinned to the bed and my ass exactly where he wanted it.

They knew how to make me fall apart and they knew how to keep me on the edge as long as they wanted. I lost all sense of time and space, giving myself to them completely. We had nowhere else to be and no one else to worry about, and they made it clear.

Over, and over, and over.

By the time they'd finished with me, there wasn't a part of me they hadn't fucked or tasted, and I was dizzy with pleasure and exhaustion. We bathed together while they had the bed cleaned.

"That was the wedding night we should have had," I said, letting Everett pin me to the tile wall to keep me upright.

"Everything happened the way it did for a reason, little nymph. And if *this* had been our wedding night, I never would have seen you eat that first banana."

I rolled my eyes as he kissed me the way he sometimes did, like he was trying to leave a lasting mark. They already had. No going back now.

We didn't bother to dress when we climbed back into the fresh bed. I was sleepy and satisfied and I never wanted to leave this bubble of happiness and peace we'd created.

"The last time we were here," Micah said, fingers grazing my hip. "You had a nightmare. Do you remember?"

"Yeah."

He winced. "I still think about that sometimes."

"He does," Cam confirmed. "Makes him a grumpy bastard at work."

"Even grumpier than me," Everett said, making us laugh.

I snuggled down between them all and sighed. "You don't have to worry. I don't have nightmares anymore. Not ones like that."

"Really?"

"Not since that night."

Micah pressed his face into my neck. "Why not?"

I still had bad dreams. There wasn't anyone in the world who didn't. But it was the truth. I'd never woken up panicked because they were gone or like they'd never existed, because it was unthinkable and impossible. My mind was no longer afraid of the possibility.

"Because," I whispered. "I know now what I didn't know then. That you'll always be there."

The silence was full of what they felt. Love and nothing but love that drowned out every other sense and thought. One by one I reached for their hands and found their rings. I tangled all their fingers together with mine and the symbols of what we had. Forever.

"I love you," I said, closing my eyes.
Before I drifted off to sleep, they said it back.

The End

There will be more in the Clarity Coast world soon!

Want a little more of Ocean and her guys? Sign up for my newsletter to get a bonus epilogue from one year later!

*H*ello beautiful readers!

Writing Ocean's story was a deeply personal journey. It took me to places in my writing that I'd never had to go or face before. I won't pretend it was easy, because it wasn't, but it was cathartic, and I hope Ocean's journey helped you as much as it helped me.

Trinity's story is next in this world, and I can't wait to see what kind of messes she gets herself into!

In the meantime, I'd love to meet you! Sign up for my newsletter for updates and sneak peeks, and the occasional dessert recipe!

I also have a Facebook group where we share memes, I share snippets of works in progress, and everything in between. Come join the Delightful Deviants! I hope to see you there, and there will be more books very soon!

Devlyn Sinclair

FLORIOGRAPHY REFERENCES

THE COMPLETE LANGUAGE OF FLOWERS
A DEFINITIVE AND ILLUSTRATED HISTORY
By S. Theresa Dietz

FLORIOGRAPHY
AN ILLUSTRATED GUIDE TO THE VICTORIAN LANGUAGE OF FLOWERS
By Jessica Roux

FLOWERS AND THEIR MEANINGS
THE SECRET LANGUAGE AND HISTORY OF OVER 600 BLOOMS
By Karen Azoulay

PLAYLIST

This is a playlist of some of the songs I listened to while writing *Priceless*.

You can listen to the playlist here, or scan the QR code below.

- **21 Gun Salute** — Catch Your Breath
- **All of Your Lies** — Morgan Clae
- **ALWAYS BEEN YOU** — Chris Grey
- **ALWAYS BEEN YOU (With Josh Makazo)** — Chris Grey, Josh Makazo
- **ALWAYS BEEN YOU (With Josh Makazo) - Slowed + Reverb** — Chris Grey, Josh Makazo
- **among the stars** — .diedlonely, Etsu
- **Anything** — Griff
- **The Apparition** — Sleep Token
- **Atlantic (Asleep)** — Adam Dodson, Anders Johanson
- **Azure** — Adrian Walther
- **Backseat** — Daniel Di Angelo
- **Better Off** — Sunsleep, Jonny Craig

- **The Best I Ever Had** — Limi
- **Be With Me** — Ramin Djawadi
- **Birds of Paradise** — Gísli Gunnarsson
- **Break Free** — Roniit
- **Burial Plot (Reimagined)** — Dayseeker, Seneca
- **COLD BLOODED** — Chris Grey
- **cry** — vowl., Kol
- **Daydreams** — We Three
- **Dead In The Water (feat. Zack Gray)** — Falling North, Zack Gray
- **Demons** — PLAZA
- **Desert Rose** — Lolo Zouaï
- **DIFFERENT** — Chris Grey
- **Eyes On You** — SWIM
- **Fatal Attraction** — Reed Wonder, Aurora Olivas
- **fever dream** — .diedlonely, Etsu
- **The Fight Within** — Memphis May Fire
- **For The Dreams That Have Faded** — Owsey
- **God's Promise** — Daniel.mp3
- **Holding Me Down** — Picturesque
- **I'd Rather Die (feat. Caroline Romano)** — Lost Stars, Caroline Romano
- **If I** — Limi
- **I Loved You From The Day You Died** — Owsey
- **Intrusive Thoughts** — Natalie Jane
- **I See My Evil** — Owsey
- **JADED** — Fordo
- **Kitchen Fan Lullaby (Raw)** — Claire Boyer
- **Lie To Me** — LUVIUM, KOIH, Donna Tella
- **Lose Face** — Daniel Di Angelo
- **The Machine** — Reed Wonder, Aurora Olivas
- **MAKEUP** — Chris Grey
- **Manipulate** — maze, Clarei
- **Medicate Me** — Rain City Drive, Dayseeker
- **Mór** — Sigur Ros
- **My Immortal - Acoustic** — Dayseeker
- **My Name** , Reed Wonder, Aurora Olivas
- **The Night Does Not Belong To God** — Sleep Token
- **night drive (200mph)** — arya x
- **night drive (50mph)** — arya x
- **Nightmare (The Devil)** — Fame on Fire
- **Novocaine** — Too Close To Touch, Bad Omens
- **Now We Are Free (from "Gladiator") - Piano Version** — Jacob's Piano

- **Not to be Dramatic** — Zoe Clark
- **obsessed** — zandros, Limi
- **Obsession** — Mellina Tey
- **ONE MORE NIGHT** — Chris Grey
- **pay for you** — Psylosia
- **Phantom Pains** — Break My Fucking Sky
- **Please Don't Go** — Barcelona
- **The Promise - Slowed and Reverb** — Owsey
- **The Return** — CLANN
- **Rumors** — Adam Ulanicki
- **THE SILENCE** — Morgan Claw
- **Sleepyhead** — Jutes
- **Solas (with Sarah Cothran)** — Jamie Duffy, Sarah Cothran
- **Spellbound** — Baby Jane
- **Still Alive** — Aaryan Shah
- **The Walls** — Chase Atlantic
- **Where's My Love - Slowed** — SYML
- **Who I Am** — Alan Walker, Putri Ariani, Peder Elias
- **Winner** — Ellie Goulding

ABOUT THE AUTHOR

Devyn Sinclair writes steamy Reverse Harem romances for your wildest fantasies. Every sexy story is packed with the right amount of steam, hot men, and delicious happy endings.

She lives in the wilds of Montana in a small red house with a crazy orange cat. When Devyn's not writing, she spends time outside in big sky country, continues her quest to find the best lemon pastry there is, and buys too many books. (Of course!)

To connect with Devyn:

ALSO BY DEVYN SINCLAIR

For a complete list of Devyn's books, content warnings, bonuses and extras, please visit her website.

https://www.devynsinclair.com/

Romance for life

INFINITE ENDINGS

PUBLISHING